G000154388

ODYSSEY

of

HOMER

Jerome Whitcroft

All rights reserved. No part of this work may be reproduced or transmitted by any person or entity, including e-mail, internet search engines or retailers, in any form or by any means, electronic or mechanical, including photo-copying, recording, scanning or by any information storage and retrieval system without prior written permission of the author.

Jerome Whitcroft asserts the moral right to be identified as the author of this work.

Copyright © Jerome Whitcroft 2018

Zeus Press

Ithaki, Greece | Melbourne, Australia

ZEUS PRESS
is an imprint of
KEYRIGHT PUBLICATIONS

ISBN: 9-781-79072-563-2

V: 05/02/19 PB

Enquiries: jw@keyright.com

Ideas you *think* are yours,

However, *all* thoughts are placed into your experience.

Homer

*

Know your future; read history.

Myths are metaphors, and,

Beliefs are mill-stones, not milestones.

J. W.

*

Homer does not describe myths,

But historical events and tangible realities.

Heinrich Schliemann

*

Always help and show kindness to others,

Because they are Zeus in disguise.

Homer

This work is dedicated to Michael A. Whitcroft.
Without his insight and inspiration it would not have started,
Nor my *Ithaki* found.

*

I am grateful to the faculty, lecturers and mentors of
La Trobe University, Australia,
Where the ground-work for this journey into self began.

*

A. A. B. and D. K. you rock my world.

Always keep Ithaca in your mind.
You are destined to arrive there.
But don't hurry your journey at all.
Far better if it takes many years,

And if you are old when you anchor at the island,
Rich with all you have gained on the way,

Not expecting that Ithaca will give you wealth,
Then Ithaca has given you a beautiful journey.
Without her you would never have set out.

She has no more left to give you.
And if you find her poor, Ithaca has not mocked you.
As wise as you have become, so filled with experience,
You will have understood what these Ithacas signify.

C. P. Cavafy

The Ages of Man

The first written account of the evolution of humans was detailed by the Greek historian, Hesiod. His poem, *Works and Days,* defines five epochs, each having a unique *cosmogony.*[a]

The fifth epoch commenced around 1,100 B.C. and is known as the Iron Age. Iron signifying rust and decay, a devolution from its precursor, the Heroic Age[1] in which Homer's allegory,[b] *Odyssey*[c] is portrayed. The evolutionary ascendancy through that era was toward physical maturity.

In the Iron Age, according to Hesiod's warning, the vast majority of humans, epsilons (the fifth-kind) live miserable, anxious existences. Lack must be overcome by toil. Dishonour, violence, deceit, betrayal, arrogance and anxiety prevail. Humans no longer feel shame or indignation at wrong-doing; liars and thieves are rewarded, if not glamourised. It is the age of power and destruction; might overcoming right; *glamour*[d] eclipsing the *metaphysical.*[e]

The evolutionary challenge of this current era is toward emotional maturity.

Perhaps, as Albert Schweitzer and others have suggested, despite its many technological advances, humanity is slowly devolving.[f]

One reason this age may be in a state of decline is because the ancient mandate of respect for the: *host-visitor* principle of *xenia*[g] - the personal obligation of kindness to others - has been subordinated to self-interest.

---

a   A *cosmogony* is any model for understanding the *source* of human experience of the world, or universe; a mental or theoretical construction of existence, a world-view, an order to things, or simply, beliefs.

b   An *allegory* is a story which can be interpreted to reveal a hidden meaning, typically revealing a moral, educational or metaphysical message. A story within a story.

c   The word *Odyssey* is derived from *Odysseus* which is derived from *"odoszeus"* a compound of two ancient Greek words: odos, meaning: *way,* and zeus, meaning: *mind.* In translation: Way of Mind.

d   *Glamour* is the quality of fascinating, alluring or attracting especially by the apparent or superficial.

e   *Metaphysics* is the enquiry into the origin of being; of thought and mind.

f   Albert Schweitzer, philosopher and humanitarian, suggested: "It will ever remain incomprehensible that our generation, so great in all its achievements of discovery, could be so low spiritually as to give up thinking."

g   *Xenia* is pronounced: ex - enya. It is the root of the English word: *saviour.*

Xenia, is the responsibility of kindness, the evolutionary challenge for humanity. On a personal level it involves mutual respect and kindness between host and visitor. It imposes the duties of protection, generosity and courtesy to be given to any visitor, whether a foreigner, a stranger or an associate of the host.

Xenia must be reciprocated by the visitor; it must not be abused. If so, retribution from Zeus is compelling and suffering is inevitable. The modern notion of *karma*[a] has its origin in the Hellenic concept of justice (Zeus-tice).

As a metaphor, the *spirit* of xenia[b] is venerated in the primary force: Zeus, the "All-knowing, Self-pervading" influence which enforces this principle. It is a fundamental paradigm underlying Western culture,[2] and its instruction is: *Help those in need; give!* Be an xenophile,[c] an example in thought, word and deed. Embrace otherness with kindness.

The opposite, or perhaps the *correspondence*, of an xenophile is an xenophobe.[d]

*

---

a   Karma means action, work or deed; it also refers to the spiritual principle of cause-and-effect where intent and actions of an individual influence the future of that individual. Good intent and good deeds contribute to good karma and future happiness, while bad intent and bad deeds bring suffering.
b   The word xenia is borrowed from the ancient Hellenic - and the modern Greek - concept of *philoxenia*, meaning: attracted to: kindness, caring or giving.
c   An *xenophile* is one attracted to foreign things, such as different styles or people, and appreciates the quality or intrinsic value of that object.
d   An *xenophobe* is one unduly fearful of what is foreign, especially of people of different origin, and who fails to appreciate the quality or intrinsic value and significance of that object, and its place within one's reality.

The Ancients, their Beliefs and Ours

The ancient Hellenistic people's world-view[a] is today known as, pan-en-theism,[3] meaning: *all-in-thought*, or, *all-of-mind*. The notion of thoughts - thinking - being the experience of a supreme, primary power, known as God, Mind, the Subconscious or Nature, which the ancient Hellenes named, Zeus.

Panentheism maintains that the Universe is a mental construct - a concept - and includes the experience of appearances of an "external" world, which are reflections of one's subjective[b] thoughts. It is mental and material simultaneously: however time, space and matter are only concepts for understanding one's "experience". Closely related to panentheism is "monism" the theory[c] that only one thing exists, one's experience of being.[d]

The "All-knowing" and "Self-pervading" influence, Zeus, was the metaphor[e] used by the ancient Greeks for the concept of "Mind". Zeus's domain is the Universe[f] and is inseparable from thought.

Zeus is primary. It is Mind. It uses eleven gods, thought-spirits, known as a pantheon.[4] Together they are the invisible Olympians. Zeus' mandate to the individual and humanity is: Kindness to others; *no harm*!

Human interaction with these gods (thought-spirits) yields feelings, emotions, sensory responses, faculties, rationale, perception and cognitive experience. Where do thoughts come from? Mind. The notion that one is separate from Mind leads all "individuals" to *trouble* and suffering.

In Homer's words: "Ideas you *think* are yours, however, *all* thoughts are placed into your experience."

The modern world's cosmogony is known as "realism". The vast majority of people believe that the universe is made of an infinite number of things. Concepts

---

a A world-view or *cosmogony* is any model for understanding the *source* of human experience of the world, or universe; a mental or theoretical context for existence, beliefs.

b *Subjective*, in philosophy, means: relating to the nature of an object as it is known in the mind as distinct from a thing in itself. *Subjective*, in language, means: existing in the mind; belonging to the thinking subject rather than to the object of thought.

c Monism, the concept that only one thing exists: Mind.

d Perhaps this is the elusive "singularity" that science and technology are looking for.

e A *metaphor* is a name or label used to represent something else; an emblem or symbol.

f The word, *Universe*, meant: one song, poem or one thought; one thinker.

(ideas) are used to explain the relationships between the apparently different things which form the separated world.

What it comes down to, is this: Is one's experience of life physical or mental, or both? Ponder on Parmenides[5] conclusion:

"Through the journey of experience, you will learn these things:

The notions and ideas of mortals are illusions, you'll find,

Which lead to one's true identity, self-pervading Mind."[a]

*

Today, another common belief is that the Ancient Hellenes worshipped gods. Nothing could be further from the truth. Hellenists believed in Mind, and Zeus was its name.

Zeus, from the Roman era onward, has been portrayed as the master-father God.[b] However, originally, it was the metaphor for Mind. The name, Zeus, translates to: *Mind*, or *nous*, or, *en-lightener by thought; thought giver, the genesis of thought.*

In ancient cultures, Zeus' god's were the thoughts that create one's mental activity. All of one's mental life is directed by the source of thought, the all-seeing, self-pervading, Mind.

Below is a list of the main gods – thought-spirits – that represent Mind's pantheon of thoughts and their respective qualities and attributes; metaphors, concepts and ideas:

God, Nature, Mind, One

Zeus: Mind. The genesis of all thought.[c] Oneness. Existence. The Way. The force. It enforces xenia, through life experience.

Mind works through its agents: gods or thoughts, ideas and concepts:

---

a   Parmenides of Elea was one of the original philosophers. His writings invoke the ideas of the self - being - is the only thing that can exist, or be experienced. He was an inspiration to Plato and Socrates.

b   It is interesting to note that the modern concept of the Christian "*God*" and the Islamic "*Allah*", were induced from the Hellenic concept of "Mind".

c   Modern versions of the "Christian" Bible, and literature of other organised religions, refers to the *Logos* (word or thought) being the fundamental nature of their God. Refer to Genesis1:1 and Gospel of John.

Athena: Inspiration, imagination, intellect, practicality, reason, consensus, wisdom, courage

Those *thoughts* oppose:

Poseidon: Fear, doubt, terror, anxiety, grief, panic, crisis, despair, desperation, hardship, punishment, devastation, dread, isolation

Then, the lesser "gods"...

Hermes: Conscience, empathy, shame, pity, guilt, confusion, introspection, clear thinking, originality

Apollo: Distance, place, space, multiplicity, separation of things, context

Artemis: Femininity, procreation, protection, perspective, attraction

Aphrodite: Female emotion, love, beauty, sensuality, eroticism, female pleasure

Hera: Domesticity, envy, jealousy, revenge, female pride, anger, scorn, gossip, security

Demeter: Prosperity, bounty, nature, appreciation, generosity, replenishment

Ares: Force, conflict, violence, deceit, betrayal, stealth, intrigue

Hephaestos: Creativity, artistry, male anger, persistence, effort, toil, fulfilment

Dionysos: Pleasure, desire, ecstasy, revelry, fertility, eccentricity, excitement, male eroticism, male emotion

*

The Curse of the Atreus Family

(An ancient, dysfunctional family)

Around 1,250 B.C. twin sons were born to Pelops,[a] the King of Olympia.[6]

Those sons were named Atreus[7] and Thyestes.[8] Because the twin brothers murdered their step-brother, Pelops banished them from his kingdom with a curse upon them, that they - and all their off-spring - might perish by each others' hands.

The two brothers took refuge at Mycenae,[b] in the kingdom of Eurystheus,[9] who was engaged in war against Athens, where he was killed. Atreus and Thyestes, who had remained in charge during his absence, took over his kingdom.

Guilt-ridden and seeking a clear conscience for the murder, Atreus took an oath to sacrifice his best sheep to Artemis,[c] one of the Invisibles, the gods of Olympos. However, when Atreus searched his flock, he discovered a magical, golden-fleeced ram and wished to keep it, thereby violating his oath to the goddess. Instead he gave it to his wife, Aerope[d] for her to hide it from Artemis.[10]

Aerope cunningly convinced Atreus that whoever would possess the ram in the future would become the new king of Argos. She immediately gave the golden lamb to her secret lover, Thyestes, Atreus' twin brother. Thyestes produced the ram and claimed the throne as king.

---

a   Pelops, coincidentally, was the originator of the Olympic games.

b   Mycenae is now an extraordinary archaeological site near Mykines, in north-eastern Pelopennese, located about 85 kilometres south-west of Athens. The site is 20 kilometres inland from the Saronic Gulf. It is built upon a hill 900 feet above sea level. In the second millennium BC, Mycenae was one of the major centres of Hellenic civilization. It was a capital, controlling military and economic interests in Greece, Crete, the Cycladic islands and parts of Anatolia (Turkey). The period of Hellenic history from about 1600 BC to about 1100 BC is called Mycenean, referring to the influence of Mycenae. Its decline coincided with the reign of the House of Atreus, from about 1250 BC.

c   Artemis, the goddess - or thought-spirit - that protects and regulates the Animal Kingdom on behalf of Zeus, the All-knowing One.

d   The name *Aerope* meant: high hopes, high-reaching ambition.

Atreus, later, took back the throne using advice he received from the thought-spirit, Hermes.[e] Thyestes agreed to give the kingdom back only when the planet Venus moved backwards in the sky,[11] a feat performed by Zeus. Atreus ascended to the throne and banished Thyestes.

Later, Atreus learned of Thyestes' and Aerope's adultery and plotted revenge. He butchered Thyestes' sons then cooked, smoked and cured their remains as dried meat.

Atreus invited Thyestes to a pretended reconciliation dinner where he was served - and ate - the cold-cuts and innards of his own sons, and was then taunted with their atrophied[b] hands and feet. Revenge is a dish best served cold.

Thyestes[c] was again forced into exile. Wanting to retaliate, he asked an oracle what to do and was advised to have a son through his daughter, Pelopia[12] who would eventually kill Atreus. The son of this union was named Agisthos[13] and he was abandoned at birth by his mother who was ashamed of the incestuous act.

A shepherd found the child and gave him to Atreus, who unwittingly raised him as his own son. When he entered adulthood Thyestes revealed the truth to Agisthos: that he was both father and grandfather to the boy, thus kindling a hatred for Atreus, his unknowing, adoptive father.

Atreus and Aerope bore two sons, Agamemnon[d] and Menelaos.[e] The two brothers married two sisters; Agamemnon married Klytemenstra[f] and Menelaos married Helen[g] who would become the infamous Helen of Troy after she eloped with a visiting foreigner, Prince Paris[h] of Troy. Troy was located on the far western shore of Asia, today's Turkey.

Agamemnon, as Commander-in-chief, united the many Greek states to invade Troy, in order to bring Helen home and satisfy Menelaos, who insisted that she had been kidnapped.

Prior to sailing off to war against Troy, Agamemnon had angered the goddess Artemis, because he killed a sanctified deer in her sacred grove, and then boasted that he was a better archer than her.

When the time came to leave, Artemis stilled the winds so that Agamemnon's fleet could not sail. A prophet named Calcus[i] told him that in order to

---

e   Hermes, the god - or thought-spirit - that rights wrongs and restores balance through clear thinking and originality, on behalf of Zeus, the all-knowing one.
b   The word: *atrophy,* meaning to be ill-fed, un-nourished or shrivelled, is attributed to the deeds of Atreus, as are the English words: *outrage* and *curse.*
c   The word: *thigh,* meaning the thick or fat part of a leg, is attributed to Thyestes. The word: *thirst* has its roots in Thyestes' desire.
d   The name *Agamemnon,* meant: unyielding and proud.
e   The name *Menelaos,* meant: power over others, dominator, despair and meanness to the people.
f   The name *Klytemenstra*, meant: manipulative or persuasive. The word: menstruate is attributed to the blood-letting which took place as she murdered Agamemnon, Cassandra and others.
g   The name *Helen*, meant: proud, virtuous, essence of femininity.
h   The name *Paris*, meant: favoured or charmed.
i   The name *Calcus*, meant: exact and meticulous. It is the origin of the words: calculate and calculus, a branch of mathematics.

appease Artemis, Agamemnon would have to sacrifice the most precious thing that had come into his possession in the year he killed the sacred deer. That was his first-born daughter, Iphiginia.[a] Agamemnon at first refused but, pressured by the other commanders, eventually agreed. Iphigenia and her mother Klytemenstra were taken to Aulis,[14] where the Greek fleet was assembled, under the pretext of a marriage to the famed Achilles.[b] However, they soon realised that the marriage was a trick.[c]

Iphigenia, knowing she was doomed, agreed to be sacrificed, reasoning that Destiny[15] would not allow her to defy the will of a goddess. She also believed that her death would be heroic, as her gesture was for the good of all Greeks. Klytemenstra tried to stop the sacrifice, but was removed. After she was killed, westerly winds carried the fleet across the Aegean Sea to the coast of Troy where the war began. That year was 1,228 B.C.

While Agamemnon was fighting the Trojans, his wife Klytemenstra, incensed by the killing of her daughter, began an affair with Agisthos. When Agamemnon returned home he brought with him, the doomed prophetess, Princess Cassandra.[16] Both of them were stabbed to death by Klytemenstra at the dining table, that night.

Agamemnon's only son, Orestes, was absent when his mother killed his father. He returned seven years later.

Orestes believed he was obliged to avenge the murder of his father, but in doing so would have to kill his mother. He prayed to Apollo[17] to resolve the dilemma and was instructed to kill them. After Orestes murdered his mother and Agisthos, he banished himself from his kingdom, and sought forgiveness for his crimes from the Invisibles. Eventually, Athena, the Spirit of Inspiration, dissolved his guilt by telling him that he had done a noble act and that neither he, or any of his descendants, would be driven to seek revenge again. The curse over the House of Atreus had ended,[18] so it was thought.

*

---

a   The name *Iphigenia*, meant: strong, fertile, motherly.
b   The name *Achilles*, meant: alert or active. The word: *agile*, is derived from the name.
c   In some versions of the story, Iphigenia remains unaware of her imminent sacrifice until the last moment, believing that she is led to the altar to be married.

Odyssey, a Reluctant Hero of the Trojan War

Odyssey,[a] the King of Ithaki,[b] and Menelaos, the King of Sparta, were friends.

When Menelaos' wife, Helen, ran off with Prince Paris of Troy, Menelaos called upon Odyssey, being very clever and resourceful, to help retrieve her.

Odyssey tried to avoid helping Menelaos because an oracle[c] had prophesied that if he participated in the war, he would not return home for twenty years. So he pretended madness and yoked a mule and an ox together and commenced ploughing a field covered with stones. Because the two animals had different stride lengths the plough moved in a circle. To make the spectacle more absurd, Odyssey, ranting and raving, started to sow the furrows with salt.

However, Palamedes,[d] an envoy of Commander Agamemnon, suspected Odyssey's madness was a ruse and placed his infant son, Telemakis,[e] in front of the plough, forcing Odyssey to stop, exposing his deception. Odyssey, honour-bound, and perhaps shamed, joined the Greek naval forces with his own ships and sailed for Troy to emerge as one of history's greatest heroes.

*

---

a   The Latinised "Odysseus" has been restored to *Odyssey* in keeping with the Homeric original. The name: *Odyssey*, meant: *trouble, struggle*. The name was given to him by his grandfather, Autolycos, because of the boy's precocious fearlessness, intelligence and aptitude. Today, *Odyssey* means: travel, adventure or wanderings.

b   *Ithaki* is pronounced: ith - ar - key, or as the locals say: *tharki,* pronounced: *thar – key.* The island of Ithaki lies in the Ionian Sea, west of the mainland of Greece.

c   The Oracle was Halithersos, a countryman of Ithaki.

d   Palamedes was an enemy of Odyssey.

e   Telemakis was less than one year of age.

A History of Homer's *Odyssey*

Prior to Heinrich Schliemann's discovery of Troy in 1873, Homer's *Iliad* and *Odyssey* were considered stories based on myths, fiction.

With the discovery of Troy these *stories* became historical evidence. However, they are more than stories: they are allegories.

Their hidden messages warn humans and human-kind of a fall from grace, which was also reflected in Hesiod's predictions which are over 2,500 years old:

> " ... *the modern era is the age of suffering ... Mind created a fifth generation of beings, and with it began, after the Bronze and Heroic Ages, the Age of Iron. It is said that all evil burst forth into this baser age, which is our own: Men never rest from labor and sorrow by day, and from perishing by night. Modesty, truth, and faith leave the earth, and in their place comes tricks, plots, traps, violence, and unbridled desire to profit from others. The ground, which had been common possession, is now neatly marked with boundary-lines. Men demand of the fields, not only the sustenance provided from its surface, but also what is in the very bowels of the earth, bringing to light the wealth buried and hidden.*
>
> *Iron and Gold: Not only will hard iron come with this age; but also gold, which is even worse than iron. And with both war will come, and so men will find it natural to live on what is plundered from others.*
> *The guest won't trust his host, and affection among brothers will became rare. The husband shall start longing for the death of his wife, and she for the death of her husband. Piety will be vanquished, and Dike[a] - the last of the Invisibles - will abandon human-kind.*
> *Doomed to destruction: If the duty-of-care principle is not honoured, Zeus - Mind - will destroy this race too: For the*

---

a   Dike, the "goddess", is the metaphor of the spirit of moral order, ethics and fairness, based on ancient traditions and socially enforced conventions.

father will not agree with his children, nor the children with their father, nor guest with his host, nor comrade with comrade, nor will brothers love each other as once they did. Humans will dishonour their parents as they attain old age, without repaying them the cost of their nurture. Might shall be right, so that one man may sack another man's city. There will be no merit for the man who keeps his word, or for the just, or for the good; rather, all will praise the evil-doer and admire his audacity and violent dealings. Strength will be right, and respect will vanish as an empty word. Peace being banished, the inspirational thoughts will cease, leading to a life of anxiety. The wicked will hurt the worthy, speaking false words against them; therefore will envy walk along with them. Anxiety will forsake mortals, letting bitter sorrows fall upon them; being defenceless like children in the wilderness, they will not find any help against all evil they themselves created."

Since the composition of these works, from 800 B.C., original documents were changed to suit the political, historical and cultural agendas of organised religions, most significantly by medieval Catholics. In turn, this led to the corruption of language and beliefs.

These "Classical" works are still considered to be based on myths: however, nothing could be further from the truth.

*

Prelude to Homer's *Odyssey*

The year is 1,228 B.C.

Helen of Sparta has eloped with the Trojan, Prince Paris, compelling, for the sake of honour, or ego, many Greek colonies to unite and seek Helen's return to her husband, Menelaos.[19]

Menelaos' brother, Agamemnon, was the Commander-in-Chief who unified the Greek forces and launched 1,186 ships[20] to invade Troy, including the support of Odyssey and his mariners. On the day of his home-coming from the war, King Agamemnon was murdered by his wife and her lover.

Victory over the Trojans had taken the Greeks almost ten years. The war ended in the spring of 1,218 B.C.

Odyssey, who contrived the Trojan Horse[a] was the master-mind behind the final victory and the hero of the destruction of Troy.

Of the Greek chieftains and warriors who survived both the war and the perilous homeward voyages, all have returned home except Odyssey, the King of Ithaki, an island in the Ionian Sea west of the Greek mainland.

Odyssey's return is prolonged by another ten years, according to his destiny. At home he is presumed dead; he has been missing for twenty years.

Nobles from Ithaki, and other regions, are vying to marry his beautiful wife, Penelope, and have over-run his palace. These *Suitors* have corrupted the servants and are eating up his estate, by abusing the privilege of hospitality, represented in the tradition of *xenia*, fundamental to harmonious social relationships.

Xenia, or *host-visitor principle*, is the unwritten social obligation of hospitality. It involves mutual respect between host and visitor; two parties. It imposes the duty of care through the protection, generosity and courtesy to be given to any guest, whether a foreigner, a stranger or an associate of the host. Metaphorically, the *spirit* of xenia is venerated in the primary deity Zeus, the "All-seeing" entity and the enforcer of this principle. It is the way to harmonious social and cultural relationships. Xenia is a fundamental paradigm underlying Western

---

a   The Trojan Horse, or Wooden Horse, is the tale from the Trojan War about the trick that the Greeks used to enter the City of Troy and win the war. After a fruitless 10-year siege, they constructed a huge wooden horse and hid a select force of men inside. The other Greeks pretended to sail away, and the Trojans pulled the horse into their city as a victory trophy. That night the Greek force crept out of the horse and opened the gates for the rest of the Greek army, which had sailed back under cover of night. The Greeks destroyed the city of Troy, ending the war.

culture, and its aspiration is: Help those in need, for help brings contentment - happiness - to both parties.

Penelope has stalled the Suitors for time, but is finding it increasingly difficult to deny their demand: That she must marry one of them.

Odyssey's son, Telemakis, is approaching his twenty-first birthday and has become resentful of the Suitors' dishonourable behaviour endured by his household.

Homer's story details the last forty days of Odyssey's quest to reach his home, revealing his trials and exploits during that ten-year period of his twenty-year absence.

*

How to enjoy this work...

What you are about to read was originally a poem. A very long poem.

It was composed so that each two lines rhymed. That format allowed performers, known as rhapsodes[21] to remember their lines more easily and to develop the rhythm and cadence[a] of the verses to give the maximum effect to their *live* performances.

Rhapsodes were highly sought-after and would earn their living by travelling city-to-city, to entertain in palaces, private homes and public places. They would tour with an entourage, who would re-write, rehearse and perfect the poem and its performance. They were paid by episode, all twenty-four of them, which would provide the troupe with a paying audience and the hospitality of their hosts and audiences for weeks, if not months.

Throughout ancient Greece and beyond, festivals were common and so were contests between rhapsodes. The entertainers would improvise and polish their performances so that their work evolved through competition and rivalry over time, into the masterpiece that we have inherited.

This version of Homer's *Odyssey* attempts to reconstruct the work to a poem that *can* be read, and enjoyed easily. The work has been restored to rhyming verse in the dialogue between all characters, except for straight-talking Zeus.[b]

Perhaps you shall discover why this ancient tale is alive and well, and more relevant to the modern world than it was to the ancients, and those in-between, for the last twenty-eight centuries.

*

---

a   The difference between *cadence* and *rhythm* is that, cadence is the act or state of declining or sinking, while rhythm is the variation of strong and weak elements (such as duration of pauses or other effects) of sounds over time; the verse's beat or meter.

b   Throughout this work be mindful that references to "gods" are synonymous with "thoughts". Zeus being the genesis of thought.

An Invocation to Athena, the Spirit of Inspiration

Muse, Athena, inspire me to understand the true story of that man, masterful in all ways of cleverness, that troubled wanderer, vexed in misery for ten years after he destroyed the Trojans and their nation's stronghold. He, who saw remote lands and cities and learned the ways of foreign men; weathering bitter nights and anxious days in the deep sea's heart, battling to save his own life and to bring his crew-mates home. He, whose determination, courage and good sense could not save them, for Destiny compelled their excesses, their doom was sealed before birth. For those fools feasted on the cattle of noble Helios, the Sun, He that colours Day from black Night. So, He erased the Dawn of their homecoming day, and their lives.

Spirit Athena, favoured daughter of Zeus, the Enlightener, inspire in me Odyssey's story, beginning at the scene of your choice ...

*

EPISODE ONE

THE INVISIBLES

*

THE SPIRIT OF INSPIRATION AND A PRINCE

War between the Hellenes[a] and the Trojans,[b] ended in June, 1,218 B.C.[22]

All who had escaped *Death*[c] on the battlefield, or on the rugged seas, have returned to their homes, except Odyssey.

Although longing to return to his wife, family and country, Odyssey is detained by the nymph *Kalypso,*[d] who lives in a cave on the island of Ogygio.[23] She wishes to marry. The years pass and the *Time*[e] allotted for the Olympian gods[24] to allow his return home to Ithaki has come. However, Poseidon,[25] his nemesis, is intent on persecuting Odyssey for his transgressions, and thwarts any progress; his suffering continues as he makes his way toward his home.

Poseidon[f] is in the Ethiopian Highlands, to receive tributes at a festival dedicated to himself, and hosted by the Egyptians. They are grateful to him for

---

a   Hellenes is a term used to denote the collective Greek civilisation's identity. In ancient times it included the Chastens, the Daanans, the Argives and other minor tribes.

b   The Trojans were the inhabitants of the City of Troy. Its ruins can be found near the shores of the Aegean Sea in western Anatolia, Turkey.

c   *Death* refers to Hades, ruler of the Underworld and its dead.

d   The name, *Kalypso*, translates to: *She who conceals; the veilor or eclipser.*

e   Time or *"Kairos"* the Hellenic concept meaning the right or destined moment. The ancient Hellenes had two concepts of Time: *chronos* and *kairos*. The former refers to chronological - or sequential - experience of reality. The latter signifies the ordained *moment* when an event within one's reality is experienced. The distinction lies in the belief that one's experience of reality is predetermined - and primary - as all "moments" are subjective. Sequential time is not subjective, but nominal, and used as a concept, or label, for sharing the experience of *kairos*.

f   The name, *Poseidon*, translates to: *Placer, positioner or situation. Poseidon* is a metaphor for the sense of doubt, fear, anxiety and crisis.

creating the volcano which formed the source of the bountiful *Nile River*[a] at Lake Tana.[26] The Nile splits the world into two halves, defining East from West.

The other Invisibles, the Olympian gods, are attending a meeting without him in the palace of Zeus,[27] the En-lightener, on Mount Olympos.

Zeus,[b] has been meditating on the revenge killing[c] by Orestes,[28] who killed Agisthos.[29] Agisthos had murdered Orestes' father, Agamemnon,[30] seven years earlier. He says to the other gods:

"Olympians! Immortals, what pathetic, shameless things these mortals are. They blame *us* for their sufferings, how they take us to task. Desire and self-interest, double their woes. Yet, they do not respect Destiny.[31] They refuse to understand that their lives are forged on the anvil of desire, and self-interest. They won't understand that wrong thinking must be righted, and then blame us for all their miseries. Wrong thinking leads to wrong actions, and they have consequences."

"There is nothing else than Mind, as Invisibles know, but from which mortals continue to stray. By reasoning? Wrong thinking more likely. Ha! What stupidity gods endure. What does man-kind believe is the source of thought?"

"Here's another example of mortal transgression leading to earthly misery: You all know about cursed Atreus[32] and Agisthos' shameful sin and the revenge by Agamemnon's son, Orestes. Bad family business, indeed!"

"It was not Agisthos' destiny to mate Agamemnon's wife and murder her husband. No, he knew the consequences of desire. I even sent Thought-spirit, clear-thinking, Hermes,[33] to warn his conscience with this command: *Don't get involved with Agememnon's wife, or harm her husband!* But he would not heed his conscience, or my spirited counsel, and now he has been killed by Orestes."

"Of course, you all know that mortal-minds can't stop when disaster can be repeated. Once is never enough for mortals. Have they not been schooled in the Delphic[34] Oracle's[35] wisdom?[d] To, *Know oneself, first;* and, *Nothing to excess*, is what they need to heed."

Athena,[36] the Spirit of Emotion,[37] says to her father:

"Zeus, Truth; Father of the Invisibles, son of Titan, Kronos,[38]

---

a The *Nile River* was believed to have a divine source created through an uplift of the Earth's crust; Poseidon's handiwork.

b The name, *Zeus*, translates to: *Illuminator of mind,* or, *en-lightener by thought; thought giver.* He is the enforcer of the principle of xenia. The words, *truth* and *just* are derived from Zeus.

c While the Hellenic commander Agamemnon was away fighting against Troy, Agisthos entered into an adulterous union with Klytemenstra, Agamemnon's wife; they murdered him on his return. The murder was later avenged by Orestes, son of Agamemnon and Klytemenstra, and is told in Aeschylus' trilogy of plays known as the *Oresteia*.

d The *Delphic* maxims are a code for right behaviour and wisdom to live by. Yes, there is a guidebook - an instruction manual - for life. It is based on the principle of "No Harm" and it is inscribed in the stone walls of the sanctuary surrounding the ruins of the Temple of Apollo at Delphi, Greece.

Compeller of deeds, provider to all needs; wielder[39] of the Aegis,[a]

Agisthos deserved his fate, his way was outrageous;
And his appetite for murder was satisfied by the scheming of Orestes,[40]

But that matter is over at long last;
So why punish yourself by enduring the past?

Enjoy the ever-present now;
Not hurtful history's furrowed brow,

Gods, all, hear this plea: the mortal deserving *now*, is Odyssey;
Shrewd, unfortunate and luckless, and all else that he may be,

He's captive on Kalypso's island, in mortal-mind belief;
That he has no hope for his release, or relief,

Twenty years he has been torn from his friends and family;
Can it be, that he is to be lost to eternity?

Should his future, not be his fate?
Life's wheel of Destiny doesn't wait,

It is true, that Atlas's[41] daughter, Kalypso, the seductress;
Attends to his every want, from the cave's shelter to her mattress,

She offers sweet words, and marriage is often her persuasion;
Yet he pines for his home, Ithaki is his true love and destination,

---

a   The Aegis, is "reality" being mirrored by our thoughts. A metaphorical shield, a symbol of Mind's work which mirrors an apparently external world. It is the working out of the plan through one's experience, and it is said to contain the destiny of all. Zeus is the minder of Mind and uses the dynamic of xenia to control behaviour. The word: *age,* is based on the concept of experience through Time.

Did his work on the plains of Troy, father; satisfy you, or annoy?

Father, Greatest of all the gods;

With Odyssey, why are you still at odds?"

Zeus, Truth, says:

"Nonsense, Daughter! What strange words escape your teeth. When shall I ever forget clever Odyssey and his generous respect for us, the Olympians, Destiny's guards? There is no greater hero alive than wily Odyssey."

"However, you know that Poseidon, the Earth-shaker, is hell-bent on keeping him away from Ithaki. You can't deny that gods must do their work too. Odyssey should not have blinded his son, Polyphemus,[a] the one-eyed Cyklops. Although Poseidon is relentless in pursuing Odyssey, keeping him in perennial exile these twenty years, he stops short of killing him through respect for *Destiny.* "

Zeus, all-knowing, continues:

"Yes! Daughter, now is the moment to act. Poseidon will respect the might of the Olympians and Odyssey shall find *Fate,*[b] that is, if I'm not over-ruled by *Moros.*"[c]

Athena, the Spark of *Emotion,*[d] replies:

"Zeus, Truth; Father of gods, Compeller of deeds, and provider to all needs,

---

a   The name: *Polyphemus,* meant: much famed, famous.

b   The *Fates,* mythological women who determined the span of a human life by spinning, measuring, and cutting the thread symbolic of it. See note, on the Moirai, below.

c   *Moros* is the omnipotent being who dispenses everyone's life through pre-determined fate. He "compels" mortals to their death. The Moirai (Fates) asserted that not even Zeus could question Moros, because he *is* destiny. Moros was the only force that Zeus truly respected and dreaded. Because of this, Moros was also considered as the God behind god. Moros' opposite is Elpis the personified Spirit of Hope. She and the other spirits were trapped in a jar by Zeus and entrusts them to the care of the *first* human woman Pandora. When she opened the vessel all of the Spirits escaped except for Elpis (Hope) who remained behind to comfort mankind.

d   *Emotion (synaisthima)* is a *feeling* derived from one's perceived circumstances, mood or relationships with others, which may be instinctive or intuitive as opposed to reasoning or learned knowledge.

If Odyssey shall return to Ithaki, as is your pleasure;

Then let us send clear-thinking Hermes, as our messenger,

To ask the sea-nymph to set him free; that home-yearning, unfortunate Odyssey;

And I shall journey to Ithaki; to encourage his son to draw an assembly,

There, in his palace, are the *Suitors*[42] and his resources are being drained;

Their disrespect for xenia[a] and their excesses must be restrained,

His mind must be directed to Odyssey's plight;

Dead, alive; where is he? He must know which is right,

But, not knowing is three times the hurt;

Dread, strife and endless doubt, the worst,

I shall send him to sandy Pilos, then Sparta;[b]

To seek knowledge of his far-flung father,

It is possible that there he shall hear of him;

And, so, he may win the praises of men."

Athena,[c] Inspiration Itself, binds gold sandals to her feet which send her at the speed of thought to the island of Ithaki in the Ionian Sea.[43] She carries her well-balanced, bronze-tipped spear which she wields at great warriors when they need pointed persuasion of Zeus' work.

---

a   *Xenia, or host-visitor principle*, is the unwritten social obligation of hospitality. It involves mutual respect between host and visitor; two parties. It imposes the duty of care through the protection, generosity and courtesy to be given to any guest, whether a foreigner, a stranger or an associate of the host. Metaphorically, the *spirit* of xenia is venerated in the primary deity Zeus, the "All-seeing" patron god and the enforcer of this principle. It is the way to harmonious social and cultural relationships. It is a fundamental paradigm underlying Western culture, and its aspiration is: Help those in need, for help brings contentment - happiness - to both parties.

b   Pilos is a city on the Ionian Sea's coast, once ruled by Nestor. Sparta is the inland region ruled by Menelaos, both are allies and friends of Odyssey.

c   *Athena*, the name suggests: *pointed words, inspiring, emotive and passionate.*

Instantly she stands at the door of Odyssey's palace. She is disguised as a family friend, Mentes,[a] the Chief of Taphia,[44] with her spear in hand.

The insolent Suitors sit near the door, lazing and gaming. The servants offer them food and wine from Odyssey's own estate.

Telemakis,[45] the son of Odyssey, sees her first. He sits in despair among the Suitors imagining that his revered father might return out of nowhere and rid his domain of these freeloaders. With these imaginings he steps toward the doorway, not wanting to ignore this dweller on the threshold. He goes straight to the visitor and grasps his right hand, saying:

> "Welcome, friend, I trust you had a pleasant trip here;
>
> Enjoy my hospitality and let me take your spear,
>
>
> When you've had your fill of food and wine;[b]
>
> Please tell what matter brings you to this house of mine."

Telemakis[c] walks to the high-walled Great Hall, Athena, Emotion, behind him. He takes the spear and puts it in a wooden rack, where the spears of his father, intrepid Odyssey, rest. He offers her a beautiful carved and decorated chair. He sits, next to her, away from the rabble of the Suitors, so that the visitor will not take offence at their ill-mannered behaviour and lose his appetite. He is curious too; perhaps this visitor knows something of his long-gone father.

A maid is present and pours scented water from a silver[d] jug over their hands into a gold basin. The house-keeper draws a table to them and brings bread and delicacies from the busy kitchen. A steward serves cut meats carved on his board. He places gold goblets and fills them with wine. The restless Suitors swagger about the dining hall, finding chairs to sit upon. The squires pour water on their hands and the maids pile bread onto plates and pour wine to brim their cups.

The Suitors feast on the generous provisions. Satisfied, they turn their thoughts to music and dance, which they know adds so much to the pleasure of banqueting. A herald brings a lyre and hands it to the minstrel Phemios,[46] who the Suitors force into their service with demands for song. As he breaks into a delightful tune Telemakis speaks quietly to Athena, Sparkling Emotion, disguised as Mentes, saying:

> "Please don't be angry for me saying wrong;

---

a   *Mentes*, the name translates to suggest: *imagined spirit, apparition or phantom.*
b   The principle of xenia-based hospitality involves etiquette. In this case: *Eat, rest, then converse.*
c   The name, *Telemakis*, translates to: *shy, passive, shuns conflict, avoids violence.*
d   Silver was used as an antiseptic and water purifier by the ancient Hellenes.

But this rabble think only of food, wine and song,

They live free off another man;
Long dead, perhaps, in some other land,

His white bones may rot on shore, or roll under sea;
It would be a different story if he returned to Ithaki,

These Suitors would pray for fast escapes;
And not gorge freely on that man's meat and grapes,

No, that day surely cannot be;
He is dead, and shall never again set foot on Ithaki,

Thoughts of his well-being we must refuse;
No-one on Earth can bring such news,

Guest, tell me, who are you, and where from?
What matter brings you here, and for how long?

By what ship did you come, and where is your crew;
Is this your first time here, did you know my father too?"

Athena, speaks to him quietly:

"My name is Mentes,[47] Chief of the Taphians, Telemakis;
I'm a son of the wise prince Anjialus,

Our boat lies in Rithron Cove[48] under the Neion woods;
With a full hull's cargo of metal goods,

We sailed here, bound for far Temesa;[49]
To trade iron for bronze, in good measure,

Our families do go back far in time;
I know your father, the son of Laertes' line,

Ask Lord Laertes,[50] but I gather he stays away from town;
It is the welfare of your father, that has worn him down,

A miserable life on that remote farm;
Suffering, like you, Odyssey's peril and harm,

Why am I here, you well ask?
It is me that must perform this good task,

Your father is alive it has been said;
Red-haired Odyssey lives, he is not dead,

But some god hinders his return home;
Twenty years, a score he was fated to roam,

Saved from certain death in the Trojan war;
Marooned, perhaps, on some lonely island's shore,

Many adventures and exploits has he;
Life has been hard on ill-fated Odyssey,

The gods indeed put this into my head;
Odyssey's true story has not yet been said,

Alone, he shall return to tell his tale;

Soon, bound for Ithaki, under wind and sail.

I am certain – as are thoughts – it is done;
By Zeus, Odyssey's return shall come,

Destiny will not be re-arranged;
Mind's intent cannot be changed,

So tell me, are you really his son?
Clearly, manhood you have won,

God-like head and caring eyes;
Likeness to your father is no surprise,

But I have not seen him since he left for Troy;
Then you'd have been a very young boy."

Telemakis politely replies:

"My friend, I shall be honest with you;
My mother says I am Odyssey's son, true,

But for myself I cannot tell;
No-one of this Earth knows parentage that well,

If only I was the son of a lucky man;
Who could enjoy life and family in this sweet land,

No, I endure the most unfortunate father that has ever been;
And to make it worse, one that I have never seen,

I've inherited nothing but sorrow and tears;
And an estate now falling down around my ears,

Mentes, I hope you are as right as you seem sure;
But, if he does not return, tell me how to endure?"

Emotion, Eye-sparkling Athena, replies:

"Dear man, your fate and domain are not doomed to calamity;
Have faith and hope in your mother, Penelope,

She is more capable than any woman ever known;
Her discretion and resilience mean that you are not alone.

But tell me now of another matter;
Who are all these people, why the din and the clatter?

Is it your birthday, are you now twenty-one?
If you've come of age, let's have a celebration,

Or, is there a wedding feast about to begin?
And why are there so many men?

They eat and drink like there is no tomorrow;
Does their presence here add to your sorrow?

Only one thing exceeds their arrogance;
A wild desire for food, wine, women and dance,

Decent folk these cannot be;
How they behave so disgracefully,

Surely you feel much disgust;

An uneasy host to this shameless lust."

Thoughtful Telemakis, replies:

"My friend, you have noted my dilemma well;

A story of disrespect that I am ashamed to tell,

In my father's time this palace was the envy of every city;

Now it is mocked with shame and pity,

How the gods conspired in the death of my father;

Now I am besieged with these Suitors' ardour,

It is with my mother, Penelope[51] they pretend to be devoted;

But eating and drinking, and stealing this estate, is their true motive,

Each afternoon they arrive empty handed;[a]

Whilst mother sits in her room; gloomy and stranded,

She hates the idea of re-marriage;

And any courting she is quick to disparage,

So, the Suitors drink wine to the very last drop;

Even their bellies groan and belch at them to stop,

And once the bounty of kitchen and cellar are gone;

The Suitors then stumble out, often it's well past dawn.

---

a   In ancient Greece it was customary to always bring a gift to a host, if possible.

Woe is me, what am I to do;

Mentes, father's friend, may I have advice from you?"

Emotion Itself, Athena, is moved:

"How disgraceful! What a different place this would be;

If these wretched Suitors saw the return of Odyssey,

If he presented himself at the palace gate right now;

What a scene to behold, Oh what a row!

Battle dress, bow, arrows and his spear;

In this rabble, nought else but deathly fear,

Odyssey, brave and true, god-like and tall;

What a sorry wedding it would be for the Suitors, one and all,

Just as I saw him when he first visited my house, and family;

After a long stay with Mermerus' son, Ilus,[52] in Ephyre,[53]

Where he went to get poison to smear his arrows' tips best;

But he was a god-respecting man; his conscience refused your father's request;

So, my father, who loved him like a true son;

Gave him the secret poison, and his mission was won,

Alas, all that is a matter for the Invisibles and the Master plan;

As a different fate is written on the brows of each and every man,

Meanwhile, I urge you to rid the palace of this vermin;

Tomorrow, call an assembly[a] and deliver this sermon,

Tell them to leave: They must not return!
The gods are offended, Zeus's wrath they will earn,

As for your mother, if she wishes to marry;
Send her to her father, he will arrange a suitable dowry,

As for you, find and fit the best ship in Ithaki;
Crew her with the strongest oarsman, numbering twenty,

Go to sandy[b] Pilos and seek many-worded Nestor;[54]
Then to Menelaos - the last man home from Troy, - in Sparta,

From these two you shall find truth;
As seekers learn, it is laid out by Zeus,

If you hear your father is alive and making home his course;
He'll probably make it by the end of Autumn, then it will be time to rejoice,

But, if he doesn't arrive, is dead, and cannot be found;
Return home and build an honourable monument high on a burial mound,

Give your lost father the greatest funeral in his home-land;
And to the *best* man, give your mother's hand,

Now, all that being settled and ready to be done;
Find a way to unsettle the Suitors, and their wicked fun,

---

a   An assembly usually takes place in the a*gora*, or the *plathia*, a public place where people gather to converse and socialise. Every village, town and city of Greece continues this age-old tradition. An agorazein is someone who hangs-out in the agora.

b   The use of "sandy" is a reference to the monolithic, sandstone rock located at the entrance to Pilos Bay.

By cunning or might you must destroy this mob;
Or, of your estate, they will continue to plunder and rob.

You are no longer a child;
Have you not heard of Orestes' revenge? So wild!

My friend, into a man you have well grown;
Now, avenge these Suitors and take your rightful throne!

Be bold and assert your power;
The Invisibles are with you, bring on the hour.

Now I must go before it gets too late;
My patient crew must be pondering my fate,

I leave with this matter in your hands;
Rely upon Zeus, planner of plans,

Let the good within be your God;
Then the God within will be your guide."

Telemakis, says:

"Good Mentes, your words are pure and true;
How can I ever repay you?

Let the maids bathe you and comfort your needs;
You have travelled long on the lonely seas,

Please stay a little longer, you lift my heart;

Or, at least take this gift to remember me after we part."

Telemakis reaches to a shelf above the spear rack and takes down a gold statue of Athena, saying:

"Mentes, take this gold figure of Athena, my father's favourite god;

It shall keep you safe wherever you may sail and trod."

Athena, sparkling-eyed Emotion, says:

"No! I must go now, my mind cannot change;

But I will take your fine gift wherever I range,

Athena, Spirit of Emotion, is most dear to my heart too;

Each time I look at this I'll pray for your father, and for you."

With these words she vanishes, like a bird through a hole in the roof. The spear rack finds Telemakis' eyes. The spear has gone. *'Is this real?'* he asks the silence.

He grows with confidence and daring. He imagines his father and that nurtures his pride. He realises that he has been visited by some god, whose words flutter in his heart the wings of a bird.

He finds that the Suitors are listening in silence to their bard who sings of the Trojan war and the trials and sufferings that Athena, Emotion, inflicted on the Hellenes, and the Trojans.

In her room upstairs, honourable Penelope,[a] daughter of Ikarius,[55] listens to the stirring ballad. She descends the stairs with a maid at each side. She draws her veil across her face to hide her tears and says:

"Phemis, why must you regale me with that ballad;

You know each time I hear it, I become ever more sad,

There are scores of other dirges you could play;

a   The name *Penelope*, translates to: *weaver of tears.*

It is me that mourns the best of husbands, every day,

You know how I grieve for beloved Odyssey;
Please, Phemis, please, play some other ditty."

Prudent Telemakis, intervenes:

"Mother, why grudge our loyal bard his right to play and sing;
It is his work to raise our blood and let emotion ring,

He is not to blame for Zeus's work on Earth;
But to fill our hearts with sorrow and mirth,

Many men did not return from that fateful war;
It is right that he plays, so we remember and endure,

We too have tasted the fruits of that war and its tragic fate;
If all this is too much distress, go upstairs, it is late,

Return with the maids to the quiet of your rooms;
And do your work with the spindles and looms,

These decisions are for me to make;
While I am master of this estate."

Prudent Penelope is shocked at Telemakis' bold, assertive words. But, realising that he has spoken sensibly, she retires to her upstairs bedroom, weeping for her beloved Odyssey until Athena, the Spirit of Emotion, closes her eyes in sweet sleep.

Meanwhile, the Suitors are in uproar that an opportunity to court the beautiful Penelope has again vanished. Each Suitor secretly offers a prayer for the chance to seduce her.

Thoughtful Telemakis calls the Suitors to order:

"Gentlemen, you who court my mother, this is a disgrace;
I'll have no more uproar in this place,

So listen in quiet and in my hospitality rejoice;
For tomorrow at noon you shall hear me in another voice,

You all shall assemble and hear as I think fit;
For the time has come for all of you to quit,

From tomorrow on, feast somewhere else;
You will not be welcome again in this palace,

For I pray that Zeus allows me to destroy you Suitors all;
And not to mark this dynasty for Time[a] to befall."

The Suitors are astounded at Telemakis' new-found audacity. Most cringe at this exuberance of youth, others bite their lip.

Finally, Antinoos[b] speaks:

"It seems that the gods are speaking in this tone, so bold and new;
But Telemakis, they may have other plans for you,

Yes, you are heir to this island's throne;
But I pray to heaven that it won't be your home,

---

a   Time or *"Kairos"* is a Greek word meaning the right or destined moment. The ancient Hellenes had two concepts of Time: *chronos* and *kairos*. The former refers to chronological - or sequential - experience of reality. The latter signifies the ordained *moment* when an event within one's reality is experienced. The distinction lies in the belief that one's experience of reality is predetermined - and primary - as all "moments" are subjective. Sequential time is not subjective, but nominal, and used as a concept, or label, for sharing the experience of *kairos*.

b   The name, Antinoos, translates as: *antagonistic; of hostile thoughts.*

You are not yet this kingdom's king;

Do you wear the crown, the sceptre and the ring?

Whilst you may be lord of this estate;

To be our king, I pray, may not be your fate."

Telemakis replies:

"Antinoos, if all you say is in Zeus' hand;

Then, I might not become king of this land,

This island has would-be kings, it is very clear;

Many wish to improve their lot, just look around here,

But, of this house I am master and I am lord;

My father's line defended it in battle, with shield and sword.

Suitors, stop and take warning from your ruinous ways;

If not, then fear that Zeus will short-number your days."

Diplomatic Eurymachos,[a] son of Polybos,[56] intervenes:

"If it shall be Zeus that determines our life's course;

Then no-one - ever - can have any recourse,

Our future cannot be changed, just like the past;

The truth is that mortal plans never last.

Whether or not you'll be the son-king of Odyssey;

---

a   The name, Eurymachos, translates as: *wide-skilled fighter, experienced combatant.*

I hope your home shall always be Ithaki.

Now, Telemakis tell us plain and true;
Who was that guest that just visited you?

Tell us who he is, and where from?
What matter brings him here, and for how long?

By what ship did he come, and where is his crew?
Is this his first time here, did he know your father too?"

Shrewd Telemakis answers him:

"Now I am certain my father will never return to this home;
I need no more rumour of his death or where he may roam,

It is now clear that by the gods my father's life is dealt;
As for the visitor, he knew him and his end he plainly spelt.

He introduced himself as Mentes, one the Taphian[57] chiefs;
An honourable son of the wise prince Anjialis,

His blue-eyed[a] boat lies in Rithron Cove under Neion woods;
With a full hull's cargo of metal goods,

He sailed here, bound for far Temesa,[b]
To trade iron for bronze, in good measure,

---

a   Blue-eye symbol. Every culture has superstitions of which some originated many thousands of years ago. A look can cause pain, injury, or bad luck to anyone on the receiving end. People who are envious or simply believe that a person does not deserve the good fortune bestowed on them also open the evil eye unconsciously. A popular belief existing in many corners of society is that the blue-eye symbol protects against evil. The symbol can be seen throughout the Mediterranean to this day.

b   Temesa, a port in ancient Italy, known today as, Catanzaro in Calabria.

Our families do go back far in time;

He knows of my father, the son of Laertes' line."

That is what Telemakis said. But in his heart he knows that this is the work of a god.

*

From then until Dawn the Suitors surrendered to the pleasure of gorging and wenching, music and dance.

Telemakis retires to his bedroom. It's a lofty room with a view in each direction over his estates. He is escorted by faithful Eurykleia.[58] She carries a burning torch. She is the daughter of Ops. Laertes had traded her when she was a girl, for twenty oxen. She had been given all due respect and privilege in Laertes' palace and treated like a daughter of the king. She had nursed Telemakis as her own son. Of all the household women she loves him the most.

He opens the heavy bedroom doors, removes his clothes and puts them in the wise woman's hands. She hangs them and leaves. There, all night long, under the sheepskin fleece, Telemakis plans his course and the journey that his fateful visitor inspired.

He ponders the god's words:

Let the good within be your God;

Then the God within will be your guide.

*

DEBATE IN ITHAKI

*

Mortals delight with the red sky of Night

But gods warn with a red sky from Dawn

Dawn appears fresh and crimson fingered. Odyssey's son rises from his bed and dresses. He binds sandals to his feet and slings a sharp sword from his shoulder. He steps god-like from his bedroom. He orders his heralds to summon people from the town and the villages to come to the agora at noon.

Telemakis walks toward the agora, being led by his herald,[a] Peisenor, who clutches the King's mace.[b] One of his hunting dogs follows. Athena, Emotion, has endowed Telemakis with a new-found boldness. All make way for him as he strides through the crowd to take the Speaker's place.

Aegyptios, an old lord bent with the burden of life, but rich in wisdom and the ways of men, is the first to speak. His son, Antiphus, had accompanied Odyssey on his voyage to Troy, survived and crewed with him again after the war only to be killed when the savage Cyklops' devoured him. Aegyptios has three other sons, one of them is Eurynomous, who keeps company with the Suitors and two others who work at their father's farm.

Aegyptios is inconsolable at not knowing his son's fate. It is with passion that he rises to address the gathering:

"My fellow-countrymen listen to what I must say;

We have not been summoned here since Odyssey went away,

---

a   A *herald* is a messenger of official business.

b   A ceremonial mace is a highly ornamented staff of metal or wood, carried before a high-ranking official in civic ceremonies intended to represent the official's authority. The mace, as used today, derives from a weapon. Processions often feature maces, as on parliamentary or formal academic occasions.

Is it a young man who calls us together?

Or one of the elders, who has some news to deliver?

Is there news of some army's advance;

Or another important matter, per chance?

Whoever it is, good man is he, I say in any case;

So give him his voice and give him his place,

Let us wish for him Zeus' good intent;

And let's hear the reason for why here, we are all sent?"

These auspicious words delight Telemakis. Without further ado he stands in the middle of the assembly. His herald, Peisenor, a shrewd and experienced counsellor hands the speaker's staff to him. Telemakis, first turning to Aegyptios, says:

"Venerable sir, you will have the truth you seek;

It is I who wish you to listen to what I must speak,

You know me, the proud son and heir to Odyssey, Ithaki's king;

And you should know that his kingdom and I are suffering,

Firstly, I have lost my father to destiny and mortal fate;

Secondly, a crowd of Suitors infests my estate,

They pester my mother for her hand in matrimony;

With complete disrespect for all our hospitality,

These Suitors are sons of many fathers that here now stand;

Too cowardly to ask Ikarius for his daughter's hand,

If it be only Ithaki's men to bring to account for our loss;
But no, men from all over the world waste our wealth and our flocks,

I'm unable to defend my father's estate, as I am bound;
The Suitors out-number us, one hundred and eight, I have found,

Yet, I will gladly fight them, one or the lot;
For I have lost hope, to further bear the things they do, I will not!

Or, is it against my father a grudge they all bear;
Was his reign as your rightful king, oppressive and unfair?

They hanker for my mother's hand, harming her health;
But their real ambition is to capture this kingdom by stealth,

The destruction of my house is a very grave mistake;
Zeus, the Hospitable One, must be outraged, revenge he will make."

With this Telemakis throws the kings' mace to the ground and bursts into tears. Everyone is very sorry for him, but they sit still, no one venturing to answer. Eventually, Antinoos, says:

"Telemakis, you speak with high arrogance and low cunning too;
You try to cast fault with the Suitors, how dare you,

It is your artful mother that must shoulder the blame;
This three years gone, she has played a devious game,

She forces each Suitor to vie for her hand;
By maid she sends sweet messages to every love-struck man,

Tugging at heart strings while playing the field;
I hope to live long enough to see her yield,

And there is a greater trick she has employed;
Another scheme by which our advances are toyed,

With the help of her maids they set up a great loom;
Rarely seen, all day and night she's in her room;

By working fine needlework she can't marry just yet;
As she labours to make Lord Laertes a burial blanket,

And whilst Odyssey is indeed dead, and never the two shall meet;
The widow is not prepared to marry until the blanket is complete,

So, by day she embroiders to make it right;
And at night she unpicks it by the candle's light,

A slave-maid told us so, the reason is unclear as yet;
The game is now up, but not over I'll bet,

We are the fools that for three years and more;
Have wasted our time in this palace of yours,

The Suitors now make this reply, a demand of you;
For we are the aggrieved in this matter, it is true,

Send your mother back to her father, Ikarius;
And bid her to marry the best man of *his* choice,

If Penelope's beauty is a curse;

Then Suitors all, are destined for the worse,

She is the most desirable, her beauty is stunning;
And Athena[a] has schooled her well in the art of cunning,

She has put all other women to shame;
To Ithaki, Penelope is legend and fame,

But to the Suitors, just as Helen was to Troy;
She's *trouble* and mischief, and mastered by a boy,

The Suitors, our name now and forever tainted;
Make this demand with which you are again acquainted,

In good faith we ventured here to win her hand;
No Suitor shall leave until she marries the best man."

Patient Telemakis answers:

"How can I drive my mother from my father's house?
Be reasonable, we don't know my father is dead, Antinoos,

I do not have the bride-price[b] that a marriage will spend;
To Ikarius, my mother - widow or otherwise - I will not send,

If you take these words as offence;
Then I bid each Suitor get out and good riddance!

Go, waste and feast on some other man's estate;

---

a   Athena, was the "metaphor" used for the mental states of *inspiration* and *imagination* etcetera.
b   Bride price, or bride-wealth, is money, property or other possessions given by a groom or his family to the parents of the woman he is to marry. Bride-price is the opposite to a dowry which is paid to the groom or the groom's family.

It's time for all Suitors to leave, there's the gate."

Zeus, Compeller of deeds, has sent two eagles and they fly on the wind, sailing side by side in quiet flight. They fly over the middle of the assembly and wheel and circle around, beating the air with their wings and beaming terror into the eyes of those below. They fight fiercely and tear at each other as they fly off towards the palace.

The people are in wonder, and ask what all this is about. Halithersos,[a] the best prophet and reader of omens among them, spoke to them plainly:

"Hear me, men and Suitors of Ithaki, and beyond;
Of this eagle-winged omen you will not be fond,

My advice is that you make amends and then leave;
Great *trouble*[b] is on its way to visit you, I don't deceive,

Everything about Odyssey, that I foretold has come true;
The twentieth year has arrived and he will come too,

Odyssey will bring fame to Ithaki and Phortune Harbour[59] renowned;
And these infamous Suitors, in his Palace, will be downed."

Eurymachos, son of Polybos, says:

"Go away old man, and tell those children's tales to another;
Your prophesy only confounds all this bother,

Your omens create ill feelings, and your words stink!
Do you believe anyone is interested in what you think?

---

a   The name, *Halithersos*, is the origin of the word, halitosis, meaning bad breath. It can result in *anxiety* among those affected. It is also associated with depression and symptoms of obsessive compulsive disorder.
b   *Trouble*, an allusion to Odyssey and his thwarted return. An *allusion* is an incidental mention of something, either directly or by implication.

I can read omens just as well as any man, too;
Birds fly in the skies, that is what they do!

Eagles are often seen flying about this place;
It doesn't change the fact that Odyssey is dead, without a trace,

It's a pity you haven't suffered his fate too;
Adding to Telemakis' anger and defiance is not right of you,

Here is my warning to him and I mean no alarm;
But, he must return to his mother, and offer the Suitors no harm,

There are other women that perhaps we should marry and satisfy;
But we can't, it's for the rare and perfect Penelope that we want, and vie,

Alas, it is by tradition that the Suitors court for this marriage rite;
Whether you like it or not, Telemakis, the gods send you this blight."

Then thoughtful Telemakis, relying on Athena's wisdom, says:

"Eurymachos, and all other Suitors, I shall say no more;
But grant me a blue-eyed[a] ship and men, numbering a score,

To sandy Pilos and Sparta we will be bound;
To seek news of where my father's house, or grave, may be found,

If I hear he is alive and making home his course;
Then once he arrives it will be time for all to rejoice,

---

a   The blue-eye symbol is a superstition with its origin dating back to the legend of the Argonauts. The
Argo, Jason's ship, was able to navigate itself away from harm as its prow had eyes which could see
its safest course.

But if Odyssey is dead and cannot be found;

I will return home, and build him a burial mound,

Give my father the greatest funeral, in this his true home-land;

And to the best man, I shall make sure, Ikarius will give my mother's hand."

With these words said, he sits.

Mentor,[60] a friend of Odyssey, who was left in charge of everything with full authority over the servants and affairs of the palace, rises to speak. He addresses them:

"Hear me, men of Ithaki, and Suitors all, whoever you may be;

I hope you are fated to never have a ruler to govern equitably,

I pray that all your future kings be cruel and unjust;

Not one of you remembers how Odyssey ruled you, as any good king must,

How can I be angry at the wretched Suitors, these drooling fools;

Their stupidity is only exceeded by their wickedness, they break all the rules,

What if he does return as all the omens portend;

Against Odyssey's wrath can you protect yourselves, how will you defend?"

Leokritus, son of Evenor, answers him, saying:

"Mentor, what folly you speak, even if he does return;

He is so out-manned, a sad welcome he will earn,

His blood will be upon his *own* head, and a sorry wife will be;

No, the wanderer's return, or not, won't be of concern to me,

I say give the lad oarsmen, boat and his leave;

Let him find what he will, on the heaving seas;

Speed him on his journey, free our midst of him;

Now, let's go back to the palace, and fill wine cups to the brim,

Let us offer great sacrifices to the gods, and feast until its late;

And trust that the Invisibles are watching, it will seal our fate."

On this, the assembly breaks up. Each man goes back to his own house or to Odyssey's palace, but for Telemakis, who goes alone to the sea and washes his hands in the blue water of Phortune Harbour. He prays silently to Athena, Inspiration Itself, with these words:

"Hear me god whose visit bid me sail the endless sea;

Questing for answers to the fate of my father, Odyssey,

Each word you spoke, was wisdom I surely cherish;

I would obey, but fear that against the Suitors, I shall surely perish,

And then what will happen to our estate and my poor mother;

A sad end to fall into the hands of one Suitor or another,

Woe is me, what now am I to do;

God, who visited me, what advice have you?"

As he prays, Athena, Inspiration Itself, now inspirited as *Mentor*,[a] visits him and says:

"Telemakis, you are neither coward or fool;

You are the *only* one who can follow your father's line of rule,

---

a   The name, *Mentor*, translates to: *Instils spirit or courage.*

You are so like your father, I can plainly see;

Fruit falls not far from this family tree,

Be bold and assert your power;

The Invisibles are with you, bring on the hour,

In time you will know that all you see, hear and find;

Is just a part of Zeus' master plan, the Mind,

So, have no thought for the Suitors, and their reckless sport;

For all their remaining days, *Doom*[a] has numbered very short,

Time has come for action, not worry, doubt and tears;

Make this voyage and your father's name shall last thousands of years,

You and me shall take this voyage, on which your father's fate depends;

So, I'll go and search Ithaki for a good boat and crew, among our friends,

There is many a fine vessel that Phortune Harbour can boast;

I'll soon have her rigged and ready for Nestor's Pilos coast,

Go to your palace now and prepare provisions well;

And make sure that of these plans, no one you tell."

Telemakis speeds home. His intuition has been awakened. He knows that this, too, is the work of a god.

He finds the Suitors butchering goats and singeing pig carcasses in the outer court. They are building an enormous fire for sacrificial offerings to the gods.

---

a   Doom, another name for Moros, the omnipotent entity who dispenses everyone's life through pre-determined fate. He "compels" mortals to their death. The Moirai (Fates) asserted that not even Zeus could question Moros, because he is destiny. Moros was the only force that Zeus truly respected and dreaded. Because of this, Moros was also considered as the God behind god. Moros' opposite is Elpis the personified Spirit of Hope. She and the other spirits were trapped in a jar by Zeus and entrusts them to the care of the first human woman Pandora. When she opened the vessel all of the Spirits escaped except for Elpis (Hope) who remained behind to comfort mankind.

Antinoos, the contrarian bully, comes up to him and takes his hand in his own, saying:

> "Telemakis, you fire-brand, bear no bad blood against us;
> The Suitors will find you a ship and crew to sail to sandy Pilos,
>
> As in the past, come feast with us, have wine and break some bread;
> And then you can leave, to find news of your father, alive or dead."

Shrewd Telemakis says:

> "Antinoos, I cannot eat in peace, or take any pleasure;
> With men like you who plunder what I have and treasure,
>
> If I sail to Pilos who'll protect this estate and my mother;
> I don't think it would be one of the Suitors, or any other."

As he speaks he snatches his hand from Antinoos.

Meanwhile, the other Suitors continue preparing their feast. Some jeer, others mock him. One youngster says:

> "Telemakis, I think, means to be the death of us;
> I suppose he'll bring an army of friends from Pilos,
>
> Or perhaps he'll go to Efyra, for poison, like his father did;
> By adding it to the wine and larder, to kill us, I'll bid."

Another says:

> "Perhaps if Telemakis sails, and is sea-tossed;
> He will share the fate of his father, and perish sea-lost,

Then we can divide up his bounty and his estates;

And his mother's house will belong to the man she marries, and mates."

This is their low talk, one trying to outdo the other, as some men do in private.

Telemakis, ignoring them, goes downstairs into the store-room. This room has strong oak doors opening in the middle. And there his father's treasure of gold, bronze and jewels lies in heaps on the floor. There, also, is linen and spare clothes kept in open chests. Fragrant olive oil and casks of vintage wine, are stacked against the wall just in case Odyssey should ever come home again.

His old and faithful house-keeper *Eurykleia*,[a] daughter of Ops,[61] is in charge of these stores, night and day. Telemakis calls her to the store-room, saying:

"Nurse, draw me off twelve jars of wine, the very best;

And fill high with barley meal that travel chest,

Then gather twenty leather bags of provisions, no less;

For tomorrow I sail for word of my father, to sandy Pilos."

She begins to cry. Speaking through her tears, she says:

"My dear child, where did these strange thoughts come from?

You are the only hope that can save your mother, and this home,

Your father is dead and gone, stop this silly notion;

This is not the time for wandering over a barren ocean."

Telemakis, answers:

"Fear not nurse, my scheme is sent by a heavenly god;

If my mother asks where I am, then tell her not,

_____

a   The name, *Eurykleia*, translates to: widely respected; well honoured.

I don't want to wrinkle her brow or grey her hair;

Worrying about me and wherever I may dare."

The old woman takes a solemn oath, and pours the wine into jars, tips the barley meal into the chest and packs the other provisions.

Telemakis goes back into the palace Hall where the Suitors remain.

In the meantime, Athena, the Spirit of Emotion, takes on the image of Telemakis. She goes around the town mustering a crew, telling them to meet at the ship, in Phortune Harbour at sunset. She goes also to Noemon, son of Phronius, and asks him to borrow a ship, which he readily allows. He offers his finest blue-eyed boat, *Sea Quest*. At sunset she slips the boat into the water, puts all the tackle on board and stations the vessel at the end of the harbour, by a stand of Pine trees. The crew comes, and the goddess greets each one with thankful words.

Athena spirits to Odyssey's palace and secretly taints the Suitors' drinks which fuddles them where they sit, throwing them into a deep sleep. Their wine-cups become invisible. When they awake, they wander back to their own homes in town to sleep off their drowsiness.

Athena, takes the form of Mentor again. She calls Telemakis outside:

"Telemakis, The *Sea Quest* is slipped and the men are at the ready;

She and her crew are waiting for the captain's rudder to steady,

If there be no wind to push onto this ship's true course;

Then our destination shall be found with twenty good oars,

A score of men are now anxious to pull towards Orion's star;

No time to waste, we have seas to cross, to ports afar."

They arrive at the blue-eyed ship and find the crew waiting. Telemakis goes aboard. Athena, has taken a seat at the vessel's helm, astern, in the guise of Mentor. Telemakis sits beside her. The crew loosen the mooring lines and take their places on the benches. Athena brings them a fair wind from the West.

Telemakis orders the crew to cast off, and they do as told. They set the mast into the socket of the keel, raise it, and tie it fast to the bow, with the fore-stays. They hoist the white sails by heaving the halyards of plaited ox hide. The crew take their places on the benches. They pull the oars along their course until Athena's hugging wind bellies out the sails. They make a heading and secure the boom and rudder. The

Sea Quest plies the blue water and foam flicks her hull. No need for oars now, so they fill their wine cups to the brim, making offerings to Athena and the Invisibles, that forever endure in bliss.

From Phortune Harbour, they sail north-east along the Gulf of Molos. On Starboard,[a] they pass the narrow, craggy Cape Skinos. Once clear, they point south and follow the coast towards the small, star-shaped island of Asteris.[62] It is midway between Phortune Harbour and the port of Sami,[63] and close to Pera Pigadi Cove on the east coast of Ithaki. It has two sheltered mooring places, on the inside of the island close to the shore. There, between the shore and Asteris Island, ships can hide from storms. As there is smooth seas and fair winds, the ship now points south-east into open water. By the Moon's light, through the night's watches, the *Sea Quest* sails into its inexorable Fate.

*

---

a   To the right lies Cape Skinos.

EPISODE THREE

PRINCE TELEMAKIS VISITS KING NESTOR

After five days, Dawn wakes to light the lantern of Day and they reach Pilos, the city of Nestor[a], the great horse tamer.

Thousands of people are gathered on the wide horse-shoe shaped beach,[b] overlooked by Nestor's palace[64]. Telemakis and his crew, flake the sails, bring the ship to anchor, and go ashore. Athena - disguised as Mentor - leads, Telemakis follows. The citizens and their army are celebrating the Festival of Poseidon, Land-maker and Earth-quaker and also the nemesis of Odyssey.

There are nine regiments with five hundred men in each. They are sacrificing 450 black bulls offering thanks for the generosity of the gods for the favourable thoughts they provide. They roll the bones in fat and burn them as an offering to the gods. Then they eat the grilled innards cut first from the beasts while the thighs roast over the spit's embers.

Athena, Inspiration, in the guise of Mentor, says:

"Telemakis, you must not be modest or nervous;

You have taken this voyage for an ordained purpose,

To find your father's house, or grave, and how he met his end;

This is not the time to be shy, your answer is with Nestor, his friend,

Go, now, and from him, ask for the truth from the king of *this* city;

He will tell no lies to you, for you're the son of revered Odyssey."

---

a   The name, *Nestor* translates to: *Home goer; returner to the nest*

b   Voidakilia Beach is an Omega-shaped land form and considered one of the world's most beautiful beaches and coves.

Coy, Telemakis, says:

"But how, Mentor, am I to address him, or converse?
For long conversations and speeches, I am for the worse,

He is a king and much my senior, I must show respect;
I might say something silly and wrong, to my regret."

Disguised Athena, answers him:

"Telemakis, trust that the right words you will speak;
Zeus watches over you from the Olympian peak,

Have faith, let the good within be your God;
Then the God within will be your guide,

The gods have been with you since your first day on Earth;
The right words will come and you shall prove your worth."

She goes quickly on, and Telemakis follows in her steps until they reach the place where the armed forces of the Pilosians are assembled. There they find Nestor sitting with his sons. His company around him are busy skewering and roasting meat and preparing the feast. They welcome the strangers and crowd around them. They offer them places at the banquet table.

Nestor's son, Pisistratus, offers his hand in health[a] to each of them, and seats them on sheepskins near his father and his brother Thrasymedes. Then he gives them portions of offal and pours wine into gold cups, first to Athena, and saluting her at the same time, says:

"Offer a prayer, good Sir, to the Earthquaker, Poseidon;
Then pass the cup to your young friend, so he can join in,

---

a   In ancient Greece, the offering of a hand-shake was a gesture of good health. Touching balanced both persons condition, reducing illness and boosting well-being.

Mortals can't live without gods, lets not pretend;

For in Mind's plan, Mortals are apart, but depend,

Let's make thanks with libations[a] and respect;

So Poseidon's protection we can continue to expect."

Athena, Emotion Itself, was impressed with this honouring of the gods and *his* wisdom. She begins her prayer:

"Poseidon, that lifts all lands above endless waters;

Grant safe lives and glory to Nestor, the Pilosians, all sons and daughters,

And after these bestial offerings that honour you by this feast;

Allow us to tell what matter our voyage brings East,

Grant, too, our blue-eyed ship and crew's safe return home;

And lessen the days that on our quest, we roam."

She hands the cup to Telemakis and he repeats the same prayer.

The other, outer, meats are cooked and taken off the embers. The carvers serve every person a portion making a bountiful banquet. Their appetites and thirst satisfied, Nestor, Knight of Gerene,[b] begins to speak:

"Now that our guests have their dinner done;

Tell us who you are and from where you've come,

You don't look like pirates, or slave traders;

And your ship and it's crew don't look like invaders,

If trading has sailed you here over the high seas;

---

a Libations, drops of wine, were poured onto the ground, the floor or fire as an offering of gratitude to the gods for the favourable thoughts they provide.

b *Greene* meant: General or commander-in-chief, in this case, supreme leader, the title he earned by default after Agamemnon was murdered. King Nestor is now the supreme ruler of the Hellenes.

Then tell us about your cargo, what do you bring as commodities?

Telemakis answers boldly, for Athena has instilled courage in him:

"Nestor, honour to the Hellene name, Hail!
You ask from what home port we did sail,

Phortune Harbour is our home, in Ithaki;
And I am here to seek news of long-lost Odyssey,

For he was my father, that I have never known;
For over twenty years, missing from his rightful throne,

He left his palace when I was but a swaddled boy;
And legend tells you joined him, to sack ill-fated Troy,

We know the fate of all who went to Ilium[a], that Trojan city;
But not for one of it's greatest heroes, my father Odyssey,

I can only hope that Athena, Inspiration Itself,
Has kept him alive, all this time, and in good health;

Dead, alive – where? I must know which is right,
Nestor, do you know where he may be, and of his plight?

Tell me straight, don't soften your words, for only truth do I care;
Not knowing his fate is true misery and utter despair."

Nestor answers:

---

a   Ilium, meant where the Sun rises, the east.

"My friend, your words stir memories, deep and pained;
From that Trojan shore where old King Priam reigned,

And even before the war, there were hard days to beat;
We crewed with Achilles, and roved every coast that we'd meet,

Plundering supplies, arms and mustering men for war each day;
Constant danger and daring escapes - or death - was our pay,

But it was in Troy that most of our best men fell in battle;
Like our offerings to the Invisibles, they were slaughtered just like cattle,

We lost the agile Achilles, Ajax and peerless Patroklos,[65] too;
But my greatest loss was a dear son, Antilochos, who I'm reminded of, by you,

And we suffered much more, but what mortal tongue wants to tell;
The whole story, many years of listening, would not do justice to how they fell,

Then you would turn for home weary of my Trojan war story;
And not have heard all about war and disastrous glory,

Nine long years we tried to overcome by every means;
Looking back, the hand of Zeus was against us, it now seems,

All through those years, and in every dire situation;
You're father excelled with persistence and determination,

He was a fearful warrior to the enemy, on the field of battle;
He easily broke their spirit, shields would shake and spears rattle,

By night, in the camps, he would rouse the blue hearts of thousands of men;

And the next morning, he'd be first in line to lead them out again,

Indeed you are his son, I can hardly believe my eyes;
You look just like him and speak so too, it does not surprise,

From camp to council, he and I never had any differences, day or night;
Of single heart and purpose we advised the Hellenes how to make things right,

After we sacked the Trojan city, and before leaving for our scattered ports;
Mighty Zeus' daughter, Athena, Emotion, had other thoughts,

She devised a quarrel between the two sons of Lord Atreus;
Their names you know, Agamemnon[a] and the younger Menelaos,

They called an assembly at sunset, and the crowd was heavy with wine;
Menelaos was for sailing homeward without any waste of time,

Agamemnon, displeased, wished to make sacrifices to Athena, first;
He should have known that the gods plans can't be changed, the fool was cursed,

There they stood exchanging curses, fast and bitter words flew;
That terrible uproar divided them, swords were drawn to slew,

That night was mostly sleep-less for anger between comrades was strong;
At dawn, we slipped our ships, with spoils and captive women, and we were gone,

But Agamemnon's men had to sacrifice to Athena, with offerings to burn;
And so they stayed and gave their thanks, foolishly, they would learn,

Our sailing went well for the gods had planned smooth water;

---

a   The name, *Agamemnon*, translates to: Stubborn, unyielding.

So, on reaching Tenedos,[66] we offered sacrifices of thanks to Athena, Zeus' daughter,

But cruel Zeus was not happy with our Trojan victory: We were mistaken;
He wanted the feuding brothers' new-found peace to be broken,

Another fight started and half the fleet turned back to Troy;
Prudent Odyssey led *those* blue-eyed ships, his diplomacy to employ,

But I foresaw the strife that always followed Agamemnon;
So, I guided our ships across the seas to Euboea[67] and beyond,

After many days we reached beloved Pilos, our welcomed home-port;
And the others of my fleet returned to their homes too, I can report,

But of the other fleet I have not seen hide nor hair;
And not a word about Odyssey, or what fate he bear,

You must have heard of Agamemnon's fated lot;
He fell victim to Agisthos's scheming plot,

But Agisthos ate justice, his way was outrageous;
His lust fully satisfied by avenging *Orestes*,[a]

He was served his just desserts and revenge;
By eating his family, what bitter ends,

It is a good thing a father leaves an able son;
I trust some day your father will know that he too, has one,

So, Telemakis, be as bold as Orestes, hold back your fears;

---

a   The name, *Orestes*, translates to: lofty heights or thoughts of grandeur.

And the future shall know your name for thousands of years."

Thoughtful Telemakis replies:

"Nestor, son of Neleus, honour to the Hellene name;
We applaud Orestes' revenge and his new-found fame,

If only Athena, Emotion Itself, would have some happiness in store;
But not knowing the fate of my father, mother and home, I sadly endure."

Nestor, replies:

"My friend, you remind me of the rumours of Suitors in your palace;
We've heard that they pester your mother, and to you, show great malice,

How disgraceful! What a different place it would forever be;
If those wretched Suitors saw the return of Odyssey,

Imagine, now, if in their presence he stands;
In battle dress, with bow, arrows and spear in his hands,

Resourceful Odyssey, brave and true, god-like and tall;
What a sorry occasion it would be for the Suitors, one and all,

He'd have them begging for mercy with a deadly end to their fun;
Your home would be peaceful again, and the wooing be done,

One hopes that Athena takes as much a liking to you;
As she did to good Odyssey, when I knew him, faithful and true."

Telemakis answers:

"Lord, you speak of the impossible and hope to change Fate;
There is no point in keeping my hopes high, it's too late;

I doubt that my father lives, I fear the very worst,
I can't expect Athena's help, for his destiny was cursed."

On this Athena, in the guise of Mentor, says:

"Telemakis, what are you saying? Yes, death is certain;
But in your father's case, he may have not seen the final curtain,

Heaven can do mighty things, that is plain to see;
Perhaps, the gods will return him when it's time, and safely,

Don't forget how Agamemnon sped on a homeward path;
To be murdered in his palace's first blood-bath,

There is always some god close enough to hear one's plea;
Trust that one is attending to your plight now, and also that of Odyssey."

Telemakis, replies, saying:

"Mentor, please, no more talk of my father's return;
His fate was sealed by the gods, of which I'm not to learn,

But of Nestor, Lord, another thing I request;
Tell me about avenging Orestes, and his blood-fest,

How did Agamemnon come to die, by what plan?
How was Agisthos able to murder such a better man?

And what of Menelaos, was he involved?

Tell me truly, how was this bad business resolved?"

Nestor, answers:

"I will tell you truly, indeed it is a shameful affair;

If Menelaos had returned home and found Agisthos there,

There would have been no mourning, funeral or prayers to the gods;

For his corpse would have been fed to the vultures and the dogs,

For whilst we were in Troy fighting for our lives and victory;

Agisthos, was wooing the heart of Agamemnon's wife with infidelity,

At first, Queen Klytemenstra[68] shunned his intentions as was proper;

And besides, her husband had arranged his minstrel to keep an eye on her,

But as heaven had destined his destruction;

Agisthos sent the minstrel off to a deserted island,[a]

There the crows and vultures fattened upon his carcass;

Then she went willingly enough to the bedroom of Agisthos,

For all his advances in the past she did spurn;

But now, she was more than ready to take his sperm,

He checked the king by mating the queen;

And so he offered sacrifices to the gods for his act, obscene,

a   Probably the island of Spetses, which can be seen from the Great Room of the palace at Mycenae. Later, Agisthos stationed his watchman on Spetses to alert him of Agamemnon's doomed return from Troy.

He heaped the altars, decorated temples and new ones he built;

With tapestries, lavish furniture, rugs and gold to dissolve his guilt,

For his desire had succeeded beyond his wildest dreams;

But his ambitions were to be cut short by revenging schemes,

Meanwhile, Menelaos and me - friends - were on our way home from Troy;

Things started to go very wrong, the gods stepped in and ruined our joy,

We got to Cape Souniun,[69] which is one of Athens' southern tips;

And far-shooter Apollo[a] with his painless shafts, stopped the heart of Phrontis,

The great navigator of Menelaos' blue-eyed ship died at the helm;

Menelaos[b] and the crew were very anxious and overwhelmed,

We had to wait and bury our comrade with full rites;

Then, Zeus sent us evil winds and waves from the Olympian heights,

He divided our fleet, and took the other five ships towards Crete;[70]

Where the Kydonians[71] dwell and the sea and the river *Iardanus*,[c] meet,

Then to a headland stretching into the sea from a place called Gortyng;[72]

Along this coast to Phaestus[73] the sea runs wild when a south wind's blowing,

After Phaestus the coast is protected and makes good shelter;

But there that part of the fleet was driven on to the rocks in a galing welter,

The ships were wrecked but the crews survived somehow;

---

a   The name *Apollo* translates to: Distance, afar. Apollo is a metaphor for the concept of space, separation between things.

b   The name *Menelaos* translates to: *meanness, despair to the people.*

c   The *Iardanus* river runs through north-western Crete, near the city of Chania.

As for the other five blue-eyed ships, I will tell you all now,

They were taken to Egypt by winds and seas so bold;
Where Menelaos gathered much treasure and the finest gold;

From those alien people, their pyramids and ancient speech;
We were not able to leave for the home ports, we wanted to reach,

Meanwhile, Agisthos had murder planned;
And Klytemenstra killed Agamemnon, her husband,

The people lived under Agisthos' kingly rule for seven years;
An unjust man who imposed oppression and constant fears,

But in the eighth year Orestes returned from Athens to be his bane;
And he killed the adulterer Agisthos, as was ordained,

For all the deeds he committed, many and atrocious;
He fell and died under the ancient curse of the House of Atreus,

Then during the funeral banquet prepared by his mother, for Agisthos;
With his ships filled high with treasure, came Menelaos,

So take my advice and don't leave your home to dangerous people;
They will eat up everything and do even more harm with their evil,

Don't allow this journey of yours to be wasted, thus;
So with all speed go and visit Helen and Menelaos,

He has just returned home from travels across vast seas;
That birds cannot fly in twelve months, even assisted by the breeze,

Go to him, by sea, and take your own men and ship's courses;

Or, if you travel by land you can take our chariots and hardy horses,

And here are my sons who'll escort you to Menelaos, in Lacedaemon;

He will tell you the truth for he is the most excellent person in his domain."

As Nestor speaks the Sun sets into the darkness. Athena, Emotion Itself,
says:

"Nestor, Sir, all that you have said was spoken well, but;

Order the tongues of these victims to be cut,[a]

And mix the wine to make drink-offerings to Poseidon, before we sleep;

People should go home early and respect for religious festivals, so keep."

All assembled, obey Athena. The man-servants pour water over the hands of
the guests, while the stewards fill mixing-bowls with wine and water and serve them
all. They stand to make their drink offerings and throw the cattle tongues into the fire.

When they had made their offerings and had drunk to their satisfaction,
Athena and Telemakis start walking towards the *Sea Quest*, but Nestor catches them
and says:

"Heaven forbid, you can't leave my house to camp on a ship;

You'll come to my palace and *there* you will both sleep,

Both of you have spent too much time sleeping at sea;

You must have the benefit of my home's hospitality."

Athena answers:

---

a   Sacrificed animals had their tongues cut out and burnt as an offering to the gods. Wine was also
     sprinkled on the embers as libations, offerings of gratitude for the generosity of the gods for the
     favourable thoughts they provide.

"Sir, you have spoken well and what you say is true;
Telemakis shall sleep at your house, and now return with you,

But to the blue-eyed ship I must go before it gets too late;
My patient crew must be pondering our fate,

This crew is not as experienced as me;
The men are but young and crew for us out of loyalty,

At Dawn, a course along the Koronian[a] coast we will be rowing;
For me to collect a long-standing debt of much money, still owing,

As for Telemakis, now that he is one of your guests;
Send him to Sparta with horses and chariots,

He should take with him one of your sons for company;
And pray to Poseidon that they arrive and return safely."

Instantly, she takes the form of an eagle and flies away. King Nestor is astonished, and takes Telemakis by the hand, saying:

"My friend I see that you are destined to become a great hero;
For that was the Spirit Athena, disguised as your friend Mentor,

She showed such deathless honour to your father, Odyssey;
Great Athena, grant fame for years to me and my family!

I'll sacrifice a young, unbroken, gilt-horned heifer;
And trust that my family lineage shall last forever."

---

a   The coast line south-west of Pilos extending to Koroni.

As he prays Athena hears him. He leads the way to his palace, followed by his sons and sons in law. They take their places on the benches and seats, He mixes them a bowl of sweet wine that is eleven years vintaged. As he mixes the wine, he prays and makes libations to Athena, Spirit of Emotion. The others go to their homes to sleep.

King Nestor sends Telemakis to bed in the room over the gateway along with Pisistratus, who is the only unmarried son. As for himself, he retires to an outer room of the house with his wife, the Queen, by his side.

At day break, rosy-fingered Dawn appears and Nestor leaves his couch and sits on a bench of polished white marble in front of his house. Here his father, Neleus, now dead, used to sit.

Nestor sits with a sceptre in hand, as guardian of the Hellenic people. His sons gather around him, Echephron, Stratius, Perseus, Aretus, Thrasymedes and the sixth son Pisistratus. Telemakis joins and sits with them. King Nestor addresses them:

"My sons, make haste, do as I bid, we were visited by Spirit Athena;

Someone go to the plains, and bring a young, wild heifer,

Another go and fetch Laerceus the goldsmith, its horns he'll gild;

Tell the maids in the house to bring logs and a fire build,

Another go to Telemakis' ship and invite the crew;

On second thoughts, summon them all except for two,

The rest of you stay where you are;

And tell the maids to bring me some fresh water."

At this, they hurry to their errands. The heifer is brought in from the plain, and Telemakis' crew arrives from the ship. The goldsmith has brought the anvil, hammer, and tongs and with the gleaming gold, gilds the heifer's horns.

Athena herself, in the guise of Mentor, oversees the preparations.

Stratius and Echephron bring the beast by the horns. Aretus has the water in a vase. His other hand holds a basket of barley meal. Thrasymedes stands by with a sharp axe, ready to strike the heifer, while Perseus holds a bucket, to catch the blood. King Nestor washes his hands and sprinkles the barley meal. He offers solemn prayers to Athena and throws a lock of hair from the heifer's head into the fire.

They finish their toasts and salutes and now Thrasymedes wields his axe at its neck and the split heifer collapses. The King's daughters and daughters-in-law, and his venerable wife Eurydice (she is eldest daughter to Clymenus) scream with delight. Then they lift the heifer's head off the ground, and Pisistratus cuts its throat. The bleeding stops and they butcher it, cutting the thigh bones and wrapping them in two layers of fat, setting the innards on the top. The King lays them on the wood fire and pours wine over them, while the young men stand near with five-pronged spits in their hands. The thighs are cooked and they eat the innards, they cut the rest of the meat up, skewering the smaller pieces on the roasting spits.

Meanwhile, the beautiful princess, Polycaste, Nestor's youngest daughter, bathes Telemakis in the royal bath.[a] She massages him with virginal olive oil blended with lemon juice. She brings a new shirt, a cloak and jacket and he looks god-like. He takes a seat at the side of Nestor.

When the other, outer, meats were done they take them off the spits and sit down to dinner where they are waited upon by some stewards who pour out the wine into gold cups. Satisfied with food and drink Nestor says:

"Sons, yoke Telemakis' horses to the chariot with haste;

For he has an Olympian mission, with no time to waste."

His sons yoke the horses to the chariot. The housekeeper has packed provisions of bread, wine, and sweet meats for the princes. Telemakis climbs into the chariot and sits besides Pisistratus as he gathers the reins. He lashes the horses and they fly forward into the open plains, Pilos behind them. They travel until Sun is replaced by Night which covers the land.

They reach Therae[74] where Diocles lives, who is the son of Ortilochus and grandson to Alpheus. Here they pass the night as Diocles entertains them generously.

At sunrise, rosy-fingered Dawn's light helps them yoke the horses. They drive out through the portico under the echoing gatehouse. Pisistratus lashes the horses on and they fly forward. Their horses perform well and soon they arrive into the corn and wheat fields in the valleys of Sparta.

Sun rises.

Light delivers Time,

Belonging to Day.

*

---

a   At the ruins of Nestor's palace the private, royal bath remains in tact, preserved as it was in the year 1,207 BC.

EPISODE FOUR

KING MENELAOS AND QUEEN HELEN OF SPARTA

They drive straight into the estate of King Menelaos. They find him in his glorious palace, in Lacedaemon[75] feasting with his many clansmen honouring the wedding of his son, and also of his daughter, Hermione,[76] who was marrying, Neoptolemus, the bold son of that valiant warrior, Achilles.

Achilles had given consent and promised her to him while he was still at Troy, and now Destiny is marrying them. Menelaos is sending her with chariots and horses and fine treasures to the city of the Myrmidons,[a] which is ruled by Achilles' son.

Menelaos, has found a bride for Megapenthes, his only son, in Sparta, the daughter of Alector. Megapenthes was born of a slave-woman in his palace. Mind has ensured that his wife Helen had no more children after she bore Hermione, who is, as many say, more beautiful than Aphrodite.

The neighbours and friends of Menelaos are feasting heartily. There is a bard singing to them and playing his lyre. Two acrobats are performing in the midst of them when the songster starts with a tune. Telemakis and the son of Nestor have tied their horses at the gate. Eteoneus, servant to Menelaos, comes out, seeing them he runs back into the palace to tell his master. He goes close and whispers:

"Two strangers have come here in a chariot, Menelaos;

These young men are god-like, for they look like sons of Zeus,

Shall I take their horses and bid them to come in;

Or turn them away for some other house to entertain?"

Menelaos is angry, saying:

---

a   The Myrmidons were a legendary people of Greek mythology, native to the region of Thessaly. During the Trojan War, they were commanded by Achilles, as described in Homer's *Iliad*. According to Hellenic history, they were created by Zeus from a colony of ants and therefore took their name from the Greek word for ant, *myrmex*.

"Eteoneus, son of Boethous, you never used to be a fool;

Have you ever seen a visitor turned away under my rule?

Take their horses and offer them our hospitality;

Bring them now and they will feast with me and my family."

Eteoneus and some servants rush to the princes and bid them to follow. The other servants take the sweating steeds from the chariots, yoke and stable them with troughs of oats and barley grains. They park the chariot against the courtyard wall.

As the two princes reach the bronzed threshold, they stop, astonished at seeing the palace's splendour. It is as if the high hall has the radiance of both the Sun and the Moon. The high walls on either side are bronze from end to end, and are inlaid with lapis lazuli[a] and gold. The doors are gold, and hung on pillars of silver that rise from a bronze floor, the lintel[b] is silver and the door handles are gold. When their wonder is content they are taken into the the bath-house and bathed.

The servants have washed, massaged and anointed them with virginal olive oil. Fresh clothes are brought; new linen tunics and over-shirts.

They take their seats by the side of Menelaos. A maid pours scented water from a gold jug over their hands into a silver basin. The house-keeper draws a table to them and brings bread and delicacies from the busy kitchen. A steward serves cut meats carved on his board. He places gold goblets and fills them with fine wine. Menelaos greets them saying:

"Welcome and please enjoy your meal and this feast;

You are honoured guests here, now that your day's journey has ceased,

Once you have had your fill of food and wine;

Please tell what matter brings you to this house of mine,

I'm curious as two men as you must be borne of kings blessed;

For you both have the handsome looks of the Immortal gods, no less."

---

a   Lapis lazuli is a deep blue, semi-precious stone with veins of pyrite giving it a brassy lustre. It has been prized since antiquity for its intense colour. It is mined in Afghanistan.

b   A lintel is a beam, or in some cases an arch-way, above a doorway or window.

He hands them pieces of roasted prime loin meat, and serves them the finest food from the table, before them. Telemakis whispers to Pisistratus:

"Man alive, can you believe this incredible treasure;
Everywhere I look gleams gold, ivory, silver and amber,

Everything is so splendid that even Olympian Zeus would be at home;
If I lived in this paradise, I should never need to leave and roam."

Menelaos overhears him, and says:

"No-one, my friends, can compete with Immortal Zeus;
Of course other men have great riches too, more or less,

But I travelled far, fought and suffered as much as any man;
For eight years after the Trojan War my fleet sailed for this home-land,

To Cyprus, Phoenicia, Egypt and Ethiopia we were ill-wind scattered;
And to Sidonia,[77] Erembia and Libya where these great treasures were gathered,

But while I was travelling and denied my homely life;
My brother was secretly murdered by his wretched wife,

So I have no pleasure in being lord over all this wealth and glory;
Your parents must have told you about the House of Atreus, and its horror story,

I'd gladly settle for a third of what I used to have before;
If only I could change what happened in this house,[a] and at that war,

I often sit here and weep for them one and all, for pained hours;

---

a   Interestingly they are all seated in the dining hall where Agamemnon (Menelaos' brother) was
     murdered by his wife Klytemenstra (Helen's sister).

Grieving is a cold comfort and one's own life soon sours,

But there's a man I grieve for the most and the dearest memory I keep;

When I brood for him, food I can not eat, and I even detest sleep,

I endure a haunting sense of loss and responsibility;

Did all his labours end in a lonely death, for the great Odyssey?

I suppose his people are already mourning him as dead;

For loyal Penelope and Telemakis, life, too, must be dread."

Telemakis begins to cry. With both hands, he holds up his cloak in front of his eyes. Menelaos sees his pain and debates whether to let him choose his own time to speak, or to ask him at once why he is so upset. While in two minds, his wife Helen, comes down from her high chamber, looking as lovely as Artemis,[78] Beauty Itself.

Adraste brings her a seat, Alcippe a soft woollen rug and Phylo brings her the silver work-box which Alcandra, wife of Polybos, had given her. Polybos lives in Egyptian Thebes, which is the richest city in the world. He had given Menelaos two baths, both of pure silver, two tripods and ten talents of gold.[a] As well as this, his wife had given Helen a gold staff, an engraved silver box, with wheels and a gold band around the top of it. Phylo places it by her side. It's full of fine spun yarn, and a distaff charged with purple-dyed wool was laid on it.

Helen sits, putting her feet on the footstool. She starts to question Menelaos:

"Do we know, Menelaos, the names of these strangers who visit us?

I cannot help saying that this young man is Odyssey's son, Telemakis,

Who was a babe-in-arms and left to the care of Penelope;

When Odyssey set sail for Troy on account of shameless me?"

Menelaos replied:

---

a   The Hellenic unit of weight corresponding to 26 kilograms (57 lbs) being the approximate mass of water required to fill an amphora, a vessel used to transport and store commodities. The value of 10 talents of gold would convert to about 20 million dollars (US).

"Dear wife, just as you, the likeness I too can see;
He does have the hair, head, eyes and feet of Odyssey,

And when I was talking about Odyssey, and saying how much he suffered;
Many tears fell from his eyes, and his sorrowed face he covered."

Pisistratus says:

"Menelaos, you are right in thinking that he is Telemakis;
And shy to come here and open conversation with you, as he is modest.

My father, Nestor, seeks good counsel for Telemakis, that is why he is sent;
For he suffers the greatest of troubles at home, where his father is still absent."

Menelaos, bawling too, says:

"The gods bless me for this visit by the son of my friend Odyssey;
Who did suffer great hardship and *trouble,* all because of me,[a]

I had hoped to entertain him with a glorious life;
After we both returned from Troy and the following sea strife,

I should have built him, and his people, the greatest city;
And made him leave his home-land Ithaki, to be closer to me,

But a nasty god stood in his *troubled* way;
He seems destined never to reach Ithaki's, Phortune Bay."

---

a   Menelaos is venting his guilt and shame for chasing after Helen which resulted in the Trojan War.

They are all weeping; Telemakis, Helen, Menelaos and Pisistratus, who cries for his brother who was lost on the voyage home from the Trojan War. Pisistratus says:

"Sir, my father, Nestor, talks about you often at home;
He told me you are one of the wisest men he has known,

We have come a long way, and I am not fond of crying when I eat;
I would like to forget how they all suffered, in victory and in defeat,

It will plague, haunt and torture our hearts in every tomorrow;
We must try to endure the middle path, between happiness and sorrow,

We can shave our heads and wring the tears from our eyes;
But can never erase from our minds, the battlefield, and its death-cries,

I too was robbed of a beloved, Antilochos, who was also lost after the war;
A valiant warrior, one you may have known, and I never saw."

Menelaos, answers:

"Your discretion, friend is beyond your young years;
It is plain you take after your father, one of history's great seers,

One can readily see a son to which Heaven and Earth have bred;
For there is more to descendants than what comes from a husband and wife's bed,

And Nestor is well blessed to have wise offspring to protect him;
So, let us dine, drink and put an end to these heavy words and weeping,

Telemakis and I can talk with one another tomorrow;
Good rest and sleep will clear our hearts and minds of all this sorrow."

Asphalion, one of the servants, pours scented water from a gold jug over their hands into a silver basin. He again offers them bread and delicacies. A steward serves cut meats carved on his board. He places gold goblets and readies them to be filled with fine wine.

But, first, Zeus's favourite, Helen, who can do no wrong, has a herb which cures sorrow and ill feelings, for twenty-four hours. This drug was given to Helen by Polydamna wife of Thon, a woman of Egypt, where they grow herbs, some good as food and medicine and others are poisonous. The people of Egypt are skilled physicians and descended from the builders of the Pyramids, the Paeons.[79]

Helen secretly adds the herb to the wine, tainting it, and tells the servants to serve it, saying:

"Menelaos, King and husband, and you all, my good friends;

All powerful Zeus, Truth, is the maker of amends,

Giving us both evil and good as he wants; damning and caring;

There are winners and losers, some are meek and others daring,

I can't tell you all of Odyssey's exploits, that number is too great;

But I must tell you of this one deed, before it gets too late,

At Troy, he disguised himself as a beggar with filthy rags on;

Frightful wounds and bruises that all people shied away from,

By this he was able to enter Priam's city gates, easily;

No-one spoke a word to him, and I alone saw that it really was he,

But he was too cunning, and would not give up his game;

Until one day he confided in me, and admitted his name,

So I bathed and massaged him and gave him fresh clothes and shoes;

Before he returned to the Hellenes' blue-eyed ships he told me of their wooden-horse ruse,

He gained much information about the city from its people's lips;
And killed many Trojans on the way back to the Hellenes' ships,

Each woman of Troy was very upset for her dead husband;
But, not me, I was yearning to return to my daughter and home-land,

For Aphrodite's spell[a] was wearing off and I had a change of heart;
Each day away from Menelaos and family was like a year apart."

Menelaos interrupts, saying:

"Yes, dear, all that you have been saying is true;
I have travelled much, and have seen a hero or two,

But there was never another man such as Odyssey, of course;
What courage and cunning he showed in that wooden horse,

Inside it, the best of us were sitting within Troy's city wall;
Ready to bring death and destruction upon the Trojans once and for all,

But you, Helen, came up to us as some god wished the *Trojans* better;
Calling out to each man's name mimicking our wives' voices to the letter,

Some of us could not decide to spring from the hollow horse;
Or, answer you from inside, either would've led to our deaths, of course,

It was Odyssey that clapped his hands over the mouth of Anticlus;
Until Athena came and took you away, and we were saved, thus,

---

a   Aphrodite promised Paris the most beautiful woman in the world, who, at the time, was Helen. They
met on the island of Kithera.

Not only that, we were then able to sack the mighty Troy;

Win that long war, and the freedom we now enjoy,

We were in the company of a hero without peer;

Without Odyssey, we all would not be sitting here."

Telemakis says:

"How sad, that after all his exploits his own life he could not keep;

I can think of it no more, let's retire, I must sleep."

Helen tells the maids to set-up two beds in the guest rooms of the gatehouse, and to make them with purpled rugs. The maids go, carrying torches, and prepare the beds. The man-servants escort the royal princes to their quarters while Menelaos lays in his bed, Helen by his side.

Dawn wakes Day.

Menelaos rises and dresses himself. He hangs his sword from his shoulder, and strides from his room with the confidence of a god. He finds Telemakis, sits with him and says:

"And what, Telemakis, has led you to take this long journey to Sparta?

Are you on public, or private business, is it about your father?

Telemakis replies:

I come to ask if you have news of my father, or of where he may be;

For it is twenty years, since he left his beloved Ithaki,

In my father's time his palace was the envy of every city;

Now it is mocked with shame and pity,

The gods must have conspired not to return my father;

Now I am besieged with one-hundred-and-eight Suitor's ardour,

It is with my mother, Penelope, they pretend devoted;
But eating and drinking is their true motive,

Each afternoon they arrive empty-handed;
Whilst mother sits in her room; gloomy, stranded,

She hates the idea of re-marriage;
And of any courting is quick to disparage,

So, the Suitors drink wine to the very last drop;
Even their bellies groan and belch at them to stop,

Once the bounty of kitchen and cellar are gone;
The Suitors then stumble out, often it's well past dawn,

What am I to do? Woe is me;
I ask you Menelaos, where is he?"

Menelaos is astonished, saying:

"So, these cowards would usurp a brave man's bed, and his estate;
Just as a doe should leave her fawn in a lion's lair, what a fate?

If Odyssey is half the man he was when he oil-wrestled in Lesbos;
It was the great Philomeleides from the oil-ring he tossed,

What a different place your palace would be;
If those wretched Suitors saw the return of Odyssey,

If he presented himself at the palace at some close hour;
What a scene, in swift death the Suitor's lives would sour,

Battle dress, bow, arrows and spear;
In that rabble nought else but deathly fear,

Odyssey, brave and true, god-sent and tall;
What a sorry wedding it would be for the Suitors, one and all.

I will not conceal a word of what was said to me;
From what I was told by Phorgyn,[80] the Old Man of The Sea,[a]

In Egypt our god offerings were lacking and they had deserted us;
Only enough to buy the winds to get to the Island of Pharaohs,[81]

Where for twenty days our ships and crews we spent;
Until the Spirit, *Eidothea*,[b] daughter of Phorgyn, was sent,

She came to me one day when I was alone;
As the men were fishing to fill their bellies and stop their hunger groans."

She asked me:

"Why do you let your men starve here, by degrees?"

I answered:

"For we have offended the gods and cannot sail the seas."

---

a   Phorgyn, the Old Man of the Sea, is the name-sake of Phorgyn Bay now known a Vathy Bay, is a picturesque safe harbour of Ithaki. It finds its way onto the English language in the aphorism: Fortune awaits the brave.
b   *Dorothea,* the Daughter of the sea-god Phorgyn, the Old Man of the Sea. She could assume many guises and was helpful to mariners in distress.

And she replied:

"Stranger, I will make it all quite clear to you, thus;
There is an old Invisible, a son of Oceanus, his name is Phorgyn,

He is my father and knows every inch of every sea;
You must trap and hold him until he tells you which way to flee,

He will direct your voyages if your home is *his* choice;
And will tell you what danger happens in your house, in a true voice."

I said:

"But how can I catch an Invisible, that's not an easy thing to do;
By what means, fair or foul, tell me, I beg of you?"

She said:

"When the Sun reaches noon, and the wind blows westerly;
Phorgyn emerges from the great depths and floats upon the sea;

Then he takes refuge in a great sea-cave, vast and high-towering;
Which has many seals and a vile stench; it is to any nose, over-powering,

At day-break I will take you to this place where Phorgyn and you shall meet;
So pick the best three men that you have in your fleet,

But I must warn you now of his tricks and his routine;
First he will count the seals on his fingers, until all he has seen,

Then to sleep he'll go as a shepherd among his sheep;

You must seize him at the moment you see him fall asleep,

He will try to get away, so with all your strength hold him tighter;

Phorgyn[a] will change into every kind of scary beast, even fire and water,[82]

Once he changes back to his natural look, then loosen your grip;

He will talk, so tell him which Invisible is angry and delays your trip."

Having said all that, she dived under the waves and was gone;

So, I turned back to the shore where my ships were upon,

My heart was clouded and black with fear as I went along;

I reached my blue-eyed ship and supper, then sweet sleep came on,

When Dawn chased away Night with a rosy sky;

I took the three best men on whom I could rely,

We prayed to every god on high Olympos;

That our mission's hopes would be favourable with Phorgyn,

Meanwhile, the Spirit fetched four seal-skins from the depths of the sea;

All flayed, for she meant to play a trick upon her father, as you'll see,

In the cave, she dug four pits for us to lie in, which we did;

Then she covered us with the skins, in each we hid,

But the fishy seal stink was the worst stench, so vile!

So she put in our noses, sweet-smelling ambrosia[b] to make it more mild,

---

a   *Phorgyn* is the original shape shifter. Shape-shifting is the ability of a being or creature to transform its physical form or shape, usually achieved through an inherent ability of a mythological creature, divine intervention, or the use of magic.

b   Ambrosia, food of the gods, gives immortality. But where do you get it?

What a bizarre creature, a strange bed-fellow;
Indeed, a man's insides, in a seal's torso,

We waited and watched the seals come to the cave all morning;
At noon Phorgyn came and counted his seals, while we waited for our warning,

Soon he laid down and started to snooze with thunder for a snore;
As we seized him he turned into a lion with a terrible roar,

Soon he changed into a sharp-clawed leopard to tear at our limbs;
Then a fire-spitting dragon that burned black our hair and our skins,

Then a wild boar with great tusks chewed us like a crocodile;
And after that he became a tree, and even water for a while,

So we gripped harder until the Old Man gave up with a wily grin;
Saying, what god hatched this plot, and what do you hope to win?

I answered him, saying:

"You know that yourself, old man, so long on this Island shore;
I am losing all heart here and only wish to return to my home, once more."

Then he said:

"'To get to your home ports soon, offer sacrifices to Zeus;
But offerings from this island will serve no use,

You must go back to Egypt and the waters of the river Nile;
And there your sacrifices will make all the gods smile,

Then fair winds will blow you on a homeward voyage;

That is the only way to escape Pharaoh Island's bondage."

("Of course I was broken hearted and in despair;

Having to make another voyage back there.")

So, I said:

"I will do all you ask, but tell me something else Old Man;

What became of our men after the fighting days were done in King Priam's land?"

Phorgyn said:

"Menelaos, it's better that you don't know this story, so wracked with pain;

Unless you wish to fill your eyes with tears to fall like rain,

Some live to tell their grim stories, but most are dead and gone;

Only two of the three most ill-fated Hellenes[a] perished, during their return home,

The third man is still at sea, alive, but hindered to return to his land;

First to die was Ajax[b], his blue-eyed ship was wrecked on Gyrae Rock[c] by Poseidon;

---

a   A reference to the three most-damned heroes of the Trojan War: Ajax, Agamemnon and Odyssey.
b   Ajax, a son of Oileus, and the nymph Rhene, (not to be confused with Ajax, son of Telamon) was also mentioned as a suitor of Helen. After the fall of Troy, he stormed the temple of Athena, where Cassandra, King Priam's daughter, had taken refuge, and was clinging to the statue of the goddess Athena. Ajax dragged her away violently and led her to the other captives. According to some statements he even raped Cassandra in the temple. Odyssey accused him of this crime, and Ajax was to be stoned to death, but saved himself by establishing his innocence by an oath. The whole charge, is on the other hand, said to have been an invention of Agamemnon, who wanted to have Cassandra for himself. Whether true or not, Athena had sufficient reason for being offended, as Ajax had violated a suppliant's plea by dragging her from the sacred refuge of her own temple, a convention which has stood from those ancient days.
c   Gyrae Rocks, or Ajax's Rocks, are two hazardous rocks 700 metres east of the Promontory of Kafireas, on the Island of Euboea off the east coast of the Greek mainland. The charming chapel of Saint Gregory overlooks this spectacular seascape.

... He got out of the water, boasting that even the Invisibles could not kill him.

As you know, Sea Smasher Poseidon, is not fond of big talk;
So he split Gyrae Rock[83] into two pieces with his Trident fork,

And Ajax slid into the salty depths, with the wrong half of that rock in his clutch;
To the bottom of the sea he surfed, and quenched his thirst too much,

The second to die was your brother, Athena saw that he should not escape;
And sent him homeward bound via Malea's Cape,[84]

For she had other plans for home-sick Agamemnon as you'll see;
But when he reached the Cape, a hurricane drove him further out to sea,

After a while the gods sent good winds and they reached their home safe;
Where Agamemnon kissed the ground, and tears of joy ran down his face,

But evil Agisthos kept a watchman to look out for Agamemnon's return;
For one whole year he watched, for two talents[a] of gold he could earn,

The watchman saw Agamemnon go by, and signalled to Agisthos so;
Who picked twenty warriors, his fiercest, and plotted an ambush, and further woe,

He placed them in his palace to lie in wait for Agamemnon;
Then he sent for him with his chariots and horsemen,

There he sat and feasted unsuspecting of the doom that awaited;
For their celebrations were short-lived, as was fated,

---

a   The ancient Hellenic unit of weight corresponding to 26 kilograms (57 lbs) being the approximate mass of water required to fill an amphora, a vessel used to transport and store commodities. The value of which would convert to about two million dollars (US).

When the banquet finished, Agamemnon and his followers;
Were slaughtered like lambs, right there in the palace cloisters."

Menelaos continues:

That is what he said and I was heart broken and wild;
I lay on the beach, wailing and weeping like a child,

Then he said to me, Menelaos, stop your grief and the crying;
Go! Bring honour to your brother's life, time is flying,

Although your step-brother Orestes has a head-start and is vengeful;
You may get to the palace in time to see Agisthos' funeral,

From the Old Man I took great comfort from what I had heard;
And asked him, 'You've spoken of only two men, what about the third?'"

He said:

"The third man is Odyssey, whose kingdom is Ithaki;
But he is captive to nymph Kalypso on an island, and sorrows bitterly,

He has no ship - nor crew – but waits for an escort to take him home;
But it is the twentieth year and soon he'll be free, again, to roam,

As for your fate, Menelaos, in Argos[85] your life will not end;
The Elysian Fields[86] is your destiny for the gods to send,

Where there is no rain, no hail, no snow, but Oceanus' kind West Wind;
Which sings softly from the sea, and gives everlasting life to all men,

Because you are favoured by the Invisibles, that is the truth;
For you married Helen, the daughter of All-knowing Zeus,

Having said all that, he dived under the waves and was gone;
So, I turned back to where my ships on the shore, were upon,

My heart was clouded and black with fear as I went along;
I reached my ship and supper and then sweet sleep came on,

When Dawn lit the horizon with a rosy sky of red;
We drew our blue-eyed ships into the water, and to Egypt the bows pointed,

When we reached the sacred waters of the Nile and the delta beyond;
We erected a huge stone obelisk[a] in memory of Agamemnon,

As we had appeased the gods and satisfied the Olympians;
They sent us home quickly, with fast and favourable winds.

So, Telemakis, for your self, stay here for a week or two, and rest;
I shall give you three horses and a sturdy chariot, my best,

And take a gold goblet to make offerings when there is strife;
So that you shall remember me for the rest of your life."

Telemakis replies:

"Gloried son of Atreus do not press me to remain here;
I would readily stay for another year,

---

a   An obelisk is a tall, stone column with four sloping sides and a pyramid pointed top, erected to honour
an important person or event.

Your hospitality and conversation delight me so;

But my crew waits for me in Pilos, and there I now must go,

Give me a metal plate to remember you by, as a keep-sake;

A thing that I can carry on my voyage, which won't break,

We can't take horses and a chariot back home in our small boat;

What's more, our land is steep and rocky and only fit for mule and goat,

We have no fields or racecourses upon which a horse can thrive;

And no pasture to grow oats, corn or barley to keep them alive,

The Ionian Islands are steep, level ground they cannot boast;

And all are covered with sharp stones, Ithaki has the most."

Menelaos smiles and takes Telemakis' hand, saying:

"Your wit and wisdom tells what a family you are from;

So, I *will* give you the most precious plate here in my home,

It is a mixing bowl by Hephaestos' hand, of pure silver, with a gold inlaid rim;[a]

King Phaedimus, of Sidonia, gave it to me, when I last visited him."

While they talk, guests come to the the palace. The men bring sheep and wine, while their wives put bread on the tables as they prepare another banquet in Menelaos' glorious palace.[b]

*

---

a   Hephaestos was the metaphor used for emotion. Fire-hot thoughts of mortal lives are beaten with hammer and tongs on the anvil of life.

b   It was customary to take a gift or an offering to a host. Arriving empty-handed was a minor violation of the xenia code.

Meanwhile, back at the palace in Ithaki, the Suitors are up to their usual antics. They are gaming again, hurling discs or throwing spears at targets in the courtyard of Odyssey's palace, with all their usual arrogance. Antinoos and Eurymachos, two of the ring-leaders are sitting together. Noemon, Phronius' son, comes to them and says to Antinoos:

"Has someone here any idea when Telemakis will return from Pilos?

He has one of my ships, and I need it to sail over to Elis,[87]

Where I have twelve brood mares, with yearling mules, unbroken;

I want to bring one of them back over here, to break it in."

They are astonished. They had not realised that Telemakis had gone to Nestor's city, Pilos. They thought he was away somewhere on the estate, mustering sheep, and pigs for their banquets. Antinoos, the most insolent, is the first to speak:

"When did Telemakis go? What men did he take?

Were they free-men or his own servants from this estate?

Did you let him have the ship, or were you forced?

Tell me true or you will end up the worst."

Noeman, says:

"I lent it to him, what else could I do for a man in his position;

He was in difficulty, how could I refuse, it was an easy decision,

His crew are the best in the land, apart from us remaining here;

And Mentor was his captain, at the helm I saw him steer,

Which is a strange thing for I also saw him here this morning;

Have they returned, or was that a god's warning?"

Noeman goes back to his father's house, but Antinoos and Eurymachos are angry. They tell the others to stop their games and sit with them. They assemble and Antinoos speaks first. His heart is furious with rage, and his eyes flash fire as he says:

> "Good heavens, this voyage of Telemakis is an outrage;
> The young fellow has got mischief in mind, I'll wage,
>
> And he picked a crew from our midst;
> Then sailed to Pilos in one of our very own ships,
>
> Such audacity of that puppy to pull off this coup;
> I hope Zeus clips his wings before there's *trouble* for me and you;
>
> So, get me a ship with a crew of twenty, to sail for Asteris Island, and lay wait;
> We'll ambush them when they head north from the Sami Strait."[a]

The others applaud him and go their separate ways.

Penelope comes to hear of the Suitors' plans through a palace servant, Medon, who overheard Antinoos plotting in the courtyard. As he crosses the threshold of her room to tell her, she asks:

> "Medon, what have the Suitors sent you here for?
> Is it to tell the maids to prepare another banquet, or more?
>
> May they neither woo me or swarm and feast here again;
> For how they waste and rob my son's estate, wretched men!
>
> Did their fathers forget to tell them how good Odyssey was as their king;
> Never offending or speaking harshly or disliking,
>
> He ruled his people with care and respect;

---

a   Asteris Island is just north of the southern coast of Ithaki where the Sami Strait ends.

Is gratitude too much to expect?"

Medon says:

> "Madam, if only what you say was the end of it all;
> But the Suitors plot something much more dreadful,
>
> I hope that heaven steps in and frustrates their designs;
> The murder of Telemakis is what occupies their minds,
>
> As he is coming home from Pilos and Sparta;
> Where he went to get news of his father."

Penelope's heart sinks. For a long time she is speechless. Her knees tremble and her eyes are full of tears. At last, she says:

> "What business had he to go sailing? Why did my son leave me?
> Making a long voyage in a small boat carrying him over a ruthless sea,
>
> Is he to die without leaving someone to carry his name?
> To perish at sea by the hand of Poseidon, will that be his only fame?"

Medon consoles her:

> "I do not know if he thought to go on his own impulse;
> Or, perhaps it was a god that sent him off to Pilos."

He goes downstairs again, leaving Penelope in an agony with grief. There are plenty of seats in her room, but she flings herself on the floor, weeping inconsolably. The maids in the house, young and old, gather near her and begin sobbing too. Finally, she says:

"My dears I am the most cursed of my age and country;
Afflicted like no other, why has heaven got it in for me?

First, I lost my brave and wondrous husband;
Our king, the pride and glory of our nation,

Of the finest lineage, but doomed to war and miseries;
And now my cherished son is thrashed by wind on merciless seas,

And all along not one word about him leaving home. How very mean!
You disloyal hussies, how could you keep that secret from your Queen?

Surely, one of you could have stirred me from my bed?
Or told me of his plans as soon as you heard,

If I knew of this voyage I'd have stopped it, one way or another;
He'd have given it up, or left behind the corpse of his dead mother,

Go, some of you, and call old Dolios, my gardener;
Ask him to go and tell everything to Lord Laertes, Odyssey's father,

Perhaps he will have some plan against the Suitors' evil design;
So my son may be saved and continue Odyssey's family line."

The old nurse Eurykleia says:

"You may kill me dear queen or let me live, whichever you please;
For it was me that gave Telemakis everything needed to travel the seas,

He made me take my solemn oath that I would not tell you anything;
Unless you asked or happened to hear that he has gone missing,

He did not want you to spoil your beauty by crying;

Or gray your hair locks by thinking he was on his way to dying,

Madam, wash your face, change your clothes and go to your chambers;

And with all your maids offer up to Athena your solemn prayers, for her favours,

She alone can save him from the jaws of death;

I don't believe that it's Laertes' line that the gods detest,

For, I am sure that Telemakis will inherit his kingship, and this estate;

He will sire offspring, and the family name will survive, as is his fate."

With these words, Penelope stops crying and dries the tears from her eyes. She washes her face, changes clothes and goes upstairs with her maids. She sifts barley[a] into a basket and begins praying to Athena, Inspiration Itself, pleading:

"Athena, Daughter of Mind, as Odyssey offered so many sacrifices to thee;

And he's still in your favour, save my darling son from the Suitor's villainy."

She cries out loud and painfully and the Spirit hears her prayer.

Meanwhile, downstairs, the Suitors are huddled together in the cloister. On hearing the scream, one of them says:

"I guess she is practising for her wedding night, with that mighty scream;

And for when she hears about her son's doom... little does she dream."

That said, Antinoos rebukes them:

"Are you mad? No loud talking, our plan may be heard;

---

a   As a ritual in ancient times, barley was sifted thirteen times to separate the good from the bad. This
     chore brought good luck to the object of prayer, but could not be used for one's own benefit. Thirteen,
     lucky for some.

Let us do our workings in silence, utter not a loud word."

He selects twenty men and leads them down to a ship, the *Sea Mist*, at the docks in Phortune Bay. They slip the vessel into the water, raise the mast and ready the sails. They tie the oars to the rowlocks with plaited leather. The footmen stow their armour and weapons. They eat their supper and wait for Night to darken Day.

Penelope lies in her bed upstairs. She is unable to sleep. She can't eat or drink, and wonders if her unsuspecting son will avoid the Suitors' evil. Like a lioness pursued by savage hunters circling ever closer, so is she roused and on edge. Finally, sleep over-powers her distress.

Athena, Inspiration, has another idea. She makes a spirit-vision, a dream-likeness of Penelope's sister, Iphthime,[88] who lives in Therae.[a] Athena tells the vision to go to Odyssey's palace and calm Penelope's sorrow. So the vision goes to her room and hovers over her head saying, gently:

"You are asleep, wise Penelope, the Invisibles wish you no suffering;

Do not weep or be sad, Telemakis suffers not, and will be returning."

Penelope, speaks into her dreams, saying:

"Sister, why did you come? You do not come here often;

Did you come to cheer me up, and my hard thoughts, soften?

I am cursed, I've lost my husband and now it's Telemakis, my boy;

That the Suitors are planning to ambush, kidnap and destroy."

The vision of Iphthime consoles her:

"Take heart, be bold for there is one who protects and saves;

I mean Athena, no less, who thwarts his enemies and stills the waves."

Penelope says:

---

a   Coincidentally, Telemakis has just spent a comfortable night in Therae where he was entertained by Diocles on his way back from Menelaos and Helen's palace, as he travelled to Pilos with Pisistratus.

"If you are a god or sent here by divine instruction;

Tell me also about Odyssey, the other *troubled* one,

Is he alive, and where does he live, or is he dead?

Please put an end to my misery and my dread."

The Spirit of Iphthime answers:

"I shall not say, alive or dead, which is true;

There is no use in idle talk, only *Time* will reveal that to you."

The Spirit vanishes. Penelope rises from her bed, refreshed and comforted by her deep sleep and vivid dream.

Meanwhile, the Suitors are aboard the *Sea Mist* furling the sails and oaring their course. From Phortune Bay they sail north-east along the Gulf of Molos. To Starboard, they pass the narrow, rocky Cape Skinos. Once clear, they point south-east and follow the coast towards the small, star-shaped island called Asteris. It is midway between Phortune Harbour and the port of Sami, a few hundred metres north of Pera Pigadi Cove in south-eastern Ithaki. It has two sheltered mooring places on the inside of the island close to the shore. At low tide it is shallow enough to walk across to the mainland. Between the shore and Asteris, ships can hide from storms. However, the Suitors have other thoughts; ambush to murder.

Son of King Odyssey, Prince Telemakis,

Beware of the risks at Asteris.

*

EPISODE FIVE

KALYPSO AND A RAFT

*

As Earth rolls toward Dawn,
Sun puts Night to Sleep,
With Light, Day is born

Again, the Invisibles meet on Olympos, in council.

Zeus, Mind, is their king and ruler. Athena, Spirit of Inspiration, his offspring,[a] begins to tell them of the many sufferings of Odyssey; she pities the great hero, as he is the captive of the nymph Kalypso. Athena says:

"Father, and all other gods that live here in eternal bliss;

Have any of you heard of a thing called justice?[b]

I hope there will be no well-disposed rulers on Earth, I implore;

And they will be all cruel and unjust, forever more,

All of you have forgotten Odyssey, your most loyal subject;

Who, on Earth, was the best example of a ruler, I suspect,

There he dwells in great pain on an island with Kalypso;

He can't return to his own country, she will not let him go,

---

a   Athena was originally sprung from Zeus' head. A thought perhaps?
b   Ironically, the word *just*, is derived from the name, *Zeus*.

He has no ship, or crew, to venture across the sea;

And now there is more peril at large for the family of Odyssey,

Suitors plague his home and plot the murder of Telemakis;

At this moment they lie in ambush whilst he returns from Pilos,

He went there and Sparta too, to seek news of his father's fate;

For his loyal son risking life and limb, it might be too late."

Zeus, the Illuminator, answers:

"What, my dear, is this nonsense you are talking? Didn't you send Odyssey there yourself, because you thought it would help him get home in time to punish the Suitors? Besides, you have the power - and more - to protect Telemakis, and to see him safely home again. Will the Suitors fail to see their opportunity and have to return from their ambush without killing him?

Ah huh! Now I see what hinders your work. The two of you, Athena and Kalypso, will never see eye-to-eye in a matter as delicate as this. What two women have ever been agreeable when a man is in the middle of their interests?

Very well then, I shall send thought-spirit Hermes to help your cause. Hermes, Ego-slayer, loyal son, I shall send you on a mission.

Destiny must return Odyssey to his home. However, he is to be conveyed by his own means. After a perilous voyage of twenty days upon a raft he is to reach fertile Skeria,[89] the home of the Phaekians,[a] whose ancestors are the gods.

They will honour him as though he were one of us and send him in a ship to Ithaki. They are to give him more bronze and gold and tapestries than he would have brought back from Troy, if he had got all his due spoils, without his twenty years of delays. This is how we have settled that he shall return to his country and his friends."

As he spoke, Hermes, god, guide and guardian, slayer of Egos, did as tasked. Instantly, as Thought itself, he binds his glittering gold sandals and flies to the cave on the Island of Ogygio where the sea-nymph Kalypso dwells.

---

a   Skeria is today named Corfu. It is in the Ionian Sea, some sixty nautical miles north of Phortune Harbour (Vathy), Ithaki.

He finds her at home. There is a large fire burning in the hearth offering a fragrant aroma of burning cedar and sandalwood. Kalypso is busy at her loom, passing her gold yarn-shuttle through the warp, singing sweetly.

Around her cave is a stand of alder, poplar, and fragrant cypress trees. All kinds of great birds; owls, hawks, and chattering sea-gulls have built their nests in the woods. A vine thriving with grapes is trained and grows around the mouth of the cave. There are four springs of running water which irrigate the flower beds and a verdant herb garden. A god could be happy in a lovely place like this. Hermes stands still and admires it before going into the cave.

Kalypso recognises him at once as the gods know each other well, no matter how far away it *seems* that they dwell from one another.

Odyssey is not there, he is on the beach, as usual, looking out to sea, teary-eyed and pining for his home.

Kalypso offers Hermes a seat and says:

> "Why have you come, Hermes? You don't often visit me;
>
> Say what you want, but first have some hospitality."

As she speaks she draws a table loaded with ambrosia beside him and mixes some red-fruit nectar. God food. He eats and drinks until he has enough, and says:

> "As one god to another, it is Zeus, Mind, that sends me;
>
> He says that you live with the most ill-starred man in history,
>
> Of those who fought nine years King Priam's battle;
>
> After the war they sailed home but killed the Sun-god's cattle,
>
> So Athena raised winds and waves, and so was their fate;
>
> That all his companions perished, and he was swept here to be your mate,
>
> Zeus, has said that you must let this man go free;
>
> He must not waste away here, but return to his family."

Kalypso trembles with rage when she hears Hermes' command. She says:

"The gods should be ashamed of themselves for their jealousy;
You all hate to see me, a Spirit, take love from mortal Odyssey,

We are happy living in love, in this beautiful place;
The gods should not destroy what has been given to us by Grace,[90]

As Artemis was sent when Orion made love to Dawn;
And killed him, so now she weeps red tears, every morn,

And what of Demeter who gave way to her decadent passion;
By three plowed furrows[a] she yielded to the love of Iasion[91],

When Zeus heard all of that, he was no more her lover;
He sent his lightning bolts and then Iasion's days were over,

Now he's angry with me, because I have a man on whom I dote;
Don't forget, I rescued him as he sat astride his upturned, blue-eyed boat,

For it was Zeus's work that capsized it in mid-sea;
All his crew were drowned and lost, except for Odyssey,

Then I became fond of him and set my heart on making him a god too;
So that he and I should never grow old, and our love remain true,

However, if it is the Olympian's wish that Odyssey must be set free;
Then I am powerless to alter Zeus' iron decree,

Then Odyssey shall leave without my helping, and he must go at once;
I've done enough, I have no boats, so I'll say good riddance."

---

a   Three furrows is an allusion to the sexual cavities of a female.

Thought-spirit Hermes, says:

"You must help him, or Zeus, will be angry;

And for the gods' forgiveness you shall pray."

Hermes vanishes.

Kalypso goes to look for Odyssey as she now realises the necessity of the situation. She finds him sitting on the beach, staring out to sea through tear-strained eyes.

He has grown wearisome of Kalypso, after all they have been together for seven years. He itches[a] for Ithaki, his home. Every night they have made love in her cavern. But now he's a half-hearted lover to an insatiable Spirit. His days are spent on the beach, exhausted, he weeps in despair and prays to leave captivation. Kalypso finds him on the beach, sits, and says:

"You *poor* man, you can't stay here any longer;

I've decided to send you where your heart will be fonder,

Come, cut beams of wood, and make a raft long and strong;

With a deck to carry you over the sea, to where you belong,

I will provision you well, so starve and thirst you'll not;

And I'll make you some clothes for when you get to your next stop,

When you are ready I will send a fair wind to guide you home;

Or, wherever the gods in heaven have planned for you to roam."

Odyssey shudders as he hears her words, and answers:

"Now Spirit, there is something hidden behind what your words say;

Do you think that a raft could take me to Phortune Bay?

---

a   The English word, *itch* is derived from *Ithaki*. The sayings: *seven-year itch* and, *itchy feet* are both attributed to Homer.

The seas and winds show no mercy on small and flimsy craft;

And gods punish stupidity by throwing thunderbolts, as they laugh,

No, I fear there is strife in your words, they offer certain grief;

You must swear an oath that you mean no mischief."

Kalypso smiles and caresses him with her hand, saying:

"You know a great deal my love, but you are wrong;

May heaven and earth bear witness I mean you no harm,

Trust me, *my* heart is not made of iron, for you I do feel pity;

You have long been on this island, seven years of captivity."

She rises and walks toward the cave. Odyssey follows her inside. He takes a seat in the chair just occupied by Hermes. Kalypso sets meat and drink for him: the maids bring ambrosia and nectar for her. God food. Now they are satisfied and Kalypso speaks:

"Odyssey, my love, your home is really where you wish to be;

Good luck, as you suffer your way towards Ithaki,

You say that you no longer wish to be my husband;

But I offer an immortal life; a goddess for a wife on this paradise island,

But that's not enough, it seems, I'm *only* a bridesmaid to Penelope;

How does this mortal woman compare to a goddess, tell me?"

Quick-witted Odyssey replies:

"Goddess, Lady Kalypso, do not be angry with me;

Penelope is only a woman and not blessed with immortality,

As such she could never compare with your beauty and grace;
Each day her hair grays and wrinkles find her face,

Do you think a man's love for you could ever grow old;
While he can gaze on the beauty that eternity will behold?

Nevertheless, I must go, my kingdom awaits its King;
Whatever the Invisibles have in store, I know there will be suffering,
For as the gods say: Life is to be suffered; enjoy while enduring."

With that he takes her in his arms and carries her to their bed. There they make love until Dawn paints the morning sky with her pink tears.

Odyssey rises, leaving Kalypso's longing arms. He dresses. Kalypso also rises and dresses in a sheer, long and graceful gown. She wears a beautiful girdle of gold under it. She covers her head with a *white* veil. Kalypso knows that he finds her very alluring and hopes that Odyssey will change his mind if she continues to seduce him.

However, her desire is short-lived; she knows that Zeus' work will be done, whether she likes it or not - even gods don't have free-will. Seeing that her desire is futile, she sets herself to help Odyssey.

She gives him a great bronze axe. It suits his hands. It is bladed on both sides, and has a beautiful olive-wood handle. She also gives him a sharp adze.[a] She leads him to the island's forest where the largest trees grow; towering alder, poplar and pine, all very dry and well-seasoned. Without sap they will float higher in the water. After she has shown him where the best trees grow, Kalypso goes home, leaving him to fell them. He fells twenty trees, and adzes them smooth, squaring them by rule in good workman-like fashion.

Kalypso returns with some augers, so he bores holes and fits the timbers together with wooden dowel pins. He makes the raft just as a skilled shipwright would. It has a wide beam to which he fixes the ribs and above them, a deck and a cockpit. He builds a gunwale around it to keep smaller waves out. He makes a mast with a yard-arm[b] and a rudder to steer with. He fences the raft all around with plaited wicker as protection against bigger waves, and then he loads a quantity of spare wood for any needed repairs.

---

a   An adze is a tool similar to an axe, with an arched blade at right angles to the handle, used for cutting or shaping large pieces of wood.
b   A yard-arm is the boom which fastens to the bottom of a sail.

Kalypso brings linen to make the sails, which he does. He also makes ropes from plaited cloth. She provides a goat-skin full of red wine, and another larger one of water, and a hamper full of provisions with dried meats.

Last of all, with the help of levers, he slips the raft down into the water. It had taken four days to complete. On day five he is ready to leave. Kalypso is impressed with his work, and looks at him saying:

"I will miss you Odyssey, you are a good and hardy man."

Quick-witted Odyssey, replies:

"Yes, Kalypso, but remember this advice if you can:

It is hard to find a good man; but good to find a hard man."

Again, he is taken by her dark, sensuous beauty. He lifts her in his arms and they enjoy their last love-making in the cockpit of the rocking raft.

She has named the craft, *Sea Horse*.

Kalypso beats-up fair winds and Odyssey, happily, spreads and hoists his sail, takes his place at the tiller and blows a kiss to her.

He doesn't look back as the raft moves slowly on his homeward voyage. He does not dare to close his eyes or look down, for he wants no more tears to drop. As Kalypso, advised him, "*Don't look back*, keep your eyes up and you shall not lose your way."

So he does, first fixing them on the Pleiads,[92] then higher on the late-setting Boötes[93] and then highest on the Great Bear,[a] which men also call the Wain, which circles in the face of Orion,[94] the Hunter, never dripping into the star stream of Oceanus.[95]

After eighteen days, feint outlines of mountains on the Phaekian coast appear, rising like the edge of Zeus' shield[96] from the placid, blue waters of the Ionian Sea. However, as Fate[b] ordered, Poseidon is returning from Ethiopia where he has

---

a   In the northern hemisphere, the Big Dipper (the Great Bear) never sets, but circles around Polaris, the North Star. For Odyssey to keep the constellation on his left would point him eastward in the direction of Skeria (Corfu).

b   The *Fates*, mythological women who determined the span of a human life by spinning, measuring, and cutting the thread symbolic of it. Life is pre-determined.

been busy with the Egyptians. From the mountains[a] of *Solymi*,[97] he sees Odyssey making good progress for his home.

Poseidon realises that he has escaped Kalypso's Island. This makes him angry. He lifts his eyes to the sky saying:

"Good heavens, I've been in Ethiopia with my nose to the grindstone;

And you gods, lounging on Olympos, have allowed Odyssey to make his way home,

I know he's destined and entitled to make it there some day;

But I'll make sure he has a plenty more *trouble* before he gets to Phortune Bay."

He grasps his Trident and smashes the sea causing great waves. He summons the clouds and the four winds to collide. Darkness descends and the earth, sea and sky become one in mighty upheaval. Odyssey's heart begins to fail him, saying:

"Woe is me, I should have listened to Kalypso;

She foretold what would happen, but how did she know?

I'm sure to die here at sea, in sight of land and freedom;

I'd rather have died four times in battle against King Priam,

Zeus, Mind, let a lightning-bolt fly now to forever stop my thrashing heart;

Keep me and Hades Halls,[b] no longer apart."

As he speaks a huge, thundering wave crashes over the *Sea Horse* . The mast breaks half way up, and both sail and boom go overboard. The raft spins and the tiller breaks off in Odyssey's hands. He is flung into the water and forced down by the weight of his wet clothes. He is submerged for a long time but now gets his head above water. He coughs and splutters the salty water from his lungs and looks for the raft which he sees. He swims towards it. He hoists himself back on board. The waves

---

a   Mountains of *Solymi* including Mt. Olympos (not to be confused with Mt. Olympos, Greece) are in the province of Antalya, Turkey. The ruins of the Temple of Hephaestos are located south of the modern coastal town of Cirali, situated in a river valley near the coast. The site at Yanartas has the Chimaera gas plumes, un-extinguishable flames leaping from the ground which have been burning for thousands of years.

b   Hades' Halls is the underworld, Hell, where the memories of the dead dwell.

and wind lift the raft and toss it like a leaf in the Autumn wind. It was as though the North, South, East and West winds were all trying to out-do each other.

The albino Spirit, Ino[98] is looking on. She had been a mortal, but was raised to the rank of a Sea-nymph. Seeing his distress, she has compassion and rising from the angry water, she glides over the waves like an albatross, landing next to him on the raft, saying:

"You *poor* man, what did you do to raise Poseidon's wrath?

And what are you doing out here on this flimsy raft?

I know this commotion is all in vain: You, Poseidon must not kill;

So, do as I say, strip, and leave your raft to the wind's will,

Swim fast to the Phaekian's coast, Skeria,[a] where your luck lurks best;

And to keep you from drowning, tie my white veil around your chest,

When you reach dry land take it off and throw it back far into the sea;

And as you do - *don't look back at me* - but go to high ground, where safety will be."

With these thoughts in his mind, she dives into the sea and vanishes beneath the dark, foaming water. Odyssey does not know what to do. Bye and bye, he thinks that Ino is luring him to destruction by advising to leave the safety of his raft. So for the time being he decides to stay on the raft until he gets closer to land. His inner debate is over and now, out loud, Odyssey says to himself:

"I'll wait, and stick to the raft for as long as her timbers hold;

And if the *Sea Horse* breaks up, I will swim for it, as Ino told."

At that very moment, Poseidon sent another monstrous wave crashing over the raft, shattering it. Odyssey flounders in the water as he removes his clothes and ties Ino's white veil around his chest. He swims toward shore and finds the top of the mast from the wrecked *Sea Horse*. He straddles it and paddles away.

Poseidon is sitting in his flying chariot, watching. With a wry smile, saying to himself:

---

a   The island of *Skeria* is today known as Corfu. The name Skeria translates to: S*ecurity, safety* or *safe haven..*

"Odyssey, I've given you mortal combat which any god would be proud;

Now swim, or ride your sea saddle, until you find King Alkinoos' crowd."[99]

Poseidon lashes his horses and flies to his palace in Aegae.[100]

Athena, too, has been watching. She halts the winds, except a tail breeze from the south-west which pushes Odyssey and his sea-horse toward the wooded, Phaekian coast.

For another two nights he paddles up each cresting wave and rides each deep trough of the heaving swells.

On the third day, Dawn lights her red lantern, putting Night to sleep. The wind drops and dead calm brings quiet. As he rises on the crest of a wave he sees land. His heart lifts with every cresting wave as the on-coming shore gets closer. He sees trees and with the heart of an excited child, paddles on with all his strength, ever closer to setting his feet upon land.

He hears thundering surf crashing onto rocks but there is a thick mist blinding any sign of the shore or a port. Again, Odyssey's heart fails him. He thinks to himself that death is at hand, saying:

"Zeus, you let me ride for three days on this rocking sea-horse;

Buffeted by wind and countless waves, with no idea of my course,

Now, I can't find a landing place, the rocks are many and bold;

And the cliffs rise into the sky, are smooth with no foot-hold,

Or, if I swim and paddle to make some other distant shore;

Certain death will offer only hurricanes or some sea-monster's jaw,

A great wave will pound me onto those rocks, harder than black steel;

Whatever happens my days are over on this life's merciless wheel,

I know that Poseidon has a long and vengeful hate;

But please, Zeus, deliver me from a watery grave and untimely fate."

At the moment he ends his plea, a powerful wave tosses him into the air, dashing him against a rock. He grips it with both hands and clings until the wave subsides. The wave returns and lifts him with great force dragging him out to sea again, where he sinks towards the sea-bed and certain death.

Odyssey would have drowned, even in spite of his own destiny, but Ino's White veil buoys him to the surface. He swims out beyond the rip of the surf and comes to the mouth of a river. Here, he thinks, is a good place as there are no rocks and the river bank is sheltered from the wind. However, dread over-powers him again, as he feels a strong current against him. Again he pleads, but this time to any god that will listen:

"Hear me Invisibles, wherever you may dwell;

Save me from Poseidon's anger which you and I know too well,

I'm at the end of my life, if this current you can't reverse;

For I have no more energy - or will - I am at my worst."

Sea-spirit Ino stills the waves and the current turns pressing him to the shore.

He reaches the shore,[101] but has no lift in his knees. His once-strong hands won't obey his grip. He is a broken man; his body bruised black and blue, and badly swollen from his water-logged ordeal. He doesn't speak, or even breathe, but lays in the shallows for what seem hours, in utter exhaustion.

He regains some strength and kneels, then stands and unties Ino's white veil from his chest. He throws it back into the sea. As he turns he thinks he sees a vision of Kalypso under the water. Looking again, the vision has vanished. Naked, he turns and staggers up the river bank. A wave throws the white veil back to the Spirit[a] and she vanishes.

Odyssey finds a clump of bull-rushes and sinks to his knees. He kisses the Earth, saying to himself:

"How is it all to end? Whatever will become of me;

Should I stay here on this river bank, or climb into a tree,

Either the damp of this ground, or some savage, wild beast;

---

a   Perhaps it was Kalypso that disguised herself as Ino, all along.

Which, will end my days: A sleepless night of bitter cold, or an animal's gnashing teeth?"

His debate is over and he thinks it best to go to the tree-line on higher ground, just as Ino had suggested. He finds a suitable place, close to a fresh-water spring.[a] There he creeps under two olive bushes that grow from a single root, one being grafted, the other natural. Perhaps their may be people in this strange land?

No wind could find him under this thick bush. Even the Sun's rays or rain could not penetrate. There is a lot of dead leaves around, so he lies down and scoops them over himself, making a blanket. Slowly, warmth comes back to him. A Spirit weighs his eyelids with sweet sleep and *trouble* is gone.

*

---

a   About 700 metres from the Ancient Port site of Corfu, is a spring which overlooks the landing place of Odyssey.

PRINCESS NAUTIKAA AND A ROYAL REFUGEE

Under the twin-trunked[a] olive tree, Odyssey, overcome by exhaustion, is being nourished by sweet sleep.

Athena is in Skeria,[b] the City of Alkinoos, King of the Phaekians.

The Phaekians once lived in the city of Hypereia, near the lawless Cyklops, their cousins. The Cyklops were aggressive and plundered them, so Nausithoos, then their king - a son of Poseidon - moved them to the safe refuge of Skeria. He had surrounded the city with a fortress wall, built houses and temples, and divided the lands among his people. After his death, Prince *Alkinoos*,[c] became king.

Athena, the Spirit of Emotion, goes directly to the bedroom of the Kings' daughter, the beautiful Nautikaa.[102] Two maid servants were sleeping near her, both very pretty, one on either side of the doorway. Athena takes the form of the famous sea captain Dymas' daughter, who is a friend of *Nautikaa*[d] and her own age. Hovering over the girl's bed, the dream whispers:

"Nautikaa, who is your mother, to have such a lazy daughter?

Here and there, your clothes are strewn in such disorder,

What if you are to get married soon, could you dress yourself?

And what would your bridesmaids wear to show off your wealth?

---

a   Twin-trunked refers to a natural tree trunk with a grafted branch. People - or monsters - could exist nearby.
b   Skeria is today named, Corfu, and is in the Ionian Sea, some sixty nautical miles north of Phortune Harbour (Vathy), Ithaki.
c   The name, *Alkinoos*, translates to: Master-mind; respected intelligence.
d   The name, *Nautical*, translates to: wrecker of ships, perhaps an allusion to the impending stone "shipwrecks" in Skeria (Corfu) harbour and Rithron (Dexia) Cove, Ithaki, which Nautikaa will be indirectly responsible for. The English words, *naughty* and *nautical* are derived from Homer's Nautikaa. Skartsoubo (Sock) Island is just off Dexia Beach, Ithaki, and is said to be the petrified remains of the Phaekian ship and its crew that delivered Odyssey to Ithaki

A good name for your loving mother and father you should make;

So tomorrow, we should have a laundry day, let's start at daybreak,

All the best young men will be coming soon to woo;

You won't be unmarried much longer if I help you,

At sunrise, ask your father for a wagon and mules;

It's a long way from town to the washing pools."

*

Athena spirits back to Olympos, the everlasting home of the gods, where no wind blows and rain and snow have never been. It offers everlasting sunshine and peaceful light. Here the Invisibles are radiant with contentment.

*

Rosy Dawn, the revealer of Day's thoughts, wakes Nautikaa. She wonders about her dream. She walks to her parent's bedroom. Her mother sits by the fire spinning purpled yarn with her maids. Her father is leaving to attend a town-council meeting, but she stops him, saying:

"Dearest father, may I have the use of a good wagon and mules;

I want to take all our dirty clothes to the river's spring and wash them in the whirl-pools,

You are lord here and your noble shirts should be clean;

And this household too should have white, bright linen seen,

Your three bachelor sons should also look the part;

When they go reveling, in search of a lady's heart."

She does not say a word about her wedding dream. On that she is silent. However, her wise father understood her motive, as fathers are closer in thought to their daughters, than their sons. He was surprised that someone may be wooing her. However, he says:

"Fair daughter, you shall have the mules and a fine wagon to hitch;

That might hold and carry the royal laundry, to the last stitch."

He orders servants to prepare the best wagon and mules. Nautikaa summons her maids. The virgins collect the palace's laundry and linen and carry it downstairs. The wagon is loaded. Her mother, Queen Arete has prepared a picnic basket with all sorts of food and a full goat-skin of wine. There is a gold flask of olive oil for massaging their feet after the washing is done.

Nautikaa takes the reins and touches the mules' hinds with her whip. Their hoofs clatter in a lively trot as they pull Nautikaa, her ten maids and the laundry to the spring and the washing ponds.

When they reach the spring they unharness the mules and hobble them in a paddock of rich clover. They unload the laundry into the crystal-clear ponds and Nautikaa leads her maids singing arm-in-arm, stomping their feet to loosen the dirt and rid the stains. They enjoy the laundry dance and their sing-along.

They lay the garments and linen out by the sea side on the rocks. They wash and massage their feet and legs with olive oil before they lunch by the side of the spring. Sun dries the laundry.

It is hot and they remove their clothing to tan their bodies whilst they play with a ball. They take turns in singing, but Nautikaa outshines all her maids with her voice, svelte body and incomparable, virginal beauty.

As they fold the clothes and load the wagon, Athena plans how Odyssey should waken and see this beautiful girl in her feminine glory... So, the princess throws the ball at the maids and it lands in the whirl-pool. They all shriek with joy. The noise wakes Odyssey, who sits up in his bed of leaves and wonders about the commotion, saying to himself:

"On no! What kind of strange creatures or people have I landed among?

Cruel savages, wild for blood, or friendly and human?

Is that the voices of young women, or haunting witches to fear?

Either way, wherever there's a woman, *trouble* will be near."

Odyssey decides to take a look at where the voices are coming from. He crawls from the under-bush, breaking off a branch of thick leaves to cover his manhood. He looks and moves like a wild, hungry lion stalking his prey.

As he gets closer to them, the girls run, scattering like the winds, but not Nautikaa; naked, she stands her ground. Athena has instilled courage into her heart, and she is now fearless.

Odyssey debates if he should throw himself at her feet and plead as a suppliant,[a] or stay there and ask her for some clothes. He thinks it best to keep his distance and talk to the girl so that she won't take offence from him coming closer. "Besides, this is a beautiful, naked woman, why not enjoy?" he says to himself.

His suave tongue says;

"Oh radiant vision, are you a mortal, or have I found Olympos?

You have the rare beauty of a goddess, heaven blessed,

Are you Zeus' daughter, the glorious Artemis?[b]

Your beautiful face and form are the twin of hers,

I can only compare you to what I saw in Delos:[c] the beauty of Apollo's Palm;[103]

I never saw one as beautiful as you, there is no match for your incomparable charm,

Ten stone lions guard Apollo's glorious Palm, and his birth place;

They would spring to eternal life with just one gaze upon *your* face,

There is nothing that compares to you, and that youthful tree: Natural wonders!

I went there on my way to fight in the war, another one of my life's many blunders,

---

a   A humble petitioner. In the ancient world it was customary for a suppliant to kneel and grasp the knees of the person from which mercy or favours were desired. A *suppliant* craves asylum or help, from the weak to the strong, often from a third party: the suppliant seeks to be defended from a pursuing enemy or a daunting situation. It is believed that Suppliants are sent by Zeus and therefore are revered and should be protected, as per the code of xenia. Whereas, a *supplicant* craves mercy from the angered, typically from an offended ruler, usually a deity or king.

b   Artemis, the goddess - or thought-spirit - that protects females and regulates the Animal Kingdom and nature.

c   Delos is a small island close to the centre of the Cyclades archipelago, in the Aegean Sea, next to Monosomy. It is one of the most important mythological, historical and archaeological sites in Greece. The excavations in the island are among the most extensive in the Mediterranean. Delos has been a holy place for a almost 4,000 years. It is the birthplace of the mythical, and metaphorical, twins, Apollo and Artemis.

However, if you really are a mortal, three times happy are your parents;
And to your brothers and sisters you must shine like a rare diamond's brilliance,

Their pride must swell when they see you join in the festival's dance;
But the richest man will be the one who wins you with wedding gifts, and love's romance,

I don't dare grasp your knees for pity, but for twenty days I've been sea-tossed;
Captive on Kalypso's Ogygio Island for seven years, now that I'm here, I'm still lost,

You are the first person I've met in this land, I don't know a soul;
Point me to your town, there I'll find my way to my home and goal,

Do you have clothes to cover my looks, so gruesome and neglected?
So I may not be mistaken for a beggar, and my manly pride be protected,

May heaven give you all your heart desires and much, much more;
A husband, a lovely house, and a happy home with children of half a score,

For there is no greater happiness than man and wife of one mind;
It's what their enemies envy, and it's their friend's joy to share that reputation, you'll find."

Nautikaa answers:

"Stranger, you appear to be experienced, and mannered well;
There is no accounting for fate - good or bad - that is for Zeus' plan to tell,

As it is said: Life is to be endured, so enjoy what you can;
Now, your luck has changed and fate has brought you to our land,

I shall show you the way to our town, and tell you about us;

We are called Phaekians, and I am the daughter of the King, Alkinoos."

She calls out to her maids:

"Maids, where are you all fleeing to?

This fellow is not here to rob or murder you,

And I don't think he has come to harm any Phaekian;

It seems he is only some troubled man who needs our protection,

As you all should know, every stranger is Zeus in disguise;

To offer this man our hospitality and kindness, would be most wise,

Let us do the right thing, give him something to drink and to eat;

Then take him to the stream and wash him from his head to his feet."

The maids stop and return timidly. They take Odyssey to a sheltered place by the stream. They lay out clean clothes for him to wear, as well as a flask of olive oil. One of the girls asks if she can wash him in the stream, but Odyssey declines, saying:

"I am most eager to wash this salt from my scaly skin;

And ply myself with olive oil, and massage it in,

But, young ladies, please, face the other way, turn and close your eyes;

So I can wash in privacy, without revealing a manly surprise."

The maids, giggling, return to Nautikaa and Odyssey washes and oils himself. He puts on the clothes that lie by the whirlpools.

Athena, who has been looking on, has made him look taller and stronger. His hair has a thick lustre and drops in curls to his shoulders. His head and shoulders are now more defined and handsome. He walks a little way along the stream and sits down. Nautikaa watches him in admiration, her intuition is sparkling. Athena's craft is working well. She says to the maids:

"Shoosh ladies, I believe the gods have sent this man for a reason;

At first I thought him hideous, but now he looks sent from heaven,

I should like a husband just like this man I see here today;

How nice it would be if I can convince him to stay,

But, for now, let's give him something to eat and drink, before we go on our way."

They do as told, setting food and drink for him. He eats it ravenously, for it has been a long time since his last meal with Kalypso.

Meanwhile, Nautikaa thinks of another matter: She does not want to start any rumours or gossip in the town. Some of the town-folk are ill-natured and might, out of spite or envy, jump to conclusions about this new man and ask: Who is this fine-looking stranger that Nautikaa has befriended? Where did she find him? Is she going to marry him? Is he a lost seafarer - or pirate - washed ashore from some strange land? A refugee displaced by civil strife or war? Or, is he some god that at last has come from heaven in answer to her prayers? Is she going to live with him all the rest of her life? It would be a good thing if she married a stranger, because she takes no interest in the many young Phaekians who are in love with her. This is the kind of talk that could create a scandal and sully her name and it would be embarrassing for her parents if she was to associate with a man before being properly acquainted.

She has the laundry folded and loaded onto the wagon and has the mules yoked. She takes her seat on the wagon, and calls to Odyssey:

"Stranger, let's make a move toward the palace and the city;

Where you shall meet all of Skeria's nobility,

You seem to be a bright and intelligent man;

I have a plan and I'm sure you will understand;

I'll lead the way back into town, to my father's home;

So, stay by the wagon for as long as we travel past field and farm,

If you want my father to give his hospitality and help you on your way;

Then follow Athena's grove of poplars to my father's field of rich hay,

It's about as far from the town as a strong man's voice will carry;

Sit there until we can get to the palace and unload the laundry.

Then, when you think we've had time, come into the town and ask;

Even a little child, can point the way to the home of my father, Alkinoos,

But when you come to the high city wall and the harbour view;

Take a look at the port's ships and shops, and make a plea to Poseidon in his temple, too,

You'll see our sailors keeping their blue-eyed ships ocean worthy;

Phaekians have no need for weapons on the foaming sea,

But I must avoid the sea-men's cruel gossip and coarse talk;

So I'll take another way home, and turn left at the road's fork,[a]

An old-salt might spread a rumour about me being with a handsome stranger;

"A pirate or a foreigner has won her heart," would put my reputation in danger,

"She only spurns the local men's attentions, anyway!"

"And if a god has come to marry her, good riddance!" is what they'll say;

They will mock and scoff at us both, just think of the embarrassment too;

I would also find fault in any woman that behaved without virtue,

Imagine my parents' feelings and my brothers, my whole family's shame;

a   Taking the left fork was considered unlucky or dangerous. In this case, Nautikaa's hopes for marriage to the stranger may be lost.

If I, being unwed, was to befriend a man, what would become of the King's good
name?

So, when you get past the gates and through the outer court;

Go into the hall and you'll find my mother sitting by the hearth,

There she'll be spinning her purpled yarn by the warmth of the firelight;

To see her sitting against the pillar with all her maids, is a fine sight,

And close to her sits my father like an immortal god, sipping wine on his throne;

But never mind him, go to my mother, and lay your hands on her knees if you want
to get home,

If you gain her favour, you may again see your own country;

No matter in what direction or how distant it may be."

That said, she touches the mules' hinds with her whip and they all leave the
spring and its stream. The mules pull hard for their feed awaits them at the palace,
but she is careful not to go too fast for Odyssey and the maids are following on foot.
She gently pulls on the reins.

*

Sun is sinking. Odyssey takes the other road in the fork - to the *right*[a] - and
comes to a sacred grove dedicated to Athena. There Odyssey, as instructed, rests and
thinks about his prayer to the daughter of Zeus, Athena, his motivator:

"Hear me, daughter of Aegis-bearing Zeus, I beg you again, hear me!

You looked the other way last time I was wrecked by Poseidon at sea,

Have some pity now and grant that I may find many friends;

And get a warm reception among the Phaekians."

---

a   The right was considered the best, or strongest side, and usually provided good omens. Perhaps a
    superstition. The left fork in the road taken by Nautikaa did not provide her dream's promise.

Athena hears his plea but she does not show herself. She is respectful - and afraid - of her uncle, raging Poseidon, the patron god of the Phaekians, who remains determined to prevent Odyssey from reaching his home.

*

THE COURT OF KING ALKINOOS

As Odyssey prays to Athena, Nautikaa drives on to the palace. She parks the wagon at the gateway and her brothers unhitch the mules and carry the laundry into the house. She goes to her own room, where an old servant, Eurymedusa of Apeira, lights a fire. This old woman had been brought from Apeira as a prize-offering for King Alkinoos, and a nanny for Nautikaa.

Odyssey starts back toward the town and Athena makes him invisible in case any of the proud Phaekians should detain him, for foreigners have no rights and he might be en-slaved or put in prison.

As he enters the town, Athena comes toward him in the likeness of a young girl carrying a jug. She stands in front of Odyssey, and he asks:

"My dear, will you be so kind as to point the way to the house of King Alkinoos?

I am a visitor to your country, I'm lost and an unfortunate foreigner, in distress."

Disguised Athena says:

"Yes, sir, stranger, I will show you the house where you want to go;

King Alkinoos lives quite close to my own father, you know,

Follow me, but look at no-one or answer any questions;

For some people here are suspicious of a foreigner's affections,

They are a sea-faring folk, trusting things by Poseidon's grace;

Their ships glide as fast as thoughts or as sea-birds can race."

Odyssey follows in her steps. Not one of the Phaekians can see him as he walks through the town. He is in awe at the harbour, the ships, Poseidon's Temple and the high walls of the city. On reaching the palace, disguised Athena tells him:

"This is the house, stranger, Sir, which you have been seeking;
In the hall you will find a number of great people at tables, feasting,

Don't be afraid, go straight in, as a bolder man makes his point more often;
First you should find queen, Arete, it's her heart that you should win and soften,

For she comes from the same family stock as her husband Alkinoos;
Originally descended from Poseidon, who was the father to Nausithoos,

She is respected beyond measure by the people, her children and the King;
And is a very good woman, in head and heart, lofty praises her friends often sing,

And she will help her friends' husbands to settle any dispute;
So much revered and liked, for she is a Queen of the highest repute,

If you gain her favour, you may see your country again;
No matter in what direction or how far distance will send."

Athena leaves Skeria and is in Athens, near Marathon,[104] instantly, where she enters the house of Erechtheus.[105]

*

Meanwhile, back in Skeria, Odyssey enters Alkinoos' Palace. As he reaches the bronzed threshold, he stops, astonished at seeing its splendour. It is as if the high hall has the radiance of both the Sun and the Moon.

The high walls on either side are bronze from end to end, and the cornice is blue enamel. The doors are gold, and hung on pillars of silver that rise from a bronze floor, the lintel is silver and the door handles are gleaming gold.

On each side there are massive gold and silver statues of mastiff dogs which Hephaestos,[106] with his consummate skill, had made to keep watch over the palace. They protect the residents within and assure that their names will live eternally. Seats are arranged along the walls and covered with fine tapestries. Raised on pedestals, are gold statues of young men with flaming torches in their hands that light the room with a soft glow.

There are fifty maid-servants, some are grinding rich-yellow corn grain on a mill, others work looms. Shuttles go backwards and forwards like fluttering Aspen leaves in the autumn wind. Other maids twist the linen press tight, extracting olive oil that drips into jars. Just as the Phaekians are the best seafarers in the world, so do their intelligent wives excel at handicrafts. Athena has inspired them well.

Outside, there is a large sports field. Also, a garden of about four acres with a stone wall around it, full of beautiful fruit trees; pears, pomegranates, and apples. There is luscious figs and olives in full growth. The fruit never rots or fails, either in winter or summer, as the West Wind is favourable to the new blooms and the old, giving a constant supply of fruit. Pear grows on pear, apple on apple, fig on fig, and so with grapes, for there is an excellent vineyard on the level ground. Some of the grapes are being dried into raisins. In another part they are being trodden in wine barrels. On the vines, grapes have shed their blossom and are beginning to show fruit, while others are just changing colour. In the furthest corner of the garden are flower beds that bloom all year round.

Two streams irrigate the garden, one courses crystal-clear water around each bed of plants, the other carries water underground into the palace's cistern, where it is stored for the town's people to use. These are some of the splendours that the Invisibles have endowed on the House of King Alkinoos.

Odyssey crosses the bronzed threshold and goes into the palace. He sees the Phaekian nobles making their drink offerings to Hermes, the Ego Slayer, which is their custom before retiring for the night. He goes on, into the palace, still unseen from the cloak of darkness which Athena has dressed him in. He sees Queen Arete and King Alkinoos and they now see him. All present are astonished and speechless. He kneels and places his hands on her knees. Odyssey begins his petition:

"Queen, may the gods grant happiness to you and all your offspring;

And down through time heap high your treasures for passing,

I come as a suppliant to you, the King and your guests;

I am lost, an unfortunate foreigner, in great distress,

Kindly grant me an escort to my beloved country, so I can make amends;

For twenty disastrous years I have roamed away from my home and friends."

He rises, turns and sits on the fire's hearth. They are all speechless and hold their tongues. Finally, Echeneus, an old hero and an excellent speaker, an elder of the Phaekians, says:

"Alkinoos, should the ashes of your fire be this man's host?

Seat him on that silver inlaid stool where he'll find comfort most,

And have the squires mix and pour him wine and water;

So we can make a toast to all-seeing Zeus, xenia's Minder,

Who protects all deserving suppliants with his will and might;

And ask the housekeeper to give him some supper for his appetite."

King Alkinoos rises and takes Odyssey by the hand from the hearth, escorts him to a seat occupied by his favourite son, Laodamas, next to his own throne. Laodamas rises and gestures for Odyssey to sit in his high-backed chair. He does.

A maid is present and pours scented water from a silver jug over his hands into a gold basin. The house-keeper draws a table to them and brings bread and delicacies from the busy kitchen. A steward serves cut meats carved on his board. He places a gold goblet and fills it with mellowed wine.

Odyssey eats and drinks. Alkinoos asks a steward:

"Pontonous, mix and hand around a jug of wine and water;

So we can make a toast to Zeus, xenia's minder,

Who protects all deserving suppliants with his will and might;

And trust that Zeus will heed this man's desperate plight."

Pontonous mixes wine and water and serves it to each of the men. They all toast and drink the wine. Alkinoos says:

"Gentlemen, tomorrow I shall invite a larger assembly for a sacrificial rite,

We'll have a banquet to honour our guest and discuss his homeward plight,

We should resolve to return him soon, without inconvenience;
No matter in which direction or how much distance,

When he is in his home and our duty will be done;
Then Destiny in his home-land, he will serve out alone,

It is possible, however, that the stranger is an immortal from the heavens;
Visiting us to witness our feasting and our rightful offerings,

Revealing themselves to us as we are next of kin;
Like the great Cyklops' we are just as close to those in heaven."[a]

Odyssey says:

"King Alkinoos, do not hold such notions in your mind;
There's nothing of the Invisibles about me, you'll find,

Think of the poor wretches that suffer the harshest woes of life;
Then the Invisibles sent me many disasters and untold strife,

Nevertheless, let me eat in spite of all my misfortune;
For the pangs of an empty stomach exaggerate the memory of my ruin,

As for yourselves, I shall be glad if you help me get to my estate;
And, once on seeing my home, I'll be content to draw my last breath, if that be my
fate."

As he finishes speaking, heads nod with approval. They make their toasts to
the gods and then each man leaves the palace on the ways to their homes. Odyssey
sits with Arete and Alkinoos while the servants clear the hall. Queen Arete recognises

---

a   The Ephesians are related to Poseidon and also cousins to the Cyklops, their enemies.

the clean shirt and jacket that Odyssey is wearing, as she and her maids had made these clothes for her sons. She asks:

> "Stranger, tell me, who you are and where from;
>
> And who gave you the clothes you have on?
>
> Did you not say you came here from across the seas?
>
> Kindly tell us your story, if you please."

Odyssey answers:

> "Queen, it would be a very long story for me to relate;
>
> A tale full of disasters and misfortunes as the Invisibles plotted my fate,
>
> But, there is the Island of Ogygio, where the sea-spirit Kalypso dwells;
>
> She is a shrewd and powerful Spirit, as her legend tells,
>
> Misfortune, however, took me to her lonely shore;
>
> For Zeus[a] struck my blue-eyed ships with his thunderbolts, wild seas and more,
>
> So that all my brave crewmen were lost and drowned;
>
> But for nine days I stuck to the keel of my blue-eyed boat, which was upside down,
>
> On the tenth night the gods sent me to Kalypso, as I was in great distress;
>
> She took me in, and treated me with the great love and kindness,
>
> Indeed she wished to make me immortal, but she could not win my heart;
>
> I stayed with Kalypso seven tearful years, and then we were destined to part,
>
> Either she changed her own mind, or Zeus told her to set me free;

---

a   Poseidon attacked Odyssey's last ship. Perhaps, realising that Poseidon is the Phaekians patron he changes the aggressor not to offend his hosts.

So, on a raft with provisions she sent me on a wide and lonely sea,

On the eighteenth day I caught sight of your shores from my raft;
But Zeus would not let me past and raised a great storm, as is his craft,

The waves were high and smashed my sturdy raft into pieces;
So, I swam for it, against wind and wave, hoping to find beaches,

But, I was thrown against the rocks and dragged out to sea;
Soon I found a river inlet away from wind, which offered land to me,

There, I got out of the water and gathered my wits;
Night was coming quickly, and I found some thickets,

There I covered myself with leaves and fell into sweet sleep;
And into the next afternoon my slumber did keep,

I woke to find the Sun sinking and your daughter and maids at play on the shore;
I thought she was a goddess, I asked her for help, which she gave me, and more,

I was provided with plenty of bread and wine, and I washed in the stream;
And she gave me this fine shirt and purple cloak you see me in,

What I have told you is the truth that I'm pained to tell;
I am deeply indebted to your daughter for helping me so well."

King Alkinoos speaks:

"Stranger, it was wrong of my daughter not to bring you here without delay;
She should have brought you home with the maids, and not made you stay away."

Odyssey replies:

"Good King, the Princess's conduct was proper; please don't frown and fuss;
For I was ashamed to follow them, thinking, about me, you might be suspicious."

Alkinoos replies:

"Stranger, I don't get angry over small things, being reasonable is better;
But I wish by Zeus, Athena and Apollo that you would stay and marry her,

If you become my son-in-law, you'll have a house and an estate;
But, no-one - heaven forbid - should keep you from your fate,

To be sure, I shall attend to your escort tomorrow;
And shorten your homeward yearning sorrow,

You can sleep the whole voyage, no matter how far away;
My men shall row the calm waters to your home port, or any favoured bay.

Even if it's past Euboea, where my people took blonde Rhadamanthus;[107]
To see Tityus, Earth's son: That place they tell me is the remotest,[a]

Yet they swear the voyage took only a single day, to go and come;
You will see for yourself, the excellence of our ships, and oarsmen."

Odyssey, happily prays to Zeus, Mind:

"Father Zeus, grant that King Alkinoos may do all he said and has planned;
Pray he win deathless glory, and ensure I return to my father-land."

---

a   Euboea is a large island on the eastern side of the Greek mainland. A place that Odyssey had been many times.

As they speak Arete tells her maids to set a bed in the portico of the gatehouse. They make it with warm purpled blankets. The maids, with lit torches, invite Odyssey to his guest room: "Rise, Sir, and we shall escort you to your waiting bed."

Long-suffering Odyssey sleeps. The portico echoes with his deep slumber. King Alkinoos lies in the inner part of the palace, with his wife, Queen Arete close by his side.

*

PALACE GAMES

*

DEMODOKOS AND PORK CRACKLING

*

Dawn lights her red lantern,

Putting Night to sleep

Both King Alkinoos and Odyssey rise early. Alkinoos leads the way to the town square, next to the port. They sit together on a bench of polished marble.

In order for Odyssey to get home, Athena takes the form of one of Alkinoos' servants, and goes around the people one-by-one inviting them to assemble and listen to the stranger who sailed here to visit the King, and who looks like an immortal.

With her words they mill and crowd the town square until there is standing-room only. They are all impressed with Odyssey's appearance, which Athena has enhanced. He appears taller and more handsome than he really is.

Alkinoos speaks:

"Hear me, Phaekians, that I may speak what's on my mind;

A stranger, whatever his name, has found his way to this Palace of mine,

From somewhere, East or West, he comes asking for an escort home, far away;

As is our custom, let us ready one of our fine ships and deliver him without delay,

For no-one can complain that the Phaekian's detain any foreigner leaving our shores;

So prepare our flag-ship, and fifty-two youthful sailors to man the oars,

Once you are ready to sail, come to the feast in my home;

You will enjoy everything the palace can offer before the oars flick the sea-foam,

In regard to the aldermen, join me in entertaining our guest in the hall;

Where Demodokos[108] the famed bard, will sing and entertain us all."

Alkinoos leads the way back to the palace. A servant goes to seek Demodokos. The fifty-two oarsmen go to the wharf and ready the blue-eyed vessel. They tie the oars to the rowlocks and ready the sheets and halyards to set the sails. The mast is placed into its socket in the keel and tied fast with the fore-stays to the bow. They flake the white sails on the boom ready to hoist them with halyards of plaited leather. The ship is ready, so they, too, go to King Alkinoos' palace. The hall, cloisters and courtyard are filled with scores of men both young and old. The squires have prepared one dozen sheep, eight boars and two oxen. These are flayed, butchered and roasting on hot coals.

The god-gifted minstrel Demodokos arrives. He is blind,[109] but sings and plays his instrument like no other. Pontonous escorts and sits him on a silver inlaid stool with his back resting against a stone pillar. His lyre is hung for him above his head and he is shown where to feel for it with his hands. The house-keeper draws a table to him and brings bread and delicacies from the busy kitchen. A steward serves cut meats carved on his board. He places a gold goblet and fills it with fine wine. The guests begin eating and enjoying the banquet.

Demodokos[a] is inspired to sing about the feats of heroes past. He chooses a popular ballad about Odyssey and Achilles' quarrel during the Trojan War. There, Agamemnon was secretly glad when he heard the great warriors quarrelling, because Apollo had foretold him that the Trojan War would not end until the noblest Hellenes had feuded. That feud started the long line of disasters suffered by Odyssey, the returning Hellenes and the all Trojans.[110]

As Demodokos sings, Odyssey draws his purple cloak over his head, covering his face. He is ashamed and does not want the Phaekians to see his tears. At the end of each verse the bard pauses. Odyssey wipes his tears and takes a long swig of wine. The Phaekians press the bard for more verse and he plays on. Odyssey again covers his face and sobs in distress. Only Alkinoos hears the heaving sighs and notices Odyssey's covered face. He says:

---

a   Could it be that Demodokos and blind Homer were the same man?

"Aldermen and town's people, enough of this feast and the bard's verse;

Let's go outside and entertain our guest with sports of which our nation ranks first."

He leads the way.

Demodokos' lyre is hung on its peg and he is escorted outside to the sports field. There is a crowd of several thousand strong, including many great athletes: Acroneos, Ocyalos, Elatreos, Nauteos, Prymneos, Anchialos, Eretmeos, Ponteos, Proreos, Thoon, Anabesinios, and Amphialos, son of Polyneos, son of Tecton.[a] Also famed Euryalos, son of Naubolus, who is like the war-god Ares[111] and was the handsomest of the Phaekians, except for the King's favourite son, Laodamas.

Three of the King's sons are there, ready to compete: Laodamas, Halios, and Clytoneos. The foot races begin.

From the starting post they raise dust out over the track. Clytoneos came in first by a long margin, leaving the others behind by the length of the furrow that two mules can plough in a day.

The gruelling sport of oil-wrestling and Euryalus proves more artful. Amphialus excels in broad-jumping.

Elatreos is undefeated in hurling the discus. Laodamas is crowned the best boxer. He suggests that because this stranger has a powerful build, and not being too old, he might enjoy some sport. Euryalos, smiling, replies:

"Laodamas, he has not had our full hospitality: Only has he drunk and eaten;

So, ask the visitor in which sport he'd prefer to be beaten."

Laodamas makes his way to where Odyssey sits, and says:

"Sir, we would like for you to try a sport to test your skill;

For nothing does credit one's life, as a man's feet and hands reveal,

Try something and it will rid the sorrows from your mind;

Your ship is ready, and you won't be delayed very long, you'll find."

---

a   These names are word-puns and translate to: tall-ship, fast-tide, paddler, marine-man, helmer, grounder, rower etc.

Odyssey answers:

"Laodamas, how you play me with your taunts;
I'm beset with getting home, not sports,

I've had much hardship, no mortal should have to bear;
I am here as your suppliant, my home return is for what I care."

Euryalos says:

"Yes, it's obvious he is a stranger to us, and sports as well;
He's just one of those greedy trader captains, I can tell,

That spends his time laying about on vessel's hulls;
Thinking only of his freight's mission and watching sea-gulls,

Or keeping a sharp eye on his cargo when he's in port;
So to the highest bidder he can sell and rort,

Yes, it seems that there is no athlete in you;
Let him go to his home, we've got better things to do."

Odyssey answers, fiercely:

What a shameless brazen half-wit is this fellow;
What a relief that the gods don't fashion all men like you,

A man might be modest of presence, but equipped with charm;
If reasonable, he leads others wherever he goes, without harm,

Another man might be blessed, or cursed, with handsome looks;

But the Invisibles don't make better looking fools than you, Euryalos,

Your foolish words only reveal ignorance of my past;

Even from my long-gone youth my sporting records last,

I was among the best athletes and warriors of my days;

On the field of battle and against heaving seas, I was praised,

But, I take your challenge, and against anyone I shall compete;

Your disrespect has offended me and with this disc, any-one I'll beat."

Without removing his cloak he selects the heaviest discus he can see. He swings it around and around, gripped in his burly hand. He releases it. The discus whistles the air as it flies above the crowd. It lands in a burst of dust far beyond any mark of the Phaekians. Athena, Spirit of Right, in the form of a man, comes and marks the place where it has landed, saying:

"Sir, even Demodokos, the blind man, could plainly see that this throw could not be beaten;

It is so far ahead of the others, perhaps it's time for Euryalos' words to be eaten."

Odyssey is glad to have found a friend amongst the crowd. He is now reasonable with his tone and his words, saying:

"Young men, I dare you to throw the disc if you think you're stronger;

For my next throw, I'll put my back into it, and it will land longer,

I can box, oil-wrestle and run, let me have your voice;

I'm ready to take any one of you in the sport of your choice;

It was the great Philomeleides from the ring that once I tossed;

When I oil-wrestled that towering brute in Lesbos;

But I'll not fight Laodamos because I am his guest;
There is no point in challenging an equal, the gods know who is best,

One should not fight with his host, that is the root of disaster;
For I should like to return here one day, and be friends ever after,

I am handy at archery and many different sports;
For I have competed in front of Kings, in their courts,

Philoctetes[112] was the only man who could out-shoot me;
And I would not like to shoot against the dead heroes, also mighty,

With bows of Herakles[113] and Eurytos were as good as the gods;
But one shouldn't brag too much, it puts them at odds,

That was how boasting Eurytos came to his sharp end;
His challenge was answered with the angriest arrow Apollo could send,

I can throw the javelin further than an arrow can find ground;
But long distance races I should decline to run, and my tongue be bound,

As my knees lost their lift and I have sea-legs to excess;
And my strength ebbs low, so running is my weakness."

They are all surprised and silent. Except the astute King Alkinoos who says:

"Intrepid Sir, we have taken much pleasure in what you have said in truth;
And please excuse Euryalos, perhaps it was the exuberance of his youth,

I trust you will spread to your countrymen, our sporting reputation;

We don't excel in boxing and wrestling, but of running and sailing we can match any
nation,

We enjoy warm baths, and good beds and our women make fine raiment;
We love good feasts, music, dancing, wine and entertainment,

So, let us show you our talents before you go on your way;
Demodokos left his lyre in the hall, so someone run and bring it right away."

A servant runs to the palace while nine stewards clear a large dance floor.
The servant returns with Demodokos' lyre. The dancing boys begin and Odyssey is
delighted with their fleetness and agility.

The bard begins his tune, singing of the love affair between Ares and
Aphrodite, and how they secretly made adulterous love in Hephaestos's bed. Ares
gave many gifts to Aphrodite, so the Sun, told Hephaestos. Being angry, he plotted
revenge. On his great anvil he forged very fine chains which could not be broken or
untied, so that the illicit lovers would not be able to leave his violated bed.

When he had finished the chains he went to his bedroom and draped the
gossamer-fine threads over the bed-posts like a cobweb. He also hung more chains
from a ceiling beam. So fine were they that a god could not see them. Then he
pretended that he was leaving for Lemnos, his favourite destination. Ares saw him
leave and, hot with desire, rushed back to Aphrodite. She had just returned from
visiting her father, Zeus, Pride's Prick, and was eager for Ares' lovemaking. Once in
bed, they were ensnared by the fine web. They could not move and were trapped.
Hephaestos returned when Sun informed him of the lovers' dilemma. He was furious
and stood by the bed and shouted to the gods to come and witness the disgraceful
sight of them in bed together:

"Father Zeus, and all you Invisibles, hear me, my anger is heating;
Aphrodite continues to dishonour me by her wanton cheating,

She doesn't find me to her liking; ugly and lame;
But, I can't help my parentage; I am how I came,

Ares, is handsome and well built, and Aphrodite, a slave to her passion;
Now they are caught in a trap that I made by my own hands' fashion,

Come, take a look at these two lovers flaunting in my bed;

They can't escape the snare - or each other - until they are dead,

And stay this way they will - like it or not - she'll not go free;

Until all the fine works I gave to Zeus, are returned to me,

They'll soon tire of this long sleep;

Then Ares can have that two-timing bitch to keep."

The gods assemble at Hephaestos' house. Female Spirits have stayed away out of respect for *Aidos*.[a] However, Poseidon; Floater of Lands, Hermes; the Ego Slayer and the far-shooting Apollo are there. At seeing the two enmeshed lovers floundering on the bed, they burst into uncontrollable laughter. One of them says:

"Bad deeds don't prosper; how the weak overpower the strong;

Lame Hephaestos has caught the fastest god on Olympos, for doing him wrong,

Now Ares will have to satisfy Hephaestos, with an adulterer's fine;

Either way, Ares and Aphrodite are in a god-awful bind."

Apollo speaks:

"Hermes, Messenger of Heaven, if you could seduce Aphrodite, would you risk the trap?

Hermes answers:

"Yes, and I'd suffer three times the chains and the full gods' audience;

To have the chance to bond with golden Aphrodite, in everlasting romance."

---

a   *Aidos*, is the Hellenistic spirit - or sense - of shame, modesty or humility. Aidos, as a quality, is that feeling of reverence or shame which restrains one from wrong. It also confronts the emotion that a rich person might feel in the presence of the impoverished; that wealth may be more a matter of luck than merit, and their wealth may preclude them from helping one in need.

This is their low talk, one Invisible trying to out-do the other, as gods do in their own company.

Again, they wail in laughter. But their fun is short-lived because Poseidon knows that Zeus will not be amused, whether Hephaestos likes it, or not. For even gods don't have free-will.[a]

He sets about thinking how he can convince Hephaestos to free them. Poseidon says:

"Let *him* go and I will make sure that he pays you;

For you don't want to enrage mighty Zeus' wrath, true?"

Hephaestos answers:

"If I break-up Aphrodite's love tryst, and Ares goes free;

Then there's further risk for me, as a bad man's bond is poor security,

Could these chains bind you to secure the debt as the Immortals look on?

No, Ares would wriggle out of this trap - and his debt - and then he'd be gone."

Poseidon answers:

"If Ares doesn't pay what you ask, then to you I shall give;

I will pay you myself, just come to my door, you know where I live."

Hephaestos replies:

In that case, I cannot - and should not - refuse your plea;

So, now I'll retract the mesh, so he may forever flee."

---

a   Free-will is a concept that maintains that one has the ability to choose between different courses of action or thought. Free-will is linked to the concepts of responsibility, guilt, sin, praise and other judgements which apply only to actions that are supposedly freely chosen. Traditionally, only actions that are freely willed are seen as deserving credit or blame. There are numerous different concerns about threats to the possibility of free-will, varying by how exactly it is conceived, which is a matter of some debate. According to Homeric philosophy, free-will is a fallacy.

With this, Ares spirits to Thrace[a] on the eastern edge of Europe.[114] The love-lusting Aphrodite flees to Paphos.[115] There, a grove and altar are dedicated to her. The Charities[116] bathe and massage her with ambrosia oil and they clothe her in divine garments which enhance her unimaginable beauty.

Demodokos finishes his ballad and the crowd applaud.

Alkinoos asks Laodamas and Halius to dance together. They take a purple ball which Polybos has made.

One of them bends backwards and throws it high into the air. The other catches it as it descends from the clouds. They begin to dance, tossing the ball to and fro. The crowd applaud at their agility. Odyssey says:

"Your people are the nimblest dancers in the world, one will ever see.

King Alkinoos, I am astonished, I must heartily agree!"

The King is delighted and says to the Phaekians:

"Aldermen, our guest seems to be endowed with great discernment;

Let's give him proof of our hospitality without further adjournment,

Including myself, there are thirteen princes among us here, I'm told;

Let us give him keepsakes to remember us; fine clothing and talents of gold,

He shall then take his dinner with a happy and light heart;

As for you, Euryalus, an apology is in order before it's time for him to depart."

Euryalus says:

"The stranger shall have satisfaction, more than you ask, my Lord;

With a scabbard of carved ivory, to hold my bronze and silver sword."

---

a   The words, *Tragic* and *tragedy* have their root in the name of this region in eastern Europe (part of modern Turkey, west of the Bosphoros) because of the countless invasions and catastrophic wars over the centuries.

He places the sword into Odyssey's hands, saying:

"Good luck to you, Sir, stranger, if what I said was amiss, let the winds blow it away;

May heaven grant safe passage and a hero's return when you find your home's bay."

Odyssey answers:

"Good luck to you my friend, may the gods grant you every wish;

And I hope your apology and this fine sword, you shall not miss."

He slings the scabbard over his shoulder.

It is sunset and the gifts begin to arrive from the many princes and noblemen. Alkinoos' sons receive and pass them into the Queen's care. Alkinoos leads the guests into the hall and they take their seats. The King says:

"Queen, wife, bring some clean clothes and a travel chest;

Boil water for our guest's bath so at dinner he'll feel his best,

Pack all the gifts that the nobles have given in that sturdy crate;

And leave some room for this gold goblet which I'm going to donate,

It is of the finest work, and will remind him of me, when he toasts to Zeus;

Or any one of the gods from whom he'll earn his fate and the truth."

Arete asks her maids to set a large bath on the fire. They heap the fire up and it blazes away, steaming the bath water. Meanwhile, Arete brings a magnificent chest, and packs the gifts. She adds fine clothes and Alkinoos' gift, saying to Odyssey:

"Sir, tie the sealing knot of this crate, by your own hand;

That will deter any thief's work, as you sleep on the voyage to your home-land."

Odyssey fits the the chest lid and ties a special knot[a] that the witch, Circe,[117] had taught him. One of the maids escorts him to his bath. He enjoys the soapy, hot water. It reminds him of the way that Kalypso had fondly cared for him, and the pleasures of her cave. He recalls how he was just one step away from being a god.

The maids finish washing him and begin the oil massage. That finished, he leaves the bath-house with clean clothes and new shoes, and walks back into the hall. He joins the guests who are seated and enjoying their wine. He notices radiant Nautikaa standing by one of the many stone pillars. While admiring him she says:

"Farewell stranger, do not forget me after you leave this shore;

For it is to me you owe your life - and by the looks of these gifts - much more."

Wily Odyssey replies:

"Princess Nautikaa, may Zeus allow me to return to my yearning shore;

Then, because you saved my life, I shall revere you as a goddess for evermore."

He sits beside Alkinoos. Supper is served, and the wine mixed for drinking. A servant leads Demodokos, their favourite minstrel, into their midst and he sits by a stone pillar. Odyssey cuts off a large piece of roasted pork with plenty of chewy, crackled fat. He thinks it will take quite a while to eat and perhaps cut short the bard's heart-wrenching words.

He asks a steward:

"Please, steward, hand this piece of crackled pork to Demodokos;

To savour every morsel slowly, just like we enjoy each word of his verse."

The servant hands the pork to Demodokos, who took it and slowly enjoys, just as the guests eat and drink to their hearts' content. Odyssey has another idea, and says:

"Demodokos, you are an outstanding minstrel and a very gifted fellow;

Did you learn your craft from the Muse, Athena or Mighty Apollo?

---

a   Historians believe that he used the complicated "circle" knot, taught to him by Circe, which is very
     difficult to tie.

You have sung well of the Hellenes' return from that fateful shore;

It's almost like you were there, or heard it all from one who attended that war,

Can you tell us about the wooden horse which Epeius[118] did build?

Which Odyssey got by trickery into the City of Troy, with thirty men filled,

Tell that wonderful tale right and I shall sing your worldly praise;

And we shall toast to you with our goblets filled to raise."

Demodokos takes up the story at the point where the Hellenes have burnt their tents and sailed away while their best thirty men are hiding within the wooden horse, which was delivered to the fortified main gate of Troy, and then dragged to the City's main square, by the Trojans, themselves. There the wooden horse stood in the midst of the Trojan people.

There were three suggestions on what to do with it. First, some were for burning it where it stood; some for dragging it to the top of a cliff and hurling it off the precipice, and others allowing it to remain as a symbol of victory over the Hellenes and an offering to the Invisibles.

After much debate, they settled on keeping the horse as a tribute. So, the great City of Troy was doomed as they stood their admiring the Wooden Horse, gloating over their supposed victory.

Demodokos now sings about how the Hellenes' "brave thirty" crept from the horse and attacked the city. He sings about Odyssey and Menelaos fighting at the palace of Prince Deiphobos[119] where the battle raged the worst for the Trojans.

As Odyssey listens, he is overcome with grief and tears stream from his eyes, like a woman weeping for a dead husband, who fighting to defend her and their children, falls to the spear's merciless point. Holding him, she wails as he gasps for death's final breath. Then she and her orphaned children will be taken as slaves, captive to a life of misery and hard labour. So pitiable is Odyssey's sobbing, but the only one to notice is Alkinoos, sitting next to him. The king, rises at once and says:

"Aldermen let Demodokos cease this song, for some it is too distressing;

Since he began to sing, our guest has been sobbing and weeping,

He is well *troubled* and we should delight in another pleasure;

It will be more to his liking to discuss the voyage with his new-found treasure,

Sir, I wish that you now give me a straight answer and true;
Tell me the name by which your father and mother call you,

For there is no one, rich or poor, who has no name to carry through life;
And tell me, too, your country and city so we can take you there, without strife,

For Phaekian ships need not rudders or even men;
Although guided by thoughts, they still need a destination,

And we can sail any sea covered in cloud or mist, in gale or calm;
With no danger of being wrecked or coming to hazard or harm,

Although my father did say that Poseidon can be angry;
For giving some people escorts, much too readily,

He also told that one day a fine ship of ours will be destroyed;
And our city will be buried under the mountain's land-slide,

It might be just a rumour of men, and come to no end;
Or, maybe we shall feel the wrath of mighty Poseidon, again,

Now, where have you travelled, from where have you been driven?
Tell us of the friendly or savage peoples, and the strange cities you have seen,

Why are you so unhappy at the Hellenes' return from Troy?
Surely victory over an enemy is something for us to enjoy,

The gods make these disasters so that future generations will sing;
Of hardship and lack, and the lessons to be learned within,

And so end the selfish deeds of mortal fools;
To learn to play life by the Olympians' rules,

In Troy, did you lose a country-man, some distant relation of your wife?
Or did a son-in-law or father-in-law or some brave friend lose his life?

*

ODYSSEY AND THE CYKLOPS
IN NO-MAN'S LAND

Odyssey replies to the King:

"King Alkinoos, it is a good thing to hear this bard's voice;
As there is nothing better than a banquet to give thanks, and rejoice,

The table is full with fine breads, meat and wines to please;
Indeed it is a lovely sight, as any man can see,

However, you ask about the story of my sorrows;
And my sad life and fate that only heaven *really* knows,

Firstly, I am the son of Laertes and my name is Odyssey;
I am known on Earth, and in Olympos, my home is the island of Ithaki,

It is in a group of islands with Kefalonia, Lefkada and Zakynthos;
There is a high mountain named Neriton, covered in bright green forests,

Below the headland are three bays, Molos, Skinos and Phortune, the deepest;
Poseidon forged the land into a trident's three-pronged fork, slanting north-west;

Hidden twice is a harbour refuge, steep shadowed in Neriton's lee;
Ithaki's port lies on Phortune Bay's edge, furthest west from the open sea,

Of all the islands, it sees an early sunset and first a dawn;
It is rugged and stony, where brave and handsome men are born,

A man's own country is the best sight and memory he can know;
But, it was the Spirit Kalypso that kept me seven years, in her cave on Ogygio,

As did the cunning Queen Circe, who also wished to marry me;
But they could not win my love, whilst my heart remains in Ithaki,

Now, to the many adventures with which Zeus entertained the other gods;
These twenty years have robbed me of a cherished home, with a life at odds.

My twelve ships sailed from victory at Troy, the winds sent us to the Cicones, in Ismarus;[120]
There we killed the men and divided the women and plunder, between us,

I was then for leaving and making sail for our next port;
But the others wanted to stay drinking, eating and for other sport,

Meanwhile, the Cicones re-grouped their forces and their might;
Better men and hardy fighters came in droves, ready for the fight,

They came in chariots and on foot as thick as Spring's grass is green;
Fate, too, was against us, with the fiercest fighters I have ever seen,

Near our moored ships, the bloody battle ranged;
Volleys of bronzed spears, were many times exchanged,

We fought all day and into the night, we were lucky to escape after they broke our flanks;
But seventy-two, six men from each ship, were lost forever from our ranks,

We sailed with grieving hearts for the brave men we cherished;
But glad to escape certain death, for we all might have perished,

Then Zeus weltered the North wind into a black hurricane;
Land and sky were hidden in thick clouds and driving rain,

Howling winds shredded the sails, so we took to the oars;
And rowed our hardest towards land and friendlier shores,

We were stranded for two days, beaten by exhaustion, on the seaside;
Then we raised our mast again letting the wind be our guide,

We should have gotten home with those fair winds, so straight;
But after Cape Malea the wind pushed us past Kithera.[121] That was our fate![a]

For nine days we were driven by menacing winds and steep seas;
And on the tenth day we reached Libya, land of the Lotus eaters,[122]

There we landed for fresh water and food, we were weak;
What place and people are these? I asked, and sent three men to seek,

They found kind people that plied them with all the Lotus[b] they could smoke and eat;
So that they lost all desire to sail for their homes, or even return to our fleet,

I found them chomping on the Lotus flowers in child-like happiness;
And they wept like children too, as I dragged back to the ships in distress,

---

a   It is on this island that Menaloas and Helen had a summer palace. When Paris visited the sanctuary
dedicated to Aphrodite, he met Helen. They eloped and sailed to Troy. At the shrine, in the sanctuary, a
statue of Aphrodite crumbled into rubble when Helen first entered, so stunning was her beauty,
according to legend.

b   Lotus, another name for cannabis, which lulls one into a state of apathy, sleepiness and confusion.

There, tied with leather ropes to the benches and oars, they were yoked;

And with every sulking pull, they turned the blue sea white, as they stroked,

*

Morale was low for many days, then we reached the land of the wretched *Cyklops*;[a]

These savages live off what the land provides: wild wheat, barley and grapes,

They have no plows or tools to till the land, they are too lazy to work crops;

With no laws or rules they live in caves, on the mountain tops,

Each is his own king, lord and master of his family, without a care;

And they take no interest in another living thing, the Invisibles or prayer,

Not too far from their harbour is a green and fertile island;[123]

It's inhabited only with many wild goats, it is unmanned,

The Cyklops don't go there, they are too lazy to hunt for goats;

They have no desire or even the skills to build the simplest of boats,

Every thing they need is within their hairy reach;

But those brutes are idol, won't learn and have nothing to teach,

They have no want to travel or visit another's land;

They dwell in their own world and care not for a god-fearing man,

What man or god sired them? Less man, more beast!

On mortal men these one-eyed giants devour and feast,

Zeus, Mind, alone knows how we found an island's shore that black, moon-less night;

---

a   The name, *Cyklops*, translates to: Round eyed or narrow of outlook or vision.

We could not see our own noses, and left was no different to right,

Our eyeballs served no purpose, and were as useless as a deaf ear;
For the sea was deathly quiet and all twelve crews were dumb with fear,

But soon we glided onto a sandy shore and camped on its beach;
Until rose-fingered Dawn splashed the morning sky with crimson and peach,

We mustered into three bands to hunt goats that Zeus' nymphs provided;
And a mighty massacre of the four-legged islanders was evenly divided,

In all, we killed or caught one-hundred-and-eight goats;[a]
A good day's hunting was shared between our dozen blue-eyed boats,

All day we feasted on roasted goat flesh and bones;
And slaked our thirst with the glorious wines we took from the sacked Cicones,

As we feasted, our eyes spied the land, where the Cyklops dwell;
We heard strange voices; bleating sheep, goats or giants, we could not tell,

Next day my crew rowed me across to the savage's island, just a little to the south;
On a cliff overlooking the sea, was a gaping cavern with laurel trees each side of its mouth,

There were pens a-many for sheep and goats, all walled with stone;
And this was the where the great monster lived with his animals, alone,

But that one-eyed beast was out shepherding his flocks in some valley below;
What a horrid sight, like a lurching rocky crag was this unnatural fellow,

---

a   Odyssey's palace is over-run with one-hundred-and-eight Suitors of his wife Penelope, and their entourages. A coincidence?

I took a dozen of the best men, the others to guard our blue-eyed ship;
In bags we took food and a large goatskin of purple wine, to sip,

That wine was given to me by Maron, son of Euanthus;
He was the temple priest of Apollo, the patron god of Ismarus,

When we sacked his city we spared him, his child and wife;
He offered me precious gifts - not much choice - his treasures or his life,

A mixing bowl of worked silver, rich jewels and of gold, seven glowing bars;
And wine, of the most exquisite flavour - fit for gods - in all, twelve jars,

No-one but himself, his wife, and a maid knew of this rare wine;
Heavenly sweet on the tongue, but so intoxicating to the mind,

Even blending it by twenty parts of water to one of the grape's juice;
The bouquet from the mixing-bowl was still impossible to refuse,

No mortal - perhaps no god - could resist its heavenly taste;
No virtue in abstinence, that would be a man's folly, and sacred libations an earthly waste,

It was of a quality that was simply too good to be shared;
But some charitable god, for us, must have truly cared,

"Take a goat-skin of that wine with you!" was whispered into my ear;
Just as I had a foreboding that we would meet some monstrous fear,

The brute was not at home, but with his flocks down in the valley,
Inside the vaulting cave, we were dumb-struck by what we did see;

Pens full of lambs and kids, divided into sucklers, yearlings and two-tooth;

And his racks of cheese were stacked up to the vaulting cavern's roof,

As for his dairy, all the jugs and buckets, brimmed with curds and whey;

My men begged me to leave and drive the animals down to our boat, without delay,

In hindsight it was good advice, but we had a god looking over us, what could go wrong?

No need to worry, we out-numbered the wretch, thirteen to one,

Perhaps when we met he might be friendly, and have a present for me?

However, that was not the case – a menacing eyesore he turned out to be,

His cavern stunk of animals and dung, to the nose a stench far from floral;

So we piled leaves from the trees by the cave's mouth, sweet-scented laurel,

After lighting a fire we sat and ate our fill of his lovely cheese;

Then waited for the beast, resting on the piles of laurel leaves,

We didn't have to wait long, and we woke to a startling sound;

A huge load of firewood hurtled into our midst, we found,

We ran for cover to the furthest end of the cave;

One thing in mind: Our own souls to save,

The giant herded the milking sheep and goats inside then;

Leaving the males, the rams and he-goats, outside in their stone pen,

Then he rolled a huge boulder into the cavern's jaw;

So big that twenty-two, hitched oxen could not draw,

He sat and milked the ewes and goats, and passed them on to the lambs to feed;
Curdled half the milk and set aside the rest for his supper, should his thirst need,

He went to light the fire, but noticed it was already flaring;
It was then he searched for us, his solitary eye glaring,

"Strangers, who are you?" he shouted. Where do you sail from? Merchant traders?
Or, do you spend your lives ruining others, are you pirates and raiders?"

We were scared out of our wits, by his booming voice and hideous look, but
I managed to say:

"We are all Hellenes on our way back from Troy's long war;
High seas and brutal winds have washed us onto your shore,

We didn't plan to come to your home-land today;
It was a just a mistake by us, or All-seeing Zeus must have intended it this way,

We are proud and victorious warriors, Agamemnon is our king;
We sacked the great City of Ilium and look forward to our home-coming,

You are our kind host, we are suppliants at your knees;
Treat us to your good nature, grant us respect, and may Zeus it please."

He gave me a pitiless answer with his gawking eyeball:

"Stranger, you know nothing of this country or our ways, you are *trouble,* and a liar;
I don't fear the gods: Heaven means nothing to me, nor does Hades' fire,

We Cyklops do not care about your Olympian gods - or Zeus - who you revere;
And if invisible Zeus cares for you, why did he send you to die here?

Now tell me where your ship is moored, on which beach?
Is it far around the point, or is she lying down below us, at easy reach?"

That dumb oaf could not outwit - so easily - a man of the world, such as I;
So, I answered:
"Cruel Poseidon[a] dashed our ship upon lee rocks far away from here," was my lie.

He made no reply, but jumped up and seized two of my crew by their feet;
And slammed their heads into the ground, like helpless puppies, they were mince-meat,

Blood splattered all about us, as he tore them limb from limb;
Then he dropped his huge jaw, and stuffed that gory meal in,

"What bitter ends" I thought, as we all screamed like women;
We wept and howled, lifting our hands to Zeus and his Heaven,

Then the loathsome brute swilled down his meal, with warm milk curds;
Stretched himself, rolled onto his side and slept, without any more words,

First, I wanted to draw my sword and stab his stony heart;
But, we were trapped by that huge rock, how could we depart?

As we sobbed I prayed to the Invisibles, until Dawn delivered Day;
When the monster woke, stoked the fire and steered his stern eye our way,

He sat on his stool and milked the goats and ewes, quelling their bleats;
And then passed them on to the lambs to feed, eager for their mothers' teets,

---

a   Here Odyssey makes an allusion to his own ignorance of Cyklops being Poseidon's son. Or was he goading him?

When his work was done, he seized two more men, and made his morning's meal;
He tore each into pieces, rolled them into a bloody ball, then his teeth made them squeal,

Soon, he rolled away the rock door, from where it had been;
Walked out with his flocks at his back, then rolled it shut again,

He whistled the flocks down the mountain, for fresh grass to find;
And I got to scheming revenge for my men, I had malice on my mind.

The best plan I could think of was this:

The beast had a huge wooden club lying near the pigs' sty;
Of green olive-wood to shape as a walking stick, once it was dry,

It was so big it could be used as a mast of a twenty-oared merchant ship;
So I cut off about a fathom,[a] and the men whittled a fine point at its tip,

We charred the stick's end in the fire, to make it hard enough to bore;
Then buried it in the piles of laurel leaves that hid the dung, on the cavern's floor,

We drew lots to blind the monster, by drilling the stick into his sleeping eye;
The lots fell to the four very best men I'd have chosen, and me, myself, made it five,

Later, the beast returned, droving all his flocks - even the rams - into the cavern;
There was none left outside: By a whim or some god's prompting him?

Again he rolled the stone back, sealing the cave and our escape;
Then he sat on his stool and milked the goats and ewes until late,

---

a   A fathom is about six feet, or two metres.

When his work was done, he snatched two men, and made two more meals;
He bit off their heads, stretched them thin, the last things he ate was their heels,

I went to him with an olive-wood bowl, full of purple wine to deceive;
Saying: "Cyklops, you have eaten well, drink this, our gift, if you please,

As visitors we brought it from our ship, as a present for you;
How do you expect visitors to return, if you treat them the way you do?"

He took the bowl and drank, delighted by its taste; he asked for more;
"And tell me," he said, "what is your name, as I wish to make you a present for sure,

We have wine in this country, for our soil and Sun grows grapes well;
But this is like Nectar and Ambrosia - made for the gods - as far as I can tell."

Three times I filled his bowl, and three times he drained it to the dregs;
When the wine got into his head, the monster lost the use of his legs,

Cyklops, you ask my name, my family calls me No-man, and my friends too;
"Here's your present then," he said, "I shall eat No-man's crew first, then I'll eat you,"

He moved to grab another man to snack upon, but his feet were drunk;
He toppled backwards, with a mighty crash, into the ground his head sunk,

From his gaping gob, wine, curds and men's flesh spewed up like an angry volcano;
So we thrust the sharp stick back into the fire, heating its point to an ember's glow,

Fear started to cripple the men's work, so I rallied them with a rousing cry;
And with high hearts we drove that stick, deep into the monster's eye,

With all our might we screwed it, like an auger's drill, round and round;

The red-hot poker hissed all the way, until the back of his eyeball was found,

His eyelids and eyebrows were on fire, the eye hissed with protest;
Just as a blacksmith plunges a molten spear-head into cold water, it tempers best,

Hot iron gains strength from a quenching swim;
But that hot stick meant that the Cyklops' world, was now invisible to him,

Then came the frightful screams, that rang out through the cave;
As he plucked the skewered eyeball from its socket, his sight he could not save.

Soon the other Cyklops gathered, coming from the head-land and afar, asking:

"What is wrong with you Polyphemus? Why do you bellow, scream and curse?
You spoil our sleep. Are you being robbed - treachery or violence - or something worse?"

Polyphemus[a] replied:

"Countrymen, it's No-man's treachery! No-man's violence is doing me in."
"Well then," they said, "if no man is attacking you, then you must be ailing,

Zeus - Mind - makes people's heads sick, no earthly help for you;
Pray to your father Poseidon, he'll know exactly what to do."

So, as they went away I laughed to myself and the idea of "*No man's*" cunning;[124]
But, it must be said - we were still prisoners - no closer to our home-coming,

The Cyklop's turn came, believing we would escape with his sheep;
So he sat in the doorway, stretched arms to catch us, to keep,

---

a   The name, *Polyphemus*, translates to: much famed; well known or talked about.

That great eyesore could not outwit - so easily - a man of the world, such as me;
So I schemed how I could save my men, and we all could flee.

This is what I planned:

The rams were bushy with thick, black wool, and very well fed;
And I bound them three across, with saplings from the brute's bed,

So each of my men would hang, under every middle sheep;
But my ram was bigger than the others, so in his wool I could hide deep,

We waited until rosy Dawn sent the Sun's rays to wake us;
That's when the males bolted from the cave, to the pastures,

The ewes stayed bleating, waiting to be milked, their udders full;
That stupid Cyklops felt only their backs, he didn't check their under-wool,

So my men got out from that dreadful cave, except the six that were dead;
But the giant took hold of my ram, with me riding underneath, and he said:

"My favourite ram, why are you the last to leave our cave today?
You like to lead the mob into the dewy grass and the green hay,

Do you take pity on your master and his missing eye, taken by a dirty trick?
Blinded by that *trouble*-maker, No-man, with evil wine and his red-hot poker stick,

I'd like to feel his skin in my hands; if you only had a voice, tell me where he might
be;
And I'll dash his brains out on this ground, and avenge what *No-man* has done to
me."

He pushed my ram outside, and after a fair distance from the cave, I let go;
Then untied each of my men, and we drove the flock down to our ship below,

The joyful crew applauded at seeing us, the men who'd cheated ghost-hood;
Then wept for the six victims of the cruel Cyklops, and his no-good,

Time was against us, I hushed their crying, and they mustered the sheep on board;
We pushed off and the fourteen men turned the blue sea white, as they oared.

We could see the monster near his lair, so I shouted back to him:

"Cyklops, you should have taken care of your visitors, and not eat us;
You dumb wretch, don't you know that we are protected by mighty Zeus,[a]

Here's some advice: Don't get *blind* drunk next time you have guests;
Look after them, be hospitable and live without regrets."

Hearing all that, he turned his blind eye our way;
His manner was for revenge, with our lives he wanted us to pay,

Furious, and with one hand, he tore off the mountain's[125] top;
And flung it straight at our boat, almost smashing the bow, it came to a stop,[126]

The men screamed as the sea quaked, and threw up its mightiest waves;
Which pushed our blue-eyed boat back towards the shore, and our certain graves,

But I snatched a long oar and pushed the boat back onto it's fleeing course;
My men put their backs into it, and rowed for dear life, with all their force,

When we had got twice as far as before, I jeered at him again;

---

a   An allusion to the principle of xenia, enforced by Zeus.

But the men pleaded and prayed that my tongue would no more offend,

"Do not," they begged, "provoke this savage creature more;
He has thrown one rock at us already, which drove us back to his shore,

If he heard our voices he'd have come down for us, we'd all be killed;
He'd pound our heads to jelly, and with sea-water this ship would be filled,

The rock he threw is all the proof you need of his power;
We are still within easy range, please don't make this our final hour."

But I would not listen as my rage was up, words could not console me:

"Cyklops," I said, "Should someone ask you who stole your eye and your beauty,
Tell them it was bold Odyssey, son of Laertes, who lives in Ithaki."

At this he groaned, long and hard, and then bellowed out;
"Alas, then the old prophecy about me did come about,

There was a prophet here once, a man both brave and of great stature;
Telemus, son of Eurymus, an excellent seer, he revealed all about my future,

He told me all this would happen one day, in some time hence;
That I should lose my sight by Odyssey's hand, and his dark offence,

One imposing man of super-human power shall come, was what I thought;
But you, a puny weakling, blinded me by deception and the powerful drink you brought,

You have robbed *your* host: My eyesight lost, my eyeball plucked and burnt;
"Beware a Greek bearing a gift," was foretold, and now the lesson sorely learnt,

Come here, then, Odyssey, I'll show you my gifts and what a host I want to be;
If not, I'll urge Poseidon to follow you on your long, hard journey,

I am the Earth-shaker's son, and he is my devoted father, true;
If it's his will, he shall heal my blindness, as no other god - nor man - can do."

Then I shouted back to him:

"I wish I could be as sure of killing you, and damning you into Hades' fire;
As your missing eye will not see again, even if Poseidon is your sire,

You have offended Zeus and now must live in darkest misery;
It's a pity that the sweet tears of our joy you cannot see."

At that, the cruel Cyklops lifted his enormous hands to the sky and prayed:

"Hear me mighty Lord Poseidon, who suspends the lands above the seven seas;
Grant that Ithaki shall never be found again, by Odyssey, son of Laertes,

Or, if he is destined to reach his port, let him suffer hard and lose all his men;
And if he should reach there in a foreign ship, let there be grave *trouble* within."

Well, Poseidon must have heard his plea, for my journey homeward became hard won;
As the Cyklops' father treated me very badly, for the pleasure of his blinded son.

Then, he hoisted a huge, long boulder[127] high above his hideous head;
He speared it with great speed, almost smashing the rudder, missing me by a thread,

The men screamed as the sea quaked, and threw up mighty waves;

Which pushed our boat away from Cyklops' shore, and our certain graves,

We soon reached Goats Island, where the other ships lay in wait;
Our comrades were lamenting, and anxious about us being so late,

We beached the vessel on the golden shore, and unloaded the sheep;
Then divided them fairly between the crews, for every man to keep,

My companions gave the big ram to me, for keeping them away from harm's reach;
So I sacrificed it to Zeus by roasting its thigh bones, on that sandy beach,

But the All-seeing son of Kronos did not notice my offering, or had some other plan;
For he was keen to destroy me, our blue-eyed ships, and every other man,

As the Sun sank into the flat sea, we feasted on roasted sheep and mellowed wine;
We camped on the beach, until Dawn showed her pink lace, pretty and fine,

We pulled the anchor stone, and the men churned the oars through the sea;
As we sailed with heavy hearts for our lost friends, I dreamed of my home in Ithaki.

*

EPISODE TEN

AEOLUS

*

CANNIBALS

*

QUEEN CIRCE, SORCERESS

"We sailed on, coming soon to Aeolia,[128] the home of Aeolus;[129]
Favoured by the Olympian gods, he is the son of Hippotes,

It is an island that appears to float upon the sea;
For its dark cliffs look like the upturned hull of a great ship, to me,[130]

Aeolus has six daughters and six grown sons, a large family;
And he joined the sons and daughters, in matrimony,

They have the very best that a charmed life can provide, so refined?
At night, on elegant beds in the best blankets and rugs, together they all reclined,

For one whole month, Aeolus entertained me in his wondrous palace;
Interested in my adventures in Troy, and our thwarted return by Destiny's malice,

I told him everything and he treated me with the highest respect;
And when it came time for me to finally leave, he made no fuss, and he did not object,

On the contrary, to speed my journey he made a sack from prime ox hide;
And all the roaring winds - from every direction - he packed inside,

Zeus made him master over all the winds that the skies will ever know;
He controls them at a whim; how, when and where they blow,

In our blue-eyed ship he placed the windbag, sewed up tight with silver thread;
And ordered the West wind to blow our blue-eyed boats, to our home, to head,

But it came to nothing, for we were doomed as you will see;
For nine days and nights we sailed south toward our home, Ithaki,

And on the tenth day we saw it clearly on the horizon, so close at hand;
We even saw my people tending their stubble fires, on their land,

That's how close we were to being home, our loved ones again to meet;
But I was so exhausted and fell into a long-earned sleep,

Having sailed ten long days, with the tiller alone in my hand;
Anxious that I might find, sooner, our beloved home-land,

Alas, the men talked amongst themselves, in their idle leisure;
They contrived that the sack did not contain wind, but must have been full of treasure.

I can only imagine that their conversation went something like this:

"Is it fair that a captain, welcomed in every port and given gifts by kings;
Should find his home - courtesy of his crew - and does not share those precious things,

Are we to return, with nothing, just as we went to Troy, with only shield and sword?
Or are these blisters from the oars and the rowing benches, our just reward?

While he sleeps, let us see what fine gifts, noble Aeolus gave to him;
That bag is full enough, there must be gold and silver for all, within."

So, they loosened the silver thread and the captured winds, whirled and spread;
A vicious storm galed down upon us, and we knew it was time to join the dead,

It was then that I thought to jump from my ship and end it all, there and then;
But I just covered my head in despair asking myself, "Who will save the men?"

We were blown away from our home-land, every man in tears, our hearts adrift;
Until the sight of the Aeolus' island - again - gave our spirits a lift,

Calm settled that heaving sea and blasting wind, a quiet shore we found;
After a hearty meal, to King Aelous' palace two men and I were bound,

There we found the King feasting, with his family and many guests;
We went in and stood by the stone pillars, their faces went white as ghosts.

Astounded, King Aelous said:

"Odyssey, what brings you back here?
Some evil-minded god has been treating you badly, I fear,

We went to great lengths to send you on your way;

Was our hospitality so good, that you have returned for another stay?"

That is how he spoke, and I appealed to him, mournfully:

"Good King, a mutinous crew and reckless sleep was my undoing;
Please put things right for me, once again, so we can get going."

There was quiet, not a word was said, until the King answered:

"Get off this island at once, be on your way, for you the gods have only hate;
In deed, they damn you, so it would be improper for me to meddle in a fool's fate,

I cannot help you, or your foolish crew, all have heaven's curse;
Trouble, leave us now, or you shall be for the worse."

(That was how one king spoke to his counter-party;
What, on this earth, has happened to honour and hospitality?)

So, we did, as bid.

"From his island we rowed six long days and nights, over flat seas;
Punished for our stupidity, we were denied any breeze,

The seventh day brought us into the rocky harbour fortress of Lamos;[131]
The port of the Laestrygonians, who need no sleep, is called Telepylos."[132]

Still captivating his audience, his gracious host Alkinoos and his court, Odyssey now breaks with the accounts of his travels and entertains with a humorous sidelight:

"In that land of daylight,[a] shepherds range sheep until Dawn's hour and return home;
Then become a herdsman, to take out his cattle to dewy pastures to graze and to roam,

If only a man could shepherd his flock, muster his herd *and* avoid all sleep;
He could earn double wages, working day and night, with more pay to keep."

He resumes the adventure for his amused audience:

"So it was that we reached a sheltered, stone-ringed cove by a cliff, high and steeping;
This harbour knew no winds, its stillness - we thought - bode safe keeping,

A narrow entrance between two headlands kept waves from any craft;
So my captains anchored their blue-eyed ships, side by side, together as a raft,

But, I moored my ship to a rock at the end of the point, less east;
Where I scaled the menacing crag, looked around, but could not see man, nor beast,

Only wispy smoke rising from the ground in the distance, far away;
So I sent three of my crew, one a messenger, to find what sort of people were they,

The men followed a logging track leading from a mountain;
Until they met a young, buxom woman going to fetch water from Artakia[133] fountain,

My men asked her about her countrymen and who their ruler was?
She was the daughter of the Laestrygonian king, his name, Antiphatas,

So she pointed out the high tower of her father's great palace;
On reaching it they found his wife, an ugly giant filled with malice,

---

a   Laestrygon was the son of Poseidon and king of the Laestrygonians. It is likely that his kingdom was the island of Corsica. Traditionally, sheep flocks were grazed at night and locked away during the day, when cattle pastured.

She summoned her husband from the palace's dining hall;
Antiphates, too, was a giant cannibal and his intention was to feast on them all,

Two escaped[a] and ran to my ship, as fast as their shadows could chase them;
Then a thousand of them sprang up from every flank. These were giants, not men,

And with boulders that ten mortals could not lift;
They showered the rafted ships, from the towering cliff,

We heard the boats splinter and the death cries of the men's grisly fate;
As the giants skewered them like fish, to carry home to their dinner plate,

With my sword I cut our anchor line, each second might be our last;
And commanded my men to row for dear life, with all their force, and fast,

We churned the water white, 'til we were out of range and breath;
Again, we had escaped. As fugitives we had fled a dreadful death,

We got away with our lives, we all might have perished;
So, we sailed with stricken hearts for our brave dead, so cherished.

In due course we came to the Island of Aeaea,[134] home of Circe, the cunning goddess;
She is the daughter of Sun and Perse,[135] and has a brother, the evil Aeetes,[136]

Our ship found - as if some god guided it - what seemed a safe harbour;[137]
For two nights and two days, exhausted in body and spirit, we camped upon its shore,

On the third day with spear and sword I climbed the high cliff to have a look around;
Only wispy smoke rising in the distance, far away, was what I found,

---

a   Eurylochus and Polites escaped to Odyssey's ship, the other man perished.

As it turned out, that smoke belonged to Circe's house in a forest clearing;
It was then I reckoned all this seemed too familiar; I had an ominous feeling,

I reasoned it best to send out an exploring party, and me alone not make that trip;
So I set off, returning to my waiting crew and our last blue-eyed ship,

On my path, some god sent a high-antlered stag, as if in a shimmering dream;
The heat drove him down from the forest, to drink from the cool stream,

I struck him in the middle of the back, with my bronze-tipped spear;
He fell bellowing in the dust, then death consumed that mighty deer,

I set my foot upon him, drew the spear from his wound, and laid it on the ground;
Then cut grass and rushes to plait a fathom of braid, his hooves I then bound,

I yoked the sling around my neck, and using the spear to steady my trip;
Dragged that massive beast down to the crew, and the waiting blue-eyed ship,

On reaching the beach I went around, rousing the men from their grief;
Saying, "Listen friends, it's not our time to die of hunger, today our lives we'll keep."

The blankets came off their moping heads,[a] they were all shocked at the stag's size;
When they had feasted their eyes enough, they made a fire and roasted its thighs,

All day long we sat and enjoyed water-mixed wine and the roasted stag's meat;
Until Sun met Sea, and darkness brought our beds friendly sleep.

I awoke early and called a council. I said, "My friends we are in *trouble* deep;
For today Dawn did not light her lantern to put Night to sleep,[b]

a   The ancient Greeks veiled their faces when in despair and sorrow.
b   They are in the midst of a very heavy fog.

The Sun has abandoned us, who can tell me where East is, or West?

I can see no way out of this, but we must find one, nevertheless,

We are on an island, for when I climbed the crag I saw to the horizon, only blue seas;

But in the middle of this land I did see smoke rising from a forest of oak trees."

"Their hearts sank, recalling the Laestrygonians and the Cyklop's evil wrongs;

They cried bitterly - but nothing is earned by tears - so I divided them into two throngs,

With a captain for each, I gave one company to Eurylochus,[138] the other I kept;

Then we shook lots in a helmet; as his name came out first, his men knelt and wept,

So, in darkness he set off with twenty-two sobbing men just like those that were left behind;

Dawn came, so they tracked the smoke to Circe's house,[139] and the strangest things that one will ever find,

In the middle of a forest glade was her palace, built of polished marble;

There were bears, wolves and lions all prowling around it, free to roam - a true marvel,

These wild animals were tamed by *Circe's*[a] magic potion;

They did not growl or attack the men, but snuggled up to them with a pet's devotion,

Just as dogs crowd around their master coming home from a feast;

For they know his pocket will bring them something, even some scraps at least,

Though those great bears, wolves and lions fawned and licked my men;

Their huge claws and teeth still frightened them,

---

a   The name, *Circe*, translates to: Circling hawk; sharp-eyed, watching, vigilant.

They reached the gates of the goddess' house and heard her within;
Working fine fabrics on her enormous loom, she was humming and singing,

Polites,[140] usually a shrewd man, who I trusted most, announced what he had heard:
"There is someone inside working a loom, and singing like a bird;

The whole palace echoes with glorious heavenly tones;
Let's call out to her and see if a woman - or a goddess - this palace owns."

So they called to her, and she came at once and unlocked the gate;
Foolishly, they all followed her, except Eurylochus, who was timid of fate,

When she had seated them and laid out cheese, honey and bread to feast;
She served them Pramnian[141] wine laced with a potion[142] that changed man into beast,

Her gold sceptre turned them into pigs with a single airy stroke;
And she drove them off to their sties, with a kick and a poke,

They were like hogs - snouts, ears and sprung tails - with grunts, too;
But their senses and memories were the same as any man, just like me or you,

And when the witch Circe flung them acorns and forest nuts to eat;
They stopped squealing and foraged in the muck around their feet,

Then Eurylochus rushed back to tell me about our friends and their fate;
But he was so exhausted and distressed that we had a long wait,

He was crying and could not find words for what he had seen and learned;
Until at last we drew out his story, and why his party had not returned.

This is what he said:

"We followed, as ordered, the wisp of smoke to the forest's open ground;
A huge stone palace, that could be seen from afar, is what we found,

There a witch, or Spirit, was working her fabric loom, and singing sweet;
So the men shouted to her, and she came to the gate for all of us to meet,

She invited us in, but as *trouble* - always - follows a woman's charm, I hid outside;
I waited a long time, but from then 'til now, I've not seen any *man's* hair, nor hide."

Then I slung my bronze sword over my shoulder, with my bow;
And told Eurylochus to come with me, so the fate of my men we could know,

But he sunk to the ground and grasped my legs and begged, with pitiful pleas;
"Favourite of Zeus, do not force me to go back, let us escape now, over the blue seas,

They are not coming back, and her evil intentions you won't survive;
Now only twenty-four of us remain, so keep us alive."

Stay here then, I answered, eat and drink 'til your belly bends;
But I must go, it is my duty, I am bound to make amends.

So I turned my back on the crew, ship and sea, and followed the whispy smoke;
Until I found the grove, Circe's great house, and more of what he spoke,

There on the road, I met Hermes, Athena's herald, with his gold mace;
He was disguised as a youth with a fluffy young beard on his face,

He came up to me, took my hand and asked:

"My unfortunate friend, you are alone and lost, where do you rove?
This is a dangerous forest, and why are your men in pigsties at Circe's grove?

They are penned like hogs, tail to jowl, do you think you can free them?
If you are not careful, you'll not see ship or crew again,

But, I can protect you and keep all from Circe's cunning and strife;
Eat this herb, it will defend against her potions and save your noble life,

Now, about that witch's crafty ways, and what you shall find:
She'll mix you a tonic brew with a drug to intoxicate your mind,

But she and her spell will be powerless if you do what I say;
For I have given to you the antidote to strip its power away,

When Circe tries to strike you with her long, thin sceptre;
Draw your sword, lunge forward as though you intend to kill her,

She will cower in fear, quiver in distress and cover her head;
Then she'll speak to you gently, and tempt you into her bed,

You must do as she wishes, satisfy her every loving need;
If you wish to see your men again, and have them all freed,

But first have her swear a binding oath to Zeus and all the gods, too;
So that no peril shall come to your men, or to you!

If you don't, your nakedness will be shy of its manhood, she will amputate!
Eunuchs have no courage, and as lovers, no point to mate."

So I ate the herb that gods call Moly with white flowers and black roots;[143]

Mortals must not tear it from the ground, but the Invisibles do whatever suits.

Then Hermes vanished fleeing the wooded island on his way to Olympos;
And I walked on toward the witch's estate, my heart was in a tempest,

On reaching her palace I called to her. She came at once and unlocked the gate;
I followed her, cautious of her cunning ways, Hermes' warnings were made straight,

I was offered a chair, inlaid with silver and there was a footstool too;
The tonic was mixed in a gold goblet, and she smiled as I drank that brew,

But its spell was useless against Hermes' antidote, and his sage advice;
Then she struck me with her sceptre, saying, "Take that, and join your friends in the pigsties."

As I rushed forward with my drawn sword ready to kill her dead;
She fell to the floor screaming and shaking, "Why did the spell fail?" she said,

"Who are you? Where are you from? What is your name, pray tell?
No man has resisted my charm, *no man* is immune to the magic of my spell,

Or are you a demon - or the demigod Odyssey - who Hermes said would come one day?
With ship and crew oaring their way from Troy to my home, to stay,

Let's be friends and learn to trust and love each other, until the day we part;
Come to my bed now, let me sheathe your eager sword with all of my heart."

So I asked the cunning Circe: Should a friend turn my men into swine?
Does a friend deceive with a cursed potion in tainted wine?

I think you mean further mischief by taking me as a bed-mate;

You intend to steal my courage, its my man-sword you want to castrate,

If I do, my nakedness will be shy of its manhood, you will amputate!
Eunuchs have no courage, and as lovers, no point to mate.

I shall not bed you without a solemn oath to Zeus, and the other gods too;
So promise that no peril shall come to my men and me, by you."

With that she swore to free the men and protect us, as I asked;
So I went to her bed, and she was satisfied, just as Hermes tasked.

Meanwhile, her four hand-maidens took to their house keeping duty;
They are the nymphs of the grove, each one of exceptional beauty,

One spread a rare purple cloth over the chairs and damask cushions to seat;
Another brought tables of silver and laid them with gold baskets of bread to eat,

The third brought gold cups and mellowed the sweet wine with water;
And the last maiden filled a bath from a large cauldron boiling over a fire,

She poured cold into it, just as I liked and she eased me into the tub;
And massaged oil into the stiffness of my limbs after a wash and a scrub,

She dressed me in new clothes, a fine shirt and a purple cloak;
And led me to a chair with an ornate footstool made of silver and oak,

Scented water was poured over my hands from a gold jug by another maid;
And she drew a table beside me, as another served tempting food on the table laid,

Then Circe pleaded to me: "Odyssey eat!" But I would not, I had no stomach for
food;

"Odyssey, why do you sit dumb-struck, your aching heart has you in a sorrowful mood,

Why do you refuse my hospitality? Are you suspicious? I have already sworn no harm."

So I said, "Circe, whilst my men are pigs in your sties, *no man* can enjoy your charm,

If you want me to eat and drink, my men - your swine - must go free;

Bring them to me now as men - not hogs - for my own eyes to see."

So she strode through the palace and out to the sties, with her magic stick;

Flung open the gates and drove her hogs out with a poke and a kick,

The hogs came out and stood gazing at her as she went along their row;

Pasting each hog's brow with a new drug to restore them to the men I'd know,

Their tails and bristles fell clean off, they were men again;

Younger and taller than before, and much more handsome,

My men hugged me and were weeping with joy, so much that Circe's hard heart eased;

She said, "Go to your blue-eyed ship and beach it, Odyssey, noble son of Laertes,

Then, hide your ship's gear in the cave above the beach on the mountain's side;

And come back here with all your crew, in my palace you may reside."

So agreed, I went back to the ship and found the crew weeping with woeful bleats;

When they saw me they were excited as calves' anxious for their mothers' teats,

As when they come home to be milked after feeding all day in the field;

And the dairy echoes with low soothing tones, as their mother's udders yield,

They were just as glad to see me as Ithaki's harbour's shore;

Where they were born and bred, but haven't seen since the start of the war,

"Odyssey, Sir" said the mournful men, "We are so glad to see you back here again;

But what of our comrades and friends, did they meet with an unhappy end?"

I spoke with a comforting voice, "Let's haul the ship onto the beach, away from the sea;

And hide the cargo and gear in that cave, then come with me to the palace of Circe,

There you will find your comrades and friends alive and well;

They'll be eating and drinking with the maids, with great stories to tell."

The men rallied and moved to my order, as fast as they could;

But Eurylochus tried to hold them back, he was up to no-good,

Saying, "Fools, don't rush so fast to your certain ruin;

If you go to Circe's house you'll be turned into a hog or a lion,

You'll be penned in her sties or stand guard at her gate;

Remember the Cyklops and how our comrades found their grisly fate,

You can blame that hot-head Odyssey for those men losing their lives;

Don't follow him ever again, if you ever want to see your wives."

I drew my sword ready to cut off his mutinous head;

But the men restrained me, as close kin,[a] he was worth more alive, than dead,

Saying, "Sir, if it be your order, let him stay and guard our ship alone;

But take the rest of us to Circe's house now, let us be gone."

---

a   Eurylochus is Odyssey's brother in law.

So we left the ship and went inland to the palace in Circe's wooded land;
And soon enough Eurylochus followed, shame-faced by my reprimand,

Meanwhile, Circe's maids had washed and massaged them with olive oil;
Clothed them in linen-wear, and set them a banquet most royal,

It was in the dining hall that we all met and enjoyed each, and every face;
The men cried for joy and the festive din burst throughout the palace,

Then Circe came to me saying, "Odyssey, noble son of Laertes;
I know how much you all suffered in the war, and on the seas,

And how you have battled cruel savages who meant only harm;
But now it's time to eat and drink 'til you are strong, healthy and calm,

Just as when you all left Ithaki so very long ago;
For now you are battle weary and your spirits low,

Your hearts need lifting so that joy may return to you all;
So stay here until you are again fit to travel and your home shore will call."

I agreed, and we stayed enjoying the food, the wine and the pleasures of her home;
One year passed, Summer came again, and my men thought it time to roam,

Saying, "Captain, it is now time to think of your Kingdom, home and family;
If it is your fate to sit upon your throne again and see beloved Ithaki,

Reluctantly I agreed and on that last day we feasted and drank, and with heavy heads;
Sun set on our festivities and we retired to our chambered beds,

When I got into Circe's bed, I hugged her at the knees;

And the goddess listened patiently to my desperate pleas,

Circe, keep your promise, it's time to leave your circus, the men seek their homes in Ithaki;

Pestering me when your back is turned, they long to see their wives and family.

The goddess answered:

"Odyssey, noble son of Laertes, don't stay here: Go home if that is what you desire;

But first you must journey to the House of Hades and the vault of hell-fire,

There you will meet dreaded Persephone[144] and consult blind Terisias,[145] the ghost;

The greatest seer - even in *Death*[a] - his wisdom and predictions are revered the most,

At this my spirit was crushed again, I wept as I knelt by her bed;

I had no need to live or see another sunrise, I wished I was dead,

But once my whimpering stopped and the teardrops failed;

I asked her: Circe, who will helm that voyage? Hades is a port that no ship has sailed."

"You need no guide," she said; "Raise your mast, set the sails wide to a broad reach;

The West Wind will blow you along Oceanus' star-stream[b] until you find Persephone's beach,[c]

That barren country[d] has groves of tall poplars and willows that wither and die too soon;

---

a   *Death,* in this context, refers to Hades, ruler of the Underworld. Persephone is his consort.
b   Oceanus' Stream is the Milky Way. Ancient mariners referred to sailing on Oceanus, the sea of stars, as a metaphor for observing or navigating the night sky.
c   Ammoudia is now a small fishing village located on the Ionian Sea coast, south-east of Parga, Greece. The mouth of the river Acheron flows through the village.
d   It is a river delta, lake and wetlands. Because the delta periodically flooded, no vegetation could survive. Dead trees appeared to be human arms reaching from the swamps.

Beach your ship and go straight to Hades' dark halls,[a] by the light of a dim Moon,

Follow the Acheron,[146] the Stream of Woe, to where two roaring rivers mate;
The River of Fire and the River of Tears, fork into The Styx,[147] the Torrent of Hate,

You can enter Hades at the place where a white crag looms high in the air;[b]
Dig a pit about a fore-arm's length and depth, and make it square,

Pour in honey blended with milk, then wine and water as well;
Then mix in sparkling barley beer as an offering to all those in Hades' Hell,[c]

And voice solemn chants for every listless ghost and ghoul's sake;
Then roast a prized heifer, if a return to Ithaki *you* wish to make,

You must load the fire with treasures cherished in your heart, most;
And for Terisias alone, you must kill your best black-sheep, to roast,

When you have honoured the ghosts with your prayers, sacrifice a ram and a black
ewe;
Turn their heads toward Erebus[148] of the Underworld, but bend *yours* to Ocean's view,

Then, your midst with countless ghosts will be filled;
So tell your men to skin the two sheep you have just killed,

Burn them and offer prayers to Hades and to dreaded Persephone, as well;

---

a   Referring to the subterranean caverns and chambers in the Nekromanteion complex. It is interesting to
    note that the enduring notion of "hell" in many organised religions is based on this reference to Hades.
b   On this elevated site is the Nekromanteion, an ancient Greek temple of the oracle of necromancy,
    devoted to Hades and Persephone. It is located overlooking the Acheron River in Epirus, near the
    ancient town of Ephyra (Messopotamo). This site is believed, by devotees, to be the door to Hades, the
    realm of the Dead.
c   Ritual use of the Necromanteion involved elaborate ceremonies wherein celebrants seeking to speak to
    the dead would start by gathering in the temple and consuming a meal and a psycho-active narcotic.
    After a cleansing ceremony, and the sacrifice of sheep, the faithful would descend through a maze of
    corridors leaving offerings as they progressed to the cavern and its vaults. The *nekromanteia* would
    pose a series of trials, consisting of questions and chants.

Then draw your sword and guard their blood until Terisias goes, he has something to
tell,

He will predict the hazards of your homeward voyage and the route to take;
Do as I say or the shore of Phortune Harbour you will never make."

With those words Dawn showed her rosy cheeks and sat on her gold throne.

I dressed in my sea-garb and Circe donned a glimmering gossamer shawl;
Fastened with a girdle of gold around her trim waist, her head with a veil of tulle,

Then I strode through the halls rousing the men from sweet sleep;
For they had too much fun the night before, and now slumbered deep,

I said to each man, you can't laze any longer, we must sail now;
Queen Circe has told me of the journey home, and shown me how,

So they mustered, but we did not get away *trouble*-free that day;
Even from Circe's house I could not get them all safely away,

It seems that Elpenor, the youngest of our crew, and a strong oarsman;
Who was known for his fondness of wine, not judgement, or heroism,

Drunk, he had strayed from his chamber seeking the cool night air;
Upon the rooftop veranda he had rested until Dawn, without a care,

So startled by the rousing and the commotion of the mustering men;
That he missed the top step, plunged head-first, and his neck was broken.

I did not know then, but his soul flew straight down into Hades.

On our way back to the beach, I gathered the men;
Saying, you think we are headed for our dear home again?

It is true, but Circe has set a much different course, for us;
First we must go to Persephone in Hades, to visit the ghost of Terisias.

At this the men broke down, terrified with fear, tearing out their hair;
What can be gained from suffering? Sometimes dread is too much to bear.

Weeping and lamenting our fate, we reached the seashore;
There Circe had readied our blue ship with provisions near the water, what's more!

Nearby on the beach, Circe had tethered the ram and ewe to a rock;
Unseen, she moved amongst the men, as Invisibles do when they shepherd their flock.

THE DEAD

"We dragged the ship from the beach into the surfing sea;
Set the mast in the keel and rigged the sails for the anxious journey,

Loaded were the sheep and the distressed crew;
Circe sent us a wind over the transom, and hard it blew,

The boom went wide and the sails bellied full;
The tiller-man held a running course, no need for the oars' pull,

All day the blue prow pointed over a dark, oily sea;
But when the Sun sank, blackness found our eyes and we could not see,

We were in Oceanus' Stream where the Cimmerians[149] live each day in endless night;
The Sun or Moon doesn't visit those gloomy people, eternal darkness is their blight,

We found Persephone's beach and moored the ship on its sand;
Perimedes and Eurylochus led the two sheep, tethered in hand,

We followed the Acheron, the Stream of Woe, to where two roaring rivers mate;
And the River of Fire and the River of Tears, did fork into The Styx, the Torrent of Hate,

Looking up we saw a crag looming high into the dark air;

So we dug the pit about a fore-arm's depth, and made it square,

And poured in honey blended with milk, then wine and water as well;
Then mixed in sparkling barley beer, an offering to the Dead, close-by in Hades' Hell,

And made the solemn promise to sacrifice a prized heifer to Terisias' ghost;
If I was ever to return to Ithaki and gaze upon my beloved island's coast,

My incantations over, toward the Underworld I turned each sheep's head;
And looking up to Oceanus I slashed their throats over the pit until they were dead,

Then, from Erebus, ghosts appeared and gathered around us, their numbers vast;
They came from every corner of every land, many from the ancient past,

Young, old, fathers, mothers, maids and their lovers, and soldiers bold;
Their armour and weapons stained with blood, their stories never told,

Thousands of howling ghouls swarmed around the pit, and fear took hold of me;
The men flayed the sheep that my heartless blade had just killed, as told by Circe,

They roasted the sheep and offered prayers to Persephone, the dreaded one;
I kept my sword unsheathed to guard the blood until Terisias' favour was won,

To my horror, the first ghost that came near was Elpenor, our crew-mate;
He was only half a ghost, for a burial and funeral he still had to wait,

I was very contrite and cried when I saw his ghoulish form;
Saying, Elpenor, how fast you have flown down here into Hades' gloom?

"My captain," he groaned, "it was the luck of a drunk. That I'm dead is my own affair;

On the roof of Circe's house where I had rested all night, without a care,

But being startled by the early rousing and the commotion of the men;
I missed the top stair and flew head-long onto the ground, where my neck was broken,

Now I beg you that on the lives of your relatives not here to witness this strife;
Your father Laertes, son Telemakis and Penelope your virtuous wife,

Do as I ask, and when you leave my Limbo hell, course the ship back to Circe's coast;
And do not leave there without giving me due funeral rites, a wake and a toast,

But in my full armour, burn me on that beach and on the funeral pyre, place my rowing oar;
And leave a tombstone to tell what a luckless fool I was, to all that visit that sea's shore."

I consoled him:

"My poor fellow, I will do all that you have asked of me, but I can't say you were a fool;
For Destiny has many different verses to voice, and life can be very cruel,

We sat facing each other across the pit, gloomy were our words, and few;
And as I held my sword guarding the blood, my dead mother's ghost close drew,

I had left her alive and well when I set out for war with Troy;
Tears gushed from my fearing eyes revealing all my grief, not joy,

My sword kept her away from the blood in the pit;
For I had not asked my questions of Terisias yet,

Then he came, Terisias's terrifying ghost, with a gold sceptre in hand;

Saying, "Odyssey, why have you left the Light of Day, and come to this nether-land?

Sheath your sword and retreat from the pit that the sheep's veins have drenched;

And I'll drink their blood so that your curiosity may be forever quenched."

I drew back, sheathing my trembling sword, he drank the blood from his cupped hand;

Saying, "About your return, heaven will make it hard to reach your home-land,

Poseidon keeps an eye out for you, you can't escape *his* watch;

I see he nurses a bitter grudge for his blinded son, the Cyklops,

If all have self control, after a dire voyage, you just might get home to tell your tale;

For when your ship reaches Thrinakia[150] you'll find Helios' sheep and cattle,[a]

Leave the flocks and herds unharmed, make your way to Ithaki, and don't delay;

If not, your boat and crew will be destroyed and you'll be seven years a castaway,

Even if you do escape death, you will return in a strange ship to your *troubled* land;

To find your estate consumed by Suitors, all vying for your wife's wedding hand,

When you do get home, kill those foes by force, take revenge;

Slashing sword, flying arrow and hurling spear will dishonour, avenge!

Then carry a well-shaped oar 'til you reach a country where people know nothing of the ocean;

They don't mix salt with food, have not seen ships, or the oars that keep them in motion,

Here is a clear sign that your destination has been made;

---

a   Thrinakia is modern-day Sicily.

A traveller will meet you and say the oar is a windmill's blade,

Then and there, bury the oar within the earth and sacrifice a ram, a bull and a boar;
To Lord of the Sea, Poseidon, first and then all the other Olympian gods, in proper order,

So that you will avoid Death by Poseidon's hands and will pass into a ripe old age;
Your respected life will be taken peacefully, if you heed the words of Hades' sage."

"This," I answered, "must be my destiny, and only Heaven knows why;
But tell me one thing more, I see my dead mother's ghost close by,

She sits by the pool of blood not looking at me or uttering a word;
I am her only son but she does not speak to me, and I'm not heard,

Sir, how can I make her know me, the man – her son – and true?"
He said, "Any ghost that tastes the blood will talk with you,

But if you deny them blood their spirit withers and fades."
And with that Terisias vanished back into the House of Hades,

His prophesies spoken, I watched as my mother came for the blood;
At once she knew me and wailed out in grief, her tears in flood,

Saying, "My son, you are alive in the House of Death, how did this come to be?
It is difficult for a mortal to visit this un-mapped place, as no man's feet can walk Oceanus' sea;

You must have a brave crew, a sturdy ship and able captain at the helm;
Or are you still on your way from Troy to Ithaki, Penelope and your royal realm?"

"Mother," I said, "I was forced here to consult the ghost of Terisias, the seer;

I've never been close to my beloved Ithaki, my absence is in its thirteenth year,

Misfortune and hardship from the very first day is what I've had to endure;
Since we left Agamemnon's land of noble steeds to fight the Trojan war,

Enough of my fate, in what way did you die, tell me truly?
Did you have a long illness, or did heaven allow your passing mercifully?

Did Artemis shower arrows that stopped your heart, so kind?
If I am to return home, what am I to find?

My father, my son are they alive? Do they still keep our royal line?
Has my domain been plundered by doubters of my return?

Tell me, please, about Penelope and her mind's state;
Does she live with my son and still protect our estate?

Or, has she wed some prince or countryman?
"Your wife," my mother said, "In your house she does remain,

But in great distress as she spends her life in tears, day and night;
No one has possession of your estate, Telemakis upholds your royal rite,

Each day he entertains the Suitors as they roast, toast and boast;
For these lofty lords gloat at inviting the company of their own host,

As for your father, he's at his old farm and has no want to visit the town;
He has no luxuries, his sleepless bed has no blankets, his face is a frown,

Through winter he sleeps on the ashen floor in front of the fire;
As with the servants he dresses in rags, for he has lost all desire,

In summer, he rests out in the vineyard on a bed of vine leaves;
He is wretched with worry about you never returning, and so he grieves,

Each day brings more suffering as it did for me, No! Sharp-eyed Artemis;
Did not take me swiftly with arrows to my heart, nor by an illness,

Which strikes down the body and mind by ebbing its mortal energy;
It was my longing for you, radiant son. That was the death of me!

You and your cleverness, and your gentle, loving ways;
Grief tore my sweet life apart, and ended my earthly days."

Then I tried to embrace the ghostly form of my poor royal mother;
Three times I sprang to clasp her in my arms, but she was a dream, a vapour,

Grief cut into my heart and I cried out to her, but my trembling words were an echo;
"Mother be still, I must embrace you, even here in Hades we can exchange comfort
for sorrow,

Or is this Persephone's ill-will, does she send a phantom to taunt and mock me?
Piling more sorrow upon my grief, she makes my heart ache for thee."

"Ill-fated son" she said, "it is not Persephone that deceives you;
When life leaves one's body, the soul flitters away too,

Flesh will not hold sinews and bone; the funeral flames forbid it;
By the time the cinders cool, each dead person is a spirit,

Now, to the light of day, run for your life;
And remember these things to tell to your wife."

So we spoke to each other, confiding and saying our good-byes;
Then Persephone assembled the ghosts of famous women before my eyes,

As they swarmed around the blood-pool, I considered how to question each;
I deemed it best to draw my hipped sword, to keep them all at arm's reach,

So, one after the other, each told me of their ancestry and where she had come from;
The first was Tyro, daughter of Salmoneus and wife of Cretheus, Aeolus' son,[151]

She fell in love with Enipeus, the beautiful river god, who was always in her dreams;
Obsessed, she stalked him by dwelling on the banks of his clear, glinting streams,

But Poseidon, disguised as Enipeus, lay with her where river and sea surged;
The Earth Shaker arched a huge blue wave to hide the love-lust as woman and god merged,

The imposter snatched her virginity and ravaged her into a deep weariness;
Whispering, "Tyro, rejoice in our love, the efforts of this god are not fruitless,

Your lover was Poseidon, I rock the world! Now go home, bite your tongue and do not tell;
And you shall have fine twin boys before the end of this year, rear them well!"

Then he dived under the sea and within that year she bore Pelias and Neleus;
Both of them served Zeus well; Pelias lived in Iolcus and the other in sandy Pilos,

Noble Tyro, to her husband Cretheus, bore three sons more;
Aeson, Pheres and Amythaon, who was a great charioteer and mighty in war.

"Next to her was the daughter to Asopus, Antiope, who was one of Zeus' bed mates;

She bore him two mighty sons Amphion and Zethus who saved Thebes with its seven gates,

Cadmus' city was so vast that even they could not shield it from invaders;
So the brothers built a high strong wall around it, which rewarded their labours."

"Then came Alcmena, Amphitryon's wife, who also slept with Zeus;
The fruit of their union was the indomitable Herakles,

Then Megara[152] came along. She was the daughter to great King Kreon;[153]
She had married Herakles the illegitimate son of Amphitryon,[154]

Then I saw the beautiful Queen Jocasta[155] mother of ill-fated Oedipus[156] once a king;
Innocently, she married him - her son - who killed his father, an abominable thing,

And the gods revealed to the world their unnatural plight and shame;
So the king of Cadmus' people was banished and suffered eternal anguish and pain,

In unbearable distress she hanged herself, and Oedipus inherited the horrors of his parents' faults;
So Jocasta's cursed soul was hurled down to Hades where Death guards its vaults;

"Then I saw Neleus' wife Chloris,[157] and her dazzling beauty;
He wooed and won her heart with beautiful gifts; every man's duty,

Chloris was youngest daughter of Iasus' son Amphion ruler of the Minyans, Orchomenus;[158]
She was queen of Pilos and bore three sons: Nestor, Chromius, and Periclymenus,

And also bore a lovely daughter Pero,[159] who was fancied by all the young princes;
But Nestor would only give her a suitor who could recover the cattle stolen by Iphikles,[160]

To return these long-horned, wild cattle from Phylace was a very difficult task;

Only the valiant soothsayer, Melampus,[161] was prepared to attempt what had been asked,

But, the gods spun a different fate, cattle rangers captured him, to prison he was sent;

Days became months and soon a year passed, the four seasons came and went,

Then his captor set him free for he had revealed all of Heaven's decrees;

And so the god's will was done, and Zeus was pleased."

"Then came Leda, wife of Tyndarus,[162] to whom twin sons[163] she bore;

One was Castor the mighty horse breaker, and the boxer Pollux, the other,

Both these heroes are buried alive in the earth;

Each day, as one brother dies the other is given a re-birth,

As Zeus only allows each twin to alternate one day alive, the next day dead,

But both are still honoured in the ranks of the gods," is what to me, Leda said."

"After her I saw Iphimedeia, wife of Aloeus, who had an affair with Poseidon;

She too experienced the pleasure waves of the Sea-lords love and affection,

She bred two sons, Otus and Ephialtes, but both were not long for living;

Except for Orion, they were the finest children ever born, and the best looking,

They were the tallest men - by far - ever born upon this earth;

At nine years of age they were nine yards high and nine yards around the girth;

They even threatened to bury Mount Olympos by piling Mount Ossa[164] on its top;

And then Mount Pelion[165] on the top of Ossa, but Apollo brought those plans to a stop,

The son of Zeus, who Leto bore, killed both of them for their sins;

His arrows cut them down before they could grow hair on their chins."

"Then I saw Phaedra[166] and Procris[167] and the fair Ariadne,[168] cruel Minos's[169] daughter;

She loved Theseus[170] who eloped with her from Crete, but he could not seduce her,

Before they could reach his home, on the island of Ntia,[171] by Artemis she was slain;

For Dionysos[172] claimed he was already married to Ariadne, so *their* wedlock should remain,

I also saw Maera[173] and Clymene and the loathed Eriphyle[174] in disgrace;

Who betrayed her innocent husband, Amphiaraus,[175] for a gold necklace,

I could never name every wife and daughter of the heroes that I saw in Hades' Hell;

And now sleep creeps upon me and I have not the strength for more stories to tell,

I must retire either here, or on board a ship with my new crew;

My future rests with the Invisibles, and with all of you."

Odyssey pauses and sits. The enthralled guests are spellbound throughout the palace hall. Queen Arete says:

"What do you think of this man, Phaekians? He's tall and good looking, and bold;

He is my guest, but all of you share in this honour and the stories he told,

Let us not be in a hurry to turn him away, or miserly with his going-away booty;

For heaven has bestowed us with riches in abundance, to share it is our duty."

The revered hero, old Echeneus speaks:

"My friends, what our queen has said, as usual, is both reasonable and just;
But the decision, in word or deed, rests in the end with King Alkinoos."

King Alkinoos rises and declares:

"Yes, as long as I'm alive and Phaekians oar the sea, this is what I say;
Our guest longs for his departure to home, but he must wait for one more day,

So that we can collect and stow his parting gifts from every noble's hand;
But most shall come from this palace, for I am the King of this land."

Wily Odyssey answers:

"King Alkinoos, if it is your wish I shall stay here for even another twelve months, gladly;
It would be to my advantage, for I would return with more of your treasures to Ithaki."

The King replies:

"Odyssey, with far-fetched yarns many crooks and fiends come here to con us by plan,
But it is obvious, you're not a pretender, we know you won't cheat us, you are a noble man;

You have the bard's skill with language and the confidence in the stories you tell;
I don't doubt that all those misfortunes and disasters led you into Hades' Hell,

But, come now, tell me truly, did you see any war heroes that met with death at Troy?
The evening is young, Sun still floats in the sky, what more can you tell, for us to enjoy?

We are your captives and will listen to your adventures until Sun rises from its
watery bed;

Your daring and valour beggars belief, but you must tell more of the heroes you met,
alive or dead."

Odyssey responds:

"Your majesty, there is a time for speeches, and a time for sleep as well;

If you really wish to hear the tragic tales of my comrades, then to you all, I shall tell,

About the heroes that did not die at Troy, but before returning home lost their lives;

All because of the infidelity of Helen, one of history's most wicked wives,

Now then, just as dreaded Persephone expelled all the women ghosts, left and right;

The ghost of King Agamemnon, marched toward me, a sad and sorry sight,

He came close with all the other men who, by Agisthos' hand, also met a bloody fate;

Stooping he tasted the blood and then recognised me; we tried to embrace, but it was
too late,

For the bursting power of his prime had fled long ago, there was no body to hold;

Tears flooded his cheeks and beard - and mine too - if the truth be told,

How, great King, did you come down into Hades' Halls, what brought you to your
end?

Were your boats destroyed? Angry seas did Poseidon's Trident send?

Perhaps your foes on land slaughtered you for plundering their cattle and sheep?

Or, were you slain by defenders of a some great city whose treasures and wives you
hoped to keep?"

King Agamemnon's ghost then said to me:

"Odyssey, my noble friend, I was not slain by nature's wind and seas; my death was not Poseidon's pleasure;

Nor did my foes on land destroy me for taking women slaves, or looting their city's treasure,

No, Agisthos, hatched my unnatural end, together with my treacherous wife;

But *she* killed me, that's how I came to be here, and this is how *they* took my life:

He invited me to a banquet in his palace, as I sat down she ran me through with his sword;

Like a slaughter-house, the butcher prepares the unsuspecting ox, to be stabbed and gored,

All around my friends lay slain like sheep or pigs killed for some grand celebration;

A public feast or wedding breakfast in a great hall set for a king of a prosperous nation,

Your travels have revealed hundreds of deaths in combat and war;

But you never saw anything so awful as what lay on *my* palace's floor,

They died where they sat or fell, sprawled over the tables and carpets, blood in streams;

But the worst thing was Priam's daughter, Cassandra's frightful screams,

As I tore the blade from my writhing body, Clytemnestra killed her right next to where I lay;

I raised the sword to kill the murdering bitch, but I was weak and Death had the last say,

The coward turned her back and ran, having not the heart to close my lips or eyes;

There is nothing more vile than a woman when she is exposed for her guilt and her lies,

Fancy murdering her own loving husband! I thought my return was to a good home and life;

To enjoy my children, friends and servants, and to live happily with my dutiful wife,

But there she sits in my palace, bathing in stained glory, the greatest of outrages,

Her abominable crimes will bring shame to all women - even the good ones - down the ages."

And I said to him:

"It is plain how Zeus, Mind - greatest of gods - has long-hated the house of Atreus;

His best weapon, from first to last - its women - have been its wicked curse,

How many of us suffered and died because of Helen's faithless act?

And whilst you were away Klytemnestra hatched mischief against you in a lovers' pact."

The King's ghost continued:

"Odyssey, don't be too trusting with your own wife, that will suit you best;

Never reveal the whole truth, tell her only part and keep to yourself, the rest,

Not that Penelope will murder you, she is an admirable wife;

Her loyalty runs deep, from her you can expect a long and happy life,

I recall that day many years ago when we left for the war in Troy;

At her breast she nursed Telemakis, your infant boy,

Your son, no doubt, is growing into a man and will be honoured in your estate;

He hopes for your joyful homecoming, but many more years he will have to wait,

But my wife never let me see my son, she killed me first, on my homecoming day;

So, bear this in mind, when you reach Ithaki, don't sail into Phortune Bay,

Go ashore in a secret place and your identity should not be made known;
The time for trusting women is over; all men are on their own,

Now, enough of women and wives, tell me about my son and his life;
Where is he? In Orchomenos away from *trouble* and strife?

Perhaps he's with Menelaos on the Spartan plain;
Or, at sandy Pilos with Nestor in his kingly domain,

Don't tell me my son, Prince Orestes is dead, too;
That would be the worst news I could ever hear from you."

So I cut his questions short, saying:

Agamemnon, I know nothing of Orestes' fate,[a] why do you ask me?
It would be wrong of me to lead you on, how could I know where he could be?

As we sat weeping and grief stricken the ghost of Achilles came to us;
He was with brave Ajax, Antilochos and fearless Patroklos."

The ghost of the fleeted-footed Achilles greeted me first:

"Odyssey, noble son of Laertes, where will your daring deeds land you next?
You've ventured down into the House of Hades amongst us pathetic wrecks."

I replied to Achilles:

Son of Peleos,[176] I was forced here to consult the ghost of Terisias, the seer;

---

a   Odyssey could not be aware that Agamemnon's son, Orestes, has already murdered Klytemenstra and
    Agisthos to avenge his dead father.

I've never been close to my beloved Ithaki, my absence is in its thirteenth year,

Misfortune and hardship from the very first day is what I've had to endure;
Since we left Agamemnon's land of noble steeds to fight the Trojan war,

But Achilles, no man was ever more respected than you;
You were adored as a god, and even down here you are revered among the dead too."

Your life was not in vain, your spirit should not grieve any longer;
Glorious Achilles, by each day your reputation grows stronger."

He answered:

"Don't talk words that glorify Death. I would rather be the slave of a poor man
instead;
And be living above ground, than a nobleman of Hades, ruling over its dead.

Now, enough of this horrid place, give me news, where is my valiant son?
Is he in some distant war shining as a great soldier, or is his life done?

And what about my father, Peleos, does he still have the Myrmidon's respect to
show?
Or, is he now resented in Hellas and Phthia, since age has weakened his body, yes or
no?

Oh! give me the chance to stand by his side, my revenge would be seen and heard;
In front of those men that would dishonour my father, a hero, and his royal word,

With the same strength that killed our foes on the Trojan plain;
Heaven help any man who with threats and violence, would wrest away his reign."

I spoke peacefully to Achilles' ghost:

"I have heard nothing of your esteemed father, Peleos;

But I can tell you about your son, Neoptolemus,[177]

For I took him in my own ship from Skyros[178] to join our army on doomed Troy's shore;

On the way we debated many things about our prospects, and the tactics of war,

His judgement was sound and he was always the first to speak true;

Nestor and I were the only two who could teach him anything new,

And, when it came to combat, he was always the first to lead;

He would dash out from the front lines, foremost in word, *and* deed,

Scores of men he killed in battle, all their names I could never list;

But every foe he met, he slew, with a spear, a sword or his bloodied fist,

However, there was one famous victim that I remember well, Eurypylus;

The most handsome man I ever saw - even as he lay dead - in blood and swirling dust,

And his comrades too, slaughtered around him, were victims of his mother's[179] betrayal;

For King Priam bribed Astyoche, so her son would fight for the Trojans, a folly destined to fail,

At Troy, when the bravest of us hid in the wooden horse,[a] which Epeus made;

It was left to me when the door should be opened, and our ambush played,

The other thirty-eight chiefs sat trembling, teardrops on their cheeks, except your son who showed no fear;

---

a   At least thirty soldiers hid in the Trojan horse's wooden hulk with two look-outs in its eyes or mouth. Other sources give different numbers: The *Bibliotheca,* fifty and Quintus Smyrnaeus names thirty, but suggested there were more. In later traditions the number was conventionalised as forty.

He kept urging me to break out of the horse, gripping his sword and bronze-tipped
spear,

He muttered curses upon the Trojans as his eager body pented with rage;

Your son, was a legendary warrior, a man ahead of his age,

After we sacked Troy, I gave him your armour and weapons, and he sailed away in
his own ship;

His body was unscathed, not even a scratch from close combat's sword, or arrow's
flying tip,

Be a proud father Achilles, for he was the gallant son that you deserved;

Protected by Ares, War's god, loyal to his comrades, who his noble heart served.

With that, Achilles' ghost flitted off, across the fields,[a] rejoicing in the words I had
said;

Then, up and around me, came swarming the rest of the famous dead,

Each ghost asking about the thing to which his grief would not yield;

Only the sullen son of Telamon, Ajax,[180] the great defender, kept himself afield,

He was still angry with me for winning Achilles' weapons and armour;

For he carried noble Achilles' corpse back to our camp, but *my* fighting was harder,

The Trojan prisoners and Athena judged me the better, and all agreed;

To the eternal gods I now wish that day had not brought Ajax's shameful deed,[b]

---

a   The Asphodel field, or meadow, is the vast marsh-land adjoining the Nekromanteion, the ancient
Greek temple of the oracle of necromancy, devoted to Hades and Persephone. The Acheron River in
Epirus, near the ancient town of Ephyra (today's Messopotamo) flows through the site. This site is
believed, by devotees, to be the door to Hades, the realm of the dead. The area near the
Nekromanteion is, to this day, profuse with these endemic plants. In legend the asphodel is one of the
most famous of the plants connected with the dead. It was planted on graves, and its general
connection with death is due to the grey colour of its leaves and its yellow flowers, which suggest the
gloom of the underworld, and the pallor of death. The roots are eaten by superstitious Greeks because,
as food, it was thought respectful for one's dead ancestors.

b   Ajax killed himself by falling on the sword that Hector had given to him. As their one-on-one combat
had not had an outcome, the fight was stopped and gifts of weapons and armour were exchanged
between the warriors. Perhaps Hector had the final victory.

For he was slain by his own sorrow as he fell disgraced, upon Hector's blade;[181]
Great Ajax's pride could not live with being second best, and so his end was made."

Then I shouted to him:

Ajax, old friend, forget, and let bygones be what they are;
Let death bury the memories that those accursed weapons mar,

It cost us dearly to lose the tower of strength you brought to the battle field;
We loved you as much as Achilles and our sorrow to this day refuses to yield,

The blame must go to Zeus, he imposed great harm against us all;
Don't blame anyone else, it was he who fated your downfall,

Come over here, now is the time to talk and conquer your deathless pride;
But he sauntered away toward the ghosts that Erebus' shadows hide,

I should have stopped him, and made him talk at least;
But now I longed to know the other ghosts that around us had increased."

"I then saw Minos, son of Zeus, in his hand a sceptre of gold;
He was presiding over all the dead, judging them, seated or standing, young or old."

"Then there was Orion, the gigantic hunter, away in the asphodel fields;
He was herding the spirits of wild beasts with the deathless, bronzed club that he
wields."

"Also, I saw pitiable Tityus,[182] son of Gaia,[183] staked out on Tartarus' old plains;
He covered nine acres laying on his back, while two vultures gorged on his liver's
remains,

Their heads were soaked red with blood, as his hands flapped like wings;
But he could never beat them off, as he was doomed to Zeus' endless sufferings,

For he raped Leto,[184] as she travelled to the ridge above Pythos[a];
Which overlooks the horse-shoe waves of the Bay of Phocis."[b]

"And I saw also, damned Tantalus,[185] and the torture he endured for his sin;
He stood in a lake's depth and tried to drink the water lapping at his chin,

But whenever he stooped and nodded his head to slake his thirst;
The water vanished and dried up, as was heaven's eternal curse,

Nothing but dry, black ground lying at the old man's feet;
And above his head dangling from tall trees was ripe fruit, fresh and sweet,

There were pears, pomegranates, apples, olives and figs hanging on all the limbs;
But every time he reached up to take his pick, the fruit was scattered to the four winds.

"And I saw Sisyphus[186] at his hopeless task, pushing a boulder up to a mountain's summit;
In dust or rain he hauled and heaved, but only to see that rock plummet,

For every time he got close to the ridge, heavier the rock became;
So he was doomed, destined to repeat forever that futile game,

Although he was feasting on Olympos, I saw the great, Herakles, his double,[187] I mean;
He was with his youthful wife Hebe,[188] daughter of Juno, Hera,[189] Zeus' vengeful queen,

a   Modern-day town of Delphi, Greece.
b   Modern-day Bay of Itea, its horse-shoe shape and unusual ringed waves can be seen from Delphi.

The other ghosts screamed around him like screeching birds, he looked dire;
He ranged around, an arrow grooved on his bowstring, ready to fire,

About his breast a marvel of wonder, a gold sword-sash adorned with scenes of war;
And slain men, bears, boars, lions, wild-eyed animals and many things more,

The man who made it must be an artist without rival,[a] greatest in fame;
For the quality is unsurpassed and its power and glory put all others to shame,

Herakles knew me at once and spoke with cold pity in his voice;
"Odyssey, you *poor* man, leading the same life I did on earth, is that your choice?

I am the son of Zeus, Mind, no less, but I went through an infinity of suffering too;
Yes, I sacked Troy before your time, but left Priam's skin for you,

And for my honour to a resentful father, he enslaved me to twelve un-godly labours;
He even sent me down here into Hades' Hell to fetch its great hound, Cerberus,[190]

He thought that I could not accomplish the most difficult order ever tasked;
But Athena and her herald, Hermes with his gold mace, helped me as soon as I asked."

At that, Herakles - his double - I mean, turned away into the darkness and fled;
I hoped that Theseus and Pirithoos[191] might come too, but their memories were dead,

Then many thousands of ghosts teemed around me all shrieking like bats in the air;
I was panic stricken for I thought Persephone may send the dreaded Gorgon[192] to fix her stare,

It was then I ordered all the men back to their benches in our blue-eyed ship;
For time and tide had come for us all, this was the last moment of our Hades trip,

a   Perhaps an allusion to Hephaestos.

Past the high-looming crag and then to the fork of the raging Styx we ran;
Beyond the Acheron, we found Persephone's beach and our ship on the sand,

With my sword I cut the mooring line, each second might be our last;
And commanded my men to row for dear life, with all their force, and fast,

We followed Oceanus' Stars, churning the sea, 'til our sails bellied full with a fair wind's breath;
Again, we had fled peril, as fugitives from Hades' Hell, we had escaped certain death.

*

THE SIRENS

*

SCYLLA OR CHARYBDIS?

*

THE CATTLE OF HELIOS

"We followed the River of Stars, Oceanus, and met with the Tyrrhenian Sea;[a]
We headed east where Dawn makes way for the Sun, and the island of Aeaea,

We hauled our ship onto the beach, it was in the darkest of night;
And there we slept 'til Dawn's lantern threw out its pinking light.

I ordered some men to Circe's house to fetch Elpenor's dead body;
The others prepared a funeral pyre on the headland that juts sharp into the sea,

There, tears filled our eyes and beards, as we wept that he was gone;
After his body and armour burned, we erected an inscribed stone,

Its epitaph told of his luckless life for all who visit that shore;

---

a   The Tyrrhenian Sea is part of the Mediterranean Sea off the western coast of Italy.

And for his last request, his grave-mound bore his well-worn rowing oar,

Our return from Hades Hell did not escape Queen Circe;
Smiling, she ran to us in her finest garments, a vision of beauty,

Her maids followed with trays of fine wine, meats and bread;
She stood, among us, radiant with joy, and said:

"Intrepid men, you have ventured into the House of Death, and returned;
Most die only once, but two chances at life you all have earned,

You followed my instructions and have now survived to face another day;
Sometimes it is good for men to heed what a woman has to say,

Now you must take meat, bread and clear wine, then rest until Dawn's rise;
When you shall sail a safe course that I shall plot, free from danger or surprise."

"Her charm won over our gloomy hearts, and we took joy from what she said;
After all, we had no choice, for without the Queen's wisdom we'd all be dead,

We agreed, and celebrated until the Sun gave way to the stars that shine,
Then the weary men made their beds on the beach by the ship's mooring line,

Circe took me away by the hand and we reclined in the bushy littoral;[a]
She was eager to know about our adventures, every detail I had to tell,

"So far, so good" she said, once my story was over, "But you must heed what I now
have to say;
Your intuition will confirm what I tell you as the truth, follow it and you will be safe
along your way,

a   The seashore above the high-water mark of a beach where vegetation grows.

First on your course, the island of the Sirens will rise from the horizon;
Those sea-maids will come close, and can entice the most hard-hearted of men,

If any one gets too close and hears the Sirens wailing they'll surely lament;
Never again shall he see wife and family, as Death will be fast sent,

For their lulling warbles lead only to a rock piled high with rancid corpses of men;
All around are heaps of the dead's bones, with the flesh still rotting on them,

Go straight onward, for they are wretched and evil, despite their innocent charm;
And soften bee's wax to press into your crew's ears, deafness will do them no harm,

However, if *you* can't resist the temptation of their intoxicating sound and sight;
Have the men bind you to a cross-piece nailed to the mast, with sturdy ropes, tied tight,

But if you are filled with desire and beg the men to loosen the ties;
Then they must wind more rope around you, and cover your bulging eyes,

When your crew have rowed past the Sirens, *you alone,* between two courses, must choose;
I cannot tell you which one is best, only one will decide if *your* life you keep, or lose,

One line will take you along a wild rolling swell, the Clashing Rocks[193] to thread;
Where Amphitrite's[194] foggy mist will blind you, and fill you full of dread,[a]

Raging winds whistle as they race through these rocks, numbered seven;
They seem to move about, called the Wanderers by the gods in Olympos' heaven,

Even birds, carrying Ambrosia to Lord Zeus, get lost in flight;
For the singing rocks confound any creature's sense of sound and sight,

---

a   Amphritrite was Poseidon's wife.

Upon the bronze-hard rock walls, one bird will be dashed, at least;
So Zeus, Mind, sends others to keep his flocks complete,

These rocks, waves and screeching winds have never known calm;
Never was there a ship that made it through without grief and harm,

They've witnessed only drowning men and shipwrecks aplenty;
Except for the famous *Argo,*[a] the only vessel to run the gauntlet to safety,

For only Queen Hera's love for Jason, and her helming hand;
Were these wild rocks denied the Argonauts, on their way to Aeete's land,[195]

Then sail south to two islands, one has a black cloud hiding its menacing peak;[b]
For no man has seen its summit, not even in summer's sweltering heat,

No man could climb it, even with twenty hands and feet;
For on its smooth polished sides, there is no foothold to greet,

There is a wide-mouthed cave, looking out to Erebus, due west;
Half way up the crag's bluff, where only death and misery infest,

Rudder your ship that way, past the cave, it's so high an archer's arrow would fall short;
Inside it dwells Scylla, the dreaded monster, with a puppy's whelp and piglet's snort,

---

a   Argo, was constructed by Argus, and its crew were specially protected by the goddess Hera. According to a variety of sources of the legend, *Argo* was said to have been built with the help of Athena. According to certain sources, *Argo* was the first ship to sail the seas. It was Athena who taught Typhus to attach the sails to the mast and boom, as he was the steersman and would need an absolute knowledge of the workings of the ship. According to other legends, she contained in her bow a magical piece of timber from the sacred forest sanctuary of Dodoni, which could speak and render prophecies. Odyssey's father had sailed on the Argo.

b   A reference to the islands of Panarea and Stromboli, with its still-active volcano.

But she is a gruesome beast, and no man - or god - could face her hideous sight;

For she has twelve deformed arms and six, long necks with ghastly heads to fright,

Each head has three mouths lined with sharp fangs, three rows at least;

She lurks there, waist-deep in gore, ready to attack and kill any god, man or beast,

From her yawning cave she springs out, her heads flailing, teeth chattering, with a harpy's[196] shrill;

She dives down into the sea depths, catching many fish - even whales - and chomps them into gristle,

No sea captain has sailed by without losing at least one man to each ghastly head;

Six-at-a-time Scylla plucks them up into her grisly lair, then returns for her next round of dead,

The other crag is not as tall and about an arrow's flight away;

A great straggling fig tree sits on its top, course your boat that way,

Under that towering rock lies the huge whirlpool and blowhole of Charybdis;

Three times a day she sucks down and then vomits up foaming black water, she is your nemesis,

Even your patron Phorgyn[197] would be of no help to you, against this formidable foe;

Better you lose six men, or more, to Scylla, then row fast, that's the only way to go..."

Odyssey interrupts, pleading:

"Surely there is some other way of escaping Charybdis and Scylla too?"

And Circe says: "Are you the world's greatest fool? I am here trying to help you,

I was sent by the the Olympians to save your neck, here I stand;

But you are headed for Hades again, if you don't change your mortal ways. Do as I command!

How many battles do you need to fight? Why do you persist, your ways are futile?

So stupid! You have no power against these supreme monsters, they are invincible,

Haven't you learnt that your destiny can't be changed, it is written on your furrowed face;

You are deaf to your heart, listen to the voice within, if you want to stay in the human race,

Scylla is a wild, savage beast that lives on the flesh of men;

Against her you have no chance, just get past as quick as you can,

Don't dawdle near her rocky lair, or think about fixing for a fight;

For she'll strike, her anger is as severe as her hunger, and her deathly might,

Drive your ship at full speed past, and pray to Crataeis,[a] who suckled her;

She might favour you and stop the second death raid on your men, but you can't be sure,

Next you will come to the shore of Thrinakia[b] where Helios' cattle and sheep range;

Seven herds of ox and seven flocks of sheep, with fifty head in each, and they never change,

They don't breed, and never die, tended by the children of the Titan Sun god, for eternity;

Mothered by radiant Nearea they are the beautiful nymphs, Phaethusa and Lampetie,

Nearea moved them to those remote shores to care for Helios' wide-horned beasts;

Make sure these herds are kept safe and your men make no feasts,

---

a   Crataeis was Scylla's mother. Her father was Phorgyn, the patron of Ithaki, by which Phortune Bay (Vathy) is named.

b   The triangular shaped island of *Sicily*.

Leave the flocks and herds unharmed, make your way to Ithaki, and don't delay;
If not, your boat and crew will be destroyed and you'll be seven years a castaway,

Even if you do escape death, you will return in a strange ship to your *troubled* land;
To find your estate consumed by Suitors, all vying for your wife's wedding hand."

With that, her words ended. Dawn broke-out a golden Sun. Circe returned to her home.

*

"We dragged the ship from the beach into the surfing sea;
Set the mast into the keel and rigged the sails for the anxious journey,

Loaded were our supplies and the distressed crew;
Circe sent us a wind over the stern, and hard it blew,

The boom went wide and the sails bellied full;
The tiller-man held a running course, no need for the oars' pull,

After a while, with great reluctance, I said to the crew;
It's not right that only I know what Circe's prophecies have in store for you,

I must tell you so that we can live or die knowing what will be our fate, before too long;
First, we must steer clear of the Sirens on their seaweed rafts, singing their seductive song,

I, alone, are to hear the Siren's song, you men must be deaf to their serenade;
So lash me tight to the mast with ropes and knots that cannot be unmade,

And bind those ties tighter if I beg or command you to set me free;
Then the wind died and not even a ripple could be seen on that dead-calm sea,

The crew flaked and furled the sails and quickly stowed them below;
And the dark, oily sea was thrashed white with the oars, as they rowed,

So I cut up some wax, warmed it in the Sun god's rays, and my hands kneaded it soft;
Then pressed the wax into my crew's ears, one by one, as they churned the sea to froth,

The men lashed me tight to the mast with ropes and knots that couldn't be undone;
As we got closer to land the Sirens noticed us and began singing their strange song:

"Come closer pride of the Hellenes, the hero that Troy's downfall made;
Great Odyssey, steer this way and listen to our serenade,

For you will be famous for all time, if you hear;
The words and the tune that soothes the soul, and charms the ear,

Come, now, and let your spirit rise and ecstasy will be filled;
And hear the sweet wisdom that we have for your mind, to be instilled,

We know the pain that you have suffered, but those days have gone;
Come, now, and listen to the craft of the Sirens' song,

Power and immortal fame are close at hand;
Come here, now, if you wish to see your home-land."

Their song so sozzled my senses that I gestured to the men, with my frowning eyes;
To untie me, but they quickened their strokes as Eurylochos and Perimedes pulled harder on the binding ties,

When we were well clear of the Sirens' sight and sound;
The men picked the wax from their ears, and I was unbound,

Suddenly, we heard the roar of crashing waves and saw the billowing sea-spray;
The men were so terrified, they dropped their oars and began to pray,

There we lay, dead in the water, with not a man willing an oar to pull;
So I went up and down the gangway rousing their spirits full,

Friends, I said, this is not the first time we've been in danger or under threat;
What about the Cyklops and the *trouble* in his cave, did you all forget?

It was my courage and cunning that got us away from that mess;
And we shall live to look back on all this with a smile, no less,

Now, trust in Zeus, Mind, and row with all your grit and might, and don't forget;
To turn the tiller toward those crags - away from the whirlpool - or there will be
regret,

So they took the oars in hand and plied the sea white;
But I did not tell them about Scylla, she would be an unexpected fright,

For, if I did, the men would cower and huddle in the hull's hollow;
And refuse to row toward her lair, and mutiny would surely follow,

Now there was one thing that I disregarded from Circe's advice;
I put on my noble armour and raised my spear, perhaps Scylla would think twice?

I ranged up and down the gangway hoping she'd be ready for the fight;
But I could see nothing, the crag's cliffs were barren and its peak out of sight,

My armour clattered with fear, and good it was that the men couldn't hear it, I
thought;

For as they pulled on the oars, their backs faced Charybdis to Starboard, and Scylla
to Port,[a]

Like a boiling cauldron Charybdis spewed up a streaming storm into the mist on
high;

And then sucked and gulped it back down again as it fell from the towering sky,

We saw into the whirlpool's abyss, it was all mud and black swirling sand;

The men were frozen with fear, all wished we were on dry land,

Suddenly, Scylla pounced from above as we were gawking over the ship's side;

She snatched up my best six men in her jaws, and hoisted them on a terror ride,

Up she flew, the men's arms and legs flailing, fast into her den;

They were screaming out my name, but I could do nothing to save them,

Just like a fisherman angling on a jutting rock or shore, barbed spear, ready handed;

He throws bait into the water so unsuspecting fish can be lured, and landed,

The little fish are seized and flicked up onto the beach, wriggling and gasping for air;

So it was with my men, panting with pleading arms, she devoured them in her lair,

This was the most gruesome sight one could ever see;

Those memories shall forever haunt and stay with me,

The remaining men rowed hard, for fear forced their oars fast;

All we could think of was finding the refuge of friendlier shores at last,

We had passed the Wandering rocks, Scylla and Charybdis, as Circe said;

---

a   Port and Starboard; left and right.

And soon we saw the shores of Hyperion's Thranacia, with its sheep and cattle, pure bred,

Still at sea we could hear the beasts bleats and bellows, as clear as day;
And it reminded me of what blind Terisias and wise Circe had to say:

"... If all have self control, after a dire voyage, you just might get home to tell your tale;
For when your ship reaches Thrinakia, you'll find Helios' sheep and cattle,

Leave the flocks and herds unharmed, make your way to Ithaki, and don't delay;
If not, your boat and crew will be destroyed and you'll be seven years a castaway,

Even if you do escape death, you will return in a strange ship to your troubled *land;*
To find your estate consumed by Suitors, all vying for your wife's wedding hand."

I was for sailing on, and putting that place astern, morale was low, the men distressed;
So, I said: "Men we must not land there, it is our greatest danger." They were not impressed,

I continued:

"Remember in Hades, the Theban told us of this place, and Circe had advice too;
Point the bow away from this island, now, if we are to escape, our numbers are too few."

Eurylochus gave me an insolent answer:

"Odyssey, you are a hard man, iron from feet to head;
You never seem to toil, your spirit is god-like and many men at your hands are dead,

Look, your crew is exhausted, and they want food and rest on the closest beach;

But you want to deny us this land, right under our noses, in arm's reach,

You want us to abandon this god-given shore, and all it could provide;
Night is near, and you want us to navigate the sea, and the rocks, that darkness hide,

By night all winds blow hardest, and ships and crew find watery death more often;
And who knows what *your* enemy has in store for *us*, we all know the wrath of
Poseidon,

If he's watching he'll send winds and waves to break this ship in two;
A hurricane will gale winds to wreck our boat, end our lives, us *and* you,

No, let's respect Night and avoid certain sorrow;
Find our supper on this shore and see another Dawn, tomorrow."

So Eurylochus spoke, and the men approved with a cheer;
But I knew that *trouble* would follow, it was very clear.

Then I said:

"You force me to yield to your way, for you are many and I'm only one;
But first make a solemn oath, that you'll not harm the cattle of the god of the Sun,

Do not kill a single ox, or even a sheep, that graze on that lush land;
And all must be satisfied - only - by the food Circe made by her own hand."

They swore the oath, and to a sandy shore, the bow of the boat was tied;
There was a spring of fresh water, so we drank and ate 'til all were happy and
satisfied,

Then they spoke of our crew-mates that Scylla had plucked up to devour;
Like children they wept themselves into slumber, until Dawn's daylight hour,

(That night, in the third watch, Zeus *did* align the stars sending winds of hurricane force;

Which joined the sea and sky into darkness, and no captain could have found a ship's course.)

When rosy-fingered Dawn sent her pinking light, we hauled the boat on shore;

Into a high-vaulted cave where Water Nymphs once met and held court,

There I called my own council, saying: "Friends, we have plenty of corn and beer[a] in the ship;

So, remember your oath, and don't be tempted to touch Helios' oxen and sheep,

For the Sun reveals and sees all things, rays of light are his means, so take care;

And they all agreed not to offend Helios, and again to their oath they did swear,

But then, the Sirocco[b] blew hard, we couldn't move the ship for a whole month long;

The stranded crew remained happy, until Circe's beer and corn were gone,

They were forced to hunt and fish, with spear and crooked hook;

But they were slowly starving, and lost the will to look,

I ventured inland to pray to the gods and summon their help, one day;

Hoping that one of them might return me home to Phortune Bay,

When clear of the men, I knelt in a sheltered place, and rinsed my hands in a stream;

But some Invisible had another plan, my eyelids got heavy and I drifted into a dream,

Meanwhile, Eurylochus had hatched his foolish, fatal plan;

"Listen", he said, "hear me friends, each and every man,

---

a   Beer is one of the oldest beverages humans have produced, dating at least 7,000 years.
b   The warm wind that blows North from Africa, across the Mediterranean Sea.

There is no virtue in dying before destiny has its place;

Starvation is the worst way to die, when food is staring us in the face,

Let's pick the best from Helios' herds, and sacrifice them to the Olympians, one and all;

And if we ever get back to Ithaki we'll build the Sun god a temple,

But if saving our *own* skins offends lord Helios, and he sinks our boat on homeward seas;

Then I'd rather die from gulping sea-water, than starving here by degrees."

So Eurylochus spoke, and the men approved with a cheer;

But I knew that *trouble* would follow, it was very clear,

The herds were grazing near the blue-eyed ship's cave, in easy reach;

So, the men mustered the best of the sheep and oxen onto the beach,

Praying to the gods that they would understand, they formed in a ring around them;

And cast young oak-shoots over the beasts, as all the ship's barley had been eaten,

When they had finished their prayers they killed and butchered the oxen;

Cutting out the bones, and wrapping them in two layers of fat and raw skin,

There was no wine for libations or to baste the roasting meat;

So they drizzled it with a little seawater, and it sizzled in the heat,

Then cut what was left into small pieces, and skewered with a spit;

And from the roasted bones scooped out the marrow, down to the very last bit,

By this time I woke from my deep sleep, and I made my way back to the men;

As I got near I smelt the roasted meat, so I groaned out a prayer to the Invisibles, again,

All-knowing Zeus, Mind, and all you other gods who live in everlasting happiness;
Again, your cruel gift of slumber has lulled me into another mess,

What is this terrible crime you have allowed, and my crew have done?
Instantly, Lampetie, in her shimmering robes, spread the news to her father, the Sun.

Then Helios, outraged, said:

"Father Zeus, Mind, and all you other gods who are omnipresent[a] in Time;
I must have revenge on the crew of Odyssey's ship for their insolent crime,

They killed my sacred cows, my pride and joy, all gone, all that I loved;
If you withhold vengeance and don't repay me with their blood,

Then I will go down into Hades and shine there among the ghosts of the Dead;
And fruitful Earth, for all eternity, shall be bathed in darkness and dread."

"Sun," said Zeus, "Go on shining upon Olympians and mortals of Earth;
I will splinter their ship with a bolt of lightning as soon as leave the shore, for the surf."

Then I had a flashback: as Circe said,

...For seven long years I was to be marooned with Kalypso;
The story came straight from Hermes' lips, she warned me so ...

As soon as I got to the ship I reprimanded each one of the men;
But the cows were already dead, how could we make amends?

---

a   *Omnipresent*, means: Ever present, everywhere.

Then the gods worked their menacing tricks, the ox-hides began to creep around;
And the meat, cooked or raw, on the spits started to bellow with a moo-ing sound,

For six days the men feasted on the Sun's butchered cattle;
On the seventh day Zeus - Xenia's Minder - stilled the Sirocco gale,

We went aboard the ship, raised the masts, hoisted the sails, and put to sea;
As soon as land was out of sight, Zeus raised a thunderous sky, dark and murky,

We didn't get much further, then the forestays snapped as we were hit by a Westerly squall;
The sails and rigging fell onto the deck as the mast toppled, smashing the helmsman's skull,

He went overboard, just as a diver does;
His soul had left him, bound for Hades,

Then Zeus, let fly with his thunderbolts, and the ship reeled about;
She was ablaze from the lightning strike, so the men jumped out,

They bobbed up and down, for a while, like sea-gulls, drifting over the sea;
But, Zeus deprived them all of a homecoming, and the shores of Ithaki,

They all thrashed their arms and screamed out to me, 'til out of breath;
But I could do nothing to save them, one by one each sank into the depth,

However, I clung to the hull which had its gunwales ripped away;
And then lashed the mast to the keel, with a sturdy ox-hide stay,

Exhausted, I climbed aboard that craft and let the wind blow me as it bid;
The Westerly gale was spent, so the wind blew again from the South, which I feared;

Was I being pushed toward Scylla - or Charybdis - and her churning whirlpool again?

All night I was smashed by waves and wind, then Dawn's red sky gave a grave warning,

There she was, opposite Scylla's rock, Charybdis, the dreaded whirling drain;

She sucked me down into the swirl, mud and water covered over me, again and again,

What remained of my raft sunk into her mouth on the sea bed;

My breath left me and I was drowning from the sand and mud,

But then, she vomited me up from the depths, high into the air, she spat;

I landed in a huge fig tree and clung to a bough like an upside-down bat,

There was no place for my feet, the ground was too far below;

The other boughs were out of arm's reach, nowhere could I go,

So, I hung there, holding on for dear life, a long time passed;

Then, just as my grip gave out, she spewed up the keel and the mast,

At last! I thought, just like the court's judge that settles the vexing suits of unworldly men;

Exhausted, his day's work done, he slowly walks towards his home and supper, again,

So, I let go and leaped into the furious surfing waves below;

I climbed aboard the flotsam,[a] and fast my hands began to row,

I thank Zeus, Righter of Wrongs, that Scylla didn't see me hanging;

For death would have been certain, and here I would not be standing,

---

a   Flotsam is floating wreckage of a ship or its cargo.

I drifted and paddled for ten days and landed on the island of Ogygio;

There dwells the great and powerful Spirit, Kalypso,

She took me in, loved me and was a kindly friend;

But why am I telling you this, now, again?

Just yesterday, right here, you and your gracious wife learned about my years with Kalypso,

It's not like me to repeat a tale, plainly told; one that you already know.[a]

*

---

a   Perhaps an allusion to Homer's observation that liars lose credibility when they repeat stories with different details. In this case, perhaps, it is a good idea for Odyssey to cease the story telling.

ODYSSEY RETURNS TO ITHAKI

So, with his tale ended, he sits.

All through the hall there is quiet; his audience is charmed by his story. Eventually, King Alkinoos speaks:

"Odyssey, you have suffered, and now that you have reached my palace in safety;
I doubt that any misadventure - or god - can keep you from your deserved Ithaki,

To all you others, who come here each night for enjoyment;
Drinking the finest wines, whilst the bard provides entertainment,

Do as I ask, already our guest has gifts of gold and other fine treasure;
Packed in sea chests stacked ready for his home-going pleasure,

Let's grant this hero more: Each man must donate his largest cauldron and tripod;
By doing so we shall earn the respect and favour we deserve, from our patron god,[a]

We will recoup from the public, by way of a tax, the cost of our kindness;
For noblemen should not have to bear all the expense of being generous."

They all approve heartily and leave for their homes and beds. Night spangles the sky with *his* pink light. The noblemen arrive at the ship and the bronze-ware is boarded. King Alkinoos goes aboard and sees that the gifts are secure, lashed under the oar benches so that nothing could become loose and harm the rowers.

---

a   An allusion to Poseidon, the Patron of Skeria.

They walk back to the palace where a feast is being prepared. In honour of Poseidon, the Earth-shaker, a prized ox is roasted, while the gathered fall into merriment. The tables are soon spread with the bountiful banquet. All seated, the bard, Demodokos, starts a favourite song.

Odyssey is restless. His eyes are on the setting Sun. Inside he is yearning to get underway, but must endure this delay. Just like a farmer who pains for his supper having spent the day behind his oxen as they plough his fallowed fields, and finding his last legs he plods toward home and slumps upon his favourite chair at the dinner table. So, Odyssey welcomes the setting Sun and wastes no more time. He rouses the nobles, saying, first to the King:

"My Lord, King Alkinoos, you shine out when you are among your court;

You have over-filled my heart with all these presents and by granting me an escort,

May the Olympians bless these precious gifts, and I find my wife's love strong;

Let's celebrate my farewell, it's time for me to leave, for I have stayed too long;

My dear friends, may your wives and children satisfy, and all live long too;

And the gods extend all the graces, and harbour no harm towards you."

The crowd's applause sounds throughout the hall. The King says:

"Pontonous, top up everyone's goblets with more wine for a toast;

To Poseidon to ensure that Odyssey returns safely to Ithaki's coast."

Pontonous mellows the wine and pours a full measure to everyone in turn. They each tip a libation onto the floor as they toast to Odyssey's safe journey home and offer thanks for the generosity of the gods for the favourable thoughts they provide.

Now he places the twin-eared goblet in the hands of Queen Arete, saying to her:

"Farewell, great Queen, 'til age and death, the common fate of us all, takes you;

Be happy in this house with your children, your friends, and with King Alkinoos."

Odyssey strides out through the palace. The King sends a man to escort him to the harboured ship. Queen Arete sends maids with him, one with a clean shirt and cloak, another to carry his strong box, and a third with cornbread and wine. When they get to the dock, the crew stows the goods in the hold. The maids layout a mattress with damask sheets and cushions on the transom deck, so that he can sleep soundly. He goes on board and lays on his day-bed. He can see the oarsmen fitting the rowlocks. They pull the spring-line through the eye of the stone cleat and begin rowing out of the harbour. Odyssey falls into a deep sleep.

The ship planes through the water, like a four-in-hand chariot flying over its course, just as the horses feel the whip's lash, so her blue-eyed bow, curved like a stallions foaming neck, bounds over the cracking waves, leaving a bubbling white wake. So quickly the ship moves through the waves, unswerving on its course, that not even a darting falcon could keep pace.

On its deck he sleeps, the man favoured with the gods' wisdom, who suffered for twenty years; tormented by separation, traumatised by war and menaced by wrong thinking. He rests in peace as the ship now points south-west into open water. By the Moon's light, through the night's watches, they sail into Destiny.

*

Dawn's awakener, Phosphorus the Morning Star,[198] rises from the sea and the ship finds Ithaki's coast, at last!

Ithaki was the home of Phorgyn, the old man of the sea. There is a heavy fog that lies over the island. Instead of landing in Phortune bay, the captain moors close-by in Rithron[199] Cove,[a] a ship's haven for it is sheltered from all winds by the high Mount Neriton to the north, the Aetos Ridge[b] to the west and two sheltered bays to the east, Phortune and Skinos, being the closest to the open sea.

On the point above the foreshore of Rithron beach is an ancient olive tree. To the south is a hill rising to a mysterious cave[c] belonging to the Naiads,[200] the Water Nymphs. Inside is a treasure trove of sacred artefacts: Gold mixing bowls, double-handed amphorae[201] filled with nectar and ambrosia, brass tripods and cauldrons, great stone looms that the nymphs weave their purple robes, so beautiful to see, and there is a fountain that has the purest, sweetest water in the world. Many bees hive here too.

The cave has two entrances, one facing north for mortals, and to the south an opening that only the Invisibles can find to enter.

---

a   Rithron Cove (Dexia Cove and Dexia Beach) is located just north of the Nymphs Cave (Naiad's) adjacent to Phortune Harbour, or as it is known today, Vathy. It may have been Rithron Cove in ancient times. Skartsoubo Island is just off Dexia Beach, Ithaki, and is said to be the petrified remains of the Phaekian ship and its crew that delivered Odyssey to Ithaki.

b   Eagle Ridge (neck), as it is known today.

c   Many caves are known to exist in the area near Rithron Cove.

The captain knows this place and runs the ship up onto the beach with almost half the hull's length out of the water. Such is the oars-men's power.

They lift Odyssey, still fast asleep, with his mattress and cushions and carry him onto the beach.[a] They take all his precious gifts, the treasure that Athena had secured for him from the Phaekians - more plunder than he ever took from Troy - and they stack the cargo on the beach. The Phaekians return to their blue-eyed ship and push it back off the pebbled beach. The oars thrash the water toward their home.

*

Poseidon, the Sea-smasher, not forgetting the very first threat he made to Odyssey,[b] implores Zeus:

"Brother Zeus, I shall no longer be honoured by the Invisibles after this affair;

The Phaekians, my own flesh and blood, show towards me, very little care,

I said I would let Odyssey get home, once he had suffered for his crime;

For I knew that once you had nodded, pledging your word, it would be just a matter of time,

But now look, they have brought him in a ship fast asleep;

And landed him in Ithaki with treasures by the heap,

He blinded my one-eyed son, why reward him for that monstrous crime?

Are you going to over-look his dark offence again, this time?"

So, Zeus, Mind, answers him:

"Earthquaker, what are you whining about, have you gone mad too?

Brother, you've earned the gods highest respect, it's the mortals that insult you!

---

a   This is the second time he has been asleep on his arrival to Ithaki.
b   *"... I know he's destined and entitled to make it there some day; but I'll make sure he has a plenty of* trouble *before he gets to Phortune Bay."*

If you're dissatisfied with their insolence and respect has been lost;

Then punishment is what will work best; show them who's boss!"

"Yes, I should have done so at once," replied Poseidon;

But, Mighty Zeus, Mind, it was you that I was afraid to offend,

I'd like to wreck that Phaekian ship before it returns to Skeria;

That will stop them from escorting my *enemies* in the future;

And perhaps I'll bury their city and port under a mountain;

That will make my heart proud, and restore my reputation."

Zeus answers Poseidon's plea:

"No, brother, wait 'til the city's people are watching the vessel and crew's return;

Then turn it into a rock resembling a ship, a lesson to stay at home, one they must learn,

Next, with your best earthquake, shake and rumble the Earth, as hard as you can;

And to remind them to honour you, raze the walls and palace of Alkinoos to the ground."

In Rithron Cove copy the stone ship to remind Odyssey not to offend you anymore;

When he wakes he'll think their ship and crew have been turned to stone, just offshore"

They both laugh at the plan.

The Earth-shaker takes flight to Skeria Harbour, in Corfu, and waits for the ship to arrive. As it gets closer he goes forward and with the flat of his hand drives the ship down rooting it to the sea bed and turning it - and crew - to stone.[a] He

---

a   Pontikonisi, or, Mouse Island, in Corfu Harbour, is said to be the remains of the ship and crew that
     returned from Ithaki. Local folklore on Corfu have long claimed it is the ship that carried Odyssey
     back to Ithaki, but was turned to stone by Poseidon, to punish the Phaekians for helping his enemy.
     The "sister" rock is located in Rithron Cove, Ithaki, and is now known as Skartsoubo Island (Sock
     Island) and also said to be the petrified remains of the Phaekian ship and its crew that delivered

vanishes. The ground trembles and the people are terrified. Alkinoos' palace is razed to the ground.

The Phaekians, astonished, begin talking among themselves, each turning to the next person, "What has happened? Just a moment ago our ship was sailing into port, now it's stone, and our beloved brothers, too. The earth quaked and the palace is now a mountain of rubble. What god has worked this outrage against us?"

King Alkinoos, distraught, comes forward, saying:

"Now I remember my father's prophecy;

That Poseidon would resent us and be angry,

For we overstepped our hospitality by ferrying strangers home;

And now, by suffering for our generosity, we must never again roam,

No more shall we offer the right of passage, as was our tradition;

Let us sacrifice our best twelve bulls to Poseidon, and end this destruction."

His people prepare the ceremonial offerings to the Earth-Shaker. The King and family, the nobles and the people mill around the ruins and the sacrifice begins.

*

Odyssey awakes on Rithron Beach.

He has been away from Ithaki for twenty years. He does not recognise this place for in the cove is a rocky outcrop that looks like a wrecked ship. Can this be his beloved home of Ithaki, or is he lost again?

Wise Athena has lowered a thick fog which clouds his sense of place. Athena has made Odyssey invisible. She intends to explain to him, when the time is right, the circumstances of his return and prevent his wife, son and friends from knowing he has found his home. Amends must be made against the Suitors too.

Everything seems different; the steep hill paths, the mountain's green foliage, the pebbled beach don't remind him of Ithaki. Distressed, he stands, slaps his thighs and screams out:

Odyssey to Ithaki.

"Alas what manner of people over this land reign?

Uncivilised savages, or are they hospitable and humane?

I wish the Phaekians had taken me back to Skeria with them;

And not leave me here on this abandoned beach, a castaway again."

Now, he must find a place to hide his belongings, so they are not stolen by some passer-by. What a disappointment to be deceived by the Phaekian King and his lords who, he thought, were honest men and promised to set him ashore on Ithaki. He thinks he's been dumped on some strange land's beach. He curses the Phaekians and hopes that Zeus - Xenia's Protector - shall repay them for their broken promise.

He starts to count the treasure that has been left there. Have the captain and crew robbed him? He checks all the chests finding, to his astonishment, that everything is there.

Odyssey grieves for his home-land, Ithaki.

He is inconsolable at the thought that he is marooned again. He mopes up and down the beach distraught with home-sickness, then sits, by his hoard of treasure, dejected.

Athena walks toward him, disguised as a young shepherd boy with the countenance of a prince, clothed in a cloak, double-folded over her shoulders wearing fine sandals and with a spear in hand. Odyssey is glad to see the shepherd and yells out, saying:

"My friend you are the first person I have met on this strange land;

I trust you will be kind and protect me, and my belongings from a thief's hand,

I honour you just as if you are an Invisible yourself;

Please tell me, truly, what land and country is this?

Who are its people? Is this an island?

Or the shore of some continent's mainland?"

Disguised Athena answers:

"Stranger, you must have come from a long way off, or be a half-wit at best;
This country is famous, and known by everybody between east and west,

This land can only be reached by boat;
This island is bold and rocky and only fit for mule and goat,

We have no fields or racecourses upon which a horse can thrive;
And no pasture to grow oats or hay to keep them alive,

Our island is steep, level ground it cannot boast;
And covered with sharp stones, this island has the most,

But it is a good place to grow grapes, corn and grain;
With fast-flowing streams that are well watered by rain,

All kinds of timber grows here, both soft and hard wood;
To find a better place to live, I doubt *you* could,

Even as far away as Troy the name of this island is renowned;
And Troy is a very long way from here. Sir, Ithaki you have found!"

His heart begins to race. Although glad to his core, wily Odyssey does not divulge who he is, for fear that the shepherd will betray him and steal his treasure. Instead he lies with a cunning story to intimidate the young man:

"I heard of Ithaki when I was far beyond these seas, to the south, in Crete;
And here I am now, having reached it safely, with all this treasure at my feet.

I left just as much behind for my children, but fled because now I'm a fugitive;
I killed Orsilochus, Idomeneus'[202] son, the best runner in Crete, which the law did not forgive.

He tried to rob me of my plunder, hard-won from Troy's wretched war;

I've been to Hades and back, through war and angry seas, to land upon this shore,

Just because I refused to serve his father at Troy and set up my own brigade;

So, with a friend, we lay in wait for the ambush in a road-side glade;

In the darkest of night, as he left his field, I killed him with my pitiless spear;

And once his life had flittered away, I headed for the harbour and a ship to get me clear,

I begged and bribed the greedy hands of a Phoenician captain to take me to Pilos;

Or Elis, where the Epeans rule, but to this shore is where that wild storm blew us,

We reached this cove at Midnight, rowing for dear life against the angry sea;

We were famished but too exhausted to eat, so we slept on the beach, under that olive tree,

This morning, while I slept, they took my goods and stacked them here for me;

Then sailed away for Sidonia, leaving me here with my *troubles*, as you can see."

As his story ends, Athena, with her bright and wide eyes, caresses his arm and smiles. Casting off her disguise, the Spirit reveals herself in her womanly form; slender and beautiful, saying:

"You are a shifty liar Odyssey, that even a god could not out-do;

All the limits of craftiness, deceit and guile have been exceeded by you,

Even here, in your own country, everything you say is a cunning and devious lie;

Let's not discuss it anymore, for both of us can get our own way, if we try,

For conniving tactics and deception - of all mortals - you are the best;

And on Olympos, for wisdom and shrewdness, I am most blessed,

To think you expected me to believe anything that a Cretan might say;
They are the worst liars the world has known, and will be forever, and a day,

But you don't recognise me - your faithful protector - Zeus's daughter;
In all your trials and exploits, I was the one who got you here, over land and water,

Even at their own peril, I made the Phaekians like you, and escort you here;
And, again, I am going to help you by hiding your cargo and treasure, near,

You can't imagine the *trouble* that awaits you in your Palace;
Only you can face it and suffer in silence. You must prepare for malice."

The wily Odyssey says:

"A man can't be blamed for not knowing all the forms and ways a god can employ;
But I am certain you protected me in those first ten years, when I was at war in Troy,

But from the day we left Priam's wrecked city, I've been at odds;
Athena, I saw nothing of you coming to my aid against the wrath of the gods,

Ten years I wandered with a sick and sorry heart, until I reached the Phaekian shore;
Where you met me and took me into Alkinoos' palace disguised as Nautikaa,

Now, you must tell me true, am I really back in my own country?
Or are you mocking me? Have I made it back to my home, Ithaki?"

Wise Athena says:

"You are capable and shrewd, so worldly wise and self-possessed;

But your thoughts are always thrashing through your head, never knowing what is
best,

You never know when to trust and so you have been afflicted long with strife;
Now is the time for you to believe that what I have said is true, and live a happy life,

Anyone would have returned after all the suffering eager to see your wife and son;
But not you! You are only interested in protecting your plunder, hard won,

Has your heart hardened so much that you don't care for your stoic[a] wife;
Who pines and weeps her days away, and wastes sleep over your wretched life,

It was Zeus, Mind, that ordained your return, but twenty hard years was the wait;
I never had any doubt that you would come back, it was your fate,

I could not quarrel with my uncle, Poseidon the Earth-shaker, he had it in for you;
You blinded his son, Polyphemus, the Cyklops, so revenge was due,

Now let me convince you that you have reached your home-land;
Follow me and you will see that this really is Ithaki upon which you stand."

The fog lifts as they walk to the top of the point above Rithron Cove. She
points to the south, saying:

Look, down there is Phortune Bay, named after Phorgyn, the old man of the sea;
Up there is the green-wooded Mount Neriton, sheltering Molos Bay, in its lee,

Over there is the sacred cave of the Naiads, the nymphs that you must worship;
Behind it is the vaulted cavern that you made sacrifices before your twenty-year trip,

---

a The word, *stoic*, meaning: Accepting of one's fate, non-complaining and virtuous, perhaps like the
   Stoics, a Hellenistic philosophical way of life, who believed that virtue and kindness are the most
   important aspirations for humans. Material values such as health, wealth, and pleasure are not good or
   bad in themselves, but have sacred value in leading people to a fulfilled life.

And there, to remind you of your trials and exploits, in every place you did rove;
Zeus and Poseidon made a copy of the Phaekian's ship offshore of Rithron Cove."[a]

Odyssey, over-joyed with emotion at knowing he has reached home, kneels and kisses the ground. His hands maul the soil. Lifting his arms to the sky, he says:

"Naiads, daughters of Zeus, Spirits of the waters and springs;
You will never know the joy that the sight of your cave brings,

I make heart-felt thanks and prayers to you, and the finest offerings I'll make good;
If Zeus's glorious daughter will grant me life here, and bring my son to manhood."[b]

Athena says:

"Have heart, do not *trouble* with all that, let us find a home for your treasure trove;
Come, follow me to the Nymph's cave, there is a safe place in the sacred alcove."

Athena, the Spirit of Inspiration, sets a stone against the door of the cave hiding its opening. The two sit by the root of the great olive tree and plot the revenge against the Suitors. She says:

"Odyssey, by cunning or might you must overcome this mob;
Or they will kill you, and your estate they will continue to plunder and rob,

For three long years they have courted your wife and consumed your palace;
Noble son of Laertes, how will you destroy these wretched rivals and their malice?

Penelope has encouraged the vying Suitors so as to not give offence;
But she has remained faithful whilst suffering twenty years your absence."

---

a   About 150 metres off shore in Rithron Cove is a rocky islet which looks remarkably like a ship. Today it is known as Sock Island.

b   Telemakis is not quite 21 years of age.

Odyssey answers:

"I'm glad for your warning, for Agamemnon and I might have shared the same fate;
And bled to death in our own homes, if a woman's betrayal lay in wait,

Let's devise a plan so I can rid the Suitors once and for all;
Stand by my side and put your courage into my heart so against them I can stand tall,

Just like that day when we knocked Troy's crown from her fair brow;
I could defeat the Three Hundred,[203] if you will be by my side now."

Athena says:

"I'll not forget you when the time comes, trust me!
There will be blood and gore awash in your palace, you'll see,

First, you'll be disguised so that no mortal can recognise you;
Your head of red hair must be bald, and your skin wrinkled too,

I'll clothe you in rags that even a beggar would not wear;
And as for your eyes, I'll dim them so they look lifeless and won't scare,

Even your wife, and the son you left behind, will have not a clue;
First, go to your loyal friend the hog-handler, who raises the palace's pigs for you,

You'll find him at his farm, by *Raven's Rock*,[a] close to the well of Arethusa;[b]
There he fattens the hogs and sows with acorns, and the spring's sweet water,

---

a   Also known today as *Korax* Rock.
b   Arethusa Well still drips pure water and can be reached after a twenty minute walk from the Vathy Road.

Stay with him and find out everything he knows about life in your palace;
And I'll go to Sparta and talk to your dear son, who is staying with Menelaos."

Odyssey says:

"Wise one, why don't you just tell him that I'm alive at home, where we both belong;
And stop him from roaming like his foolish father, while others do his estate wrong."

Athena answers:

"Never mind about your son, I went with him so his confidence would be stronger;
He is safe from the *trouble* that was sent for you, he can stay there a little longer,

The Suitors have other thoughts, they will try to ambush him near Asteris;[a]
But will not succeed, for they are marked for death: Telemakis is not at risk!"

As she speaks, Athena touches Odyssey with her wand. He is suddenly covered with wrinkles, his auburn hair has gone; he is bald, his eyes are bleary and deep-set. He is dressed in rags, filthy and tattered having a smoky stench. Draping from his shoulders is a rotten deer-hide and a beggar's frayed knapsack. Finally she gives him a walking stick.

Having made their plans, Odyssey starts the long walk to Eumaios' hut.

*

The Spirit vanishes to Sparta to fetch Telemakis.

*

---

a   Asteris Islet is today known as Ligia or Pera Pagadi. This tiny island is overlooked by Arethusa's Well and Raven's Rock, near the site of Eumaios' piggery. Close by is Eumaios' Cave, a curious refuge for adventurers.

EPISODE FOURTEEN

ODYSSEY AND EUMAIOS

Odyssey walks south from the Nymph's cavern along a rising track through the forest. He reaches the ridge line of Mount Nerovoulo.[a] He stops at the place called Merovigla and looks back toward the cavern and Rithron Cove. He can see the three bays lying below, opposite Mount Neriton: Molos, Skinos and Phortune.

He can see, just off the shore-line of Phortune Harbour's port, the tiny islet of Lazareto.[204] From where he stands he can also see his palace,[b] lying above the thin wrist of land which holds Ithaki's two halves together. He wonders what is going on there. Above, to the west, atop Mount Aetos he sees the Temple of Apollo[c] in all its splendour. He knows he is home.

He rushes on, over the ridge-line to an open, stony plain and there, in the distance, he sees Eumaios' pig farm. Eumaios[205] is his most loyal worker and has served his master's estate for many years. His father, Ktesios, son of Ormenos, was king of the island of Syros.[d]

When he was a young child a Phoenician trader seduced his nurse, a slave, who agreed to deliver him, with other stolen treasures, in exchange for her escape and freedom. The nurse was killed on the voyage, but the slavers continued to Ithaki where Odyssey's father, Laertes, adopted him. From then on he was brought up with Odyssey and his sister Ctimene, and was treated by Antikleia,[206] their mother, as a son and an equal brother.

Eumaios, despite his heritage, is a modest man. He sits at the gate of his farm, in front of the stone-walled holding pens he built himself, and sometimes with the help of Laertes, Odyssey's father, who used to visit him when his wife was alive. The pens are large and comfortable for the pigs. Around the pens is a run so that they can be moved easily. A thick hedge of wild Prickly Pear borders the pens and protects the pigs from wind, rain and shades the Sun.

Outside the pens he built a yard. It has a strong fence of oak posts, split and spaced evenly. Inside he built twelve enormous sties for the sows to nurse their

---

a   The highest mountain on the southern half of the island at 669 metres.
b   The ruins of the palace are today known as Alalkomenes near Aetos, Ithaki
c   The ruins of the temple may be visited after a steep climb to the summit of Mount Aetos. The views and the "Cyclopean" masonry walls erected 300 metres on the mountain's side are astounding.
d   The island of Syros, located in the Cyclades group of Islands, in the Aegean Sea.

piglets. There are fifty breeding sows in each sty. The boars live in the holding pens, but now their numbers are fewer for the Suitors keep demanding more for their daily feasts.

There are only three-hundred-and-sixty boars remaining. Eumaios' four hounds, fierce as wolves, roam around the farm guarding the pigs.

Eumaios is busy, cutting up some dried ox-hide to fashion into sandals. Three of his men are out herding pigs into pens. His other worker is delivering a boar to the palace for the nightly feast.

The hounds see Odyssey, bark and run at him. Cunning Odyssey sits down and drops his walking-stick, so that the dogs won't attack. Even so, without the help of Eumaios he'd have been torn to pieces. He drops his leather work and whilst pelting stones at the dogs and cursing, he races toward Odyssey, yelling to him:

"Old man, these dogs would have made mince-meat of you;

And that would have landed me in a lot of *trouble* too,

The Invisibles have given me enough to worry about, without your safety as well;

For I am grieved, I've lost the best master a man could enjoy, to Hades' hell,

Here, I have to breed hogs for the free-loaders, to gorge and feast;

While my master starves in some distant land, who knows, west or east,

Now, come inside and have your fill of pork and bread;

Then tell me about your hardships, and where you were bred."

The swine-handler led the way into his hut. He scoops up a thick pile of laurel leaves and lays a shaggy goat skin over it. A most comfortable seat. Odyssey sits. He is pleased at being made so welcome, and says:

"Sir, may Zeus, and the rest of the gods, grant your heart's desire;

In return for your kindness. Do you do this for every stranger?"

Eumaios answers:

"It would be wrong to send any stranger away;

Many poorer men than you, have come here before today,

Kings and beggars are all sent from Zeus, for we must aid all those in need;

I should be thankful that he sends them to me, for I can help in thought, and in deed,

We must take what we are given, no point thinking we can change our fate;

But I would dearly love to see the return of my master, before it gets too late,

For the Olympians have hindered his home-coming, if he still has a life;

He'd have looked after me, with a pension, some land with a cottage, and a wife,

And everything else that a good and honest master would provide;

To a loyal servant that has worked all his life, but I must face it, long ago he died,

If only he'd lived and grown old here, instead of dying on a strange shore in a hostile war;

And, whose to blame? Helen of Sparta of course. Many a good man died for that whore,

For it was my master that was urged to fight for her foolish husband's pride;

So he sailed to Troy, twenty long years ago, and since I've seen nothing of him, hair or hide."

Eumaios stands, tucks his jacket into his belt and goes out to the sties. He kills two suckling piglets and returns. He singes their hair on the fire and butchers them, cutting the flesh into small pieces. Next, he skewers and cooks them on the embers. Now cooked, he sets the hot meal in front of Odyssey. Then he mellows some wine in a cup of olive-wood. He sits opposite Odyssey and encourages him to eat, saying:

"Stranger, dine with me on these small suckling piglets, it's all I can spare;

As the fat boars go to the gluttons in the palace, for their evening fare,

In my master's time his palace was the envy of every city;

Now it is mocked across the world, with shame and pity,

The Suitors don't care about the shameful things that go on there;

But the reckoning day will come. Even as to god-less pirates who pillage without a care,

For Zeus, Mind, allows them spoils, and also their share of regret, guilt and more;

Conscience haunts them, as they wait nervously for the Invisibles to settle the score,

The Suitors must realise their arrogance won't be tolerated by the Lightning Bolter;

Or, perhaps, some divine rumour reached them telling that my master is no longer?

Yes! That explains why they pretend to court Penelope the Queen;

As an excuse for free-loading on the Royal estate, like you have never seen,

Not a day or night comes from heaven, that a boar - or two - isn't killed;

And the cellar is being drained away, because of the wine that's daily swilled and spilled,

My master was very rich, no-one could match his wealth, monarch or king."

Eumaios begins to tell about the vast herds of cattle, sheep, pigs and the many men employed to manage the animals on Ithaki and the mainland. But Odyssey eagerly chews the pork and gulps the wine. His mind is racing. He plans revenge. Eumaios brims his cup with wine again. Odyssey is thankful and gladdened by the loyalty of his long-lost friend and brother.

It's Odyssey's turn:

"My friend, tell me about this powerful and famous man, who was once your master;

You say he perished in the cause of King Agamemnon's Trojan war disaster;

Tell me who he was, just in case I have met him, he may not be a stranger to me;

Heaven knows, I may have news of him, for I have travelled far and wide over land and sea."

Eumaios smiling, answers:

"Old man, Odyssey's wife and son will never believe another traveller's story;

Grifters and fraudsters often come from afar, seeking lodging and glory,

Mouths full of deceptive lies, the queen has listened to them for years;

Desperate for news of her husband's fate, she clings to false hopes, which end in tears,

But what would you expect from a woman who loves him, and has avoided any scandals?

Even you, old man, would exchange one of *your* stories for a fresh jacket, and new sandals,

But why pretend, long ago the wild dogs and vultures picked his carcass clean;

Or, fish ate him up and his bones roll around the deep sea. No, he'll never be seen!

For all who knew him, his death has meant nothing but heartache and strife;

Especially or me, for I'll never have such a master, not in this world, or the after-life,

Even if I go home to my loving mother and father where I was born and bred;

Yes, I am homesick to see them again, but I grieve the most for Odyssey, though he's dead,

He was very fond of me too, and took care of me, our bond could not have been stronger:

I cannot speak more highly of any man, past or present, even though he is here no longer."

242

Patient Odyssey, now says:

"My good friend, you are so positive about your master's peril and his death, as well;

That you won't accept what I have wanted to say. But hear this now, what *I* have to tell,

I now swear on my life that your master is coming, and you'll be the first to see him, too;

And when he sets foot in his own house, then provide me with clothes and sandals, all new,

As you see, I'm in need; new clothes would help me here-after;

But I'll take nothing until you see red-haired Odyssey, your master;

For I detest any man, just like I hate Hades Hell;

Who lets poverty and desperation breed lies, that he should not tell,

I swear by Zeus and the Invisibles, and by the threshold of Odyssey's throne;

What I have said will happen, and to you, your master *again* will be shown,

He will return and avenge those who dishonour his family and friends, very soon;

The palace can expect him between the waning and the waxing of this coming moon."

To this Eumaios answers:

"Old friend, you will never get paid for that bet, or for bringing news, good or bad;

Odyssey is dead and buried, drink in peace and we'll talk of something else, less sad,

As for your oath, forget such thoughts, let's just dream of his return, and the joy;

Of what it would be like for his wife, his old father and Telemakis, his boy,

I am upset about his son too, who was rising into manhood, to be the next king;
A handsome man - much better looking than his father - he went to Pilos, searching,

Someone, god or man, deprived him of his senses, now he's gone to trace his father;
And the devious Suitors will ambush him at Asteris Island, from here, it's not far,

Arcesius' line[207] won't have a male heir, for Telemakis may soon be dead;
Then the kingship of Ithaki will go to one of the Suitors, whom Penelope must wed,

But let us say no more about the perils of young Telemakis;
We should pray that he escapes and returns home, by the kind hand of mighty Zeus,

Now, you old battler, tell me your story, where do you come from, and who are you?
Tell me about your city, king and parents. I know a liar if I see one, so tell me true,

And, what ship did you arrive on? Where was the vessel from, and who were its crew?
What lands have you travelled to in the past? Stranger, I'd like to know more about you."

Shrewd Odyssey answers:

"I would tell you all if only there were meat and wine to last a year;
But that would not be long enough for all sorrow and misfortune that you could hear,

However, I am a Cretan by birth, my father was a prosperous and happy man;
With many sons and a dutiful wife, but I was born a bastard to his concubine,

Anyway, my father, Castor, son of Hylax, adopted me as an equal in his family;
But when Death called him to Hades, his sons divided the estate, without me,

Except for a meagre allowance and a bare plot of worthless land;

But, my good looks and charm won me a well-to-do maiden's heart, and her hand,

Alas, the good times were over long ago, but it wasn't all bad;
From the stubble you now look upon, you can see what a great harvest I've had,

But since then, Ares, the war god, picked me for my combat skills, I had no fear:
I was the first to lead the battle forward, with sword, shield and spear,

Many men were sent to Hades straight from my sword's sharp end;
And as the cowards bolted into the distance, they fell into the dust, from the arrows
I'd send,

No! Farm work was not for me, nor boring chores around the house;
Tending animals and children is for the women; I'm a man, not a mouse,

Give me a ship with a bold crew ready for the fight;
With javelins and lances, Oh! that is a lovely sight,

Most men would tremble at the thought of combat and action;
Each to his own, but from domestic chores, I get no satisfaction,

Long before the Achaeans[208] went to Troy, nine times I was a captain in command;
Of a navy in foreign waters, and I amassed a great fortune from every visited land,

"My estate grew in abundance, and on Crete I became a great man, honoured and
feared;
But it was all short-lived, as from all-seeing Zeus, another campaign appeared,

So many of us perished, for all Cretans were required to invade the Trojan shore;
Idomeneus and me had to lead ships there, where we fought the ten-year war,

When, finally, Priam's gleaming city was destroyed we sailed for my home in Crete;

Then, Zeus, Mind, devised more mischief and disaster for me, it was the fate I had to meet,

I had barely spent one month with my happy children and wife in my own estate,
When I had the idea of making a raid on Egypt, Zeus made it my fate,

So I provisioned the nine ships of the fleet, they were in their prime;
And crews flocked to them for the adventure - some their last - of a lifetime,

For each of the six days before we departed, we celebrated with a feast;
On the seventh, we sailed Boreas' wind,[a] east,

It was plain sailing for the next five days, and then we got to Egypt's river Nile;
We anchored the ships and I sent out scouts to explore for a while,

But the men disobeyed my orders and weakened to their own greed;
They killed men, slaved women and children, and robbed beyond need,

News of the invasion soon carried itself to the city, then came the war-cry sounding;
The huge army assembled at dawn with cavalry and foot soldiers abounding,

When Zeus showed my army the foe's gleaming arms, they left their hearts in the retreat;
The Egyptians killed many of us, and took the rest as slaves, so was our defeat,

I wished I'd have died there too, but Zeus, Mind, gave me an idea which saved my skin;
I took off my helmet and shield, dropped my spear, and went straight up to the King;

He was in a fine chariot and I clasped his knees and kissed his ring, he offered me a ride;

---

a   The Greek god of the North wind.

Pitying me, he spared my life and drove me to his palace, I was weeping for joy,
inside,

Many of his angry soldiers tried to kill me with their ashen lances;
But the King defended me, for he feared Zeus' wrath, for not protecting strangers,

I stayed there for seven years and made a fortune trading with the Egyptian nation;
But in the eighth year I befriended a villainous Phoenician, with a bad reputation,

He persuaded me to sail with him to his home in Phoenicia, and I stayed a year;
Then we sailed to Libya, to take cargo for trading, was what he made clear,

But I suspected he had another plan: to steal my wealth, and, as a slave, sell me;
The Southerly wind pushed our ship far beyond Crete, from the Libyan Sea,

Where the Lightning Bolter wanted to even the score;
And raised a black storm, with galing winds, steep seas and more,

By letting fly with his lightning bolts, the ship went round and round, fast;
Fire filled the cabins and the brimstone[a] exploded into flames higher than the mast,

The whole crew jumped into the sea, bobbing up and down, like drifting sea kites;
For a while. But Zeus, put a swift end to them; their watery grave had no last rites,

Incredibly, Zeus took pity on me and thrust into my arms the mast of that ship;
For ten dark days I clung to it, as the angry seas tossed me along that water-logged
trip,

Then a great wave beached me on the Thesprotian[209] coast;
There Phaedon, the King, entertained me; *he* is a wonderful host,

---

a   Brimstone is sulphur, which burns fiercely.

His son was walking the beach that day, when he found me half dead;

And carried me to his father's house, gave me clothes and sandals to wear, and a warm bed,

It was there that I heard news of Odyssey, for he had been there too, the king did tell;

Who entertained him with such hospitality that it was hard for him to say farewell,

He showed me the treasure that Odyssey had given him for safe-keeping;

Enough to keep a family for ten generations, is what he kept saying,

He also said that Odyssey was curious to learn more about his destiny;

So he went to Dodoni to listen to the rustling leaves of the Oracle's oak tree,[a]

He wished to ask the Oracle if it was safe to return to Ithaki;

And if he should go back there - in disguise - or openly?

And the King made a solemn oath, with libations, in front of me;

That a ship was in the harbour ready to ferry Odyssey to the island of Ithaki,

Before Odyssey returned, Phaeton sent me off in a grain ship, Kefalonia[210] bound;

And he told his captain to look after me until we got there, and King Acastus[211] was found,

But, as Zeus, Mind, would have it, the crew hatched a plot against me;

Again life's bitter blows reduced me to unrivalled misery,

For when the ship had gone over the horizon, they took me as their slave to sell;

Stripped off my shirt, jacket and sandals, and gave me these rags in which I dwell,

---

a   This ancient site lies close to the modern city of Ioannina, in Epirus, Greece. In ancient Greece, priestesses and priests in the sacred grove interpreted the rustling of the oak (or beech) leaves to determine the correct actions to be taken. According to a new interpretation, the sounds originated from bronze objects hanging from oak branches and sounded with the wind blowing, similar to a wind chime, and were interpreted by the oracles. The Cyclopean Walls of the sanctuary are of an impressive scale.

As night fell, we could see the outline of Ithaki's rugged landscape;
Then they tied me to the rowing benches so I could not escape,

And while they went ashore to make their dinner on the beach;
I untied the ropes, wrapped these rags around my head, and swam out of reach;

They couldn't find me, for I was invisible, hiding in a forest thicket;
They were very angry and went back to the ship, darkness made them quit,

It was not my time to die, the gods had a hand in it, that's for sure;
And that is how, my good friend, I came to arrive at your door."

The swine-handler's turn:

"Poor friend, I have found the tale of your misfortunes curious, indeed;
For it reminds me of my own story, for I was sold by slavers, and also freed,

But about Odyssey you are plainly amiss, of my master the gods despised;
I'll never believe that he lives, he's dead! Why should a man like you tell me lies?

He wasn't killed in battle at Troy, or even after that wretched war's finishing;
For then the Achaeans would have built a memorial over his tomb, fit for a hero king,

He is only memories now. The pitiless gods have stripped his son's honour, forever;
Hades has hold of him, and his glory. You want me to believe he's alive? Never!

As for me, I live out here with my pigs, I don't go to town unless Penelope sends word;
Of some traveller coming with news of Odyssey, then I go to listen, to the lies, to be heard,

Then we all sit in court and ask questions, those that grieve and suffer Odyssey's fate;

And the Suitors, too, who rejoice at him being lost or dead, so they can squander his estate,

I lost all interest after a liar from Aetolia[212] came to my farm one day;

He wanted me to believe that he had killed a man there, and ran away,

He, too, had seen Odyssey with Idomeneus in Crete, fixing ships which had been in a storm;

He said Odyssey would return - bringing treasure - in the following Autumn,

And now the gods send you, a pitiful old man, to upset me with false hopes, too!

I should kick you out, but I respect Zeus, the god of guests, and I do pity you."

Artful Odyssey, smiling to himself, answers:

"I see that you look for *trouble,* where truth is;

I gave you my solemn word, what's wrong with my promise?

Again, let's make a bargain, and call all the gods of heaven, as my witness;

If Odyssey comes, as said, then send me to Dulichium[a] with cloak and shirt of your best,

But if he doesn't come, as I have made in my gravest pledge;

Then you and your men can throw me off Raven Rock's cliff edge,

As a dire warning to rogues that come here to your sties;

Don't try to deceive an Ithakan, by telling groundless lies."

Eumaios, vexed by Odyssey's taunts says, sarcastically:

---

a   Dulichium is an island, west of Ithaki, close to the mainland, although a new theory suggests it may have been the northern or southern part of the island of Ithaki.

"And a great reputation I would have, such honour and glory, now and forever more;

And Zeus wouldn't be offended, either, if I was to murder a visitor who comes to my door!"[a]

It is dinner time. Eumaios rises and walks into his hut. He starts to prepare a meal for his men. They hear the pigs being driven along the paths to their pens. They are squealing and grunting as they race toward the fodder laid out in each feed stall. They fight for the best position and gorge the corn kernels, grains and hay. Eumaios yells out to them:

Men, bring that old long-tusked boar which remains, the ugliest;

I'll kill it, for we have an extra mouth to feed, Zeus has sent us a guest,

Only Zeus - Mind - knows how many years we raised and cared for that beast;

Why send it to the palace for the drunken Suitors to feast?"

He sharpens his axe and chops firewood. The fire builds. The others drag the huge five-year-old boar to the hearth. Eumaios, ever respectful, begs the gods to one day return his beloved master to his home-land, or at least inform him of Odyssey's fate. He plucks a handful of bristles from the animal's snout and throws them into the fizzing fire. With the ceremony complete, he clubs the boar with a length of oak-wood. It drops to the floor, dead. The men butcher it. Eumaios cuts out the bones and wraps them in two layers of fat and offers it to the Invisibles by tossing it into the fire.

Some of the meat is spiked and placed on the embers to grill. They roll the joints in layers of fat and sprinkle them with barley meal, so they won't burn, and lay the cuts on the embers to cook slowly. The spiked meat sears and cooks quickly. Ready to be eaten, unstinting Eumaios divides the meal into seven portions, one is set aside for Hermes, the son of Maia,[213] and the Nymphs, offering thanks for the generosity of the gods for the favourable thoughts they provide.

Eumaios serves each man, thanking them for being there to share with him. For the guest, he gives the choicest loin slices.

Odyssey, now much pleased to be in the company of his true friend, says:

"I trust, Eumaios, that All-seeing Zeus will look upon you just as kindly;

For it is noble to be gracious, in thought and deed, to a man like me."

---

a   This remark is regarded as the first use of sarcasm in Western literature.

Eumaios replies:

"Eat up my good man, enjoy your supper, as modest as it is;

It is not me, but Zeus, Mind, that gives and takes anything he chooses."

As he speaks he burns another piece of pork as sacrifice to the Lightning Bolter. He tips some wine onto the floor as an offering and pours more into Odyssey's cup. He sits at Odyssey's side, as is the custom when guests dine.

Their bread is brought by Mesaulius.[214] He was saved from slavery by Eumaios who had taken pity on him and paid a Taphian trader, from his savings, during Odyssey's twenty year absence. Eumaios acted alone, and did not seek help from Laertes and Penelope, such is his kindly way.

They all began to eat and drink to their fill. Mesaulius clears what is left over. They prepare for bed.

The night is stormy. The moon hides from the cold. Rain pelts. Wind zephyrs hard from the West. Zeus cracks lightning bolts above the hut.

Odyssey thinks he will further test Eumaios' limit of generosity. Would he give up his cloak on such a cold night? Or, maybe he'll ask one of his men to oblige. He says:

"Eumaios, and friends, I've had more than my share of wine tonight;

And its made me boastful of when I was in Troy, on another cold night,

Wine to excess makes any brain boggle and brag, which ends in regret;

Even the wisest of men do - and say - what they should always forget,

But, as I've now started it would be wrong not to settle your curiosity;

When I was a warrior, young and strong, we set up an ambush near Ilium, Priam's city,

I was in command, Menelaos and Odyssey were the leaders, too;

When we were close to the city walls, under cover of the marshes, and out of view,

The frost chilled our bones and the north wind was the coldest ever sent by Boreas;
We wore our shields like hats and they were high with the snow that covered us,

All the others had woollen jackets, even so, the cruel cold kept them awake;
But I, like a fool, had left my jacket behind, and began to shiver and shake,

I laid there watching the stars, until the third watch, when I nudged cunning Odyssey;
Who was close to my frozen elbow, and he asked what was wrong with me,

Odyssey, this cold will kill me, for I have no jacket to wear, my life is lost;
Some Invisible fooled me into setting out in my shorts, now I'm bitten by frost,

Odyssey said to me, keep quiet, or the others will hear your plight;
Then he raised his head and said to the men, I've had a dream sent by Heaven, this night,

We are a long way from the ships and will need more men for battle, tomorrow;
One of you take flight and return soon, or our lives will be remembered in sorrow,

Then, Thoas,[215] son of Andraemon,[216] dropped his jacket and ran off to warn Agamemnon;
So, I took it, put it on and lay cosy and snug until the light of Dawn,

If Odyssey was here *I* wouldn't go cold, a blanket *he'd* provide - Zeus knows!
He had respect for age and bravery, but here I'm loathed, because of my clothes."

Eumaios answers:

"Old man, friend and brother in suffering, what you have said to us is true;
So here's a jacket to protect you from the bitter night, that, as a guest, you are surely due,

But tomorrow morning you'll have to wear those rags you brought along,

For we have no spare clothes here, each man has only one,

If Odyssey's son comes home soon, he'll give you what you need;

Cloak, shirts and sandals, and he'll send you wherever, with god-speed."

Eumaios rises then makes a bed for Odyssey. He places goat hides and then thick lambskins on the floor in front of the fire's hearth. Odyssey lays down, and Eumaios covers him with his only heavy woollen jacket that he keeps for very cold, wild weather.

Soon Odyssey falls asleep, his deceptions have exhausted his mind. Around him the young working men sleep. Eumaios, however, thinking of the frightened pigs, puts on a coat and a thick goat fleece to keep out the wind and rain. He slings his sword over his shoulder. He takes his lance in hand. His pigs may need protection from poachers and wild dogs who stalk under the cover of wild storms. He walks into the blasting North wind to huddle with the pigs until Dawn, in a sheltered corner of the pens.

Odyssey has a true ally that he is proud of; his adopted brother, his most loyal friend.

*

ATHENA AND TELEMAKIS

*

TELEMAKIS AND THE SOOTHSAYER[a]

*

TELEMAKIS RETURNS

Athena is in the fertile plains of Sparta speeding to Menelaos' estate, to tell brave-hearted Telemakis that he must return home at once.

He and Pisistratus are sleeping in the forecourt of Menelaos's palace. Pisistratus is fast asleep. But Telemakis lies there, thinking. His mind is vexed over the fate of his father. Athena, Inspiration, goes to him and says:

"Telemakis, you should go to Ithaki your island home, today;

There are dangerous people in your house, wasting your estate away,

Return now or there will be nought left to save, do you realise what you are abandoning?

And this mission will yield for you a fool's reputation, don't you wish to be Ithaki's King?

---

a   The word, *soothsayer* derives from: *Zeus* and *sayer*; a person who can predict the outcome of an event or the future.

Ask Menelaos to send you home if you wish to find your mother freed from vice;
Her family urge her to marry Eurymachos,[217] who overbids the highest bride-price,

You should hope that nothing precious farewells your estate too;
For women always want the best for a husband, who'll take priority over you,

That is if you have a home to go back to, it might be too late;
Go home, and put everything right, leave now, don't hesitate!

When you get there, go to the most trusted house-maid with whom you can confide;
And all your treasures you wish to keep, have her hide, until you find a bride,

Now, another matter, the Suitors are ready to ambush you near Asteris;
But will not succeed, for *they* are marked for death: Telemakis you are not at risk!"

Your guardian god will direct the breezes you'll need to find your home-land;
Sail day and night north following the mainland's coast, and pass by Oxeia Island,[218]

Then point due west to Ithaki's coast, there - you alone - get off at Pera Pigadi Bay;
As for your crew, send them north passing Asteris Island, that's where the Suitors will lay,

I will send a thick mist to blind the murderers' sight, which will hasten their disaster;
Tell your men to sail into Molos Bay, in Neriton's lee, they'll find Phortune Harbour,

You take the track leading up to Raven's Rock, Arethusa's Well is not far away;
Continue 'til you see Eumaios' hut, he'll be there tending pigs as he does everyday;

You know he loves you like a son, so keep him company for the night;
Next day, send him to your mother to tell you're back from Pilos, and everything is alright."

Athena vanishes, returning to Olympos. Telemakis stirs Pisistratus with a toe to the ribs, saying:

> "Wake up Pisistratus, to the chariot and harness the horses;
>
> For we must make for Ithaki now, over land and waters."

Pisistratus protests:

> "No matter, what's the hurry? We can't drive in the dark;
>
> Dawn can't be seen yet, why the haste to embark?
>
> Menelaos has presents to fill the chariot for us;
>
> And let him say good-bye as a host does in kindness,
>
> One never forgets a heart-felt send off, so let's wait a while."

With that Dawn sat upon her morning throne and shone a golden smile.

As he spoke Menelaos, who had already risen from Helen's bed, walks toward them noticing Telemakis dressing himself hurriedly.

Telemakis says to him:

> "Menelaos, courageous spearman, I think it's a good idea for me to leave here;
>
> For when I get back to Ithaki, *trouble* will be there, and the Suitors have plans for me, I fear."

Menelaos answers:

> "Telemakis, if you insist, go if you wish, I won't detain you any longer;
>
> I disapprove of any host who is too kind, or not kind enough, to any visitor,
>
> Moderation should prevail, it would offend if I asked you too leave too soon;
>
> And to detain a beloved guest who is anxious to go in order to avoid his ruin,

One should treat a guest well, for as long as he can stay;

And when it does come time, give him his leave and speed him away,

But, hold your horses, in your chariot I have fine gifts to load and stack;

And I'll ask the kitchen to make a banquet for us all to enjoy, before you go back,

It is a great privilege to travel the world on such a long quest;

But don't go on an empty stomach you won't get far, come to the dining hall, that's best!

Perhaps you might like to see the sights of Hellas, or the Peloponnese;

In that case I'll harness my horses too, and give you a tour of their best cities,

We won't return empty handed, I'm well known in those places;

You can count on our hosts for bronze tripods, statues, and gold cups by the cases."

Telemakis is impatient:

"Menelaos, mighty King and host, my property is at risk, I must go now;

The estate is under siege; the Suitors press my mother for her wedding vow."

When Menelaos hears this he tells Helen to order the servants to prepare a meal in the dining hall, immediately. Eteoneus, his man-servant, joins him in the palace courtyard. Menelaos asks him to light the fire quickly, and cook some meat. Menelaos goes down into the basement's treasure vault, with Helen and his son Megapenthes. He picks a double-handled cup and Megapenthes chooses a silver mixing bowl as gifts.

Meanwhile, Helen goes into the cedar-scented linen room to a chest where she keeps her most beautiful clothes, most made by her own hands. She takes the boldest dress,[a] which has been hidden, for safe keeping, at the very bottom of the chest. It is embroidered with gemstones and glitters like the stars.

They go upstairs through the house to Telemakis. Menelaos says:

---

a   Some suggest that this robe was her wedding dress when she married Paris of Troy.

"Telemakis, may Zeus, Xenia's Minder, make your home safe as you grow old;

And take with you the most precious piece in all my household,

It is a mixing bowl by Hephaestos' hand, of pure silver, gold inlay and rim;

Phaedimus, King of the Sidons,[a] gave it to me when I last visited him."

Into Telemakis' hands he places the mixing bowl and the double-handled gold cup. Helen is standing by. She moves forward to hand him the robe, saying:

"Young man, have something coming from the hand of Helen of Sparta;[b]

For it is a gift for *your* bride to wear on her wedding day, and thereafter,

Let your mother have it, until you find a deserving woman;

And I too wish you a joyful, safe return to your home-land."

She gives him the robe. He thanks her gladly, but thinks of his distressed mother, Penelope, whose wedding hand is being pursued by the Suitors. Perhaps, this might be her wedding dress.

Pisistratus packs the presents into the chariot. His eyes are alight with envy as he admires them. Menelaos takes Telemakis and Pisistratus into the palace and they sit at the dining table. A maid brings them water in a gold jug. She pours it into a silver basin and they wash their hands. She draws a table close for another servant to place a platter of breads and savoury tit-bits. Eteoneus carves the meat and serves their portions, while Megapenthes pours the mellowed wine.

They satisfy their hunger and then move to the chariot. Menelaos comes after them with a gold wine goblet to make a libation to the safety of the princes returning to their homes. He stands in front of the straining horses and pours the breakfast beer onto the ground, saying:

"Farewell, my beloved princes, give my best greetings to brave Nestor;

He was as kind to me as any father, when we fought together in the Trojan War."

---

a   Sidon was a port in the western end of the Mediterranean Sea, now part of Lebanon.
b   Another Homeric irony as it comes from the hand of Helen of *Troy.*

Respectful as ever, Telemakis answers:

"Of course, Sir! We will tell him everything as soon as we see him, certainly;
And I wish I could be as positive of finding my father returned back to Ithaki,

That I might tell him about the kindness you have shown to us;
And of the many presents you have given to me; you are very generous."

Whilst he speaks an eagle flies over his right shoulder and straight up into the sky. In its talons is a large, white goose which has been plucked up from the palace's courtyard. The servants run after it shouting. It circles back, swooping past Telemakis, from the right. The horses are startled and the crowd's spirits are lifted at seeing such a sight.

Prince Pisistratus speaks first, asking:

"Menelaos, leader of men, was this sent from heaven?
What does it mean? Is it for you, or us? Is it an omen?

Menelaos thinks of the most prudent answer, but Helen is quicker to reply, on his behalf:

"I will tell this matter as Zeus, Mind, has intended it to be read;
I can say with all my heart, this is not a bad omen, but one you'll like instead,

Eagles come from mountains afar, where they breed and have their nests;
And that bird of prey snatched up the goose, being fattened for our family and guests,

Just like Odyssey who travelled far from his home, through great suffering;
So he will return to take revenge on the Suitors, and again wear the crown of a king,

Or, perhaps already he has arrived home and is rejoicing, safe and well;
And planning *trouble* for the Suitors, that will see them all in Hades' Hell."

Telemakis is overjoyed, and says thankfully to Helen:

"May Zeus, Mind, grant that what you foretell, shall come to be;

And I shall honour you as much as all the gods of Heaven, when I get home to Ithaki."

As he speaks he lashes his horses and they burst through the inner gateway and under the echoing portico of the outer court, through the town and into the open plains. They gallop until sunset, reach Therae, where Diocles lives[a] who was son of Ortilochus, the son of Alpheus. There they stay the night and are well treated.

When Dawn arrives, they go, driving out through the inner gateway and under the thundering gatehouse. Pisistratus lashes his horses, not holding back with the whip. Sweat streams from their withers as they race towards Nestor's Pilos palace.

Telemakis says:

"Pisistratus, I hope you will promise to do what I ask of you;

We are both the same age as was our fathers when they met, too,

And this journey has made us closer than friends, you are more like a brother;

So, avoid Nestor's Palace and take me straight to my ship, in the harbour,

For if I go back to your father's home now for more hospitality;

His enthusiasm for banquets, speeches and talk, will further delay me,

I would be biting my tongue and chafing at the bit to get to the ship's bow;

You must allow me to go straight for home, so let's go to the *Sea Quest* now!"

Pisistratus considers what has been said. He agrees with Telemakis and reins the horses toward the port. They arrive at the blue-eyed *Sea Quest* and stack Menelaos' gifts in the ship's aft lockers. He says:

---

a   In the Kalamata district of the southern Peloponnese peninsula of mainland Greece.

"Go aboard and muster the crew before I get home and tell my father;

You know how unyielding he is, he won't let you go, he'll be angry and in a bother,

I'm sure he'll come down here to get you in person;

And won't go home without you, then your delay will worsen."

After he farewells Telemakis, he steers the horses to the palace, hoping he has time time to get underway before his father realises they have returned from Sparta.

Telemakis, anxious to embark, calls out to the men, and orders:

"Men get everything on board, make haste;

We must sail for Ithaki now, we have no time to waste."

*

The men go aboard and prepare the rigging, and set the oars in the rowlocks, ready to row windward. But, just as Telemakis finishes his prayers to Athena and prepares to launch, Theoklymenos,[219] approaches the ship. He is a fugitive and on the run for killing a man whose family seeks revenge. They have pursued him to Pilos.

He is an oracle, descended from Melampus who once lived in Pilos, the best sheep-breeding land in the world. Melampus was very rich, owning a prized estate. The King of Pilos, then, was Neleus, Nestor's father and Pisistratus' grandfather.

Neleus had a daughter, Pero,[220] whose beauty attracted many Suitors. Melampus wished to win her hand to give to his brother as a bride. However, Neleus refused to allow a marriage unless a bride-price was paid: Melampus had to recover the cattle stolen from Neleus, by Iphikles.[221]

The agreement provided that Melampus' estate was turned over to Neleus until he returned with the cattle. The Invisibles had other plans. He was captured by Iphikles' rangers and imprisoned in Phylacus[222] until a prophecy he made came true. It took one year. In prison he suffered depression and had a mental breakdown - at the hands of the Erinyes[223] - from the anguish of his predicament; not only was he furious that he had suffered so much for Pero, a woman he could never marry, but also couldn't accept that as a seer, he did not foresee his own destiny.[a]

---

a   The Erinyes, or the Furies, are a metaphor for the curse of unwanted, persistent thoughts which lead to anxiety and depression.

Iphikles pardoned him and he recovered the cattle and drove them to Neleus in Pilos. He gave Pero to his brother, Bias,[224] as a wedding gift. He then went to Argos, where he ruled as king. He married Iphianeria[225] and had two famous sons: Antiphates and Mantius.

Antiphates became father of Oicleus, and Oicleus of Amphiaraus, who was protected by Zeus and Apollo, but died young, for he was betrayed by his wife Eriphyle and killed in Thebes.

His sons were Alcmaeon and Amphilochus. Mantius, the other son of Melampus, was father to Polypheides and Cleitus. Dawn was so enamoured with Melampus' beauty she fantasised that he was really a god and that they would live together with the other Invisibles on Olympos.

Apollo made Polypheides the greatest soothsayer in the world. He quarrelled with his father and went to Hyperesia,[226] where he remained.

*

And so, his son, Theoklymenos, approaches Telemakis' ship, the *Sea Quest*, just as Telemakis finishes his prayers to Athena and prepares to launch. He is a fugitive, and on the run for killing a man. The slain man's family and friends seek revenge and have pursued him to Pilos. He is an oracle, descended from Melampus. He says to Telemakis:

"Friend I find you preparing for the journey you are about to go on;

As you pray to your gods, I pray to you for truth, who are you and where from?

Tell me about your parents and the port from which you hale;

And why are you leaving sandy Pilos, so quickly, under oar and sail?"

Telemakis says:

"Stranger, I can answer your questions better than any other;

I am from Ithaki, my father is Odyssey, and Penelope is my mother,

I am searching for word of him, in Sparta and Pilos, or wherever the gods send;

If he existed at all, and is not just a myth, then he's found a *troubled* end;

So this ship and its crew are proof of the adventure at hand;

But it's been twenty years since he saw me, or his home-land."

Theoklymenos replies:

"Well, I'm in exile too, and a fugitive on the run, there's a bounty on by head;

For I killed a countryman, and his brothers and friends want me dead,

They have chased me from Argos, I'm a wanted man;

And now that I have reached you, I've run out of land,

I must get away, they are breathing down my neck;

Take me with you now, please allow me to come on deck."

Telemakis replies:

"You are in need, I can't refuse a plea for help, Zeus sent you, and it's my duty;

If you are ready to travel now, then come aboard, for you are on your way to Ithaki,

There we will treat you to hospitality, like no others can;

Make haste, get aboard now, and we'll flee the dead man's clan."

He stows Theoklymenos' spear on the deck and shows him to the helm at the stern where they sit together. Telemakis orders the crew to cast off the mooring lines, and they do as told. They set the mast into the socket of the keel, raise it, and tie it fast to the bow, with the fore-stays and the back-stay.

They hoist the white sails by heaving the halyards of plaited ox hide. The crew take their places on the benches. They pull the oars along their course until Athena's hugging wind bellies out the sails. They make a heading and secure the boom and rudder. The *Sea Quest* plies the blue water and foam flicks her hull.

Heading north, following the mainland's coast, they pass Crouni and Chalcis, then Pheae and Elia, where the Epeans rule.[a]

Sun sets as they pass Oxeia Island. Telemakis points the bow of the ship due west toward the coast of Ithaki. He wonders if they shall escape death at the hands of the ambush party, lying in wait at Asteris Islet.

*

Meanwhile, Odyssey, Eumaios and his men are eating their dinner in the hut. Odyssey is curious to know if the old pig-handler will continue to treat him kindly, and ask him to stay, or give him a send-off to the capital. He taunts his unsuspecting step-brother more, asking:

"Eumaios, and all you men, tomorrow I want to go to the town;

For I am *trouble* to you all, you must be tired of me, am I getting you down?

Can one of you guide me there, for whilst I'm on this side of the grave, and not too old?

My heart longs to see Ithaki's fabled harbour, for I've heard that: *Phortune favours the bold,*

I will go around the city begging for a cup of water and a crust of bread;

And I'd also like to meet Queen Penelope, to tell her that Odyssey isn't dead,

Perhaps, while I'm in the palace, I'd like to visit these men you call the Suitors;

I'm sure they will take pity on me, and allow me some of their left-overs,

And they'll employ me for any type of work around the palace, I'm guessing;

I'll make an excellent servant in every way, for I have Hermes' blessing,[b]

He, who favours all men that take pride in their art, and in their occupation;

---

a   From Pilos, the *Sea Quest* courses north along the mainland's coast.
b   Hermes is also a patron to workers and skilled craftsmen. Hermetic thought is the contentment one receives from doing a job well, or completing an "original" work.

But for me, *no-man* is more deserving to be in that palace, even the king of this nation,

I'll show them real help, like the proper way to flame the torches in the fire;
To cook, carve and serve wine - to *quench* them - will be my first desire."

Eumaios is very distressed at what the stranger is saying:

"Who in heaven has put such foolish ideas into your head?
Go near the Suitors and you'll wind up dead,

Their arrogance extends to the heavens, and far beyond;
Trust me brother, of your type of man, they will not be fond,

Their servants are young, well dressed, wearing the proper apparel;
They are groomed, faces shaved and barbered hair, they don't look feral!

And strong, they stand at the Suitors' sides, heavy trays in their arms;
I do not mind if you stay here, any more than the others, I have no qualms,

If Odyssey's son comes home soon, he'll give you what you need;
Cloak, shirts and sandals, and he'll send you wherever, with god-speed."[a]

Odyssey answers:

"I hope Zeus is as good to you, as you are to me;
There is nothing worse than being a beggar, on land or sea,

Being homeless is the worst fate, it's difficult to survive;
For a bellyache forces him to wander and beg, just to stay alive,

---

a   God-speed is the speed of thought, meaning instantaneously.

So, since you press me to stay, and you are sure that I'm not *trouble*;

Whilst we wait for Telemakis, tell me about Odyssey's parents, are they a happy couple?

I'd like to see them too, if you can arrange it so;

Are they still living or among Hades' dead? I'd like to know.

Eumaios replies:

"I can tell you about them, Laertes lives and prays to heaven for a quick end;

For he is so distressed about Odyssey and the death of his wife, his life-long friend,

The anguish for her lost son, sent her to an early tomb;

For Odyssey was her favourite child, and she could not accept his doom,

I was adopted by her and she mothered me, Odyssey and her daughter Ctimeine,[227]

It was hard to bear, watching Antikleia endure such a miserable decline;

Ctimeine[a] was sent to Same, a very high bride-price was paid for her marriage hand;

And I received a good shirt, jacket and a pair of sandals, and taught to live off this land,

But the past is where it belongs and I'm grateful for what I do, and how I live;

I have plenty to drink and eat, and to strangers I can afford to give;

But I miss Penelope's kindness in words and deeds, and her beautiful face;

For the palace has fallen to the Suitors, and now its a treacherous place,

As Penelope's servant it was nice when I visited, and we often dined together;

She was always in a good humour, those were the days that are now lost forever."

---

a   *Ctimene* was married to Eurylochus, who accompanied Odyssey to Troy, but was killed there in war.

Odyssey answers:

"Eumaios, you must have been a very young boy then;
Tell me about your home-land and parents, how were you taken?

Tell me the truth, did your city's invaders come by land, or boats?
Were you kidnapped from your home, or while in the hills tending your goats?

How did you get here, and why Ithaki?
Tell us about your adventures over land and sea."

Eumaios begins...

"Stranger make yourself comfortable, this is your home too;
Drink some wine and listen to how I came to be here, now with you,

These winter nights are long, there's plenty of time to talk and listen;
And there's no need for you to go to bed early, for tomorrow *you* can sleep in,

The others can sleep now, for they make breakfast and tend the hogs before Dawn;
Too little sleep is as bad as too much, so we can stay awake into the early hours of
the morn,

For when a man has suffered much, and been blown around the world;
He can, eventually, overcome his sorrows by letting his memories become unfurled,

You wish to hear my story, as painful as it is?
Then you shall, my friend, so hold your tongue and open your ears,

For my misfortunes are what you are about to hear next;

And, perhaps, someday, someone will write these words on a stone or in a text,

You may have heard of a place called Syros;[228]
It lies north of Apollo's birthplace, the island of Delos,[229]

It's in the middle of a circle of islands known as the Cyclades,[230] in the Aegean seas;
It is fertile and yields cattle, sheep, grapes, wheat and grains, and the best olive trees,

From the bounty of the land the people have a healthy life;
And they live for a very long time, they have no stress, or strife,

But, when, at last the final day comes along, and it's time for each to depart;
They die peacefully in their sleep, for Apollo sends the arrow which stops each heart,

There are two towns on Syros Island, one on the east side, and one west;
My father was the king, and the son of the demi-god Ormenus,[231] his name is Ctesius,

Long ago, sea-merchants came from *Phoenicia*,[a] for they are famous for sailing;
And for their cunning ways, they had a cargo of jewelry and gold for trading,

In my father's palace was a Phoenician woman of great beauty;
Very tall, graceful and an excellent servant, she could do any duty;

One day she was washing clothes in the stream, near their ship in port;
And one of these rogues lusted after her, tempting with jewelry if she would court,

The sailor sweet-talked her and soon enough, seduced her in the ship's hold;
For she could not resist his charms and beauty, so dashing and bold,

---

a   *Phoenicia*, in ancient times, was the region at the eastern end of the Mediterranean. The Phoenicians were the first state-ranked society to make extensive use of alphabets for communication. The Phoenician alphabet is the basis of modern alphabets. By maritime trade, the Phoenicians spread the use of the alphabet and written language throughout the Mediterranean where it was adopted by the Greeks, who in turn transmitted it to the Romans.

But Zeus only reveals Truth, so perhaps she, wanting to go home, saw a way to benefit;

You and I know that *trouble,* always, follows a woman's charm, maybe *she* got affectionate!

Being from Sidon, she told the sailor that her father was the wealthy *Arybabas,*[a]

And that one day, whilst walking home, she was kidnapped by Taphian pirates,

She said the pirates brought her there, and sold her to the King of Siros;

He paid a very high price and she looked after me, his son, for I was Prince Eumaios,

The sailor asked if she'd like to return to Sidon, to her home and family;

And told her they were alive and well; "Of Course!" she said, "I'll go gladly,"

But first the sailor and crew must swear a solemn oath, she'd be returned safe and sound;

And they all should look the other way when she was seen at the stream, or in town,

For if someone became suspicious and her master heard about the affair;

He'd put her in prison, and the sea-merchants would be hanged in the public square,

So they should keep quiet and finish their trading as quick as could be;

Then send word to her, when the ship and crew, were ready to flee,

She agreed to bring as many precious things from the palace as one hand could hold;

And to make it worth their while she'd bring me, the prince, for I was only four years old,

---

a Perhaps her father was a wealthy Phoenician trader, or she may have invented the character to win favours from the slavers and escape her servant life. Here is also an allusion to the ancient story: *Ali Baba and the Forty Thieves (*in, *One Thousand and One Nights).* In that story, Ali Baba is a poor woodcutter who discovers the secret of the thieves' den, entered with the phrase, Open Sesame! The thieves try to kill Ali Baba, but his faithful slave-girl foils their plots. Ali Baba gives his son to her in marriage and keeps the secret of the treasure. That story has a correspondence with Eumaios' life as a child. The story may have been lifted from Homer's *Odyssey.* Food for thought.

I was like a son to her and always stayed by her side in the palace where we did dwell;

She claimed that they'd recoup a fortune for me in any foreign land, for I'd be easy to sell,

So she went back to the palace and waited patiently to hear what they would attend to;

But the mariners were busy trading, and it took a year for the word to come through,

One night they sent a messenger to my father's home, with a cunning ploy;

He brought a gold necklace strung through amber stones, for my mother, as a decoy,

Whilst she and the servants where handing it around, before she paid for it;

The rascal eyed a wink to my nanny, then went to the ship, to further the gambit,[a]

A little later, she took me by the hand and led me toward the front entryway;

As we were leaving she noticed some gold goblets used at lunch, that day,

My father had dined with his friends, he often did, he was a great entertainer;

But now they all had gone to a public debate in the town's amphitheatre,

So she snatched three goblets and hid them in her blouse;

I could not have known better, so, hand in hand, we left the house,

It was dusk as we ran through many a dark backstreet, and alleyway;

Down to the harbour where the Phoenician ship was moored, ready for our getaway,

The kidnappers were ready, hoisted us aboard and rowed 'til the sea was churning;

No time for departing ceremonies or prayers, those Arabs were of pagan learning,

---

a   A gambit is a ruse, a ploy or a trick.

Zeus, sent us a stiff breeze and we got fast away, by their bold artifice;
But on the second day my nanny's heart was stopped by an arrow from Artemis,

She fell, diving like a gannet, head first into the ship's hold;
So the Arab seamen tossed her corpse into the sea, before it could get cold,

A pretty snack for the sharks, the seals and the sea-vultures too;
And I remained howling with anguish, a head-ache for the uneasy crew,

For six days I screamed, red faced, like there was no tomorrow;
No end to my temper tantrums and my inconsolable sorrow,

At the height of one screaming fit, a crewman dangled me over the stern;
By the heels and ready to drop, but he lost heart as the shrieking worsened,

But soon Zeus sent a swift breeze and stirred a favourable current within the seas;
The closest port was Phortune Bay, in Ithaki, which then was ruled by King Laertes,

When we arrived, he bought my freedom from the sea-merchants with a box of
tomatoes;
They were happy to get rid of me, and anxious to go where the west wind blows,

Hardly a princely sum, not much of a ransom, but I've had a good life, all the same;
And that's how I'm here with you brother. Now why don't you tell me *your* name?

Odyssey, amused, answers:

Eumaios, your misfortunes are tragic, clearly you have suffered too;
Zeus did send you bad as well as good, for he granted a good master to you,

His estate provides lots of work, which you enjoy;

And plenty of food and bread from when you were rescued as a boy,

You are lucky! The only abundance I have is the mean streets that I beg upon, as I
must;
We have a lot in common, and time will allow us to tell each other more, I trust."

As Dawn peeks through the curtains, they sleep.

*

In the meantime, Telemakis and his crew are nearing Pera Pigadi Cove.
Quietly they flake the sails, take down the mast and row onto the beach. They notice
that the north side of Asteris Islet is covered in a thick fog.

They drop anchor stones from the stern and tie the bow line to a rock on the
beach. On shore they make a meal and their breakfast beer. Telemakis says, pointing:

"Men, take this ship north - go quietly - as you pass Asteris Island, under that mist;

Go to Phortune Harbour, you all know the way, at Molos Bay, go left, it's west,

Leave me here, for I must go to Eumaios, and inspect that pig farm of mine;

I'll stay there and come to the palace tomorrow, we'll rejoice with pork-meat and
wine."

Then Theoklymenos asks:

"And what, my dear young friend, is to become of me?

Whom of the many lords on this rugged island will provide hospitality?

Or, to your royal mansion should someone be my guide;

And be introduced to your mother and the Suitors. Or should I hide?"

Telemakis replies:

"At any other time, friend, I'd have invited you to our palace;

For I want you to find hospitality there, not malice,

Unfortunately my mother won't see you, she rarely comes out of her room;

She retreats to her chamber with the maids, spending day and night at her weaving loom,

And stay clear of Eurymachos, son of Polybos, he's not your man;

He's popular, and at the moment the highest bidder for my mother's wedding hand,

He's a Suitor, there is one hundred and eight, all vying to take over Ithaki's monarchy;

Zeus, alone, knows whether they'll all meet a bad end, before its time for matrimony."

As he speaks a bird - a sea eagle - swoops from his right. A messenger[a] from the Far Shooter, mighty Apollo.[232] It tears apart a dove in its talons, and feathers waft below to the pebbled beach, between Telemakis and the *Sea Quest*. To this, Theoklymenos, the seer, takes him aside, by the hand, saying:

"Telemakis, that bird was sent by Heaven, some charitable god has spoken;

For it flew from your right, so it must be a very good omen,

It means that your ancestors' line will endure, soon will come the hour;

And the *trouble* you are about to meet with, will bring peace through power."

Telemakis, joyful, answers:

"I hope it proves so, for if it does, you'll be rewarded with gifts, well;

And you will become revered and legendary for the prophecy you tell."

He says to his friend, Peiraeus:[233]

---

a   An observed and recorded astronomical event, a meteor shower, which took place on 28th October, 1207 B.C. confirmed by: Papamarinopoulos, et al (2013). See: Note 232.

"Peiraeus, son of Clytius,[a] on this trip to Pilos you have been most loyal;

Please take Theoklymenos to your home tonight and treat him like a royal."

Peiraeus answers:

"Telemakis, you may stay away with Eumaios, as long as you dare;

And I shall look after our guest, Theoklymenos, with the best of care."

Pieraeus goes aboard. The others follow. They take up their positions. The men untie the moorings and cast off. They point due north, passing Asteris, still shrouded in fog, where the Suitors, in their ship the *Sea Mist*, lie in wait.

Telemakis ties his sandals, and takes his spear in hand. He strides up the steep track leading past Raven's Rock and Arethusa's Well. Eumaios' pig farm is not far away. He will be there, loyal and devoted to his masters - man and beast - day and night.

*

---

a   Clytius and Peiraeus are noblemen residing in Ithaki and friends of Telemakis.

A FATHER MEETS HIS SON

In the hut, Odyssey and Eumaios have lit a fire. They prepare breakfast. The other men are feeding the pigs.

Telemakis arrives and the dogs run toward him. Not barking, but excited, they jump up, licking his face, seeking attention. He pats and talks to each one in turn. There tails wag for joy; he has come to the farm again.

Odyssey, hearing footsteps, but noticing that the dogs are not barking, says to Eumaios:

"Eumaios, I hear footsteps, is that one of your men or a stranger?

The dogs aren't barking, *they are licking his sandals!* And he's not in any danger."

The words are hardly out of his mouth, when Telemakis stands at the door. Eumaios springs to his feet, and the table's bowls are scattered throughout the hut. He strides towards Telemakis. He kisses his head and eyes. Eumaios is beaming with joy, just as any father would, who after 20 years absence of his son who suffered many hardships in some foreign land, could now not be more thrilled at this reunion, so, like his own son, Eumaios embraces and hugs Telemakis. Tears fill his eyes and drench his beard. Softly he says to Telemakis:

"The light of my eyes! Have you really returned, is it you these arms hold this day?

I was sure I'd never see you again when I heard you went to Pilos, on harm's way,

My dearest child, come in, so my happy eyes can see you, I'm amazed!

You don't come to visit your uncle much, are you happier in the palace these days?

Telemakis answers:

"I have come here to see you, and to learn if my mother has wed;
And if the cobwebs have been swept from my father's lonely bed."

Eumaios replies;

"She is in her chamber - not wed yet - and grieving her broken heart;
Her eyes drop tears each day ever since your father and her have been apart."

He takes Telemakis' spear and leans it against the wall. Odyssey rises from his seat in astonishment at seeing his son for the first time in twenty years.

Telemakis responds:

"Stranger, old man, no need to get up, be seated and relax where you are, please sit!
I'm sure there is something else to rest upon around here, and my uncle will bring it."

Odyssey sits. Eumaios makes a pile of sweet-scented laurel leaves and places a lambskin over it. Telemakis sits.

Eumaios brings them a platter of left-overs, cold meats and bread from yesterday.

He mixes and pours beer into the olive-wood cups, and sits facing Odyssey. As soon as they have eaten, Telemakis asks Eumaios:

"Uncle, where is this stranger from? He has said nothing, can he talk?
What captain's ship brought him to Ithaki, I know he didn't walk?"

Eumaios answers:

"My son, I will tell you, as he told me;
He came in a Thesprotian ship, to Ithaki,

He claims he is a Cretan, and that he's *not* a liar!
He's a homeless beggar, and his circumstances are dire,

Once a great adventurer, and now a fugitive;
He's on the run, I took him in, and here is now where he lives,

Perhaps you should take care of him now, I'll hand him over to you;
He wants to help out in the palace, with whatever he thinks he can do."

Telemakis, distressed, says:

"I am dismayed by what you say, how can I take a stranger into our home?
I am inexperienced, how would I defend him against the Suitors, on my own?

And my mother needs all the attention she can get, each and every day;
She's in two minds; should her fidelity persist as long as my father stays away?

Or is it time for her to make the most of the highest bidder's persuasion?
And rid the Suitors siege by making her marriage the next royal occasion,

But as you say, he is a suppliant and deserves our respect, no matter what;
I'll dress him with new clothes and sandals, a two-edged sword, the best I've got,

And I'll send him wherever he'd like to go from here;
But I won't send him to the palace, there *trouble* will be near,

The Suitors, resent anyone else partaking in my hospitality;
This poor man will only experience insults and mockery,

They are looking for a reason to attack anyone, and that distresses me;
For no matter how valiant one man can be, it would be 108-to-1 against victory."

278

Odyssey finally speaks:

"Young man, may I join in? There's a few of questions I'd like to raise;
I am shocked at what I hear about these Suitors, and their high-and-mighty ways,

Will you submit so easily? Or, are your people against you with their disdain?
Or, some oracle's foreboding that dooms your ancestors' bloodline and its reign?

Can't you consult your brothers who may be able to help your quest?
For close family is where you should seek support first, when hard pressed,

If only I was your age, now, with all the experience that's in this old head!
If I was you - or Odyssey himself - and wouldn't kill them, then you can cut it off
instead,

I would be the bane of these Suitors, each and every one;
For I'd rather die fighting in my own palace, than see it overcome,

What crimes they commit and repeat day and night? Its outrageous!
Not only do they get away with the dreadful treatment of visitors and strangers,

But, the maids are molested in every corner of the estate,
They have made it a brothel! Is that the royal palace's fate?

They all feast on wine and food, pretending each is in line for a wedding vow;
They drive the estate into ruin - no end is in sight - do something now!"

Telemakis answers:

"Hear what I can tell, between me and my citizens, there is no enmity;

I am respected by my people, except for the Suitors, they are the enemy,

I can't ask my brothers for help, no matter the quarrel's size, I have not one;
Arceisios sired Laertes who sired Odyssey, and I'm his only son,

Zeus has ordained that each generation has only one son to endure;
Odyssey left me to inherit the throne, but I have not made it secure,

Because of my weakness the estate has fallen into competing hands;
From Kefalonia, Lefkada, Zakynthos and Ithaki, men have formed clans,

They are destroying the estate to gain control and force my mother's hand;
Her choices are to marry one - or reject all - but she won't make a stand,

So they continue to force her to submit by ruining our heritage and estate;
And soon they will - and destroy me too - if Zeus has scripted that fate,

Eumaios, old friend, go to my mother and tell her I've returned safe and sound;
There are many in the palace plotting evil, so tell her only when there is no-one around."

Eumaios understands and says:

"Yes, good idea! As I'm going that way, should I give the message to poor Laertes?
He used to come here, but was always gloomy about Odyssey being lost overseas,

He used to dine with his workers but since you went to Pilos he's grief-stricken;
He sits in his house, not eating or caring, he just wastes away and continues to sicken."

Telemakis answers:

"It is a pity that I can't help my grandfather now, that must be deferred;
If I could have it my way I'd wish my father was here to help me, but that's absurd,

Let our priorities work out as they must and deliver the news, fast;
Then return here without haste and leave Laertes for later, he'll last,

Tell my mother to send the message by her faithful house-keeper, Eurykleia;
But to send the news secretly and at once, for grandfather *will* believe her."

Eumaios puts on his sandals and goes. Athena watches as he strides to town. She stands at the threshold of the hut's door looking glorious and stately. Odyssey sees her, but she is invisible to Telemakis, for gods reveal themselves only to the chosen. The dogs can see her too, but don't bark, instead they run whelping to the back of the farm for they are terrified.

She nods to Odyssey and with her eyebrows, summons him outside. He leaves the hut and stands opposite her, near the main stone wall. She says:

"Odyssey, noble son of Laertes, with a nimble mind you are empowered by Zeus;
It is time to tell your son the truth and make plans for the destruction of the Suitors,

Then go to town, the Suitors' doom is near, leave without delay;
I'll be joining you soon, for I too am anxious for the battle fray."

She touches him with her gold wand. He now appears in a new shirt and tunic with a purple cloak around his shoulders. He is younger with a natural imposing presence. His hair is thick and red, his face bold with a dark, kept beard. She vanishes.

Odyssey goes back into the hut. Telemakis is astounded and turns his eyes away from the bright radiant man, who has the presence of a god.

Telemakis says:

"Stranger, how suddenly you have changed from what you were;
You are dressed differently and your countenance is pure,

Are you a god that Zeus has sent on a revenge quest?
If so, have mercy and I'll make you a sacrifice of gold, the very best."

Odyssey says to him:

"I am not one of the Invisibles, why should you take me so? Rather;
I am the man who has brought you great suffering, I am your father!"

He hugs Telemakis and teardrops fall from his cheek to the ground.
Telemakis does not believe this man, saying:

"You are not my father, but some god taunting me;
So that I will continue suffering in the absence of Odyssey,

No mortal man could make himself old or young instantly;
A moment ago you were old and in rags, a god's work if you ask me."

Odyssey counters:

"My son, don't be so surprised by my return, fate *has* brought me back;
And you have no other father by the name of Odyssey, that is a fact!

It is me! The man who wandered hard and long these twenty past years;
Who has reached his home-land and sees his beloved son through falling tears,

What you were wondering at was Athena's handiwork, for she protects me;
I was a beggar, and now I have regal clothes on my back, as you can see,

The Invisibles who live in heaven only know what is next;
It keeps the world in their control, and mortals like us, vexed!"

Odyssey sits. Telemakis throws his arms around his father and they both weep uncontrollably. They cry out like circling eagles with out-stretched talons watching villagers robbing eggs from their nests below. They sob and whimper for a long time, until Telemakis asks:

"Father, was it your own crew or foreigners that brought you back?

What type of ship was it, for I know you didn't walk, the sea has no track?"

Odyssey replies:

"Son, it was the Phaekians, those great hosts and sailors, who brought me home;

They give escorts to anyone who reaches their shores, and then wish to roam,

They sailed and rowed while I was fast asleep and landed me on Rithron Beach;

They gave me great treasures which I hid in a cave, out of harm's reach,

Now we must conspire toward the doom of the Suitors, the foe!

Give me a list of their names and numbers so that I can know;

Who they are, and by what strategy you and I might slay them;

Or, should we enlist trusted friends on whom we can depend."

To this, Telemakis answers:

"Father, I have heard of your exploits in council and on the battlefield;

But the two of us would have no chance, we'd be forced to yield,

There are not just ten Suitors, add eight after you've multiplied by ten;

There's fifty-two from Dulichium, and they have six servant men,

From Same, twenty-four came, and from the mainland, twenty;

And twelve - all of them well bred and known - come from Ithaki,

Also, there is the servant Medon, a minstrel and two scullery slaves;
The total is at least one hundred and twenty four that we'd have to put in graves,

We might rue the day we engage in combat with the Suitors' resistance;
To overcome them we will need many allies to give assistance."

Odyssey replies:

"I wonder if Athena and Zeus' help will be enough for us to win;
If they are not on our side, we are beaten before we begin,

It matters not what we think, victory or death will be our prize;
We have no choice, we are compelled to do as the Invisibles devise."

Telemakis responds:

"Those you've named are the best allies we could have in peace, and in strife;
For although they live out of sight, their mission is to script life."

Odyssey's turn:

"I hope they'll be joining us too, and as anxious for the battle's fray;
The Suitors' doom might be nearer than we think, if we get our way,

So, you return home early in the morning and mingle with those scumbags;
Later Eumaios will take me there disguised as a beggar, in rags,

If you see them offending me, quell your heart, don't take it personally;
Even if they drag me by the heels from the palace, or throw things at me,

Look on and bear it, just ask them politely to behave as hosts should;
But they won't listen to you, for their excesses beckon ghost-hood,

And I shall give you an eye's blink and a nod, when Athena stirs me;
Then collect all the weaponry and lock them in the armoury,

If, when you are removing the weapons and the Suitors ask;
Say, *'They are grimy from the smoke and soot, the maids are doing a cleaning task,*

Since Odyssey left for Troy, they haven't been cleaned, it's true;
And a god prompted me of something more menacing, too,

If the Suitors disgrace the courting feasts and guests and a drunken quarrel ensues;
The sight of weapons might tempt the men to use them, if it's the will of Zeus.'

"Son, there is a force within gold, bronze and iron that leads men on;
They gain a false mettle, and that arrogance brings their ruin,

But leave one sword and spear apiece, handy, but out of sight;
With two ox-hide shields to snaffle, ready for the fight,

Zeus and Athena will put lulling thoughts into each Suitor's head;
They won't suspect or give it a second care, until they are almost dead,

One more issue: If you are my son and it's my blood your heart does churn;
Let no-one: Laertes, Eumaios, the servants or even Penelope, know of my return,

Of the palace's women and the island's men, you and I shall select those we can trust;
We'll test them all to see who is on our side, and whose hand is against us."

Telemakis replies:

"Father, you will come to know of what stuff I am made, time reveals all;
And you'll find that I can keep my mouth shut too, for I'm not a fool,

But, I think your plan could be better, it will take a long time to find who is loyal;
Whilst the Suitors will be wasting away the palace and your estate, once royal,

Yes, we should prove which of the palace's maids and servants are honest and true;
But I am not in favour of scouting the island looking for men who are faithful to you,

That we can do once the kingdom is back in your command;
We have nothing to fear if Zeus did send a sign that our future is in his hand."

*

Into the night they discuss the best strategies that will bring the Suitors' downfall.

*

Meanwhile, the *Sea Quest* which had brought Telemakis and his crew from Pilos has reached Phortune Bay, Ithaki's harbour. They moor the ship at its dock. Servants unload the cargo and gear. The treasures from Menelaos and Nestor are taken to Clytius' house for safe keeping.

They send a messenger to tell Penelope that Telemakis has returned from Pilos, but was dropped off and has gone into the countryside to visit his farms. He had sent the ship around to deliver the message so that she would not be distressed any further.

The messenger and Eumaios happen to meet, both being on their way to visit Penelope.

When they reach the palace, the messenger blurts out for all to hear:

"Queen Penelope, I am glad to tell you about Telemakis;

Your son is alive! He has returned from sandy Pilos."

Eumaios alarmed at the messenger's indiscretion goes to Penelope and whispers in her ear what Telemakis had told him. With that he turns and walks out of the palace, striding toward his pig farm.

The Suitors are surprised and angry at what has happened. They all leave the banquet hall and assemble in the outer courtyard. Eurymachos, son of Polybos, is the first to speak:

"My friends, it is a grave matter this news of the return of Telemakis;

We had our ambush ship, the *Sea Mist*, and crew waiting for him at Asteris,

Let's send another boat and crew, and find out how he was missed,

Get them to return quickly, for we are going to need every man we can enlist."

Amphinomos[234] turns and looks down into the harbour and points to the *Sea Mist* already moored at the dock. Her crew is busy lowering the mast, flaking the sails and stowing the oars. Laughing, he says to the others in the wolf-pack:

"No need to send a search party by boat, look and see!

Some god has sent your message, they are here, already,

Perhaps the crew slept while the S*ea Quest* passed;

Or, gave chase but could not overtake her, obviously she was too fast."

The Suitors walk down to the beach to meet *Antinoos*,[a] the captain of the *Sea Mist*. While the crew unload the cargo, they escort him back to the courtyard and assemble there again, but this time only four of them attend; the ringleaders of each faction.

Antinoos, son of Eupeithes,[235] speaks first:

---

a   *Antinoos*, in Greek means: against mind; antagonistic.

"Damn the heavens, how did the gods save Telemakis?
We kept scouts on the cliffs all night and day overlooking Asteris,

And only slept when heavy mists blocked our eyes from seeing the strait;
How can we put an end to him, he must not live if our strategy is to become our fate,

Public sentiment is not all on our side, we can't count on every man;
We should move quickly before he calls his countrymen into his private clan,

He will be angry and tell the world we planned his assassination;
And failed! We'll be banished from Ithaki to seek refuge in some other nation,

Let's abduct and murder him somewhere out in the hinterland;
That will force his mother's wedding hand,

And divide all the property between the four of us;
Whoever woos her best will keep the palace,

But if this does not please you, and you wish Telemakis to remain alive;
So that his father's property and estates may survive,

Then, if that's our fate, let's not meet here and waste *his* estate, any longer;
But from our own houses make our courting of Penelope, all the more stronger,

And she can marry the man with the richest wedding-price;
Then our strategies will be fair and free of any vice."

You could hear a pin drop, for all of the four ringleaders are silent.

Amphinomos,[a] stands to speak. He is the son of Nisus, whose father was King of Aretias.[236] He is from the verdant island of Dulichium, adjacent to Ithaki to

---

a   The name, *Amphinomos*, translates to: Going about, both ways or ambivalent.

288

the east. A man of principle and liked by Penelope for his good nature. He says to them:

"My friends, I speak plainly as you all know, so give my honesty your ears;

I don't favour killing Telemakis, it is a heinous thing to die by the hands of peers,

He has noble blood, to kill a prince would need the gods' assent;

Let's consult the oracle of Zeus, to know what prophecy is meant,

Then we shall have a divine mandate: To kill or to prevent;

And I will help you all, no matter what decree is heaven sent."

They all agree, rise and walk into the palace and resume their seats in the banqueting hall.

Penelope enters the hall with her maidservants.

Enraged, she has resolved to confront the Suitors. She knows of the plot against Telemakis, as Medon, her messenger, had overheard the ringleaders' plan to abduct and murder him, and has warned her.

Reaching one of the main pillars in the middle of the room, she stops and draws her glistening veil back from her cheeks, saying to Antinoos:

"Antinoos, you are supposed to set an example, being an aristocrat;

But you are nothing of the kind, only a despicable, conniving rat,

A treacherous madman bent on bringing death to Telemakis;

Who leads others to their ruin by disrespecting even your maker, Zeus,

It is sacrilege for one who has received protection;

Not to offer it back when the time comes to repay that affection,

Don't forget, your father sought refuge in this very house to save his own skin;

He joined the Taphian pirates and raided the Thresprotians, our friends, who were after him,

They'd have butchered him and taken all his wealth, and *your* probate;

If Odyssey hadn't rescued him, made peace and set things straight,

Now you guttle his estate and force me to re-marry against my will;

While plundering my son's inheritance, who you mean to kill,

Great grief you are causing me, and my son;

Stop! And prevent the others too, before more harm is done."

Eurymachos answers:

"Queen Penelope, daughter of Ikarius, don't fret on these terrors of your mind;

No-man, born or not, shall lay *hands* upon your son Telemakis, you will find,

He is like a brother to me, I should protect him from harm, and play my part;

For my spear will be stained with the gushing blood of any *enemy's* heart,

Telemakis is watched over by the Suitors, he has nothing to worry about;

But if the Invisibles have fated his death, there will be no escape route."

He says this to placate her, but in truth his black heart lusts for Telemakis' final hour, for he is one of the ringleaders.

Penelope says nothing and goes upstairs to her chamber. She weeps until Athena puts her mind and heart to sleep.

Evening has come and Eumaios arrives back at the pig farm. Odyssey and his son have butchered a yearling piglet and are preparing dinner. Athena approaches Odyssey, and with a wave of her wand, she disguises him again as the homeless beggar that Eumaios knows. He is clad in rags and his appearance is bedraggled. It is better that Eumaios does not know of Odyssey's return for he might run back to Penelope and give the news.

Telemakis speaks first:

"So, uncle, *you* have returned, but what news do you have of the Suitor's fate?
Are they still out by Asteris hoping to ambush me, or did they give up the wait?"

Eumaios, responds:

"I had no time to go down to the port and enquire about the hijack;
My mission was to deliver the news to your mother, and come straight back,

But I did follow a messenger sent by your crew, and he spoke first to the court;
He told your mother - and all those in earshot - that you've returned unhurt,

Come to think of it, as I got to the top of Merovigla Hill and looked back to the harbour;
I did see a ship with armed men coming ashore. Was it the Suitors? I can't be sure."

Telemakis secretly smiles to his father. Each of them sits and enjoys the meal, the wine and the company. Soon pleasant slumber fills their hearts and heads.

*

ODYSSEY AND EUMAIOS GO TO TOWN

*

ODYSSEY'S FRIEND, FAITHFUL ARGOS

*

PENELOPE MEETS THE STRANGER

Dawn spangles the sky with a fresh, pink light.

Telemakis ties his sandals, takes a sturdy well-balanced spear in hand and makes for the palace, saying to Eumaios:

"Old friend, I'm going to town and to my mother to show myself;
For she will weep until her eyes prove I'm alive, and in good health,

As for this *troubled* stranger, take him to beg in the town;
Surely someone there will give bread and water, in exchange for his frown,

This fellow is *trouble*, more than I've ever seen;
If my words make him angry, so be it, but I say what I mean."

Quick-witted Odyssey says:

"Young man, I don't want to stay here, a drifter must always be on the move;

A poor man does better in town than in the country, as I shall prove,

Anyone who avoids a hobo's life, will give him something for pity's sake;

And, I'm old, there is no work remaining in me, for a master to take,

So, let me warm my bones by this fire, while the shadows grow short;

And when noon comes, Eumaios can take me into town, or down to the port,

It's a frosty morning and my clothes are thin, I don't wish to wind up dead;

For it will be a cold walk, and the city is a long way off, as you have said."

Telemakis agrees with a nod. He strides off through the yards towards the palace. He broods over his revenge against the Suitors. He reaches his home and stands his spear against a column in the outer cloister. He crosses the threshold and enters the hall.

His servant maid, Eurykleia is cushioning the dining chairs with lamb fleeces. She screams and runs toward him. The other maids also run to him embracing and kissing his forehead and cheeks.

Penelope, hearing the uproar, leaves her chamber and runs down the stairs. She is a vision of beauty, like Artemis or Aphrodite, hugging him tightly and doling kisses on his cheeks and eyes, and says:

"Light of my life, I was sure these tearful eyes would never see you again;

Without my consent, you went looking for your father. Have you seen him, then?"

Telemakis replies:

"Do not scold me, for I have survived a long journey that was dangerous;

Now go with your maids and prepare a petition to Zeus, to damn the Suitors, thus,

And I'll go to the town-square to meet a friend who came back with me from Pilos;

I sent him on with my crew, for Peiraeus to look after him until I returned from Eumaios."

She heeds her son's words and with the maids bathes and changes into her best clothes vowing to make full petitions to Zeus and the Invisibles if they make revenge on these wolves, the Suitors.

Telemakis goes out through the cloisters gathering his spear. His two dogs follow.

Athena has now endowed him with a venerable presence. Those whom he passes marvel at him. He reaches the town square. The Suitors are there and surround him. They have cheerful words in their mouths, but malice in their hearts. He brushes them aside and goes to sit with Mentor, Antiphus, and Halithersos, old friends of his father. They ask him about his excursion to Pilos and Sparta.

Peiraeus comes to them with Theoklymenos, escorting him from his home. Telemakis goes at once and joins them. Peiraeus is first to speak:

"Telemakis, I wish you would send some of your maids to my house;

To take away all those presents given to you by Menelaos."

Telemakis responds, saying:

"No Peiraeus, if the Suitors kill me in the palace, give the gifts to my friends;

It would be better if you get to keep them, than if they fall into the Suitors' hands,

However, if I manage to kill them, there;

I'll send any maid that I can spare."

With these words he takes the travel-worn Theoklymenos to the palace. They go to the baths and undress. The maids wash and massage them with lemon juice and herbal oils. In new clothes they walk to the Grand Hall and take their seats. A maid brings them water in a silver jug. She pours it into a gold basin and they wash their hands. She draws a decorated table close for another servant to place a platter of breads and savoury snacks.

Penelope arrives and is introduced to the suppliant Theoklymenos. She reclines on a lounge near them embroidering a linen table cloth while the men eat and enjoy the food and drinks. When they finish, Penelope, restless, says:

"Telemakis, I'm going to lie on my lonely bed, that's been watered by my tears;
Since the day Odyssey set out for Troy, it has now been twenty years,

But I noticed you did not make it clear if you heard or saw;
Anything of your father, or even if he survived that senseless war."

Telemakis speaks:

"Mother I'll tell you the truth. We sailed to Pilos, and saw Nestor,
He treated me well from the moment I got to his door,

Like I was one of his sons he'd not seen for a long time, but such was my dread;
For, he had not seen or heard of my father, being alive or dead,

So he sent me with his son in a chariot to see Menelaos and Helen in Sparta;
Her wanton ways brought about the Trojan War, and her reputation will persist hereafter,

Menelaos asked me what had brought me there;
And I told him the whole truth, with nothing to spare,

And he said:

'So, these cowards would usurp a brave man's bed, and his estate;
Just as a deer should leave her young in a lion's lair, what a fate?

If Odyssey is half the man he was when he oil-wrestled in Lesbos;
It was the great Philomeleides from the oil-ring he tossed,

What a different place your palace would be;

If those wretched Suitors saw the return of Odyssey,

If he presented himself at the palace at some soon hour;
What a scene, in swift death the Suitors' lives would sorely sour,

Battle dress, bow, arrows and spear;
In that rabble nothing else but deathly fear,

Odyssey, brave and true, god-like and tall;
What a sorry wedding it would be for the Suitors, one and all.'

Mother, I will not conceal a word of what was said to me;
From what Menelaos was told by the Old Man of the Sea.'

Phorgyn,[a] he said, told him that:

'Odyssey the King, whose palace is in Ithaki;
Is a captive of the nymph Kalypso on an island, and sorrows bitterly,

For he has no ship - nor crew - but waits for an escort to take him home;
It is the twentieth year and soon he should be free to roam.'

This was all that Menelaos told me. The gods gave us fair winds and safe carriage;
And I'm very glad to find your hand was not given to a Suitor, for marriage."

With these words Penelope's heart is uplifted; Odyssey may be alive.
Theoklymenos says to her:

"Madam, Telemakis does not understand these things well;
Therefore listen to me, for I am a seer, and I'll not hide what I must tell,

---

a   Phorgyn, the old man of the Sea, is the patron god of the Island of Ithaki. Phortune Harbour is named
    after him

May Zeus be my witness and just as we have shared this table's hospitality;

I promise you that Odyssey is alive and well and walks now, in Ithaki,

He goes around learning of the Suitors' evil deeds and plotting their plight;

For I saw an omen from Asteris beach, that your husband will prevail in a fight."

Penelope responds:

"I hope it proves so, for if it does, you'll be rewarded with gifts, well;

And you will become revered and legendary for the prophecy you tell."

So they spoke. Meanwhile, the Suitors are amusing themselves outside. They throw discs, or spears at a target on the ground in the courtyard while drinking and cajoling each other.

It's time for lunch. Medon, their favourite servant, greets them and as usual they file into the Great Hall, saying to them:

"Now then, my young masters, you've had your sports, now it's time to eat;

Come inside and feast, for food is welcome at noon-time, so take a seat."

They take their usual seats on the chairs and benches. Already they can smell the roasting meats. The servants have slaughtered lambs, goats, pigs and a fat heifer.[a]

Meanwhile, Odyssey and Eumaios are getting ready to walk to town. Eumaios says to his beggar friend:

"Stranger, I suppose you still want to go to town today, as my master said;

I would like you to stay here and help out around the farm, it will be safer I dread,

But I must do what my master orders, or my pay will be a cruel scold;

Let's go while the Sun is high, for later the long shadows will bring bitter cold."

---

a   A heifer is a young cow over one year old that has not produced a calf.

Odyssey responds:

"I know, say no more, let's get going, but do you have a walking stick?

For three legs are better than two, on a road that is stony and slick."

As he speaks he yokes his shoulder with the cord of a shabby, old bag. Euameus hands him a sturdy well-balanced stick. The two leave the farm, the other herdsmen and the dogs. Eumaios leads his bedraggled master along the track to town.

They walk down the steep track and get to the city, reaching a well from which the citizens draw their daily water. This was erected by Odyssey himself, with the help of Neritus,[237] and Polyctor.[238] There is a splendid grove of poplars planted in a circle around it. Clear, cool water cascades from the rocks above. Near the fountain is an altar dedicated to the Naiads, the nymphs which all travellers should pray to for fair blessings.

Here [a]Melanthios,[239] son of Dolios,[240] and two of his helpers are watering his goats, the best of his flock that are now on their way to the Great Hall and the Suitors' bellies.

As he sees Eumaios and Odyssey he insults them, swearing and cursing and making Odyssey angry, saying:

"There you go, what a precious pair you two make;

Hogs of the same leather *do* team together, for heaven's sake!

Master Eumaios, where are you taking this filthy beast?

It would make any one vomit to see such a pig at any feast,

This fellow could only hope to be paid with mockery, what a dead-beat!

Content enough to darken any doorstep and beg for scraps, if he can get to his feet,

Give him to me and I'll extract work from this lazy sod;

He'll start mucking out the sties and feeding the weanlings, by god,

And he could do with fattening himself, he's skin and bone;

---

a   The name, Melanthios, translates to: Bad speech; poor words or curser.

I'll feed him on grains and whey, and a man's body he will own,

But there is no point rescuing this miserable wretch, he's useless;
Happy to scrounge off others, with scraps to fill his pathetic carcass,

Don't let him go near Odyssey's palace, he'll get broken bones and a cracked skull;
The Suitors will throw a gauntlet of footstools, and hurl insults by the earful."

As the bully passes, he kicks Odyssey's backside. But Odyssey stands his ground and doesn't budge. He thinks to smash Melanthios' head with his walking staff, or lift and drop him head first onto the stony track. However, he overcomes his rage and endures the abuse, handing it over to Time,[a] who rights all wrongs.

Eumaios looks straight at Melanthios and chides him, lifting his hands and eyes to heaven, praying:

"Fountain nymphs, children of Zeus, surely as Odyssey made sacrifices to you;
Grant my prayer to bring him home, and to restore respect and honour, anew,

Melianthus, he would soon put an end to your contemptible deeds and words;
In the palace you boast how great you are, whilst your men are ruining your farm and herds."

Melanthios returns the abuse:

"I'm going to send you back to where you came from, tomorrow!
And I'll sell your scrawny hide to a slave-trader for just a single tomato,

As for Odyssey, he can't save you, he's dead or worlds away,
And I wish the Suitors - or Apollo's arrows - will kill Telemakis this very day."

Melanthios leaves and walks quickly away down the track towards the palace, hurling abuse and insults back at the men. Once there, he takes a seat in the

---

a   Time, an allusion to Kronos whose powers are directed through his son, the all-seeing fixer, Zeus.

Great Hall opposite Eurymachos who likes him better than the others do. The servants bring him a portion of pork meat, some bread and wine. Such is the hospitality of Odyssey's palace.

Soon Odyssey and Eumaios arrive and stand in the courtyard. They can hear the festivities inside, Phemios begins to sing and plays a beautiful tune on his famous lyre. Odyssey takes the hog-master's hand, saying:

"Eumaios, Odyssey's palace is a very fine place, to the eye and the ear;

I've travelled the world and have never felt more at home, than here,

There are many fine buildings with a stonewall around the outer court;

The double gates are sturdy and strong, well defended, it's like a fort,

I can hear many people banqueting, and there's the smell of roast meat;

And I hear the sound of music which moves dancers to their feet."

Eumaios says:

"Your senses don't lie, and your wit, as usual, works;

But keep your mind on the job, for within danger lurks,

What is best? Should you go in first, or would that be rude?

Perhaps it's best if I come out to get you as soon as I've felt out the mood."

Odyssey answers:

"Yes, I agree, you go first and leave me here where I am, is best;

I'll be less likely to be attacked outside, than within, I suggest,

Anyway, I'm used to being beaten up and avoiding things thrown at me;

I can take any punishment, for I was hardened on the battlefield and the wild sea,

But there is one thing any man cannot avoid: His desire for respect;

It is like a groaning belly aching to be satisfied, that cannot be checked,

It is what drives men, leading them on to mischief or fortune;

With the right intent, it steers them to fame and glory, wrongly to ruin,

Men go to war and drag each other down, our whole lives we must all suffer;

For it is the gods' order, *'Life is for suffering; enjoy and endure!'*

Here we stand Eumaios with the future at our feet;

Men *must* take the moment when it is served, and refuse defeat."

As they talk, Odyssey notices a dog that has been sleeping on a dung heap. The dog sees Odyssey and raises its nose, pricking his ears. His name is Argos[241] who Odyssey had bred for hunting hares, goats and wild boars. A regal dog in his day, but now he lies neglected on a dung heap in front of the stable, where - as a puppy - he lay when Odyssey departed for the war twenty years ago.

Argos is lousy with fleas. It hurts Odyssey to see him this way. Argos recognises his master and drops his ears and wags his tail. But he can't get up to greet him, his energy is sapped from years of waiting in distress. Odyssey walks to the dog and kneels, stroking it. He flicks a tear from his eye without Eumaios noticing, and says:

"Eumaios, why is a noble dog like this fellow lying here in this mess;

Does he belong to a Suitor? He's no show dog, he looks in great distress."

Eumaios answers:

"Old battler, the owner of this poor dog died long ago, in a far-away kingdom;

This is Odyssey's loyal dog Argos, his pride and joy, for *he* bred him,

His master trained him to have astonishing power and will;

There was no wild animal that he couldn't sniff-out, stalk and kill,

For the last twenty years he has sat here, against this stable door;

For it's the place that he last saw Odyssey, on his way to a fool's war,

He has fallen on hard times - like us all - since Odyssey went away;

The servants new masters are the Suitors, they make the orders, and have the final say,

For Zeus takes half the goodness from men who rule, but have no right to be kings;

And resentment runs deep when servants are forced to the wrong things."

As he speaks Eumaios walks away into the palace.

Odyssey is by the dog's side and with a whimper Argos' head slowly drops and a final smack of his tail brings Death to the loyal dog and his spirit is freed.

*

Telemakis sees Eumaios before anyone else does. He signals for him to sit beside him. He summons a servant to cease serving the Suitors and bring a plate of food for Euameus. The servant does so and brings Eumaios his serving, and a wicker basket of bread.

Odyssey appears, a picture of abject poverty and destitution that only the gods could paint. He's leaning on his staff, his clothes are in tatters. He sits on the floor inside the Great Hall near the double doors. His back is supported by a Cypress column, that was shaped and smoothed by him when he helped build the Great Hall with his father, many years ago.

Telemakis seeing his disguised father, takes a loaf of bread from the tray and says to Eumaios:

"Take this to the stranger and tell him to ask for food from each Suitor host;

For, of all beggars that be, the one who is more bashful, goes hungry the most."

So Eumaios goes to him and says:

"Stranger, Telemakis sends you this, and says you should ask the Suitors for food;

You are a suppliant in the midst of those that can help you, so it won't be rude."

Odyssey answers:

"Friend, may Zeus grant peace to Telemakis;

And fill the desire he aches for, *with happiness*."

Then, with both hands, he takes the bread and lays it on his shoulder bag, now at his feet. He starts to eat while listening to Phemios' song. When the bard finishes, applause breaks out through the dining hall.

Athena, Inspiration, goes to Odyssey and encourages him to beg for pieces of meat from the Suitors. This way he might sort the kind and hospitable from the ruthless. But this does not mean she will save anyone of the them.

Odyssey starts his round, going from table to table, his arms stretched out showing his palms as real beggars do.

Some men pity him, some show disdain and others ask who he is, and where is he from. The goat-herder, Melanthios says:

"Suitors of our noble Queen, I have seen this wretch before;

Eumaios brought him here, but I don't know why, or what for."

Antinoos, the antagonistic ringleader, starts to abuse Eumaios as he springs from his chair:

"Why bring this old battler to the palace, you worthless idiot?

Plate-lickers, free-loaders and ne'er-do-wells, we've already got!

Besides, do you have your master's consent to bring this outcast here?

To eat out his household and what is reserved as our food, wine and beer?"

Eumaios is quick to defend the visitor's presence:

"Antinoos, your hurtful words make one suspect your noble birthright;

You are an aristocrat, he's a free man, extend to him what is polite,

What visitor needs to be invited? Zeus places all men where he thinks best;

There is a reason this man has come from far off, and is now in our midst,

Does your hospitality extend only to stonemason, prophet, physician, bard or builder?

As they have some skill or service that you can employ for your own gain, and pleasure,

All those men are welcome anywhere in the world, but what about the poor man?

He, too, must eat, drink and have shelter, let's be as obliging as we can,

Don't forget, every man has a desire for acceptance and respect;

It is like a groaning belly aching to be satisfied, and it's our duty to provide and protect,

You are the biggest bully among the Suitors, picking on me the most;

But I don't care, as long as Telemakis and Penelope are alive and remain your host."

Prudent Telemakis asserts himself by taking over, saying:

"Hush, don't trade words with Antinoos, you'll never win;

He's got a nasty tongue and will make the others join in."

Then turning to Antinoos he says:

"Antinoos, are you my father? For you wish to control my affairs in this palace;

Is it *your* place to order this stranger to be turned away from *our* house?

Zeus forbids and punishes such behaviour, give him some meat from your own plate;

Mother and I won't begrudge your charity; offer him something to take,

But I doubt you will, you're greedy ways have made you fat;
You should lead by example, you are supposed to be an aristocrat."

Antinoos has a surly reply:

"Such high-handed talk from you Telemakis, you impudent pup;
If all the Suitors give what's in my mind, you won't see him until the next season is up."[a]

As he speaks he draws his footstool from under the table and waves it in the air, with a gesture to throw it at disguised Odyssey. However, the other Suitors give him meat and bread. On his way back to the hall's entrance he goes over to Antinoos and says:

"Sir, please give me something, for you're not the poorest man here;
If you are the king of the Suitors then give me a larger crust to go with some beer,

Surely you can afford to give to me, what you got for free;
Then I can tell the world, wherever I go, about your generosity,

I was once a rich man with a grand home of my own;
And *I* gave to beggars, my kindness was always shown,

I had scores of servants too, with all the trappings of wealth and success;
But it was Zeus' Mind that took it all away, now I've ended up here, in this mess,

For, foolishly, I joined a band of pirates making a raid in Egypt, on the river Nile;
We anchored the ships and I sent out scouts to explore for a while,

---

a   The season is about to change; winter is about to begin in a few days.

But the men disobeyed my orders and weakened to their own greed;

They killed men, slaved women and children, and robbed beyond need,

News of the invasion soon carried itself to the city, then came the war-cry sounding;

The army assembled at dawn with cavalry and a legion[a] of foot soldiers rounding,

When Zeus showed my army the foe's gleaming armour, they lost their hearts in the retreat;

The Egyptians killed many of us, and took the rest as slaves, so was our defeat,

I wished I'd have died there too, but Zeus, Mind, gave me an idea which saved my skin;

I took off my helmet and shield, dropped my spear, and went straight up to the King;

He was in a fine chariot and I clasped his knees and kissed his ring, he offered me a ride;

Pitying me, he spared my life and drove me to his palace, I was weeping for joy, inside,

Many of his angry soldiers tried to kill me with their ashen lances;

But the King defended me, for he feared Zeus' wrath for not protecting strangers,

Then I was sold to the prince, *Dmetor*,[b] son of *Iausus*, the cruel King of Cyprus;

All I escaped with was a hunger in my belly, these rags and great distress."

Antinoos displeased, says:

"Why would Zeus send such a tormentor to upset our dinner feast?

Get away from me, stand in the courtyard where I can see you least,

Or you'll wish you were back in Cyprus or Egypt;

---

a   In ancient times, a legion was a division of 3,000 to 6,000 men, excluding cavalry.
b   No record is found of these two characters, they are probably invented by Odyssey.

For if you don't stop your insolence, that's where you'll be shipped,

You've scrounged from the others, who have provided enough to save your health;
For they don't care, it's easy to be generous with another man's wealth."

Odyssey begins to move away, but stops, saying to Antinoos:

"Your behaviour does not match your breeding, you are a mean and miserable man;
Even here in someone else's rich home, is a pinch of salt too much to grant?"

Antinoos is red-faced with anger. Scowling he says:

"I warned you, now your words won't escape penalty;
You *were* just a worthless beggar, but *now* you are my enemy!"

Antinoos takes his footstool in hand and hurls it at Odyssey, hitting him in the back of the neck between his shoulder-blades. The chair bounces off, Odyssey stands firm as the blow did not hurt him. He shakes his head silently, for it is filled with thoughts of revenge against this shameful attack. However, he overcomes his rage knowing that Time will right all wrongs. Patience is now a virtue, and a weapon in his armoury. The stranger moves back to his place near the entry doors. Before sitting, he says:

"Listen to me, Suitors of the Queen, so that I may speak what I should state;
A man doesn't resent a bruise or two defending the things that make up his estate,

Money, sheep and cattle, his possessions, he must protect from men of greed;
But to covet what another has is like a groaning belly, aching to be freed,

Desire is a curse that yokes the world with a debt it cannot pay;
And always ends with spoiling *trouble*, winning out the day,

Antinoos pretends to court and woo the Queen's heart and hand, a snake's way!

I pray that the *Fates*[a] send him an arrow to avenge his true aim, ahead of his wedding day."

Antinoos, on his feet, screams:

"If you say another word in front of the Suitors, or your host;

I'll have you dragged out and flogged at the stable's fence post."

But many of the Suitors are concerned at Antinoos' violence and cowardly attack. One of the younger men says:

"Antinoos, you've attacked this poor fellow; it was the wrong thing to do!

What if he's a god in disguise? For they do come to our world, from out of the blue,

These roving gods *protect* those that do good;

And fix fate at its fiercest, for those who don't, but should."

That is the general opinion of the Suitors, but Antinoos pays no heed to them. Meanwhile, Telemakis is enraged by the assault against his father, but holds down his emotions, shaking his head with thoughts of revenge. "Wait, stealth is important now", he thinks.

Queen Penelope is in her chamber upstairs. A servant-maid has just whispered to her that a stranger has been assaulted in the Great Hall by Antinoos. In despair she says to the maids around her:

"I hope that one of Apollo's arrows will strike Antinoos;

Just as he has violated a visiting guest, whoever he is."

Eurykleia, her trusted maid-servant speaks:

"If only our prayers to Zeus would be fulfilled;

Then, before another sunset all the offenders would be killed."

---

a   The *Fates*, mythological women who determined the span of a human life by spinning, measuring, and cutting the thread symbolic of it.

Wise Penelope says:

"Maid, I loathe every single one of them, for they mean malice;

But Antinoos, the worst, has a heart like the darkness of Death, itself,

A *troubled* homeless man came here out of want, and to escape his own dread;

Most gave him food, but Antinoos hit him with a footstool, just missing his head!"

As she is talking with her maids, Odyssey eats his dinner. She asks Eurykleia to have Eumaios come to her chamber. When he arrives she explains that she wants him to bring the stranger to her, to apologise for the assault. Thinking, perhaps, he may be well-travelled and has some knowledge of Odyssey, or even may know him.

Eumaios arrives and says to Penelope:

"I am sorry for the disturbance downstairs, my Queen;

But you will be charmed by this stranger and the adventures he has seen,

He stayed with me for three days and nights, in my hut at the farm;

It was the first place he found after jumping ship, to escape harm,

I've not heard all his stories and misfortunes that only Time could tell;

As we sat by my fire he had me spellbound with tales of heaven and of Hell,

He says he comes from Crete where the descendants of Minos dwell;

And there is a kinship between *his* house and that of Odyssey's, which he'd like to tell,

After leaving his home and being driven from one disaster to another;

He says he knows where Odyssey is, he's alive and well and close to Phortune Harbour,

For the oracle at Dodoni[a] told him that Odyssey;

Would one day find his family and home again, in Ithaki."

Penelope is anxious and says:

"Then go and call him here now, so that I may hear his tales and speech;

If he comes here, less offence will be taken from the Suitors; every one of them is a leech,

For their households have plenty of meat, wine and beer;

Only their servants consume there, what the Suitors gorge here,

Day after day we slaughter oxen, lambs, hogs and fat goats for their bellies, swollen big;

And there is no accounting of the quantity of wine and beer they spill and swig,

No estate can stand such wanton recklessness;

As no legitimate and rightful king reigns here to protect us,

How disgraceful! What a different place it would forever be;

If those wretched Suitors saw the return of Odyssey,

Imagine, now, if in their presence Telemakis and he stand;

In battle dress, with bow, arrows and their spears in hand,

Resourceful Odyssey, brave and true, god-like and tall;

What a sorry marriage it would be for the Suitors, one and all,

---

a   In ancient Greece, priestesses and priests in the sacred grove interpreted the rustling of the oak (or beech) leaves to determine the correct actions to be taken. According to a new interpretation, the sounds originated from bronze objects hanging from oak branches and sounded with the wind blowing, similar to a wind chime and were interpreted by the oracles.

He'd have them begging for mercy with a deadly end to their fun;
And our home would be peaceful again, and the wooing be done."

As she speaks Telemakis sneezes so loudly that the whole house echoes.
Penelope laughs and says to Eumaios:

"Go and call the stranger now for Telemakis just sneezed, after I had spoken;
It can mean only one thing, the Suitors are to die and their curse will be broken,

If I am satisfied that this stranger's words are true;
I shall give him a shirt and cloak and a lot more will be due."

Eumaios goes to Odyssey and says:

My friend, Telemakis' mother, Queen Penelope, is as anxious as can be;
She is wistful, but wants to hear anything you can say about Odyssey,

If you can satisfy her with the truth, she'll give you a new shirt and cloak;
Which is what you shall need when begging among the town folk,

Then you'll get much more than you beg for, when it comes to bread, water and meat;
For clothes give a man dignity, and rags make people retreat."

Crafty Odyssey replies:

"She shall hear only the truth, for I am as familiar to Odyssey, as any man could be;
I know all about his afflictions and shared his *trouble*, and the odd catastrophe,

But this mob of Suitors frightens me, a passion for violence is high on their list;
For just now I was minding my own business, and copped an unrequited fist,

No-man came to my aid, and Telemakis turned the other way;

So tell Penelope to be patient and I'll come at the end of the day,

Let her give me a seat near her fire's hearth, for my clothes are thread-bare;

Then I can tell her everything about her long-lost husband, to end her despair."

Eumaios goes back to Penelope who sees that the stranger has not followed him. She says:

"Where is he Eumaios? Is he shy of a woman host?

Bashful beggars go without the most."

Eumaios assures her:

"The stranger talks with a level head, he is avoiding the Suitors ire;

He will meet you privately, at sundown, in front of your chamber's fire,

He will reveal to you where Odyssey can be found;

And more, he has news that is guaranteed to astound."

Wise Penelope, curious about this man, says:

My fireplace has not seen any man since Odyssey left, twenty years ago;

He's not a Suitor and he doesn't appear to be *trouble*, so let me see what he has to show."

As she finishes speaking, Eumaios goes back to the Great Hall and whispers to Telemakis:

"Prince, I'm leaving, for there is work to do at the farm;

Look after yourself and see that the Suitors do you no harm,

Let us hope that Zeus has numbered their days;

To bring a bad end to their treacherous ways."

Telemakis is assuring:

"Very well, uncle and friend, go after you've finished your dinner here;

In the morning bring back some prize pigs to roast and enjoy with our beer,

I'll attend to everything that we need for security;

So, leave heaven's work to Zeus, and me."

Eumaios takes his seat and finishes dinner. He leaves the hall and the Suitors who are engaged in revelry and wenching, for it is nearly sunset.

*

THE BEGGARS FIGHT

*

THE STRANGER'S WARNING

*

THE SUITORS BRING GIFTS FOR PENELOPE

Into the palace comes a vagrant and beggar well known through the streets of Ithaki. He is a drunk and a glutton. A big, hulking man but lacking in strength and stamina. His real name, given to him by his parents, is Arnaeus.[242] However, his nickname is Irus,[a] because he runs errands for the Suitors, earning meagre tips. As he comes into the Great Hall he begins to insult Odyssey, trying to move him out of his domain, saying:

"Be off, old man, or I'll drag you out of here by the ears;

The Suitors give me the wink, but I won't need help from any volunteers,

So, get up and get out - on your own - or we'll be swapping blows;

You'll have your teeth knocked out, and a flat nose."

Odyssey frowns at him, saying:

---

a   *Irus*, meant: move back and forward. It is the root of the English word: rush.

"My friend, What are you talking about? I don't begrudge what people give you;
I'm not greedy, and there is enough in this palace for us to share, true?

You seem to be a beggar just like me, and your luck depends on the gods, as well;
But when it comes to fighting you'll be surprised at what happens, I must tell,

For you'll be stained with blood from your mouth to the floor;
And you won't be hanging around the house of Odyssey any more."

Irus, the beggar, is very angry and answers:

"You filthy pig, your mouth runs like nagging witches at a coven;
I'd like to knock out your teeth, just like any stray boar in Cyprus would earn.[a]

Roll up your sleeves and get ready to be thrashed;
And the crowd can watch an old man's wild mouth get bashed."

They move outside to the courtyard and start to spar and throw punches.
Antinoos hears the commotion and laughs when he sees the two vagrants shaping up.
He loudly summons the revellers outside, shouting:

"This is the finest sport that we've ever seen in the palace;
Heaven never sent anything this good to entertain us,

The stranger and Irus are going to come to blows,
A boxing match we'll enjoy, although a short one I propose."

The crowd laughs as the weakling stranger appears no match for Irus.
Antinoos breaks up the fight, saying to the boxers:

"Listen to me, there are some goat loins grilling on the fire for the winner;

---

a   Historians mention a law of ancient Cyprus, that any stray animal which damaged crops or livestock
could have its teeth pulled out.

Whoever champions the other shall join my table each day, and there enjoy his dinner,

Whoever loses, will be barred from entering this palace anymore;
And he can pursue his livelihood begging on the streets of Ithaki, door-to-door."

The mob agree, but crafty Odyssey wants to make sure of the bargain, saying:

"Lords, an old man like me, worn down by life's eternal misery;
Cannot win against this young brute, who is likely to inflict mortal injury,

I should leave now, but my aching belly likes grilled loins of goat meat;
So I'll take my chances, but you must all swear not to give Irus help, and cause my defeat."

The Suitors agree and make an oath to Zeus. Telemakis puts in a word:

"Stranger, you need not be afraid of cheats, if you have the courage for a brawl;
If anyone wants to interfere with the bout, I'll protect you against one, and all,

I am the host here, and Antinoos and Eurymachos, being of the same mind;
I trust, will back you up just as much to make it a fair fight, you'll find."

Everyone is agreed. Odyssey threw off his tattered rags baring his enormous rippling thighs, broad chest and boxer's shoulders. Athena, invisible, is near and tones his limbs to make him look stronger and more intimidating.

The Suitors are astonished at the beggar's physique. They murmur to each other and trade predictions about the fight. One of them says:

"Look at those thighs, this intruder has some godly mettle and might;
If he's looking for *trouble*, there he stands and for Irus it could be an early night."

Irus is shaken by the old beggar's powerful presence. His reluctance is countered by the servants who pull and push the bigger man into the middle of the mob. Antinoos scolds him for being timid, saying:

"You sauntering ox, you'll be better dead, than fearful of this old, broken man;

If he beats you, I'll sail you off to King Echetus[243] on the mainland,

He eats every one that comes near him, he's a cannibal and likes human meat.

He will fry your nose and ears first, and cut off your privates, for the dogs to eat."

Irus is more frightened and starts to tremble. Both raise their hands and touch each others fists, signalling the fight is to begin. Odyssey considers whether he should let fly with a hay-maker punch, or just sting the big man with a light jab. He decides on the second option for there is no point in alerting the Suitors to suspect that he is not who he seems.

The fight begins with Irus hitting Odyssey with a couple of glancing knocks around his shoulders. Odyssey returns each hit with some light blows to Irus' body. Soon his opportunity opens and he lands a blow to the jaw, under his neck. The blow crushes Irus' jaw where it joins the skull. Blood and teeth bubble from his lips as he falls to the ground, his mouth set in a grin of pain. His feet are the last things to land in the dust.

Odyssey drags the brute by his heels from the courtyard. Irus is unconscious and is propped up against the stone-wall fence near the stable. The Suitors are dying with laughter.

Odyssey says to Irus:

"From now on you are the palace's scarecrow, lie here and keep the cats and rabbits away;

If you try to be king of the beggars again, then more *trouble* will be your only pay."

He slings the old, dirty bag over his shoulder and goes back into the Hall to where he sat by the entrance doors. The Suitors follow him and voice their congratulations and respect. One of them saying:

"Time for Irus to go; he's been deposed as the beggar-king, and he can't fight;

We'll ship him off to the mainland for King Echetus' appetite,

May Zeus, and the other gods, grant the stranger what he wants, at once!

And let's thank him for ending Irus' damned begging, and annoyance."

Odyssey thinks these words are a good omen foreboding the Suitors' fate.

In front of Odyssey, Antinoos places a grilled, goat-loin sausage, sizzling with fat and hissing blood. Amphinomos takes two loaves from the bread basket together with a gold cup of wine and sets them in front of Odyssey, then sits next to him, saying privately:

"Old man, life has been hard on you, here's cheers!

Let us hope that luck will be better for you in the coming years."

To this Odyssey answers:

"Amphinomos, you are young, but a man of good mind and health;

Just as your father, Nisus of Dulichium,[a] is a sensible man, with wealth,

So listen carefully to what I have to say, and heed it in your future;

Of all the things that creep upon this Earth, man is the most pitiable creature,

As long as Heaven gives him fortune, luck and strength;

He gives no thought to the harm he might endure through life's length,

But Destiny brings hardship and grief, that all of us must give way;

For there is no such thing as luck, Zeus plans our lives, day by day,

I was on my way to becoming a rich man too, like my father, such was my foolish pride;

That I committed shameful deeds, believing my heritage would always provide,

---

a   An island adjacent to the west of Ithaki. Or, it maybe the southern half of Ithaki, as another plausible theory suggests.

A man must learn to accept Zeus in every single thing he sees and hears and feels;

For it is that god's order, *'Life is for experiencing; enjoy and endure what it reveals.'*

Look around you and see what calamity you reprobates create;

How you all dishonour Penelope, and waste this estate,

Odyssey is set to make his return very soon, he is close at hand;

If you have any sense, leave now, for blood will be shed when he makes his stand."

Odyssey takes the cup and, raising it, makes a toast to Zeus. He drains the sweet wine and hands the cup back to Amphinomos who looks at the old man in dismay. Amphinomos walks through the Hall, his head shaking and his heart filled with dread; the stranger's words promise danger. Bewildered, he takes a seat again with the ring leaders in the cloister. Sometimes security is found by joining the pack: but not this time. Despite Odyssey's warning, Amphinomos can not escape certain death for Athena has already fixed his doom by the hands of Telemakis.

*

Athena, Inspiration, plants a thought in the mind of Penelope: *To address the Suitors again and win some extra time for her husband's return, and Telemakis' survival.*

So she pretends a laugh and says, sarcastically, to her elderly maid, Eurykleia:

"I have changed my mind about the Suitors, I shall go and flirt with them;

So I can pass on to Telemakis that they mean *only* to murder him."

Eurykleia answers:

"My dear Queen, what you say, on each count, is a good idea;

Beauty passes, but wisdom remains!

So let's make-up your face before you leave here,

There is no point in wearing cheeks stained with *unnecessary* tears;

Telemakis can protect himself, his beard reveals that he has reached manly years."

The Queen replies:

"You are right Eurykleia, he is old enough to look after himself now;

But since Odyssey left, make-up won't cover the distress earned by my brow,

However, tell Autonoe and Hippodamia that they should escort me under a veil;

I can't go alone among men looking like this, it would not be proper, modesty must prevail."

Eurykleia goes from the room to gather the maids.

Meanwhile, Athena has another idea. She makes Penelope sleepy and soon falls fast asleep on her couch. Athena transforms her with grace and beauty to rival even the goddess Aphrodite, who no man can resist. She washes Penelope's face and feeds her with ambrosia, which strips away time, restoring her to a youthful splendour. Her physique is taller and nubile, her skin shines pearlescent. When Athena's work is done, she vanishes just as the maids arrive. Penelope wakes to find her servants fussing around her, saying to them:

"What an exquisite slumber I have woken from, just now;

But I awake to all the misery that would wrinkle any woman's brow,

I wish Artemis would send her arrows now, to end *my* hopeless life;

For I miss my dear husband - history's *best* man - lost in the gods' strife."

Veiled, she proceeds from her chamber down the stairs, with a maid at each side. When they reach the pillars near the cloisters she stops. The noise and busyness in the Hall ceases as the Suitors and servants become aware of Penelope's presence. She is radiant and the Suitors hearts begin to race; each man besotted by her beauty. They ogle and mumble prayers, begging the gods for the chance of sharing her bed.

Telemakis goes to her. She says to him:

"I fear you have lost your sense of better judgment, are you still your father's son?
You're not as well conducted as you used to be, there is a stranger who has come,

What is all this disturbance that you seem happy to permit?
A visitor who comes as a suppliant is abused, and to bullies he must submit?"

Telemakis responds:

"Mother, I am not happy that the Suitors gang makes you feel so disgusted;
Not only is coping with hospitality difficult, but my well-being can't be trusted,

However, the boxing match between Irus and the stranger was a success;
For the Suitors were disappointed that the old battler beat Irus into a mess,

I wish Zeus, Athena and Apollo would knock all the Suitors, senseless;
Just as the stranger paralysed Irus who lies defeated, out near the stable's fences,

His head nods like a wobbling drunk, looking for his own feet;
To carry him off to search for his own home, or even his street."

As they speak, cunning Eurymachos speaks out:

"If only all Ionian men could see you now, daughter of Ikarius, Penelope our Queen;
This palace would fill with more Suitors, and more eagerness for your heart would be
seen,

For you are the most desirable woman the Earth can find;
In supreme beauty of form, virtue and wisdom of mind."

To this, the inscrutable Penelope, replies:

"Eurymachos, heaven robbed my beauty in figure and face;

When my husband sailed for Troy to undo Helen's disgrace,

But if he would return and restore the honour of my regal descent;

Then my reputation shall be respected, and I shall be content,

For now, I am oppressed with these afflictions, which I can't cure;

That for some godly reason - I too - must suffer and endure,

My husband foresaw it all, he took me by the hand before he went to Troy;

And said, *'Wife, not all of us will come home safely, Ilium will be difficult to destroy,*

For the Trojans fight fiercely with bow and spear;

And their chariots yield dire panic and hellish fear,

Nothing decides a battle sooner than those two;

While I'm away, take care of my parents and Telemakis, too,

But if he grows a beard before I come back to this palace, in time;

Then marry and live happily to the best *man you can find.'*

"And now all this *trouble* is coming true, just as he said;

The night is coming when I'll have to yield in my groom's bed,

Why is Zeus punishing me with this bitter distress?

All I desire is my true husband and happiness!

And there is another offence which stirs my vexation;

You reprobates are not courting me as is customary in this nation,

When a man woos a Queen, or any woman of good quality;

He must bring livestock and wine to feast for *her* friends and family,

And should offer the most precious gifts to her to prove his devotion;

Instead of free-loading off another man's generosity, now dead in a foreign land or ocean."

Odyssey, too, is overcome with her beauty and glad to hear her canny words. He knows that she is flattering the Suitors to get their presents and reduce the strangle-hold they have over the estate. The scales are tipping.

Sly Antinoos joins in:

"Queen Penelope, daughter of Ikarius, take all the presents you can, from every man;

For it is bad manners to refuse gifts from any one, in any land,

But our festivities will continue here without fear or shame;

Until we witness your husband's wedding name."

The mob applauds and agrees with Antinoos. Each Suitor sends his porter to fetch a gift for Penelope. Soon Antinoos' man returns with a full-length dress exquisitely embroidered having twelve brooches of pure gold as fasteners.

Eurymachos hands her a magnificent thick chain of gold, studded with rubies, gleaming like the Sun. Eurydamos'[244] two men have a pair of earrings each one crafted into three brilliant diamond pendants which sparkle like a shimmering rainbow.

Prince Peisander, son of Polyctor, offers a gold and ivory necklace of incomparable engraving and workmanship. The line of gift bearers is one-hundred deep. When Penelope had thanked all the Suitors for their generosity, she goes upstairs into her chamber, the maids carry the troves of gifts behind her.

The Suitors celebrate, believing that they have broken Penelope's refusal to re-marry and now, one fortunate man - the *best* man - will finally get to indulge this magnificent woman. Music, singing and dancing is now the business of the palace's Great Hall.

Evening comes. The revelry continues and at dusk the servants bring three large *braziers*[a] to light the courtyard within the cloisters. They are piled high with

a   A *brazier* is a portable metal or stone container for holding burning wood, coals or charcoal for lighting, cooking or scent burning.

dried, split firewood. The servants take it in turns to feed and fan the flames to keep the torches that line the cloisters alight. Then Odyssey, favoured by Athena, says:

"Maids, servants of Odyssey, who has been absent from this palace,

Go upstairs to the Queen and amuse her by spinning wool, or picking lace,

I will fan the torches to light the hall for this riff-raff, now;

Even if they stay 'til Dawn, for my stamina won't be worn down."

The maids look at one another and laugh. Pretty Melantho,[245] has a sharp tongue and starts to mock the old beggar. She is the daughter of Dolios, but has been brought up by Penelope since she was a young child. Despite Penelope's care and long devotion to her, she has no empathy for the Queen's plight. Melantho is a mistress of Eurymachos, who she believes loves her. She starts insulting her disguised king, Odyssey:

"You wretched vagabond, get out of here, and stay where you belong;

Go to the stables or the flop-house in town, instead of annoying everyone,

Aren't you ashamed of insulting your hosts with your foolish remarks?

Do you think you'll go unpunished? These men are princes and aristocrats!

Has the wine fuddled your mind? Or do you always talk like a jack-ass?

You've lost *your* wits since you beat-up your brother-tramp, Irus,

A better man might come to destroy such arrogance, so beware;

There will be blood-and-gore in flood, for those that speak without care."

King Odyssey, beetle-browed,[a] replies:

"Bitch! I'm not going anywhere, except to inform Telemakis about what you have just said;

---

a   *Beetle-browed*, meaning: bushy eyebrows adding to a menacing, glaring expression.

He'll have you torn apart - alive - limb from limb, and *your* blood will flow until *you* are dead."

The women are scared for they know Telemakis would not tolerate this dishonour. They scamper upstairs to the refuge of Penelope's company. Sometimes security is found in a pack's size: but not this time; Athena avenges betrayal.

*

Athena turns her attention back to the Suitors and their insolence. She wants hatred to bite deeper into Odyssey's heart. She makes the Suitors more drunk than they would be at this time of day. This makes Eurymachos nastier than usual. He taunts the beggar again:

"Suitors of the Queen, lend me your ears, I have something I'd like to say;

There is a good reason why Zeus sent this old battler to Odyssey's palace today,

For he flames and fans the torches at the fireside, to set the cloisters with light;

But it's the reflection from his bald head that makes the Great Hall so bright!"

Finding Eurymachos' remarks hilarious, the Suitors are killing themselves with laughter. He turns back to Odyssey, the destroyer of Troy, and asks:

"Stranger, will you work for me as a servant on my estate;

There you'll be paid well, and be certain of a full dinner plate,

Can you pile a dry-wall fence from stones, or plant a tree?

If so, throw away those rags, I'll give you a new shirt, jacket and a pair of sandals, for free,

Will you go? No! For you are too lazy; the thought of work makes your bowels run;

You're a sponger, fixed on filling your belly's hole. There was never *any* work in you, none!"

Quick-witted Odyssey responds:

"Eurymachos, if you and I would work together side by side, let's say;
When the heat from the longest summer day's Sun scorches the listless hay,

With scythes in hand mowing and reaping the long, wide field;
Without water or food, you wouldn't make noon, you'd faint in the dust, and yield,

Or, shall we take turns steering a strong ox team, yoked to a heavy plough?
Then you'll see the man who digs the straighter furrow, the one standing in front of you, now!

And suppose some war was to break out here, on this very day;
Just give me a shield, spears and a bow, and I'll be first into the fray,

Then you'd think twice about blaming my belly, which brings only *trouble,* and me;
You exploit others' misfortunes, and lesser lots in life, you are just a cruel bully!

If Odyssey was to return, there would be no escape from his wrath;
And those double doors are too narrow to allow the stampede of the coward's path."

Eurymachos is furious and screams back to the beggar-King:

"You filthy, stinking wretch you'll pay for this ill-bred humiliation;
Who do you think you are? I say you are *trouble* and damnation!

Has the wine be-fuddled your mind? Or do you always talk like a jackass?
You've lost *your* wits since you beat-up your brother tramp, Irus."

Athena works the opportunity further; Eurymachos picks up a footstool and hurls it at Odyssey who ducks. It misses him, but strikes Amphinomos who is not so agile. The missile knocks him to the floor and ricochets off him hitting his wine steward, Mulius, who is filling his cup. Wine jug, tray and cups fly in all directions ringing out as they bounce over the floor.

The Suitors jump to their feet, yelling out through the cloisters, now in an uproar. One man turns to his neighbour saying:

"If only that intruder had died in a foreign land, or sea;

Before he came here. He's outright *trouble,* plainly!

We cannot permit such disturbance from this defiant low-life;

He upsets the banqueting and our celebrations turn into strife."

Telemakis comes forward, saying:

"Nobles, are you all drunk? Can't hold your liquor? Or does some spirit possess you instead?

It is impolite to turn away guests, but your fun must give way to sleep, it's time for bed!"

The Suitors are gob-smacked by his boldness. Each looking at the other considering if they *are* more drunk than usual. Amphinomos is the first to speak:

"We shouldn't resent the Prince's words and mood, that clearly offend;

For now, let's bring the hostility against the stranger to an end,

For us, he is unfinished business for another day, and Telemakis' *trouble* tonight;

Let the stewards pour another drink, then we can go to our beds, for peace and quiet."

All nod consent. Amphinomos' servant, Mulius, brims their goblets with mellowed wine. They all make a toast to the gods for long and healthy lives. They swagger and shuffle out through the courtyard gates towards their homes and tomorrow's Fate.

PENELOPE MEETS THE STRANGER

*

THE BOAR SCAR

*

PENELOPE'S DREAM

The Great Hall is full of emptiness. However, in a quiet corner of the cloisters, father and son, King and Prince, are plotting the end of the Suitors' siege. Athena, Inspiration, provides wisdom.

Odyssey says to Telemakis:

"We must get the armour and weapons out of here tonight;
So, collect them all and lock them in the armoury, out of sight,

If the Suitors notice they are missing tomorrow, and happen to ask;
Say, *'They are grimy from the smoke and soot, the maids are doing a cleaning task,*

Since Odyssey left for Troy, they haven't been cleaned, it's true;
And a god prompted me of something more troublesome, too,

If the Suitors disgrace the courting feasts and guests, and a drunken quarrel ensues;
The sight of weapons might tempt the men to use them, if it's the will of Zeus.'

"Son, there is a force within bronze and iron that leads men on;
Metals lend false mettle, and that arrogance brings ruin upon."

Telemakis accepts his father's advice and calls to his maid, Eurykleia:

"Lock the the other maids in their quarters while I remove these old arrows and
spears;
Since my father left, no-one has used them, they are filthy with the grime of twenty
years."

Faithful Eurykleia answers:

"My child, J wish that one day you will take back the affairs of this House, now for
the worse;
And manage it so that all your property and servants can be free of the Suitors' curse,

But who will help, and who will light the storage vault and stair-flight?
The maids could, but you want them locked away, out of sight."

Telemakis says:

The stranger will help, he will hold the torch and show me the way on;
If he eats in this house he'll earn it, wherever he may come from."

Eurykleia, without another word, bolts the women inside their chambers.

Odyssey and his son hide the helmets, shields and spears. Suddenly the hall
is illuminated with a bright golden light, the work of their friend Athena. Telemakis
says to his father:

"Father, what god's work is the marvel of the light's beauty in this Hall?

Look, the walls, the rafters, crossbeams and pillars are now draped in a golden pall."

Wily Odyssey answers his son:

"Quiet! Keep your thoughts to yourself, this is the work of the gods;

Sometimes we can't understand why they do things, or their methods,

Go now to your bed and slumber, while I test the maids some more;

And I'll talk with your mother who will ask me lots of questions, I'm sure."

Telemakis with a torch-light, goes to his bedroom on the other side of the courtyard. He lies in bed, but does not sleep, anxious for Dawn's bringings.

*

Odyssey remains in the hall pondering, with the help of Athena, Imagination, his strategy for defeating the foe.

Penelope comes down from her chambers. She looks like the most beautiful of the gods; Aphrodite or Artemis. Odyssey draws a chair for her near the brazier. A chair crafted for a Queen, by Ikmalios.[a] It's curved arms inlaid with scrolls of glistening silver and lustrous ivory. It has a matching footstool attached and is covered with a sumptuous fleece. Her maids join her as she reclines upon it.

They go about their chores, first they fan the embers in the brazier and feed the fire with dry wood. The fire cracks with soft light and warmth. Next they clear and clean the tables of the Suitors' left-overs of scraps and wine jugs and goblets. The maid Melantho begins to rail at Odyssey a second time, saying:

"Stranger, you are still here, go some place where you belong, a home if you have one;

And don't hang around here, why are you ogling and upsetting the women?"

Nimble-witted Odyssey scowls at her again, answering:

---

a   Ikmalios, a cabinet and furniture maker of Ithaki.

"Young lady, what's gotten into you? Why are you angry with me?

Is it because I am a beggar and dressed like one, as you can see?

I was a rich man once, and had my own fine home, just like this;

And I gave to any suppliant that came my way, as is the call of Zeus,

I had scores of servants and all the trappings of the rich and famous;

But misfortune and Fate dealt me the cruelest blows, I'm still homeless,

Miss, be aware that Destiny can rob you of pride and your position in life;

Your Queen might turn on you, or King Odyssey might come back to his wife,

There is still a very good chance that he lives to fight another day;

And by the grace of Apollo, his son will come of age, and keep watch over each maid."

Penelope hearing the conversation, scolds Melantho:

"You impudent bitch! You'll pay dearly for your treachery;

For I told you I was coming here to ask this man about Odyssey,

He is a suppliant and by tradition must be treated like any guest of our estate;

I long for news of my husband and all you can do is insult him, and prevaricate."[a]

She asks her most-trusted servant, the house-keeper Eurykleia, to bring a seat covered with a fleece for the stranger to sit upon, which she does obediently. Odyssey sits and Penelope begins:

"Sir, tell me your story, where do you come from, and who are you?

Tell me about your city, king and parents. Do you have a wife and children? Tell me true,

---

a   *Prevaricate*, means to speak falsely or misleadingly; deliberately misstate or create an incorrect impression; to lie or manipulate.

What matter brings you hear, today?

And how long would you like to stay?"

Crafty Odyssey answers:

"My lady, on this Earth no mortal could find flaw with you, and your beauty cannot be faulted;

More, your reputation reaches into the Heavens where among the gods your name is exalted,

You remind me of a benevolent king who upholds what is good and right for all;

His people till the Earth yielding bounteous crops, and fruit trees tall,

Where sheep, goats and pigs abound, and fish within his island's seas are found;

He takes care of his prospering people and good deeds and happiness rebound,

But, as I sit here in *your* house, please don't ask about my family, and where I'm from;

For that will pull harder on the heartstrings, and reveal the distance to my love, and my home,

It would be wrong of me to be weeping here, in *your* home, your torment would only double;

You will be shocked with me and my crying, you can't see it yet, but I am *trouble*."

Inscrutable[a] Penelope answers him:

"Stranger, heaven robbed all my beauty of form and face;

When my husband sailed for Troy to undo Helen's disgrace,

But if he would return and restore the honour of my regal descent;

---

a   *Inscrutable*: meaning, incapable of being investigated, or scrutinized; impenetrable, unknowable.

Then my reputation shall be respected, only then shall I be content,

For now, I am oppressed with these afflictions I can't cure;

Which for some godly reason - I too - must suffer and endure,

The noblemen of Kefalonia, Lefkada, Zakynthos and Ithaki are wooing me;

And everyday they waste away this estate, whilst I wait for news of my husband, Odyssey,

I have not time to attend to suppliants and strangers sent by Zeus;

And I even neglect messengers who come here on official business."

She moves closer to the stranger. Her voice lowers to a whisper. She confides that the Suitors are pressing to marry her as soon as possible and that she has thwarted their advances by trickery.

She also confides to him about a thought that came to her some years before - from some god, no less, when she installed a loom in her chamber and began weaving an enormous tapestry. She told the Suitors that as her husband was dead, and would never return, that she would re-marry soon, but first must finish the tapestry which was to be a funeral shroud for Laertes, Odyssey's father. Being a skilled and artistic weaver she wanted to create the very finest work, before his death.

The Suitors agreed and she and her maids worked her loom each day, but, at night, by torchlight, she alone would unpick the stitches. For four years she got away with the deception, but her maids discovered her undoing their work and, being angry, betrayed her to the Suitors. From then on she was forced to finish the work. Now she has run out of ideas for stalling their marriage proposals, and the estate is almost ruined through their consumption.

She tells the stranger about the pressure her parents apply and that her son is outraged by the Suitors demands, although he is now old enough to look after the palace's affairs, his hands are tied until she marries. Having confided in the stranger, again the Queen asks him:

"Nevertheless, please tell me where you come from and who you might be;

You must have a family somewhere, for you didn't spring from a rock or a tree."

Odyssey answers:

"My lady, honoured wife of Laertes' son, Odyssey, you seem intrigued by my
ancestry;

So, I'll tell you despite it bringing back painful memories of misfortune and misery,

Here, then, is the tale of my woes for *your* ears to trust;

I hope it satisfies your curiosity, and can hold your interest,

There is a beautiful and fruitful island called Crete, south of here;

It is large with ninety cities of many foreigners, from far and near,

It is the original home of the ancient Pelasgians[246] who fathered the Hellenes;

The Dorians,[247] the Aeolians, the Achaeans and the Ionians,[a]

There is the great city of Knossus,[248] which was once ruled by King Minos;

Every nine years he had a conference with Zeus, himself,

Minos fathered Deucalion,[249] who fathered my brother Idomeneus, and me;

Idomeneus went to war at Troy, but I was too young for battle and was confined to
Crete,

That is where I met Odyssey and introduced myself, I'm Prince Aethon,[250] by *name*;[b]

He too was on his way to Troy, but via the treacherous Cape Malea is how he came,

For ill-winds blew him back onto our shore at [c]*Amnisus*[251] near the cave of
[d]*Eileithyia*,[252]

We got along very well, as one would expect, for he is a most-likeable character,

---

a   Crete is the original melting pot of what has become known as *Greeks*, more correctly Hellenes. The
    ancient Pelasgians fathered the Hellenes; the Dorians, the Aeolians, the Achaeans and the Ionians, all
    different tribal states.
b   *Aethon*, in ancient Greek meant: tormentor. It was the name of the eagle which tormented Prometheus,
    by eating his re-generating liver daily.
c   *Amnisos* is a public beach now, about 7 km east of Heraklion (Iraklio) but was once the port for the
    palace of Knossos.
d   *Eileithyia,* the Spirit of childbirth.

As soon as he arrived he wanted to meet with Idomeneus, claiming to be his friend;

But Idomeneus had already set sail for Troy some ten or twelve days earlier, with his men,

So I showed him around and took him to my palace and gave the best hospitality;

For I had plenty of everything such as any prince could want, and sharing came naturally,

I lodged his crew in my palace and set up an account for them at the public store;

And they all drank and ate 'til their bellies swelled, and they couldn't take any more,

They stayed with me for twelve days, while that north wind galed;

It was so strong that to stay on your feet, they'd have to be nailed,

An unfriendly god, Poseidon perhaps, wanted them kept on shore;

But luckily, the wind relented on the thirteenth day, and they set out for that dreadful war."

He goes on and on with more lies as Penelope weeps inconsolably, bawling with grief. Tears stream in torrents from her eyes. Like when the snows on the mountain tops melt and flow into cascading streams as the desert wind[a] from the south blows its searing heat. That's how her tears gush.

Odyssey feels sorry for her, but keeps his eyes as dry as horn and as steely as cold bronze, refusing to allow even one teardrop to pass. Her grief fades and she is able to speak again, asking the stranger:

"Now, stranger, I shall put you to the test and see if you and he have really met;

Tell me, how was he dressed? And what kind of a man is he to look at?

The master of deception continues:

---

a   The Sirocco is a wind that comes from the Sahara and can reach hurricane speeds, especially during the summer season.

"Twenty years have come and gone since he left my home, my lady;

I think your husband wore a cloak of purple wool, but my mind is hazy,

Was it double-breasted with gold buttons fastened in its eyelet's jaws?

And on each button an emblem of a dog tearing apart a spotted fawn, held in its paws?

Everyone marvelled at the engraving of the gold, the dog strangling the fawn;

While the fawn was looking back into the dog's eyes, struggling to escape, and run,

As for his shirt, it was soft and well-fitted, like an onion skin;

And it glistened in the sunlight to the admiration of all the women,

But I don't know if Odyssey wore these clothes when he left Ithaki;

Or if a companion gave them to him while he was on his voyage over the sea,

Perhaps someone on his journey gave these clothes as gifts, to him;

For he had many friends wherever he went, but few could equal that Achaean,

I gave him *my* own bronze spear, and *my* double-breasted purple coat;

With a fringed shirt down to his feet, and sandals to wear when he was not afloat,

And I provisioned his ship and crew with all they would need;

Sending them off after a full ceremony, wishing them gods' speed;

Another thing, he had an older servant, and I can tell you how he appeared;

His shoulders were hunched, he was dark, with thick curly hair and a beard,

His name was Eurybates,[253] and Odyssey treated him like a brother;

For he was like-minded, saw eye to eye, and was trustworthy like no other."

Penelope is moved more deeply for hearing these indisputable facts. She finds herself howling and gushing tears again. But is it for another reason, perhaps a disguised joy? Is her intuition slowly revealing that this stranger might be her husband? Eventually, she finds the fortitude to go on, saying, deftly:

"Stranger, I had respected you before; but now you shall be honoured all the more;

For you spoke the truth, it was *me* who gave Odyssey the clothes he wore,

I took them from the shelf of his cedar cabinet and packed them myself;

And *I* sewed the gold buttons on his coat! The man you describe couldn't be anyone else."

It was a black day when he sailed to that ill-fated city - *Ilium* - No! *Ill I am*;

I'd love to put my hands around his neck! I only wish for the chance to welcome him home."

Odyssey answers her:

"My lady, wife to Odyssey, do not be bitter at what appears to be lost;

Although I can hardly blame you for doing so, of course, you must,

For, you are a faithful wife and lover to your husband, and mother to his heir;

And they say that Odyssey is a god, so it is natural to be distraught through care,

Quiet your *troubled* mind, hold back your tears and lend me your ear;

I'll hide nothing from you, and can say - truthfully - that Odyssey is alive, and near!

He comes from *Thresprotia*,[a] and is bringing for you many treasure chests;

Which he gained through his adventures after he sacked Priam's fortress,

But don't expect to see his crew, or his blue-eyed ships again;

---

a   The *Thesprotians* were referred to by Homer as having friendly relations with Ithaki and Dulichium (Either Kefalonia, or an island east of Ithaki, or the southern - or even the northern - part of Ithaki). The Thesprotians originally controlled the wind chime oracle at Dodoni, the oldest in Greece.

For angry Zeus destroyed each boat and every crewman, all of them,

On a stormy sea as they escaped from Thrinakia, land of the god of the Sun;
Because his men slaughtered Helios' cattle, they were all drowned, their days done,

The Lightning Bolter wanted to even the score;
And raised a black storm, with galing winds, high seas and more,

By letting fly with his lightning bolts, the ship went around and around, fast;
Fire filled the cabins, and the brimstone exploded with flames higher than the mast,

The whole crew jumped into the sea, bobbing up and down like drifting sea kites;
For a while. Then Zeus, put a swift end to them; their watery graves had no last rites,

Incredibly, Zeus took pity on Odyssey and thrust into his arms the mast of the ship;
For ten dark days he clung to it as the sea tossed him along that water-logged trip,

Until Odyssey, clinging to the flotsam, drifted onto the Phaekian's shore;
Where they treated him as a god with renowned hospitality, presents and more."

His lies and torment continue:

"He'd have been here sooner, for the Phaekians were eager to escort him home safely;
But he wanted more wealth; there is no man alive that can enrich himself like Odyssey,

Pheidon[254] king of the Thesprotians told all this, when he entertained me;
For his ship and crew were ready to take Odyssey and I, to Ithaki,

But *he* sent me here first, on his grain ship, on the way to Kefalonia;

And he showed me Odyssey's hoard, enough for a family of ten generations to treasure;

However, as the king told, Odyssey went to Dodoni, to listen to the Oracle of the breeze;

To hear if he should return home openly - or in disguise - straight from the rustling leaves,[a]

By what I have said, you should know he is safe and close at hand;

It won't be long before his family and friends recognise their king in his home-land,

Nevertheless, I swear by Zeus, and the Invisibles, and by Odyssey's throne;

That what I have said will happen, and to you, your husband will again be shown,

He will return and avenge those who dishonour his family and friends, very soon;

The palace can expect him between the waning and the waxing of this moon."[b]

The interplay continues as wise Penelope answers:

"Friend and confidante, I hope it proves true, for if it does, *you'll* be rewarded with gifts, well;

And you will become revered and legendary for all time, for the prophecy that *you* tell,

But, now I know this: Odyssey will not come any closer to this palace, or to me;

Nor will you need an escort away from Ithaki, to your home, wherever it may be,

For now, there is no master in this house, as I once knew him;

---

a   In ancient Greece, priestesses and priests in the sacred grove interpreted the rustling of the oak (or beech) leaves to determine the correct actions to be taken. According to a new interpretation, the sounds originated from bronze objects hanging from oak branches and sounded with the wind blowing, similar to a wind chime and were interpreted by the oracles.

b   In effect an allusion to the next day, being the start of the Festival of Apollo which coincides with a recorded solar eclipse on that day. Astronomers have confirmed these events using NASA software. On the 30th October, 1207 B.C. a solar eclipse of a 75% magnitude darkened Ithaki for about one minute. Refer to: Papamarinopoulos, et al. (2012).

Only the Suitors rule here, and they mean harm; your time will be short with them,

Odyssey! *There* is the man who'd know best what to do;
Or, is he only a has-been from the past, now just a phantom between me and you?"

*

She calls the maids and asks them to wash the strangers feet and prepare a bed with rugs and cushions on one of the couches, so that he may be warm until morning. Then, they are to bathe and massage him with lemon juice and olive oil, before taking his place at breakfast with Telemakis.

Confiding again in the stranger, she says:

"I shall rebuke any one of these reprobates if they are uncivil to you again;
And they shall be thrown out forever, and have no hope of my wedding hand,

For how, sir, can *you* know that I am respected for my faithfulness, wisdom and care?
No! You can't be seen in rags, you'll have a new shirt, jacket and a pair of sandals to wear,

We all live for a short time, and if one is hard-hearted to another person;
He will be despised, and others will wish his life to be even harder, and to worsen,

And when he's dead, his reputation won't be mentioned, or preserved;
But, if he is righteous he'll be honoured in the many hearts and minds of those he served."

Odyssey answers with more skilful torment:

"My lady, honoured wife of Odyssey, rugs and cushions are not for me;
Since I sailed from the snowy peaks of Crete, into a world of misery,

No! Please let me lie without comfort, for sleepless-ness is my bed mate;

For twenty years, I've slept with one eye open, hoping Dawn would deliver a better fate,

The prospect of a young maid washing and tickling my feet, leaves me cold, you shall find;

But, if an old woman who knows *trouble* like me, washes up to my knees, I won't mind."

To this, the subtle Penelope replies:

My dear sir, since Odyssey left here, *no-man* has spoken so prudently well;

You seem to have a great understanding of this house, from what you tell,

For there *is* an honourable woman, my husband's nurse-maid, Eurykleia will look after you;

She delivered Odyssey into the world and nursed him, and she has known *trouble* too,

She is *very* old and feeble now, but she will wash your hands and feet;

Eurykleia, come! The stranger is here, he is someone you should meet,

Please wash his worn hands and feet, they seem to be from the same year as you;

How *trouble* ages us all too soon, and no doubt that Odyssey's feet are just like our guest's, too."

With these words the old-maid Eurykleia covers her face with her hands to hide her tears. Lamenting, she says:

"Our dear Queen, what am I to do with you and your hopeless situation?

There is no-one more god-fearing than yourself, and yet Zeus torments you to frustration,

No-one burned more thigh bones, or sacrificed offerings than you;

Or more often prayed just to reach a ripe old age, and see Telemakis mature too,

Yet, Zeus has denied your husband-king a fitting welcome here in his own residence;
And, no doubt other women in foreign palaces have mocked Odyssey too, with pestilence,

Just like these impudent, treacherous sluts, who slur and curse you, our guest;
It's no wonder that you prefer me to bathe your hands and feet, experience knows best!

I shall wash your feet and hands gladly, as Penelope has asked me to do;
As your appalling condition has touched my heart, and it will make *you* feel better too,

And also, of all the travel-weary strangers that have come distressed into this place;
No-man has ever resembled Odyssey like you, in feet, figure, voice and face."

Coy Odyssey says:

"Those who have seen us both before have remarked how alike we seem to be;
And what a surprise, your eyesight is so good that you too have noticed the similarity."

*

The old woman pours a little cold water into the basin which has been heating over the embers. As Odyssey sits by the fire, he turns his feet away from the fire light, for he does not want his old nurse-maid to see the scar which he has had since boyhood.

*

When Odyssey was born, his grandfather Autolycos,[255] came to visit the palace in Ithaki from his home on Mt. Parnassos.[256] He was an adept trickster, magician and master of deception. Hermes, himself, Spirit of Persuasion, had taught him, and was his accomplice in many exploits.

Autolycos[a] went to Ithaki when he heard that his daughter, Queen Antikleia had given birth to a son.

As soon as he had dined, Eurykleia set the infant upon his knee and asked if Autolycos would name the boy, his grandson, for it had been his wish that there should be a rightful heir to Arcesius' kingdom. Autolycos wanted the boy to be named Odyssey, because he had always found people, man or woman, to be difficult in some way, or another. So he named the child Odyssey, which meant *trouble*, a name-sake for his fiery personality, flaming red hair and audacity.

Some years later, Odyssey was invited to Mt. Parnassos by Autolycos to receive presents from his grandfather, and he dutifully went. His grandmother Amphithea[257] threw her arms around him and kissed and cared for him, whilst his uncles butchered a five-year old bull into joints for roasting. The rest of the meat was cut into smaller pieces, and skewered. They feasted into the night whilst the boy found joyous sleep.

At Dawn, Autolycos and the uncles set out with Odyssey and their hunting hounds. They climbed up into the wooded forests of Mt. Parnassos reaching one of its wide, windswept valleys and found a dell where the wildest boars lived. The hounds were out in front following a scent, the uncles behind and little Odyssey, with his spear in hand, tracking them. They all passed the lair of a huge, wild boar off to the right in the thick dogwood, so thick that the wind and rain would not bother to enter, nor the Sun's light could find. There the mighty beast lay on a thick bed of autumn leaves.

The boar heard the noise of the men's feet, and the hounds baying in front of them. As the boy moved along, the boar saw his chance and with flashing eyes and a bristled back he charged from his lair. Odyssey was the first to see it in the corner of his eye. He raised his spear to drive it into the brute, but the beast was too fast and its tusk struck his thigh ripping a deep gash, just missing the bone of his kneecap.

The boar was not so fortunate, Odyssey hit him between the shoulder blades with the bronze spear, it went straight through. The huge beast fell grunting and convulsing in the dust, and its soul shimmered away.

Some of the uncles bound Odyssey's wound to stop the bleeding, whilst the others butchered the beast's carcass.

Once the bleeding had stopped Autolycos lifted the boy on his shoulders and carried him down the mountain to his palace. Some weeks passed and when Odyssey was healed he was escorted back to Ithaki, arriving with wonderful presents and many stories of his adventures. There was much rejoicing for his family were glad to see him. He told them his tales and showed the palace court the scar he earned on Mt. Parnassos with his grandfather and uncles.

---

a   The name, *Autolykos*, translates to: Lone wolf, or, himself a wolf.

Eurykleia has hold of his leg. As she washes away the dirt she feels the scar and recognises it instantly. Astonished, she drops his foot which falls into the basin, spilling all the water onto the floor. Eurykleia's eyes light up. She is overcome with joy and also distressed. Her eyes flood with tears. Finding it difficult to speak, she grabs his beard, saying:

"My child, it is you! Odyssey, it *is* you, you've finally appeared!

I did not recognise you until I got close enough to hold your beard."

As she speaks Eurykleia looks towards Penelope, wanting to tell her that Odyssey has arrived, but, for some reason, wise Penelope is looking away. Has Athena diverted her attention, or does she choose to avoid the discovery? Is she curious, does her intuition know something?

Odyssey takes hold of Eurykleia by wrapping his right arm around her shoulder and drawing close to her, he whispers:

"Nurse, do you wish to be my ruin, *you* who nursed me at your own bosom?

After twenty years lost and wandering, now I've finally come home,

And since the gods want you to know now that I've returned to where I belong;

Hold your tongue! Do not say a word about it, or you'll do me wrong,

If heaven does grants me the chance to destroy the Suitors, maids and all;

I will not spare you, although you were my own nurse, if you tell a single soul."

Eurykleia answers:

"My child, what are you saying? You know very well that nothing could impair my loyalty;

This is *our* secret, my heart is made of stone and my tongue is iron cold, when it needs to be,

And when Zeus and Athena deliver the Suitors into your hands, if that's their plot;
I shall give you a list of the women in this house who should be punished, or not."

Odyssey whispers:

"Nurse, why do you say that, I'll form my own opinion when the time is right;
You just hold your tongue and leave their fate to the gods' will, and might."

As he says this Eurykleia goes to fetch more water for the basin. She washes
and massages him with olive oil. He draws a chair back near the fire's hearth to warm
himself. Penelope returns and he hurriedly hides the scar under his rags. She begins
talking to him:

"Stranger, I would like to speak with you briefly, about another issue;
It is nearly bed time for those who have peaceful sleep to take, as I'm sure you do,

As for myself, heaven has given me a life of such immeasurable suffering;
That even by day, busy with all my duties in this house, I still go about weeping,

And when Night brings bedtime, I lie there awake, restless;
Anxiety torturing my broken heart, for my life is hopeless,

Like the nightingale, *Aedon*,[258] who sings in Spring's shady trees, all day long;
Of the death of her son,[a] she killed by mistake, and now tweets and trills her endless
song,

That is how my mind works, ever tossing and turning, day-in and day-out;
Should I stay with my son and make sure of his future, which is in doubt?

And safeguard my home, servants and the memory and respect of my late spouse;

---

a   *Aedon*, attempting to murder the son of her sister-in-law, Niobe, accidentally killed her own child,
Prince Itylus, son of King Zethus. She had intended to kill Niobe's son because she was jealous that
she had fourteen children.

Or, is it best to take the Suitor with the best bride-price and treasure, and live in his house?

When my son was younger, he could not understand my dilemma, and re-marriage;
But now, he begs and prays for me to do so, for the Suitors are squandering *his* heritage,

But enough! Listen to me and interpret this dream, if you can, stranger;
It goes: A flock of twenty geese that come in from their pond to eat grain from a manger,

I dreamt that a great eagle swooped on the flock and killed each bird, then flew away;
And I wept 'til my maids gathered around me, pitying and grieving the death of its prey,

Then the eagle returned and perched on a rafter and spoke in a man's voice;
Telling me to stop crying and have courage, saying, *'Penelope now is the time to rejoice!*

This is not a dream, its an omen, the Suitors are the geese;
And I'm not an eagle, but your long-lost husband, that will restore your peace.'

But, when I awoke the geese were feeding at the manger;
Tell me what this dream means, who is in danger?"

Odyssey responds:

"This dream, my lady, has only one meaning and portends well;
The death of the Suitors is assured, their future lies in Hades' Hell."

Penelope, may be losing hope, but answers:

"Stranger, dreams are dubious things, and most times no truth is born;

There are only two gates through which visions unfold, one is of ivory, the other horn,[259]

Those that come through the ivory gate, are lies that are sent to deceive;
But those from the gate of horn predict what will happen, and are safe to believe,

I think *my* dream came through the ivory gate;
Although my son and I will be thankful if that is not our fate,

Furthermore, I dread the coming Dawn, it will banish me from this house;
For tomorrow I will hold an archery contest, and must wed the winner as my spouse,

Odyssey used to line up twelve axes in the courtyard, like stays supporting the hull of a ship;
And through all the axe-handle rings, he could fly an arrow's tip,

I'll make the Suitors compete, shoot through all the rings, after first stringing the bow:
Whoever shall do this deed will welcome me into his bridal bed, where I must go,

And leave this house, that of my rightful husband, and all the things I cherish;
But even so, I will have the wealth of my memories with him here, until I perish."

Odyssey replies:

"My lady, wife of Laertes' son, King Odyssey, don't delay the contest you've devised;
For he will string the bow and send an arrow through the rings, to the Suitors' surprise."

To that Penelope says:

"Sir, as long as you will sit here and talk with me, I have no desire for bed;

But, I can't go without sleep forever; the gods grant it to gain strength, for what lies
ahead,

So, I'll go upstairs and weep tears to water my bed of sorrows, which *no-man* has
enjoyed;
Since the day Odyssey set out for Priam's doomed city, and now *all* is destroyed!"

She goes upstairs with her maids following. On her bed she cries until
Athena seals her eyes with Sleep.

*

PENELOPE'S PRAYER

*

TWO SIGNS FROM THE INVISIBLES

*

THE FESTIVAL OF APOLLO BEGINS

*

DISASTER FORETOLD

Odyssey lies down to sleep in the cloister which surrounds the Great Hall. His mattress is a raw ox-hide covered with plush lamb-skins. The blankets are thick and quilted. He pretends to be asleep as Eurykleia places a cloak over him.

There he lies in restlessness, scheming how to kill the Suitors.

A group of maids, the Suitors' mistresses, are giggling and laughing at the old beggar as they leave the palace on the way to the arms of their Suitor mates. This makes him more angry. He debates whether he should kill each of them now, or let them have their last pleasures with the Suitors, tonight. His heart growls with fury, just as a bitch with puppies yowls and bares her teeth when she sees a threat nearby. But he quiets his racing heart and says to himself:

"Heart, be still! I have overcome worse, remember the day the Cyklops ate my friends?

I took it silently until my cunning devised a way out of his cave, and *then* I made amends."

So he quelled his fiery heart but could not stop twisting and turning, like a sausage in its own skin, hissing fat and blood as it is turned over and over on the hot embers by a man eager to satisfy his craving hunger. A man who is obsessed with hard-minded revenge cannot sleep.

Athena attends, hovering over him with her wisdom. She asks:

"My poor man, did Hypnos,[260] rob you of sleep, and steal your peace of mind?

This is your home, your wife is safe and your son is the best *you* will ever find."

Odyssey, the master schemer, says:

Goddess, what you say is true, but how am I to kill all the Suitors, alone?

And, even if Zeus and you help, where will I go to escape the revenge that will be shown?

Athena, the Spirit of Inspiration, replies:

"Are you blind? A better union of Spirit and man *you* will never see;

Haven't I always saved you from self-defeat and *trouble*? No, you won't need to flee.

Even if fifty brigades of blood-thirsty men surrounded you and me;

You would defeat them and walk away with all their possessions, free!

Go to sleep, now! It is distressing to watch the night;

Fear not, your misfortunes are over, darkness breeds light."

His eyes shut and sleep prevails. At the speed of life, Athena is in Olympos.

While Odyssey's slumber unloads his woes, Penelope wakes from her sleep. She kneels at the foot of the bed, weeping. As the tears subside, she prays to Artemis:

"Artemis, daughter of Zeus, put an arrow into my heart, slay me, before it is too late;

Or, let a hurricane snatch me up into Oceanus' stars, like *Cameiro* and *Clytia's* fate,[a]

Even so, I wish that the gods would remove me from every man's sight, because;

Odyssey's image is in my heart, I'd rather die than surrender to a man who is half of what he was,

Must grief be endured by day, and by night, as well?

For sleep divides the good, and multiplies the bad, that fate *will* always tell,

My misery haunts me even in sleep, for tonight I dreamt Odyssey was lying close by;

I am baffled, for what I witnessed was so real, but when I awoke, it turned into a lie."

*

Dawn is Light.[b]

*

Odyssey wakes to the sound of Penelope sobbing, which is puzzling, because he has just dreamed that she had *already* recognised him. Shouldn't she be happy?

*

---

a   Pandareus' two youngest daughters were named *Cameiro* and *Clytia*. After the death of their parents, Aphrodite took care of them, Hera taught them to be honourable and Athena made them capable, but when Aphrodite went to see Zeus to arrange their marriages, a hurricane snatched them into the heavens where they were forced to be the servants of the Erinyes (the Furies).

b   Today is Wednesday, 30th October, 1207 B.C. It is 6.53 A.M. and the first day of the Festival of Apollo.

He gathers his bedding, the fleeces and blankets and lays them on a stool in the cloister. He takes the ox-hide out into the courtyard, kneels upon it, lifts his hands to the sky, and prays:

"Father Zeus, you have returned me from that wretched war, to my home and family;

Now, after twenty years of hell, prove to me with two signs that I'm finished with misery."

As he prays, Zeus sends a blinding white flash with a shuddering thunderclap. Odyssey notices that there are no storm clouds, only a clear-blue sky.[a] His heart lifts.

A servant from the bakery, an older woman, appears and steps out into the courtyard, looking up into the sky. She is one of the twelve maids that grind grains and knead dough for the baker's ovens. The other servants are sleeping, exhausted, as they have finished their night-shifts' work, but this woman is slower. She was kneading dough when she heard the thunder-clap. She smiles at the beggar-king and looks up into the heavens, raising her dough-covered hands and forearms dusted with flour, and pleads:

"My god, Zeus, who *is* all, you have thundered from a sky that is cloudless;

A good omen, so here is my prayer: Let this be the last day the Suitors eat bread in this house,

They have worn me down with the labours of making bread for their bellies, every day;

And I hope that they never eat here - or elsewhere - again! That is what I pray."

Odyssey smiles at the woman. He is grateful for Zeus' omens received through the woman's plea and the bolt from the blue. He has gathered confidence in his destiny, soon the Suitors will be crushed under the weight of revenge, he thinks.

The other maids appear and busy themselves with their chores, lighting the fires and preparing for the Suitors' banquet.

---

a   A lightning strike from a blue sky is called a "positive giant" or "dry lightning". It can occur over 30 kilometres away from a storm. Because it seems to strike from a clear sky it is known as "a bolt from the blue". These powerful lightning flashes strike between the storm's top "anvil" and the Earth and carry several times the energy of a regular lightning strike.

Telemakis rises and dons his clothes. He straps his sword and sheath around his shoulder, sandals his feet, takes his spear with its sharpened bronze point and enters the cloisters. He asks Eurykleia:

"Dear nurse, did you make the stranger comfortable with food and a warm bed?
Or did you allow him to leave our house and fend for himself, instead?

My mother is a good woman, but gives more attention to inferior men;
And neglects the others who are, in reality, much better than them."

Eurykleia remarks:

"Young man, don't look to find fault, where there is no fault to find;
Last night the stranger sat and drank wine with your mother, and she didn't mind,

When he wanted to sleep, she told the maids to take him to a chamber's bed;
But, because he has been homeless for so long, he asked to sleep by the fire instead,

An ox-hide and lambskin fleeces, only, was how he wished to be kept;
And I placed quilted blankets and a coat over him as he slept."

Telemakis goes out through the courtyard to the town-square where an assembly is under way. He has his spear in hand, and his two dogs trail behind him.

Eurykleia rouses the maids, calling on them to sweep and mop the cloisters, cover the seats; and wipe down the tables, and prepare for another feast; the Suitors are coming, it is the first day of the Apollo Festival.

The entourage are here. They chop wood and light the fires. Eumaios arrives and unloads three of his best pigs, letting them graze near the courtyard. Close by is the kitchen where they will be butchered. He sees the beggar in the cloisters, goes to him and shakes his hand. He asks, unwittingly:

"Stranger, friend, are the Suitors looking after you, here in King Odyssey's palace?
Or are they as insolent as ever, and still full of malice?

Odyssey answers:

"I hope that heaven, punishes these shameless rogues, one day soon;

If Odyssey was standing here, I bet he would be planning their doom."

As they speak Melanthios, the goat-herder, comes along. He has brought goats for the Suitors' banquet. He has two helpers with him. They pen the goats in the stables underneath the gatehouse. Melanthios begins throwing insults at Odyssey:

"Stranger, you are still here. Go some place you belong, you are nothing but a pest;

And don't hang around this palace begging again, be off and make room for a proper guest,

Go and beg in some other land, otherwise you and I will come to blows before long;

Mark my words, this will be your last day as a beggar here, be gone!"

Odyssey makes no answer. He bows his head and stews on the bully's insults. A third man, Philoitios, joins them. He has brought a heifer and some lambs from the island of Dulichium[a] by ferry-boat for today's festivities. Philoitios pens the animals in the barn under the gatehouse. He walks over to Eumaios and the beggar, asking:

"Eumaios, who is this stranger that has been seen around here lately?

Is he one of your men? Where does he come from? Does he have friends, a family?

A poor fellow, down and out, but he looks as if he had been a great man;

Some are less fortunate, gods have the last say, even mighty kings bear sorrow and pain in Zeus's plan."

Philoitios offers his hand to the stranger and he shakes it, starting a conversation:

"Sir, when I saw you, my eyes filled with tears and a shiver came over me;

---

a   *Dulichium* is today an island lying to the east of Ithaki, although a recent, plausible theory suggests that it may have been another name for the southern, or northern half of the island of Ithaki.

For you remind me of my master, who's somewhere on Earth in rags too, his name is
Odyssey,

That is, if he's still alive and can see the blue sky, and can breathe fresh air like you
and I;

But, more likely he is in Hades by now, it has been twenty years since I saw him eye-
to-eye,

You see, my master made me head stockman for the Ionian clans, when I was quite
young;

Because of what he taught me, the cattle thrive like the kernels of corn they feed
upon;

Just as well, for these wretched Suitors demand more and more these days;

And they dishonour my master's son, and have only contempt for Zeus' ways,

Now that the king has been away for so long, they are all out-doing each other;

Eager to divide his estate once one of them gets the hand, of his son's mother,

And what a dilemma for me, although it would be wrong to abandon the prince, who
is in need;

But I want to escape and seek refuge in a foreign land, and maybe take some cattle to
breed;

That would be difficult, but not as hard as watching this herd of Suitors eat up all my
toil;

For I still cling to the hope that my master will return, and rid the Suitors from
Ithaki's soil."

Odyssey replies:

"Stockman, you seem to be a very loyal and sensible person, who is trustworthy;

So, I say that your king lives and returns today! I make that oath on the throne of
Odyssey,

Before you leave this place to return to your broad-horned cattle, across the water;

Your eyes will see him killing the Suitors, all 108 of them, in a bloody slaughter."

The stockman, Philoitios, confirms his faithfulness:

"If it's Zeus' will to bring my king home and rid the world of these vermin;

Your eyes will see this loyal friend in the fray, ready to help him."

And in like-minded faith, Eumaios offers the same promise.

While they speak, the Suitors ring-leaders are standing at the other end of the courtyard, hatching a plot to murder Telemakis. Between the two groups of men, a screeching eagle flies toward the conspirators from their left. It holds a dove in its talons. On this Melanthios, the goat-wrangler, says:

"My friends, our plot to murder Telemakis, by this omen, has been beaten;

We must abandon our plan, and the deed, and talk about it once we have eaten."

The others agree and go inside, hanging their coats and then taking their usual places at the dining tables in the Great Hall, where the servants are plating their meals. They are offered the innards first. There is a selection of lamb, goat, pork and beef. The stewards mellow the wines in the mixing-bowls, and the Eumaios gives each man his wine-cup. Philoitios offers bread from the baskets, while Melanthios follows him, pouring them their wine. They start their celebrations.

Telemakis has purposely set up a small table and an old stool for Odyssey near the entrance to the banquet hall, near the double doors. He has brought him a plate of meats, some bread and a gold cup filled with wine. He says to his royal father - the stranger - and to all those present:

"Sit, eat and drink your wine and share the privileges provided for all of you today;

It is not a tavern, but my father's home, and *'strangers are welcome'* is what he would say,

Therefore, Suitors, keep your hands and your tongues at bay;

I'll not permit insults and brawling to spoil Apollo's holy day."

The Suitors are surprised at Telemakis' assertiveness and all bite their lips, except Antinoos, who says:

"Such an offensive speech from the prince, we are guests here too, don't forget!

Zeus has defeated our plans; we should have shut his mouth long ago, that is my regret."

Telemakis ignores him.

Meanwhile, some stockmen are walking the sacrificial cattle through the town, they pass the shady grove of Apollo which is filling with town's people.

Back at the palace, the celebrations are in full swing. Each man has a share of the roasted meats and wine being offered by the servants. Odyssey receives the same portion as the others just as Telemakis instructed. Athena applies more pressure on the situation. She wants Odyssey to become more bitter and resentful to the Suitors.

Ctesippos,[261] of Kefalonia, is a wealthy lord. This man is a conceited and shameless bully, also trying to court the hand of Penelope. He says to the festive crowd:

"Attention, everyone, has that stranger already had his rightful share?

It's not right to ill-treat a visitor, especially one who is under Telemakis' care,

So, old man, here's something to tip the women in the bath-house with, if you know what a bath is;

A present from my own plate with the compliments of our hosts Odyssey, and Telemakis."

As he speaks, he takes a heifer's foot from the plate in front of him and hurls it at Odyssey, who moves his head to avoid it. The missile hits the wall behind him and a menacing grin takes hold of his face.

Telemakis speaks fiercely:

"Ctesippos, it is a good thing that you missed our visitor, for I'd have speared you, dead;

And your father would have to cancel your wedding plans, and arrange a funeral instead,

There will be no more violence and insults from any Suitor or guest here;
I'm not a child anymore, and I know right from wrong. From now on be respectful. Is that clear?

For too long you have been indulging yourselves, you've worn out your welcome;
I can't stop all of you, I'm outnumbered, but if you wish to kill me now, come on!

For I would rather die than witness such disgraceful acts day after day, of which you all boast;
You squander our estate, molest the maids and even threaten to kill me, your host."

Their tongues are tied with astonishment. The room is quiet. At last Agelaos, son of Damastor, says:

"*No-man* should be offended by what has just been said, was it fair?
Let's put an end to maltreating the stranger, and anyone else under Telemakis' care,

And here's a friendly word for Telemakis and his mother, which I hope you will accept;
Both of you have suffered waiting for Odyssey's return, and *he* would be angry with that,

It would have been better for you if Odyssey had returned;
But it is obvious, he is in another land where his grave was earned,

So, talk with your mother, and tell her to marry the man with the best bride-wealth;
Then you could enjoy your inheritance, while your mother attends to her new husband, in health."

Telemakis answers:

"Agelaos, I swear to you, that by Zeus, and by the sorrows of my mother's world-weary husband;

Who may have died far from here, I will urge my mother to seek her union with only the *best* man,

And I will be the first to give priceless presents and gifts on their wedding day;

But I cannot ask her to leave against her will, may the gods spare me from that dilemma, I pray!"

Athena makes the Suitors laugh uncontrollably. They are out of their minds with hysteria. Their happy faces now turn to dismay and horror as each man, separately, hallucinates that the food in front of him is spattered with blood. Indeed each man sees blood and mire throughout the Hall. Their faces wince and tears stream from their eyes. Their hearts are now heavy with foreboding. Theoklymenos, the seer, says:

"Men, you look gloomy with horror, a shroud of darkness covers you all like a flood;

I tell you that the air will be alive with ghostly voices and the walls and rafters shall drip blood,

The cloisters and the courtyard will fill with ghouls ready for a night in Hell;

Darkness will descend upon the land and even the Sun will desert you, as well."

When he finished, they all laughed at him. Eurymachos is the first to speak:

"This other stranger, Telemakis' friend, has lost his senses too, he *is* crazy;

Servants, throw him into the street, since he finds it too dark in here, to see."

Theoklymenos says:

"Eurymachos, I don't need an escort, I have eyes, ears and feet of my own *and* common sense;

And I will take them with me, but your gang may not get the chance, for all its ill-deeds and offence,

For your ruin sits close by and blocks your escape from catastrophe;

You have no chance whilst you remain in the Great Hall of Odyssey."

He leaves the palace and returns to Peiraeus' house, his host.

The Suitors are drunk and anxious. They heckle Telemakis. One of the gang says to him:

"Telemakis, you don't have much luck with guests, first you drag in that useless beggar;

Who gorges your bread and wine and can't work or fight to save himself, or any other,

And now here's another fellow pretending to be a prophet, so here's my advice;

Put them on board a fast ship to Sicily, and sell them to a slaver, for any price."

Telemakis ignores him and sits quietly, watching his father, expecting him to attack the Suitors at any moment.

Meanwhile, wise Penelope has been seated behind her chamber door, above the cloisters. She has heard the conversation and the wranglings.

*

The banquet lunch to honour Apollo, god of the bow, has been enjoyed with great celebration by the Suitors. They have eaten the innocent sacrificial cattle and drank to their limits. Their desserts are yet to come, a gory affair to be finished off by an avenging Spirit and a troubling man, for the Suitors are to face their doom.

*

THE ARCHERY CONTEST

*

WHO WILL STRING THE GREAT BOW?

*

THE GANG OF FOUR

Fire-eyed Athena has put into Penelope's mind that she should entice the Suitors to contest for her marriage by trying their skill with a bow and arrow. She senses this contest will bring about their destruction. With some of her maids she goes to the storage vault in the cellar. It's double doors are made of thick bronze and have ivory handles. Here Odyssey's treasures of gold, bronze, and silver are hoarded with his precious bow and a quiver full of arrows, given to him by a friend, Iphitus, the son of *Eurytus*,[a] King of Oichalia.[262]

The two princes became friends when they first met in the remote sanctuary at Bassae[b] dedicated to Apollo, the Helper.[263] Odyssey, as ambassador, went there to recover three-hundred sheep from Messenian[264] raiders who had stolen them and kidnapped their shepherds from Ithaki, and escaped by ship. Odyssey's father, Laertes, and the other noblemen sent him to recover the livestock when he was just a youth.

---

a   According to Homer, *Eurytus* was so proud of his archery skills that he challenged Apollo, who killed him for his audacity and arrogance. His bow was passed down to his son, Iphitus, who later gave the bow to his friend Odyssey. Iphitus was killed by Herakles. It was this bow that Odyssey, later, would use to attack the Suitors.

b   Although unknown, it is likely that *Ortilochus'* location was close to the remote archaic settlement at the beautiful Temple of Apollo, the Helper, in Bassae, Messenia in western Greece.

Iphitus had gone there to recover twelve brood mares and their yearlings, which had been stolen from his father's estate. The recovery of these mares brought on his death when he went, on behalf of his father - *who had beaten Herakles in an archery contest* - to ask for their return.

Herakles pretended to be friendly toward Iphitus, but murdered him by throwing him off the high walls of Tiryns,[265] violating Zeus' principle of hospitality to suppliants. It was before this that Odyssey exchanged his sword and a spear for Iphitus' bow and arrows. The bow was not taken to war, as it was a precious gift from his friend.

Penelope turns the key in its lock and thrusts the bolt back. The vault echoes like a bellowing bull. In there are shelves of fragrant cedar reaching up to the ceiling, all with clothes folded and stacked. She sees the leather case containing the bow hanging on a peg. Taking the bow from its case she kneels and begins sobbing. As her tears fade, she takes the bow and quiver to the Suitors, in the cloisters. The maids follow, carrying a chest containing gold and silver medals that her husband had won as prizes. On reaching one of the main pillars near them she stops and draws her glistening veil back from her cheeks, saying:

"Suitors, listen, you are all intent on abusing the hospitality shown by the House of Odyssey;

Because its ruler has long been absent, with the excuse that each of you wish to marry me,

Well, my wedding hand is the prize that any of you may compete for, lords and kings;

Here is Odyssey's bow, if you string it and shoot an arrow through the axe-handles' rings,

Then one of you will have me as your bride and from this day on I shall yield to matrimony;

And I hope *that* husband can provide me with the equal of this palace's bounty."

She tells Eumaios to give the axe handles and the bow to the Suitors. Eumaios weeps as he does so. Near him is Philoitios, the stockman, also weeping. Antinoos harasses them:

"You fools, why are *you* crying! You're only adding to the sorrows of your mistress;

Go outside and leave us, the Queen is about to find a husband, isn't that enough distress?

Leave the bow to us and let it seal our fate, for Penelope there will be only one man to enjoy;

But, friends, stringing this bow is not easy, for I saw Odyssey do it when I was a young boy."

Despite what Antinoos said, he secretly expected to be the first one to complete the tasks. However, he would be the first to taste his own blood from an arrow sent by Odyssey, the sacker of cities.

Athena rouses Telemakis. He addresses the Suitors:

"Good heavens, did Zeus rob me of my senses? My mother is telling you she wants a man;

And you are all sitting there like dumb-struck fools. If it's your fate, string the bow, if you can!

It is to win the woman who is peerless in Pilos, Argos and Mycenae;[a]

And not on the mainland, or here on Ithaki, has her likeness ever been,

You know all this too well, I don't need to sing her praises: She is a Queen!

Come on, make no excuses, if you can string the bow, her husband will be seen,

I will contest this trial too, and if I win and my mother does leave with another man;

At least I will know that I've earned the inheritance which my father planned."

He stands and throws his jacket onto his chair. With his sword he digs holes and buries the twelve axe heads so that their handle rings are lined up. Then he stamps the earth tight around their bases and everyone is amused by his proficiency. He walks back to the pavement under the cloisters and three times tried to bend the

---

a   Mycenae is an archaeological site near Mykines, in north-eastern Pelopennese, located about 85 kilometres south-west of Athens. The site is 20 kilometres inland from the Saronic Gulf. It is built upon a hill 900 feet above sea level. In the second millennium BC, Mycenae was one of the major centres of Hellenic civilization. It was a capital, controlling military and economic interests in Greece, Crete, the Cycladic islands and parts of Anatolia (Turkey). The period of Hellenic history from about 1600 BC to about 1100 BC is called Mycenean, referring to the influence of Mycenae. Its decline coincided with the reign of the House of Atreus, around 1250 BC.

bow to attach the string. Three times he fails. On his fourth attempt his father tilts his head, signalling him to stop, and he says:

"God help me! Am I a weakling, with no skills to defend myself under attack?

Who's next? Someone a bit stronger than myself should be able to bend the bow back."

He leans the bow against one of the double-doors at the entry, with an arrow. He sits in his chair, just as Antinoos says:

"Come on then, each man must take his turn, in line;

Starting from where the steward is now pouring the wine."

The rest agree, and Leodos,[266] a diviner, who is the son of Oenops, is the first to rise. He is a religious priest to the Suitors, and sits in the corner near the wine steward. Of the Suitors gang, he is the only man who despises them for their recklessness. He takes the bow and arrow, and goes back to the mark from where he must shoot. For all of his effort, he can't even bend the bow in the slightest arc; his hands are weak and not used to work. Quickly he wilts, saying to the Suitors:

"My friends, I cannot string it, this bow will stop the heart and soul of anyone trying;

But isn't it better to die of a heart attack, than to miss the prize for which we all are vying?

That which has brought us together for all this time, in this place;

If you are hoping to marry Penelope, think again, and woo another woman's face,

Perhaps Penelope won't have to re-marry a man! That destiny is yet to be revealed:

For this bow is stronger than iron, if it cannot be bent, she may not have to yield."

He puts the bow back where it was, propped against the door jamb and sits. Antinoos rebukes him saying:

"Leiodes, what are you saying? You make me angry with your monstrous speak;

How will this bow, *'stop the heart and soul of anyone trying'* just because you are weak?

Obviously, your mother didn't breed an archer, or gave you any strength;

So don't discourage the others, there are strong men in this queue's length."

He says to Melanthios, the goat-wrangler:

"Hurry, go to the fireplace and melt a ball of lard onto lambswool and smear it into the bow;

It's heat will soften the timber and we can contend this contest, so the winner we'll know."

Melanthios feeds the fire, and did as he was bid. A few men rub the hot lard into the bow and try to bend it, but they fail to get the string's eyelet near the bow's tip, but Antinoos and Eurymachos, two of the ring-leaders, are determined to win.

Trouble is brewing. Eumaios and Philoitios leave the cloisters. Odyssey follows them. Outside the courtyard, Odyssey says to them, quietly:

"Stockman, and you, swine-handler, stop! I have something to ask both of you;

Would each of you stand and fight for Odyssey if he returned now? You must tell me what is true."

Philoitios says:

"I wish Zeus himself would return Odyssey right now;

Then you would see what I could do against this mob, in a fighting row."

Eumaios nods his head and makes an oath to the gods for Odyssey's swift return.

Knowing that both men are on his side, he says:

"Well, it is me; I am Odyssey!

I have suffered much, lost for twenty years, now I'm home in my own country;

Only you two, out of all my servants, are glad, for I don't see the others praying for me,

So, I promise you both, if we defeat the Suitors I will find a wife for each of you;

And fine homes close to the palace and you will become my friends and brothers, too,

Now, I will give you proof of who I am, look at this scar, I got it on Mt Parnassos;

When a boar's tusk ripped me open, when I was hunting with the sons of Autolycos."

He draws back the rags revealing the great scar. They both start to weep and hug Odyssey, kissing his forehead and cheeks. The Sun will set and rise again if Odyssey doesn't check them. He says:

"No more crying, in case someone should see us and their suspicion grows;

We should go inside separately. Also, the Suitors won't want me to get the bow and arrows,

Therefore, Eumaios, pass it to me when you are coming down the Hall;

Then go to the women's chambers and bolt those doors, and tell them all,

That if they hear men fighting or screaming around the palace and in the Hall;

Not to come out of their rooms, keep busy with their chores, one and all,

And I charge you, Philoitios, to close and bolt the double door;

So no-one can flee into the courtyard and escape what is in store."

Odyssey goes back inside and sits on his stool. His two companions follow him.

Eurymachos has the bow and is heating it by the fire to make it more flexible, but even so he can't bend it. He is angry. Heaving a sigh, he says:

"Damn us all! It seems that we have been *divorced*, before we got the chance to marry Penelope;

But there are plenty of other women in Ithaki that we can always make brides-to-be,

What's infuriating is that we must match the *memory* of Odyssey's long-lost strength and vitality;

Because we cannot string his bow, the Suitors are destined to be disgraced for eternity."

Antinoos, is quick to protest:

"It shall not be so, Eurymachos, as you know today is Apollo, the Helper's, anniversary;

No-man should string that bow, and shoot an arrow, that would be against this occasion's sanctity,

Let's resume this contest tomorrow, when the Suitors may find the true husband. Put the bow away!

And tell Melanthios to bring more goats for tomorrow's gifts for Apollo, god of the Bow, without delay,

And, as for the axes, let them stand where they are planted over-night;

For *no-man* is likely to use them between now and daylight,

Now, wine steward, fill our cups, all to the brim;

And to Apollo, the Far Shooter, let's drink to him."

The rest of the revellers agree and make their toasts to the god. Once they had drunk their wine, Odyssey craftily asks:

"Suitors to your illustrious Queen, listen to what I ask, here is my plea;

Especially to Eurymachos and Antinoos who have just spoken so sensibly,

Yes, leave your archery contest to tomorrow and its outcome be as the gods intend;

But, let's see if *my* once-strong hands can string that bow that the others have failed to bend,

Let's see if I might have the power to curve its defiant length;

Or whether begging and neglect have robbed my youthful strength."

The mob are furious at his suggestion, for each man secretly fears that he may be able to bend the bow and be a competitor for Penelope's hand in marriage. Antinoos, always the first to bully, says:

"Wretched fool and pest! Not only are you mindless, you have no sense of decency;

Think of yourself as very fortunate by being allowed to dine with your superiors so frequently!

No other beggar has been allowed to hear what is said by us privately;

Has the wine befuddled your head as it does to all who gulp immoderately?

It was wine that inflamed the Centaur Eurytion,[267] a guest of Pirithoos, one of the *Lapiths*;[a]

When the wine befuddled *his* head, he tried to rape the bride, according to the myths,

Which angered the hero Pirithoos who cut off Eurytion's ears and nose, there and then;

And dragged him out of the palace. When he awoke he'd forgotten what had happened,

And that's what started the war[b] between the Centaurs and mankind;

All because of the wine, which deluded and disturbed his drunken mind,

Don't let *our* wine delude you, you're stupid enough! Just sit there and put your daydreams at bay;

---

a   The legendary Lapiths were an ancient tribe that lived in Thessally, in the valley of Peneus under Mount Pelion.
b   That war is known as the Centauromachy.

Drink moderately and don't try to compete with the others, or you'll be sent to King Echetus[a] today,

He kills every one that comes near him, he's a cannibal and likes human meat;

He will hack off and fry your nose and ears first, and then geld your privates for the dogs to eat."

Prudent Penelope has been listening to Antinoos' vicious words; she knows it's time to speak:

"Antinoos, show some decency! Is it right that *you* should ill-treat a guest of Telemakis?

Even if this stranger *is* strong enough to bend the bow, today in this palace,

You have a wild imagination, do you think he could take me into his home, and make me his spouse?

Even this man would not think such a thing. Is that what disturbs your feast tonight, in this house?"

Eurymachos, is quick to defend the Suitors' self-serving concern:

"Queen Penelope, we do not suppose that this man will take you away with him, impossible!

But gossip from lesser folk than are celebrating here, men and women, is probable,

They might start a scandal by saying:

'These Suitors are weaklings; not one could bend the bow for the wife of long-lost Odyssey;

But a lowly beggar sent an arrow through the ring's hearts, who she couldn't marry.'"

---

a   King Echetus, the cannibal king of a rugged and mountainous region, Epirus in the north-west area of ancient Greece, near modern-day Albania. It is where Odyssey pretends he visited the sanctuary of Dodoni, with its wind-chiming oracle, the oldest in archaic Greece, to learn his fate on returning to Ithaki. It is thought that Echetus was a mythological creation, used to scare disobedient children or used as the villain in bedtime stories. An alternate theory is that Echetus was a real king around the time of Homer, and that he was demented and possibly a cannibal.

Penelope answers him:

"Eurymachos, *some* people abuse others, and desecrate their duty of hospitality;

So, why do you care that other men, or women, speak their mind when it comes to honesty?

This stranger is strong and well-built, he says that he is sprung from a noble line of kings;

Give him that bow, and let's see whether he can string it *and* arrow the twelve rings,

Grant this man a chance, let us all see if he can live up to his claim;

For an archer is not known by his arrow, but by his aim!

Eurymachos, what have you to lose?

I promise, and mark my words, that if Apollo answers his prayers, and he succeeds;

Then I will give the man a new shirt and jacket, a sturdy sword and a javelin, to deter dogs and thieves,

I will also give him sandals, and anything else he may want, or need;

To carry him safely wherever he wishes to go, and with a blessing of the gods' speed."

Telemakis gets involved:

"Mother, I am the only man between here and the mainland who can offer or refuse this bow;

And *no-man*, including this stranger, can force me either way. Anyway, it's time for *you* to go,

Leave here now and go about your duties, to your loom and maids who you should be near;

This bow is a matter between men - and it's mine above all - for *now*, it is me who is the master here."

She takes the stairs to her chamber and maids, thinking of the desperate situation below. Penelope, "the weaver of tears", lays on her bed and sobs into sleep.

Eumaios, takes hold of the bow and quiver of arrows and walks toward the stranger, and the double doors. The Suitors rush at him from all sides of the cloisters. One of the younger men says:

"You idiot, where do you think you are taking that? Are you out of your wits like the stranger, too?

If Apollo grants my prayer, your own hunting hounds will tear apart all your pigs, and you;

That weapon is needed for tomorrow's contest;

Whose side are you on; the Suitors or the guest?"

Eumaios, frightened by the outburst, drops the bow and quiver. Telemakis shouts out, above the crowd's din, pretending to threaten him:

"Uncle Eumaios, bring the bow and don't worry about their roar:

Or, *I* will pelt you with stones back to your farm-hut's door,

For I am the better of us two, if only I had the same advantage over the Suitors, as I have over you,

I'd soon send them away, battle-beaten with their ill-starred plans destroyed, too."

As he speaks the Suitors roar with laughter to mock their host. It lowers the tension. Eumaios now brings the bow on, handing it to Odyssey, and then finds Eurykleia, whispering to her:

"Eurykleia, Telemakis says:

"'You are to go to the women's chambers and bolt the doors, and tell them all;

That if they hear men fighting or screaming around the palace and in the hall,

Not to come out of their rooms, keep busy with their chores, one and all.'"

Eurykleia does so.

Meanwhile, Philoitios has slipped out and bolted the gates of the outer courtyard wall. In the gatehouse he found a ship's mooring line made of timber fibres from Byblos[a] and ties the gates securely.

He returns to the inner courtyard and sits at his usual place, keeping an eye on Odyssey, who has the bow in his hands. He twists and turns it checking that rot or wood-worms have not eaten it since he went away. One of the Suitors turns to his neighbour and says:

"This stranger is quite the connoisseur of antique bows; do you think he has one like it at his place?

Or, does he want to make one? Either way, he looks like a *trouble*-maker to my face."

Another Suitor says:

"I hope he is more successful with other things;

Than he is at stringing this bow, it's not for weaklings."

Odyssey, has checked the bow and strings it, without effort, like a bard stringing his lyre, he loops the sheep-gut around each end of the bow. He takes the bow in his left hand and plucks the string with his right, with the skill of a minstrel. The sound is like the sweet twittering of a swallow's song.

The Suitors are shocked, colour drains from their faces.

The Great Hall starts to darken turning to an early night. There is an eerie atmosphere as the Suitors, sit in silence. The solar eclipse lasts for a minute.[b] In the darkness, a groaning thunder-clap explodes above the palace. Odyssey's heart lifts, appreciating the omen sent by Zeus, the En-lightener.

---

a   An ancient city, established over 9,000 years ago at the western end of the Mediterranean Sea in Phoenicia (modern Lebanon). It was the home of Sanchuniathon, who was one of the first historians and lived around the time of Homer, about 25 centuries ago.

b   Astronomers have confirmed these events using NASA software. On the 30th October, 1207 B.C. a solar eclipse of a 75% magnitude darkened Ithaki for about one minute. Refer to: Papamarinopoulos, et al. (2012).

Daylight returns to the Hall to find Odyssey seated on his stool, he picks an arrow from the table next to him, the rest are in the quiver and will soon be delivered to the Suitors. He places the arrow's notch in the bow-string and draws it back. He takes aim and releases. The arrow's bronze tip leads the shaft through each of the rings, flying through the double doors and lodging in a fence rail at the end of the courtyard just above Irus's be-fuddled head. Smiling, he says to Telemakis:

"*This* guest has not disgraced you, Telemakis, I strung the bow and the rings were holed;

My strength seems to have held up considering the Suitors thought me far too old,

Now, while its daylight, let's prepare this crowd's last supper at least;

These festivities should have desserts for the guests to crown this feast."

As he speaks, he blinks an eye, giving a signal to Telemakis, who stands, armed, by his father's seat.

*

JUSTICE OR REVENGE?

*

THE SLAUGHTER

*

THE MAIDS

Odyssey tears off his rags, springs to the double doors and locks them. He pours the arrows from his quiver onto the stone floor, shouting:

"This archery contest is over, but the match to seal your fate now arises;

Let us see if Apollo, the Helper, will allow me to reveal some more surprises."

He takes dead aim at Antinoos who is about to take a gulp of wine from his two-handled gold cup. No thoughts of violence or bloodshed has entered his mind, for who would be foolish enough to think that one man, however bold, would attack so many? Sometimes security is found in numbers: but not this time.

The arrow strikes Antinoos in the throat, and its bronze point goes through his neck, emerging between his shoulder blades. Dropping the cup, he falls back as a torrent of blood surges from his nostrils and mouth. He knocks the table as he goes down, scattering his meal; bread and roasted meats lie in the blood pool around him.

The Suitors are in uproar, and morose with fear, as they see that Antinoos has collapsed, dead. They spring from their seats searching the walls for arms; a shield or a spear to defend themselves, but there is none. Angrily, someone says:

"Stranger, you shall pay for making this mistake, you're a dead man too!

You've killed the most famous Suitor in Ithaki, now the vultures will devour you."

They all think that Antinoos has been killed by accident, and can not imagine that Death is prepared for every one of them. Odyssey, glaring, says:

"Dogs, you didn't believe I would come back from the war in Troy;

So, you've wasted my estate and wenched the maids in my employ;

And in front of me, each one of you tried to seduce my wife into my marital bed;

Without any fear of the gods, or vengeance of men! Now it's time for you all to join the Dead."

They are pale with fear, each man looks around for an escape, or a place to hide. Eurymachos speaks:

"If you are Odyssey, then what you say is right, we have wronged you and your family;

But Antinoos, was the ring-leader, it was all his idea, and he is dead already,

He didn't really want to marry Penelope either, that was not his real purpose;

He wanted to kill Telemakis and be King of Ithaki, but he's been thwarted by Zeus,

Given that he has paid with his life, please spare ours, we are your people;

And we shall repay what was wasted, in full, and then all should be peaceful,

Each man here shall pay you a fine equal to twenty oxen;

And we shall keep giving you gold and bronze until your heart softens,

Until we have made amends and righted those wrongs and mistakes;

You will be justified in taxing us for as long as it takes."

Odyssey glares at him, saying:

"Even if I take everything you have, and multiply it a thousand times;

It would never be enough to compensate for your arrogance, and outrageous crimes,

Now, it has come down to this, you have two choices, stay and fight;

Or, see if you can out-run Moros[a] and his looming Fates, by taking flight."

As they listen, their eyes bulge as their hearts sink. Their knees weaken. Eurymachos speaks for the last time:

"My friends, this man denies our plea, even though we are supplicants,[b] one and all;

He has no mercy, and will shoot everyone from where he stands, hell-bent on seeing us fall,

So, let us show him our mettle; draw your swords, and use the tables as a shield;

And rush at him, all of us, like the force of Thera's wave,[c] then he'll yield,

He'll have to make a retreat though the gatehouse, while I go and raise the alarm in town;

Odyssey's archery exploits are over, his last arrow has been shot, it's his time to be put down!"

---

a   Moros is the omnipotent being who dispenses everyone's life through pre-determined fate. He "compels" mortals to their death. The Moirai (Fates) asserted that not even Zeus could question Moros, because he *is* destiny. Moros was the only force that Zeus truly respected and dreaded. Because of this, Moros was also considered as the entity behind Zeus. Moros' opposite is Elpis the personified Spirit of Hope. She and the other spirits were trapped in a jar by Zeus entrusting them to the care of the *first* human woman Pandora. When she opened the vessel all of the Spirits escaped except for Elpis (Hope) who remained behind to comfort mankind.

b   Suppliants are sent by Zeus and therefore are revered and should be protected. Whereas a *supplicant* begs for mercy from the angered, typically from an offended ruler, deity or king.

c   An allusion, mine, to the eruption of the volcano on the island of Thera (Santorini) in the Aegean Sea. It occurred around 1,600 B.C. and destroyed the Minoan civilisation then based on Crete. The "tsunami" - *Thera's wave* - from the seismic event destroyed the palaces at Knossos, and many Mediterranean coastal cities and settlements. It was a cataclysmic event that fogged the Earth's atmosphere with ash clouds for five years, causing widespread famine across the world, and the collapse of many cultures, including, Minoan, Egyptian and the Xia Dynasty in China. It was the most destructive eruption in recorded history.

He draws the blade of his bronze sword, sharp-edged on both sides, and lunges at Odyssey, with a blood-curdling scream. Odyssey instantly releases an arrow into his breast, entering under his nipple, piercing his liver. He drops his sword and falls forward over a table. His gold cup and all the food fly, as he rolls off the table his face crumples into the stone floor. He kicks the stool he kept under the table, the same stool he hit the stranger with, as his last unwitting act of defiance. Silently, he writhes in pain, then his eyes shimmer into Death. The wave of the attack is stalled as the other men think again.

Amphinomos draws his sword and comes at Odyssey to maneuver him from the guarded doors, but Telemakis is too quick, striking him from behind; the spear goes between his shoulder-blades through his chest, and he collapses with his face in the dirt. Then Telemakis springs away, leaving his spear still in the corpse, for he fears that one of the foes might attack him as he pulls the spear out. He runs to his father's side and says:

"Father, I'll get you a shield, spears and a brass helmet, so your head won't be harmed;

And get weapons for all of us too, for now it's best to be well armed."

Odyssey replies:

"Don't waste a breath, return quickly and get into the fray;

Only while these arrows remain here, can I spoil their get-away."

Telemakis runs to the armoury. He selects four shields, eight spears and four brass helmets with horse-hair plumes and temple guards, and brings them back to Odyssey. He covers them while they don their amour and join him, armed. He has been killing the Suitors one by one, who've fallen into piles throughout the Hall.

All the arrows have flown and he leans the bow against the door post. He hangs a shield four hides thick from his shoulder and on his gallant head, places the helmet with its tall, menacing plume. He grabs the two bronze-tipped spears.

There is a trap-door at one end of the hall leading into a narrow passage, and an exit to the outer courtyard. Odyssey tells Eumaios to stand by this narrow door and guard it, for only one person could get through it at a time. But Agelaos is onto it, and shouts:

"Someone go to the trap-door and make a run through the courtyard; go to the town-square;

Raise the alarm, get some weapons back here, so an end can be put to this murderous affair."

Melanthios speaks to Agelaos:

"That may not work so well, for the trap-door is narrow and easily defended by one man;

But, I know what to do, I'll bring you arms from the palace's store-room, that's a better plan."

Melanthios goes by the back passage to the armoury and collects twelve shields, helmets and spears and delivers them to the Suitors, where they are distributed. Odyssey's heart sinks and his knees lose lift when the armed Suitors emerge from the cloisters bearing their weapons. He feels the gravity of the moment.

He says to Telemakis:

"One, or some, of the women are helping the Suitors;

Or, perhaps its the goat-wrangler, Melanthios."

Telemakis admits:

"Father, the fault is mine - alone - for I left the armoury door wide open,

Eumaios, go and lock it and check who's been inside: the goat-herder or the women?"

Meanwhile, Melanthios is returning to the store-room to fetch more weapons. Eumaios notices him and says to Odyssey:

"Odyssey, it *is* that roughneck Melanthios, who's looting the weapon storages;

Shall I kill him, if I can, or bring him here to pay for his outrages."

Odyssey answers:

"Telemakis and I will hold the Suitors, no matter what, they won't get passed this flank;

Take Philoitios with you and bind Melanthios' hands and feet behind him, on a plank,

Lock him in the armoury once you've strung him up, hanging from a rafter;
And let him spin there into madness, and we'll deal with him after."

They go to the armoury and see Melanthios busy searching for arms at the back of the room. With spear-points ready they wait for him to emerge. Melanthios comes out with a helmet in one hand and an old, rotted shield in the other, which was used by Laertes, but has long since been discarded. The straps are unravelled and worn.

The two seize and drag him, struggling, along the floor by the hair. They tie his hands and feet behind his body which is kept straight by a plank. They bind a rope around his belly and hoist him into the air, suspended from a rafter in the middle of the room. They wind the rope, turning it as tight as they can. They release the twisted line and Melanthios starts spinning.

The hog-handler taunting him, says:

"Melanthios, it will be a giddy[a] watch over your goats from this bed, spinning on its cable;
Until Dawn stops Oceanus' star-stream,[b] when you usually bring them here, for the Suitors' table."

He spins wildly on the whirligig[c] while they remove more weapons and go back to Odyssey. There in the cloister the four men stand, armed and formidable. Those in the Hall are just as fierce and outnumber them.

Zeus's daughter, Athena, appears in the guise of Mentor who Odyssey hasn't seen for twenty years.

Odyssey is excited, saying:

"Mentor, help me, it's your old friend, we grew up together, remember me?
And the many good turns I did for you, help us now to victory."

---

a   The Greek word for goat is: *gida*. Many Mediterranean cultures link goats to anger, anxiety and madness. The English word, *tragedy*, is derived from Greek for: *goat-song* which was named after the region of Thrace, the Goat country, where the turmoil and upheaval of constant invasion and war, drove the inhabitants mad.
b   Oceanus' Stream is the Milky Way. Ancient mariners referred to sailing on Oceanus, the sea of stars, as a metaphor for observing or navigating the night sky.
c   The whirligig was originally a torture device.

His instinct tells him it is Athena whose presence is rousing him.

The Suitors raise an uproar, cursing and abusing her, believing it is Mentor. Agelaos, son of Damastor, tries to shame Athena, further:

"Mentor,[a] don't let Odyssey fool you into joining his side, they are already defeated;

If you do, then after their throats are slashed, that's how you'll be treated,

We will seize your estates: *all* your possessions and property;

And sell your wives and children into slavery, far away from Ithaki."

These threats make Athena more furious and she goads Odyssey:

"Odyssey, your valour is not what it was, your reputation may not survive hereafter;

You fought for ten hard years against the Trojans for the sins of Helen of Sparta,

You killed countless men in those days, even sacked Priam's city by your horse's hoax;[b]

How lamentable is this scene *now*: in your own home, you face defeat from these pathetic folks,

Come on - close friend - let's stand by side, and you can *watch* how Mentor, son of Alcimus,

The Courageous One, battles your foes to repay some of *your* outstanding kindness."

But she does not allow him victory yet, she wants to prove his and Telemakis' mettle. She flies onto a ceiling rafter, taking the form of a swallow.

Meanwhile, Agelaos, son of Damastor, Eurynomus, Amphimedon, Demoptolemus, Pisander, and Polybos, son of Polyctor, are at the front of the fighting, on the Suitors' side, for many others had already fallen from Odyssey's death-winged arrows. Agelaos shouts to them:

---

a   The name, Mentor, translates to: *Instils spirit or courage.*
b   An allusion to the Wooden Horse stratagem, conceived by Odyssey.

"Friends, we'll have victory soon, Mentor has deserted them, and their spirit has fled;

Now, let's hurl six spears straight at Odyssey, he can't dodge them all, he'll be the first man dead,

Whoever lands the fatal spear shall have glory for all time, if it's Zeus' will;

The others are nothing without their commander, they'll make an easy kill."

They threw the volley of spears, but Athena made them all miss. One lodged in the door post, another into the double doors, and one sparked off the solid wall, the others flew wildly out of harm's way. Safe from that burst, Odyssey rallies the other three:

"My friends, it's our turn to attack, drive your spears into the heart of their advance;

Let's stay alive, and make sure they don't add to their list of crimes, perchance."

Sometimes security is found in a gang's size, and this is one of those occasions, for they aim straight into the front of them and hurl their spears. Odyssey kills Demoptolemus, Telemakis spears Euryades, Eumaios ends Elatos, while the stockman slays Pisander. They all bite the dust, and the other Suitors retreat into a corner of the cloisters. Odyssey's men rush and pull the spears from the dying foes.

Again, the Suitors take aim and again Athena makes their weapons useless, sending them randomly throughout the hall, except that Amphimedon's spear grazed Telemakis's wrist, slicing it open, and Ctesippos manages to glance Eumaios's shoulder above his shield, but it draws no blood.

Odyssey and his men drive into the crowd of Suitors with another volley. Odyssey hits Eurydamos, Telemakis stabs Amphimedon, and Eumaios drops Polybos. The stockman spears Ctesippos in the breast, his heart gushes blood as he is taunted:

"Foul-mouthed son of that braggart, Polythersos, time to save your speeches now;

Next time you talk it will be to the gods, and dishonour they don't allow,

So, take this spear as repayment for the cow's hoof you threw at Odyssey, your king;

When he was a suppliant beggar to you, in his own house. Is it satisfying?"

Odyssey slays Agelaos with a sword. Telemakis rams Leocritos, son of Evenor, in the belly; the spear-tip goes cleanly through him emerging from his back as he falls face first onto the stone floor.

Athena, as a swallow, holds out her deadly Aegis[a] from the rafters.

The Suitors wail in fear, for they know their time is short. They flee to the western end of the hall in a stampede, like cattle escaping horseflies in the short-shadowed heat of summer. But the gang of four chase the retreat, like sharp-beaked falcons with spread talons that swoop from the high, cool air onto bird flocks, and their weak are killed. They have no escape. Some men train these birds to kill, for they delight in destruction and blood-sports.

The four men range around the Suitors, huddled together. Their voices fall away as one-by-one they are hacked and impaled. The floor runs red with blood and gore oozing from each man. The blood-lust continues.

Leodos rushes forward and grips the knees of Odyssey, pleading:

"Odyssey I beg you to show me mercy, spare my life, let *me* be freed;

I never wronged any of the women in this house either in thought, word or deed,

I tried to stop them, but they wouldn't heed and have now paid a gruesome price;

I was only the priest, an official. Must I die for just offering holy advice?

Odyssey looks him in the eyes, saying:

"If you're their priest, you had plenty of opportunities to pray that I might come home;

And persuade the Suitors not to marry my wife, or plot to kill my son,

But you didn't, therefore you shall now die."

Odyssey plucks the sword from Agelaos' dead body, and as Leodos starts to speak again, slashes his neck, cleaving his head onto the ground, still talking as it rolls across the stone floor.

The minstrel Phemios, son of Terpes, who was forced by the Suitors to perform for them, now tries to save his own life. He is standing near the trap door, with his lyre in hand. He debates if he should flee outside to the altar of Zeus in the

---

a   Athena's Aegis, being a symbolic shield or mirror, depicts her authority to represent Zeus' mission: to fulfil Destiny on behalf of Moros. In this setting the context is that Athena holds up to the Suitors a mirror which shows each man his life; it flashes before them and they know they are doomed.

courtyard where many sacrifices had been made in the past and hide there, or go to Odyssey and embrace his knees as a supplicant. He lays the lyre on the ground between the mixing bowl and a silver-studded seat, then he goes to Odyssey and drops at his feet, hugging his knees. His words run:

"Odyssey, I beg for your mercy, spare me, don't kill the bard that plays for gods and men;

I taught myself, heaven grants me tunes and lyrics through Athena's inspiration,

I shall sing to you as a Muse does for a god, if you leave my head on these shoulders;

I never wished to play for the Suitors, but they forced me, just ask your son, Telemakis."

Telemakis hears his plea and goes to his father, agreeing:

"Father, this man is innocent, do him no harm, and let's also spare Medon;

He has been good to me all these years, that's if Philoitios or Eumaios haven't killed him."

Medon, the chief steward, hears Telemakis, as he is cowering under a seat hidden by a large ox hide. Throwing it off he runs to Telemakis, and takes hold of his knees, pleading:

"Here I am, Sir, halt your hands, and beg your father not to involve me in this bloody strife;

For I never wasted his estate's bounty, or was disrespectful to yourself, or his wife."

Odyssey smiles and replies:

"Fear not, Telemakis has saved your life, and you may live to tell another;

That good deeds always prosper, and bad deeds lead to disaster,

Medon, get out of here fast, beyond the cloisters, into the courtyard;

While we finish our work here; and don't forget to take Phemios, the bard!"

The pair leave, chasing their shadows as fast they can. They hide by Zeus's altar, still expecting to be killed if the Suitors win the day.

Odyssey searches the Hall and cloisters for anyone who may have escaped justice. No, all are lying dead, or dying, in pools of blood. Like fish which the angler has netted from the sea, and thrown upon the beach to lie gasping for water until the heat of the Sun brings their end. That's how the Suitors have fallen.

Odyssey asks Telemakis to bring Eurykleia, the senior maid, to the Hall. He does so by going to the locked women's chamber and summoning her. She follows him back to the Hall where she finds Odyssey among the bodies, he is soaked from head to toe in crimson gore, like a lion that has just devoured an ox, with his cheeks and mane dripping with blood, a terrifying sight.

As she takes in the scale of the carnage, she begins to cry for joy, for she sees what a great deed they have done. But Odyssey reprimands her:

"Old woman, don't crow! Rejoice in silence, it's unholy to gloat over the misfortunes of men;

Heaven fated these men before birth, and their wrong-doings brought their end,

For they had no respect for Zeus' work, they dishonoured all, from its kings to its poorest;

And their evil only earned early deaths, for no-man escapes the eyes of Moros,

Now, tell me which women in this house have Zeus to answer to;

And who are innocent and have remained loyal and true?"

Eurykleia, answers:

"I will tell you truly, my son, the number of women who work here is fifty;

Of them, twelve have disgraced their loyalties to this house, myself and to Penelope,

However, they showed no disrespect to Telemakis, for until lately he was just a boy;

And his mother never permitted him to give orders to any maids, in this house's employ,

Let me go upstairs and retrieve your wife to show her;

For some god has held her in the bosom of deepest slumber."

Odyssey replies, sharply:

"Do not wake her yet! Go and tell the Suitors' sluts to come here, at once."

Eurykleia leaves the Great Hall to fetch the guilty maids.

In the meantime he calls Telemakis, the stockman, and the swine-handler, telling them to remove the bodies and clean the hall, once the women arrive. And after it has been cleansed, to take the women out to the gatehouse in the outer courtyard and kill them by stabbing each with their swords, and release their lust and betrayal forever.

The women appear, all weeping remorsefully. Their first chore is to drag the corpses into the courtyard next to the gatehouse where they are to be piled.

Next, they scrub the walls, tables and seats with hot water and sponges, while Telemakis, Eumaeos and Philoitios shovel up the blood and gore into buckets. The women dispose of the blood buckets and mop the floors. The Great Hall has been cleaned, so they take the women, at sword-point, into a corner of the courtyard, where they cannot escape. Telemakis whispers to the other two:

"I won't allow these women noble deaths,[a] for they have offended Zeus;

They were insolent to my mother and me, and were the whores of the Suitors."

He takes a ship's mooring line, which had until now bound the gatehouse doors. He strings it between the roof joists and the end of the building. He ties nooses to the line and one-by-one each terrified maid is hoisted above the ground. Like *spring-snares*,[b] set for a thrush or quail, in the undergrowth where they go to nest. For a little while the maids' feet twitch and dance, but soon they are stilled by Death.

Next, Melanthios is dragged, dizzy and senseless, from the armoury where he spent the night spinning on the whirling-board. They cut off his nose and ears, and the pitiless knife gelds his genitals which are strewn to the dogs that hang around the kitchen's back-door, his hands and feet are hacked off, completing the blood-lust.

---

a   Telemakis defies Odyssey's instructions by denying the offending women an honourable death like, a ritual sacrifice of an animal, by sword. Instead he kills them by hanging.

b   *Spring-snares* are nooses, attached to bent branches, used to trap birds and other small prey.

The three staunch men, wash their hands and feet and return to the Great Hall.

There Odyssey says to Eurykleia:

"Fetch me *brimstone*[a] and *frank-incense*,[b] and bring braziers with flaming fires;

And go to Penelope and ask her to come here, with all her servants and loyal maids, if she desires."

Eurykleia, responds:

"A fair request under the circumstances, but let me bring you a new jacket and shirt;

You can't stand here in your palace with those rags drenched in blood, looking your worst."

Sternly, Odyssey says: "First light the fires to purge and purify this place!"

She lights all the braziers and brings the brimstone and frank-incense already mixed. Odyssey ignites the mixture, billowing an aromatic cloud throughout the palace and courtyards.

Eurykleia goes to the women's chamber. The maids return, pressing around Odyssey, embracing and kissing his cheeks. He remembers each one of them and is elated at this, his long-awaited homecoming. He breaks down; tears flood from his eyes.

*

---

a *Brimstone* is sulphur, which burns fiercely. In this case it is used to fire the incense to purify the atmosphere in the Great Hall.
b *Frank-incense*, an aromatic resin, when burnt produces a pungent, woody fragrance.

PENELOPE AND ODYSSEY

*

THE GANG OF FOUR LEAVE

Eurykleia, over-joyed at being the one to break news of the King's return, runs, her knees lifting and her ankles springing her up the stairs to Penelope's chamber.

On reaching her bed, the old maid is sparkling with news, saying:

"Wake up Penelope, my lady, come and see what, for twenty years, you have missed;

Odyssey has returned and killed the Suitors, their curse, and lives, have all been dismissed."

Penelope is waking from her deep sleep, but finds these words:

"The gods sometimes make sensible people stupid;

And make fools sensible, Eurykleia, have you gone mad?

That is what they must have done to you, swapped your senses for insanity, instead;

You were a reasonable person before I went to bed, but now you have goats in your head,

Why do you make fun of me, don't you think I've seen enough *trouble* already;

And you've woken me from the deepest, sweet sleep I've ever enjoyed, with this
absurdity,

I've never slept so well since the day my husband went to doomed Ilium;

Go back to the women's room before I scold you, as I should have done."

Eurykleia tries again:

"But, I am not mocking you, Odyssey has returned, as your eyes shall see;

He's the stranger who the Suitors man-handled in the hall, so badly,

Telemakis has known for days of his return;

But kept it a secret so that revenge, those dogs, would surely earn."

Penelope springs from her bed and throws her arms around Eurykleia,
weeping, she says:

"But my dear nurse, explain this: If he has come home, as you want me to see;

How did he manage to overcome all the wicked Suitors, single-handedly?"

Eurykleia answers:

"I do not know, I only heard the shouts and the groaning during their slaying;

We sat huddled in a corner of the women's room with the doors locked, praying,

Telemakis let me out and I found Odyssey standing over the corpses on the floor;

Your heart would have glowed hot to see him standing like a lion, spattered with
blood and gore,

Now the cold dead are piled up near the gatehouse outside;

Odyssey lit a great fire of frank-incense to purify the house to its former pride,

He sent me to ask you to come and join him so that both of you may be happy like before;

For now, at last, your heart's wish has been granted, and you shall suffer no more."

Penelope, less convinced, says:

"Don't get carried away! Yes, everyone would like to see Odyssey back in Ithaki;

Particularly me and Telemakis, our only son, but what you say, can't be,

Some god angry with the Suitors for their evil deeds, has made amends for us;

For they had no respect for Zeus' work, they dis-honoured all, from kings to its poorest;

And now, inevitably, they have come to disaster, for their offences spawned their fate;

Just as Odyssey is dead far away from this land, he'll never return, woman, it's too late!"

Eurykleia anxious, says:

"How can you talk this way, when he waits by the fire's hearth, below;

Besides, here's more proof, as I washed him I saw his boar's scar, which you and I know,

I wanted to tell you earlier, but he wouldn't let me, I was sworn to secrecy;

So come with me, I'll put my life on it, and if it's not him then let me die, kill *me*!"

Penelope says:

"Wise we may think we are, but one is easily fooled by the Invisibles, on Olympos;

However, I shall go and find my son, and the man who, you say, killed the Suitors."

She cautiously descends the staircase, her heart is grinding emotions; should she keep her distance and question him, or run to him and embrace?

She sees the stranger sitting by the fire's hearth his back to her, looking at the floor, thinking what his wife might do when she sees him.

Penelope, thinks to herself, "Has he seen me?"

For a long time she sits quietly in amazement, some times staring at him trying to recognise her husband in this withered old man, in rags.

Telemakis enters the scene, faulting his mother's reluctance:

"Mother, has your heart been so hardened, that you avoid my father in this way?

Go closer and sit, side-by-side, talk with him, you must have a lot to say,

No other woman could resist her long-lost husband after twenty years;

Having endured so much! Your heart was always soft and everyday wrung out its tears."

Penelope answers:

"My son, I am so astonished that no words or actions can I find, I can't even look him in the face;

But, if he is Odyssey, we'll get to know each other again, for we have secrets that time can't erase."

Odyssey overhears her words. Smiling he says to Telemakis:

"Let your mother put me to any test, soon she'll see me in a better light, I know;

She rejects me now believing I'm not the man who left here twenty years ago,

However, we must consider that we have killed others, the pride of Ithaki;

And if their avengers come, we may have to flee and abandon our family, home and country."

Telemakis answers his father:

"Consider it yourself father, for it is said that you are unrivalled in the ways of *trouble* and strife;
The three of us shall follow your lead, and not fail as long as Death does not take us from life."

Odyssey, replies:

"I say this: Tell the maids to prepare the bathhouse, let's wash and don clean clothes;
Get some loud music in the Hall, have it playing from the lyre of Phemios,

Passers-by might think there is a wedding going on, and the festivities are at their best;
And no rumours about the Suitors' deaths will get out, before we escape to the forest,

I have an idea, once we are safe there;
Let's see what opportunity Zeus will bring to bear."

They all do as bid. First the maids draw baths in the wash-house and gather new clothes for the men. Phemios takes his lyre and plucks a sweet rhythmic dance tune, singing a marriage love-song as the maids sing along in chorus. The palace echoes with the gaiety of a festive occasion, so much so, that a passer-by remarks:

"I hope that Queen Penelope has finally been courted by a husband who is the worthiest man;
But it's a shame she couldn't wait for King Odyssey to return to his home-land."

This is what was said. Sometimes there is irony in truth.

Eurykleia bathes and massages Odyssey with olive oil. He receives new clothes.

Athena makes Odyssey look taller and stronger. His baldness is replaced with thick, curly golden-red hair like petals of Hyacinth. She sharpens his features like an artisan who has learned his skills from Hephaestos or Athena, a work of great beauty enriched like an ornate silver plate.

He comes from the bath looking like one of the immortals, and resumes his seat opposite his wife, saying:

"My dear wife, heaven has hardened your heart over these past twenty years;
No other would keep away from her husband, or fail to shed tears,

Eurykleia, make-up a bed ready for me to sleep in alone;
For my wife's heart has turned into stone."

It's Penelope's turn to torment:

"Stranger, I have no want to be aloof, and I don't wish to reject you, also;
But you don't look like the man that left this house, long ago,

If you insist, Eurykleia, take the bed from my bed chamber that my husband built;
And bring it downstairs by the fire and cover it with fleeces, blankets and a quilt."

Odyssey is angry and says:

"Wife, you stab my heart with the sharp words, just said;
What man could move it from the place where I built that bed?"

He realises that Penelope is testing him, as she must be certain that *he* is Odyssey. He tells her how he came to make the bed, which he could not know, unless he had built it. He starts by confiding that there was a very old olive tree growing next to the palace, healthy and strong. Before their marriage he wished to build their bedroom around that spot. He had cut the limbs off the tree, leaving it's deeply rooted stump in the ground.

Around the trunk he built a large room of stone with a high, spanning roof, their marital chamber. He had made the doors with the olive-wood cut from the mighty tree and the bed's frame, which was dowelled to the stump. On the frame he built a base and inlaid it with ivory, gold and silver. On the frame he made a mattress upholstered from soft crimson leather. He continues:

"So, you know what I built there, and I would like to see if *it* has survived;

Or, whether someone violated our bed and *it* - our secret - has died."

Hearing this proof, her knees go weak and her heart races. She runs towards him and embraces and kisses him. Tears are streaming down her face, but she says, sighing:

"Do not be angry with me Odyssey, savvy man, both us have suffered long;

Heaven denied our happiness, twenty years we waited, but now Ithaki is where you belong,

Don't be angry with me because I didn't embrace you on that first day;

For I've been fearful that someone might come to deceive me, thinking I'm easy prey,

Zeus's daughter, *Helen*,[a] would never have slept with that stranger, Paris;

If she'd known that her sin would only return her back to Menelaos,

Zeus, Heaven's mind, wooed her heart to do wrong, with no thought of the implications;

Her infidelity became the source of all our sorrows; that shameful war between two nations,

Now, however, you shall see our bed again, that *no-man* has seen, before;

Except for my man-servant, Actoris,[b] who was given to me by my father, to protect my door,

My heart was not ready to believe you have returned;

Now is the time we've waited for, that which my fidelity has earned."

Odyssey breaks down, embracing and kissing her. Tears drop. This moment is like the brimming sight of land to a man swimming to shore, his ship wrecked by Poseidon in a fury of winds and steep waves. Alone he reaches the shore and crawls

---

a   *Helen* of Sparta, who eloped with Paris of Troy was the daughter of Zeus and promiscuous Leda.
b   The man-servant, *Actoris*, was probably a eunuch, referring to a castrated male who has no, or insufficient libido to be a sexual threat.

over the lusty warmth of its sun-burnt beach, covered in salt-sweat he collapses, elated, with no thoughts of the peril that he has escaped.

They cannot let go of each other and time seems to stand still, hugging ecstasy.

They would have continued their joy until daylight, when Dawn's chariot takes away Night by the reins of Lampus and Phaethon, she steers the two stallions that pull Oceanus' star-stream away, bringing Day.

However, Athena, again inspiring Odyssey with another plan, whispers:

"Wife, we have not yet reached the end of my *trouble*. There is more to reveal!

I have one more trial to overcome, so Terisias' ghost foretold when I was in Hades' Hell,

But now let's not keep the great root[a] in your faithful bed waiting;

It's been a long time since we shared it, no more hesitating!"

Penelope's reply holds curiosity:

"You shall show me your stump soon, now that the gods have revealed you, to me;

But Heaven's mind has prompted you to a task, which has peaked my curiosity."

Odyssey answers:

"It can wait, but you press me, so no longer shall I conceal;

What he said was that I would defeat the Suitors and then, will:

'... carry a well-shaped oar 'til you reach a country where people know nothing of the ocean;

They don't mix salt with food, have not seen ships or the oars that keep them in motion,

Here is a clear sign that your destination has been made;

---

a   A slang word for sex is: *Root* which has its origin in the unusual bed that Odyssey built.

A traveller will meet you and say the oar is a windmill's blade,

Then and there, bury the oar within the earth and sacrifice a ram, a bull and a boar;

To Lord of the Sea, Poseidon, first, and then all the other Olympian gods in proper order,

So that you will avoid Death by Poseidon's hands and will pass-on into a ripe old age;

Your respected life will be taken peacefully, if you heed the words of Terisias, Hades' sage.'"

Penelope says:

"If the gods have promised you happiness in old age;

Then, let's hope your *trouble* will soon be over, according to the sage."

Meanwhile, Eurykleia and another nurse make the bed and cover it with fine blankets. Eurykleia escorts Odyssey and Penelope to their bed by torch light. She leaves and the couple enjoy their long-awaited intimacy.

Telemakis, Philoitios, and the swine-handler have gone to bed. The Great Hall is quiet.

Odyssey and Penelope have fulfilled each other and begin to talk.

She tells him how much she endured with the Suitors, having killed thousands of goats, sheep and cattle, and of the river of wine they had drunk.

Odyssey tells her about his sufferings and how much *trouble* he has given to others. He tells her everything he can. She is captivated, hanging on every word. He begins with the victory over the Cicones, and how they were washed ashore on the land of the Lotus-eaters. He tells about how he punished the Cyklops who had devoured his brave crew-mates and how he met Aeolus, who helped them on their way. Then onto the Laestrygonian city of Telepylos where the cannibals destroyed all his ships with their crews, except his own. Then about cunning Circe and her witch-craft, and from there to Hades' underworld, to consult the ghost of the Theban prophet, Terisias, and once there, he saw old warrior friends, and his mother. Then onto the singing Sirens, and the wandering rocks and terrible Charybdis and to Scylla. Then about the destruction of his crew-men who ate the cattle of Helios, the Sun-god, and how Zeus' lightning bolts killed them. Then how he reached Ogygio island and the nymph Kalypso, who kept him in a cave, wanting to marry, and make him immortal, so that he would never grow old, but she could not persuade him, for he longed for Penelope. Then after so much suffering, he found his way to the Phaekians, who treated him like a god, and escorted him to Ithaki with a great hoard of treasure.

That was the last thing he told her, for deep sleep takes hold of his thoughts and soothes the memories of his misfortunes.

*

Athena has another matter to be dealt with. When Odyssey and Penelope have had enough sleep and love-making, she summons splashing Dawn, to escape from Night.

Odyssey ascends from the love and warmth of their bed, saying to Penelope:

"My lady, both of us have had our full share of *trouble*, you lamenting my absence;

And mine, in being denied for twenty years, your love and magnificent presence,

Now, that we are together, we must take care of what property in this house remains;

As for the livestock the Suitors wasted, I will take by force from all those wolves' relations,

But now, I must visit my father, who has grieved for me a long while at his estate;

So, don't let word of the Suitors deaths spread to the town, lock up the servants and wait."

He buckles his sword-belt and walks downstairs into the cloisters. Here he rouses Telemakis, Philoitios, and Eumaios. They arm themselves. Odyssey leads the way, through the town and up into the woodlands towards Laertes' orchard, behind the summit of Mount Neriton.

It is a bright, sun-clad day, but the men move unseen.

*

THE SUITORS' GHOSTS

*

SON MEETS FATHER

*

THE PEOPLE VERSUS THE KING

Hermes, Spirit of Guidance, rouses the Suitors' ghosts. In his hand is the sceptre-wand that seals men's eyes in sleep or wakes them, as he pleases.

They follow him along the Acheron, the Stream of Woe, to where two roaring rivers mate; The River of Fire and the River of Tears, forking into The Styx, the Torrent of Hate. They climb Leucas Crag[a] looming high in the air and then come to the Gates of the Sun[b] above the meadow where only death dwells.[c]

He leads them as they whine and screech behind him, like bats squealing as they zig-zag through a vaulted cavern. They go down into dark Hades.

Here they find the ghost of Achilles, son of Peleos, with those of Patroklos, Antilochos, and Ajax, who was the finest and most handsome man of all the Hellenes after Achilles himself. They gather around his ghost and Agamemnon's spirit joins them. Around him are the ghost-memories of his loyal servants who were murdered

---

a   On this elevated site is the Nekromanteion, an ancient Greek temple of the oracle of necromancy, devoted to Hades and Persephone. It overlooks the Acheron River in Epirus, near the ancient town of Ephyra (modern Messopotamo). This site is believed, by devotees, to be the door to Hades, the realm of the dead. The word, *leucas*, means: white.

b   The Gates of the Sun was an expression, meaning: a place of learning or experience, as the Sun, each day, reveals what one must learn through experience.

c   It is a river delta, with lakes and wetlands. Because the delta periodically flooded, no vegetation could survive. Dead trees appeared to be human arms reaching from the swamps.

in his own house by his wife Klytemenstra and Agisthos. The ghost of Achilles speaks first:

"Agamemnon, we used to say that Zeus loved you more, you had the most glory;
For you were commander over all the heroes who fought together in Troy,

Yet, death's familiar hand laid you to rest in your own home;
Better that you had fallen in combat at Ilium, you'd have more renown,

And your warriors could have built a mound over the ashes in your grave;
Then your son would be an heir to your good name, and your reputation saved."

Agamemnon's ghost-memory answers:

"Achilles, *you* were the fortunate one, dying in battle at Troy, far away;
Where our bravest warriors fought for your body lying in the dust, that day,

If it wasn't for Zeus sending that thunder-storm, we'd have fought into the night;
We wouldn't be able to have got you away and dress you in a shroud, wrapped tight,

The men tore out their hair and wept, and Thetis[a] and her Sea-nymphs came out of the sea;
Great waves thrashed and we quaked with fear, as the sounds forced us to flee,

We would have gone, if not for wise Nestor whose counsel calmed our worst fears;
Saying, *'Hold, Hellenes, don't run, Achilles' mother is coming, to shed her tears.'*

So he spoke, and soon your mother came, she wept bitterly then clothed you in gold;
And then the nine Muses each in turn chorused,[b] their sweet laments were told,

---

a   *Thetis*, the Spirit of the Sea, is Achilles' mother.
b   The *Muses* are Spirits of song, literature, and the arts.

Seventeen days and nights we mourned, mortals and the Invisibles were there with you;

On the eighteenth, fast-licking flames took you and the slain oxen and sheep, too."

He goes on, explaining the ceremony; how he was cremated with fuels of rich resins, frank-incense and honey, and how a parade of warriors and heroes on horse-back in full battle dress, clashed their armour as he burned. When the flames work was done they gathered the ashes and mixed them with rare herbs and un-mellowed wine. Thetis, poured the mixture into a gold vase, a gift from Dionysos[268] and the work of the incomparable Hephaestos, in which they are mixed with the ashes of Patroklos[a] his close friend, who died before Achilles, there on that fatal beach.

North of Troy, on a headland close to the Hellespont,[b] the sea-way which leads into the Bay of Marmara, the Old Army built a memorial tomb to their fallen heroes that can be seen by all that pass it, by land and water, as a tribute to their siege and triumph over the Trojan empire.

He tells Achilles how his mother sought gifts from the Invisibles and offered them as prizes at the contests of the funeral games. The gifts were the best ever offered by the gods to any competitors, sealing Achilles' status as the greatest warrior, ensuring his fame forever.

Now he consoles himself and his miserable fate, for while he was fighting for his home-land's honour, his wicked wife and her lover plotted to murder him, and on his return, they did so.

So they speak about their lives, and each ghost's Destiny, as Hermes draws near with the ghouls of the Suitors, slain by Odyssey. The ghosts of Agamemnon and Achilles are astonished at seeing them. Agamemnon's ghost recognises Amphimedon, son of Melaneos, who lived in Ithaki and once had been his host. It begins talking to him:

"Amphimedon, what brings all these fine young men into Hades, with early graves?

No-man could pick finer fellows, did Poseidon slay them with un-swimmable waves?

Did their enemies catch them cattle rustling, on the mainland?

Or, did they die fighting for some palace, or perhaps a woman's wedding hand?

Answer me, we are friends, I was your guest in Ithaki, along with Menelaos;

---

a   *Patroklos*, the famous warrior and friend of Achilles, who was also killed in battle at Troy.
b   The *Hellespont* is the Dardanelles, is the strait connecting the Aegean Sea with the Marmara Sea. It is located just north of Troy (Truva) in modern Turkey.

When we came to urge Odyssey to follow us to Troy, his ships and crews joining us,

We were there one whole month for he took a lot of persuasion;
And we were glad too, for he devised the Wooden Horse invasion."

Now the ghost of Amphimedon answers,

"Agamemnon, son of Atreus, King of men, I remember all you have said, and more;
So, I will tell you what cut our lives short; Odyssey had been long gone, lost at the war,

And we all were courting his wife, Penelope, who would not decide whom to wed;
Or even if she would re-marry. Penelope is the reason we are dead,

This is what happened; three years went by while she played her devious game:

She forced each of the Suitors to vie for her hand;
By maid she would send sweet messages to each love-struck man,

Tugging at heart strings while she played the field;
We all hoped to live long enough to see her bed yield,

Then came the greatest trick any woman has employed;
Another scheme by which our advances were toyed,

With the help of her maids they set up a great weaving loom;
Rarely seen, each day and night Penelope stayed in her room,

Working the shuttles and needlework was her excuse not to marry, just yet;
She laboured, she said, to make Lord Laertes a burial blanket,

And whilst Odyssey was thought to be long dead, and never the two were again to meet;

The widow was not prepared to re-marry until the blanket was complete,

So, by day she worked the loom and embroidery to make it just right;

And at night she unpicked her work by candle-light."

He continues telling the other ghosts about Odyssey's return to Ithaki and how he first arrived at the swine-handler's farm at about the same time as his son Telemakis who returned from his voyage to Pilos. There, father and son, hatched a plan to slay them. Telemakis came into the palace first, and then Eumaios accompanied Odyssey, disguised in bedraggled rags, appearing to be a miserable old beggar propped on a stick. No-one recognised him!

He was revolting and they tried to evict him from the Great Hall, first with insults, then bullying and even throwing furniture at him. Day after day they jeered and cursed him, in his own home!

Then Aegis-bearing Athena inspired him, and he and Telemakis hid all the weapons that usually lined the walls of the Hall. Next his cunning wife offered to marry the champion of an archery contest, and that was the beginning of the end for the Suitors as Odyssey, in disguise, was the only one to string the bow, and he did it with ease. Then he sent an arrow through the axe-handles' rings.

As he did that, the Hall went dark, for Zeus blackened the sky. A bad omen. When light returned, he was standing, blocking the escape doors. At his feet lay many arrows at the ready. The first to die was Antinoos, and then, one-by-one they all fell, groaning onto the bloody floor. It is plain now, that some god was helping him. He withstood it all; he's still there, and we are ghosts.

He tells Agamemnon that their bodies are still piled up by the gatehouse of the palace, and that their families are not aware that they are dead. They will be anxious to give them funeral rites.

The ghost of Agamemnon speaks:

"Fortunate Odyssey, he really is blessed with a faithful and virtuous wife;

Her fame is destined to never die, as long as mortals on Earth live life,

A good thing he didn't marry that bitch, Tyndareus' daughter, who killed *her* husband;[a]

---

a   Agamemnon's sarcastic remark is referring to his own wife, Klytemenstra, who murdered him. She was the sister of Helen of Sparta; two very troublesome women.

She'll be hated by all men, for she disgraced women forever, in this or any other land."

So the ghosts talk in the bowels of Hades' Hell.

*

Meanwhile, Odyssey and his men have reached Laertes' remote orchard. It stands in a clearing, where a forest once stood.[a] It is well established with neat fruit trees and tilled, terraced garden beds. There are many huts where the workers sleep. The central lodge is modest. It has a large dining table to accommodate all those living there.

Inside the lodge there is an elderly Sicilian woman who looks after Laertes.

Odyssey asks Telemakis to:

"Take the other two and go to the house, and kill the best pig you can find;

I will see if my father still knows me, or if his memories have left his mind."

He hands his sword and shield to Eumaios and Philoitios. They go into the house while he walks through the orchard to the vineyard where his father is pruning vines. As he walks toward his father he doesn't see Dolios, his manager, or his sons, for they are hauling rocks to make a fence far off in another field. He sees his father alone, trimming vines, dressed in an old shirt, patched and shabby. He is also wearing a leather apron and a goat-skin cap.[b] He looks weary and life-beaten.

Odyssey is surprised at his father's appearance; he is frail and stooped. He stops under a pear tree and begins to weep. He wants to run to him, embrace and tell him that he is home! But, he'll try teasing him first, as is his way. He goes up to his father who is now on his knees tending to a vine, and says to him:

"I see, sir, that you are an excellent gardener, what special care you take with your grove;

With all these fig-trees, vines, olives, pears and flower beds, it's a natural treasure trove,

If only you would take as much care of yourself as you do of this fine place;

---

a   On Ithaki, local folklore locates it near the modern-day village of Anogi.
b   A goat-skin cap signifies the maddening grief of a mourner.

Yes, you are old, but you appear to have noble heritage; it's in your form and face,

You seem to be one who should wash and eat well, and dine without a care;
So tell me true, who are you apprenticed to? Is he a good man, is he fair?

And tell me about another matter, have I really landed in Ithaki?
I just met a man on the road who said so, but he looked like a madman, between you and me,

He had no patience, for as I started to ask him about an old friend;
If he was still living, or in Hades? He just turned away, and walked around the bend,

Believe me when I tell you, this friend was once in *my* country, and in *my* home;
And what a wonderful stranger he turned out to be, the best man *I* have ever known,

He told me that his family lives in Ithaki, and that his father was Laertes;
I welcomed him and gave the abundance of *my* home, before he left for the open seas,

He took seven gold bars, a silver cup engraved with flowers, in baskets;
And, twelve tapestries, twelve rugs, twelve shirts, and a dozen jackets,

And, to carry it all, I gave him four well-endowed damsels[a] of his choice;
Skilled in all useful arts; house-keeping, cooking, sewing and one with a singing voice."

His father sobs, and sheds tears. Finally, he speaks:

"Young man, you have come to the country that you have well named;
But it has fallen into the hands of wicked people and is forever shamed,

---

a   A virginal female.

All those presents he gave you would serve you well, if you could find that man here;
He'd have entertained you hospitably, and returned the favour without a tear,

Now, tell me true, how many years since you've seen the man you seek?
For, he was *my* ill-fated son, lost in the sea's deep, or a victim of the buzzard's beak,

Neither his mother, or me, embraced him before he died, no wailing, no tears;
And his widow Penelope never had the chance to look into his eyes, after all these
years,

Now, stranger, tell me your story, where do you come from, and who are you?
Tell me about your city, king and parents. I know a liar if I see one, so tell me true,

And, what ship did you arrive on? Where is the vessel from, and who are its crew?
What lands have you travelled in the past? Stranger, I'd like to know more about
you."

Odyssey answers with more lies:

"Yes, I *can* tell the truth, my palace is in *Roam-around*, from where I have come;
I am the son of *King Discord*, grand-son of *Strife-lord*, my name is *Troublesome*,

Destiny's west wind drove me here, against my will, off course when I left Sicily;
My ship lies in a cove nearby, and it's five years since I have seen Odyssey,

Poor fellow, *if he was ill-starred*, but when he left me, sea-birds flocked from his
right;
And we rejoiced at parting ways, looking forward to meeting when we might."

A dark cloud pains Leartes' face as he listens. He fills both hands with dust
from the ground and pours it over his wearied head, groaning heavily. The heart of
Odyssey feels his pain, his nostrils quiver as he looks at his father.

He springs forward embracing and kissing his father, saying to him:

"Father, it is me, I have returned after these twenty hard years;

So, cease your grieving, there is no more time for suffering, or tears,

I should tell you that I have killed the Suitors, they are all in Hades' Hell;

As punishment for their arrogance and dishonour, and other crimes, as well."

Laertes, sceptical, says:

"If you really are my son show me proof, I find it hard to believe;

Don't forget you are in Ithaki now - we know liars - I won't be easy to deceive."

Odyssey is quick to answer:

"Look, I will give you proof of who I am, here's the scar, I got on Mt Parnassos;

When a boar's tusk ripped me open, while I was hunting with the sons of Autolycos."

Here's more proof, when I was a boy you told me the names of the trees this garden
grows;

You gave me thirteen pear trees, ten apple trees, forty fig trees and of vines, fifty
rows,

And there was corn planted between each vine row for its full length;

That yields heavy bunches of every kind when Summer's heat loses its strength."

Laertes' strength fails him, he falls to his knees, weakened by the shock of
his son's return. Odyssey has to steady him, as he is about to faint. He recovers
slowly, regaining his senses, he lifts his arms into the air, pleading:

"Father Zeus, you and your gods are really there on Olympos, after all this time;

Finally, our prayers have been answered, the Suitors have paid for their reign of
crime,

However, I am afraid that the townsfolk of Ithaki will come for revenge;
They'll be bringing mercenaries from all the cities of the Kefalonians."[a]

Odyssey answers:

"Take heart and do not *trouble* yourself, I'll deal with that issue;
Now, let's go to the lodge, Telemakis, Philoitios and Eumaios want to see you."

Father and son walk back to the stone farm-house. There they find Telemakis with the stockman and the hog-handler cutting up meat and mellowing wine.

Laertes' maid takes him to the bath-house, she bathes and massages him with lemon juice and olive oil. He puts on a new shirt and tunic. Athena gives him a younger, more imposing presence, making him taller and wider than his years. He returns to the dining room where Odyssey is surprised to see him looking so vital, saying:

"Father, one of the gods has just made you taller and better-looking."

Laertes answers:

"By Zeus, Athena and Apollo, if only I was the king of the Ionians, again;
With the power I had when we took Nerikos,[269] and their fortress, on that island,[b]

If I was today, *what I was back then*, then yesterday you wouldn't have been lonely;
With sword and shield in your house, I'd have stood by you and killed the Suitors too.
If only!"

So they talked. The others have prepared the feast and all take their places at the table. They wait out of respect for old Dolios and his sons who are coming in from the field, summoned already by the Sicilian woman. They are excited at hearing

---

a   The word *kephalos* is Greek for "head", perhaps because Cephalus was the founding "head" of a great family that included Odyssey's ancestors. One theory contends that the Kefalonians were so named because of their larger-than-average heads.
b   Nericum, is modern-day Lefkada, close by.

that Odyssey has returned and upon arriving they recognise him. All are lost for words.

Odyssey jokingly scolds them, saying:

"Gentlemen, sit down and eat your meal, and never mind the unexpected guest;

I've been waiting for twenty years to lunch with my father, and his men, Ithaki's best!"

Dolios puts out both hands, and kisses Odyssey's wrists, saying:

"Sir, we have long been praying that you would come home, here you are!

Welcome, the gods have smiled on us all. Does the Queen know you are here?"

Odyssey answers:

"She knows that I've come already, old friend;

No need to *trouble* her about that, on me she can depend."

Dolios and all his sons gather around him and embrace one after the other, then take their seats at the table and make the most of the feast, and the surprise visitor.

While they are busy with their celebration, rumours flew from the palace, into town; the Suitors have been killed. Soon there is a rabble outside the palace walls. Some take the dead away to their homes to be prepared for their funerals. Other bodies are taken to the port for the voyage home.

The mourners and families meet in the town square. The mob is angry.

Eupeithes, father of Antinoos, the first of the Suitors' ringleaders, is overwhelmed by grief. He speaks first:

"My friends, this man has done the Hellenes great wrongs, and worse;

First, *he* lost our young men and their ships which didn't return from Troy's curse,

Now, that *he* has returned he's murdered our best men, this island's pride;

Let's get after him, before he can flee to Pilos, or to Elis, where he could hide,

We would be disgraced forever if we don't seek justice for our loved ones;

Now is the time, we must avenge the murder of our brothers, and our sons,

I can have no more pleasure from this life, I'd rather die today!

So, let's find them before they escape to the mainland, and get away."

He wept as he spoke to the agitated crowd. There is pity, and revenge, in their hearts.

Medon, the palace's chief steward and Phemios, the minstrel, have arrived at the town square. Everyone is astonished at seeing them. Medon speaks:

"Hear me, men of Ithaki, Odyssey did not do these things against Heaven's will;

I saw Athena, take the form of Mentor and fought beside him, *her* heart was in the kill."

Fear grips the chattering crowd, their faces losing colour.

The revered son of Mastor, Halithersos, the best prophet and reader of omens among them, speaks:

"Men of Ithaki, it is your own fault that these things have turned out this way;

They should have listened to me, and to Mentor, and heeded what we had to say,

The Suitors knew they were abusing their *xenia*,[a] by courting Penelope, his wife;

Did they really think that Zeus would turn a blind eye, and allow this folly, without strife?

Now, a caution for you all: Do not seek revenge against Odyssey;

For if you do, the Invisibles will fast end your day in blood, you'll see."

---

a   *Xenia*, or *host-visitor* principle, is the unwritten social obligation of hospitality. It involves mutual *respect* between host and visitor. The *spirit* of xenia is venerated in the primary deity Zeus, the "All-seeing, Self-pervading" oneness, that enforces this principle.

There is a loud shout from all who revere his words and they leave, satisfied by what Halithersos has said. But the other half of the crowd are not convinced, siding with Eupeithes. They hurry to collect their weapons and soon return to the town square, armed. Eupeithes will lead them to a fight, that he hopes will dispense justice for his dead son. Little does he know that Destiny has another outcome in store.

*

Athena is with her father, Zeus, xenia's enforcer. She asks him:

"Father, answer me this question: What do you propose to do?

Will you set them to fighting each other, or will there be peace between the two?"

Zeus answers:

"My child, Spark of Inspiration, why should you ask me? All this matter is by your hand and heart. Didn't you seek revenge for Odyssey? It's up to you, do what is right. Perhaps a pact between the foes might settle this *trouble* once and for all. Settle it in the ways of their fore-fathers and let bygones be what they are. Let their memories darken and forget the deaths of their loved ones. Make them friends to live in peace and plenty. You should turn this unfortunate matter over to the future, where history shall teach generations to welcome the lessons to be learned from the virtues of xenia, their saviour."

Her father's words ring true in her heart and head. This is what Athena is eager to bring about. At the speed of thought she darts from Olympos' lofty peak.

*

At Laertes' lodge, the lunch is over. Odyssey suggests that someone stands guard, just in case avengers come. One of Dolios sons goes to the porch, where he has a clear view down to the road which rises from the island's isthmus.[a]

Soon he sees men moving along toward the lodge, armed. He alerts Odyssey who asks the men to prepare for a fight. They all clad themselves in armour and take

---

a   The isthmus of Ithaki is the thin wrist of land that separates the north and south parts of the island.

their weapons in hand. There are twelve men ready for the foe; Telemakis, Eumaios, Philoitios and Dolios, with his six sons, and Leartes, all captained by Odyssey.

Athena, disguised as Mentor appears and Odyssey's heart lifts. A sign from above, perhaps. He says to his son:

> "Telemakis, now that a fight is inevitable, every man must show his mettle and might;
>
> Be sure not to disgrace your ancestors reputation for strength and courage, in this fight."

Telemakis is eager to match his father:

> "What you say is true father, and valour from your son you shall see;
>
> But I won't be the one on which disgrace shall rest, you just try to keep up with me!"

Laertes, delighted with his family's pride, says:

> "Good heavens, what a day I am having, I must rejoice!
>
> My son and grandson are rivals for the hero's most boastful voice."

On this Athena, as Mentor, comes close to him, saying:

> "*Arceisios'* son,[a] best friend in this world, pray to the sparkling-eyed Daughter of Light;
>
> And to Zeus, Mind, poise and aim your spear, then hurl it with all your might."

As Mentor speaks, Athena infuses a new vitality in him, endowing great power. He gives tribute to her and aims the spear. It leaves his hand and its iron tip cracks as it penetrates Eupeithes' helmet, entering through the temple guard. His knees buckle and his armour clatters as he falls, dead.

Odyssey and Telemakis are in the front line of the attack. Their combatants fall in the flurry of their broad-swords. They would have killed them all, preventing any witnesses returning to the town, except that Athena raised Mentor's voice, booming he pleads:

---

a   *Arceisios,* was Leartes' father.

"Men, cease this blood-shed now and respect xenia; the time has come to forgive!

Be an example for the future of all men: *Make peace, live, and let live!*"

Fear seizes every man, frightened they drop their weapons. Those from the town turn and flee for their lives. Odyssey, picking up his spear pursues the bolters, swooping after them like a screaming eagle. Zeus is watching, and sends a lightning bolt and thunder-clap, landing at his feet. Athena gives Mentor his voice, saying:

"Odyssey, noble son of Laertes, why are you at war with Zeus?

Haven't you learned your lessons? Stop this war against yourself!"

Odyssey obeys.

Athena assumes the form and voice of Mentor again, and soon a pact is reached between enemies, which is meant to last for all time.

Ithaki, and all, should now be ruled by xenia, in peace.

*

Always show kindness and help others,

Because they are Zeus in disguise.

Homer

Reading and Reference List / Endnotes

A new astronomical dating of Odysseus' return to Ithaca. Papamarinopoulos, et al. Mediterranean Archaeology and Archaeometry, Vol. 12, No 1, pp.117-128 (2012)

A Travel Guide to Homer, On the trail of Odysseus through Turkey and the Mediterranean, John Freely, I. B. Tauris, 2014

Complete Poems of Cavafy, C. P. Cavafy, Translated by R. Dalven, Harvest, 1976

Greek Mythology, K. Servi, Ekdotike Athens, S. A., 2012

Homer and the Epic, G. S. Kirk, Cambridge University Press, 1974

Ithaca and Homer: Why Homer Matters, A. Nicholson, William Collins, 2014

Ithaca and Homer: The Truth, The Advocacy of the Case, C. Tzakos, Translator: Geoffrey Cox, 2005

Mediterranean Passages, Readings from Dido to Derida, Edited by: M. Cooke, E. Goknar and G. Parker, UNC Press, 2008

Memoirs of Heinrich Schliemann, L. Deuel, Harper & Row, 1977

No-man's Lands, One man's odyssey through the Odyssey, S. Huler, Three Rivers Press, 2008

Sailing the Wine-dark Sea: Why the Greeks matter, T. Cahill, Nan A. Talese, 2003

The Consciousness of the Atom, A. A. B. Bailey, Lucis Press, London, 1922

The anatomy of a complex astronomical phenomenon described in the Odyssey.
Papamarinopoulos, et al. Mediterranean Archaeology and Archaeometry,
Vol. 13, No. 2, pp. 69-82. University of Patras (2013)

The Art of the Odyssey, H. W. Clarke, Spectrum Books, 1967

The Authoress of the Odyssey, S. Butler, University of Chicago Press, 1898

The Hero with a Thousand Faces, Joseph Campbell, New World Library, (Third
Edition) 2008

The Odyssey, A modern sequel, Nikos Kazantzakis, (Translated by K. Friar), Simon
and Schuster, 1958

The Odyssey, Homer, translated by R. Fagles, Penguin Classics, 1996

The Odyssey, Homer, translated by R. Fitzgerald, Houghton Mifflin Company, 1965

The Odyssey, Homer, E. V. Rieu, Penguin Books, 2003

The Odyssey of Homer, T. E. Shaw, Alan Sutton Publishing, 1932

The Perennial Philosophy, Aldous Huxley, Harper & Brothers, 1945

Theogeny and *Works and Days,* Hesiod, translated by M. L. West, Oxford University
Press, 1988

The Story of the Odyssey, S. V. Tracey, Princeton University Press, 1990

The Tale of Troy, R. L. Green, Puffin Books, 1961

The Unity of the Odyssey, G. Dimock, University of Massachusetts Press, 1989

The World of Odysseus, M. I. Finley, Pelican Books, 1954

Three Magic Words, U. S. Andersen, Nelson, 1954

Throwing Light on Homeric Ithaca, Dimitis Paizas-Danias, Stavros Community
Association of Ithaca, 2013

Ulysses Found, E. Bradford, Hodder & Staughton, 1964

View from Olympus, A history of ancient Greece, M. Kelly, Longman Cheshire, 1984

1   The Ages of Man: According to Hesiod's predictions, the modern era is the age of suffering: "… Mind made a fifth generation of men, and with it began, after the Bronze and Heroic Ages, the Age of Iron. It is said that all evil burst forth into this baser age, which is our own: Men never rest from labor and sorrow by day, and from exhaustion by night. Modesty, truth, and faith leave the earth, and in their place come tricks, plots, traps, violence, and unbridled love of profit. The ground, which had been common possession, is now neatly marked with boundary-lines. Men demand of the fields, not only the sustenance they provide with their surface, but also what is in the very bowels of the earth, bringing to light the wealth buried and hidden away by the gods.

Iron and Gold: Not only hard iron came with this age; but also gold, which is even worse than iron. And with both war came, and so men found it natural to live on plunder: The guest cannot trust his host, and affection among brothers became rare. The husband started longing for the death of his wife, and she for the death of her husband. Piety was vanquished, and Dike - the last of the invisibles - left the Earth.

Doomed to destruction: If the duty-of-care principle is not honoured, Mind will destroy this race of mortals too: For the father will not agree with his children, nor the children with their father, nor guest with his host, nor comrade with comrade, nor will brothers love each other as once they did. Men will dishonour their parents as they attain old age, without repaying them the cost of their nurture. Might shall be right, so that one man may sack another man's city. There will be no merit for the man who keeps his word, or for the just, or for the good; rather, men will praise the evil-doer and admire his audacity and violent dealings. Strength will be right, and respect will vanish as an empty word. Peace being banished, the inspirational thoughts will cease, leading to a life of anxiety. The wicked will hurt the worthy, speaking false words against them; therefore will envy walk along with them. Anxiety will forsake mortal men, letting bitter sorrows fall upon them; and being defenceless like children in the wilderness, they will not find any help against all evil they themselves created."

2   Western culture (Iron Age culture) is based on the foundational works of art and literature known as the Western Canon, of which Homer's epics, the *Iliad* and *Odyssey* are the most significant.

3   Panentheism, see: *The Perennial Philosophy*, Aldous Huxley (1945). As Huxley stated, "The metaphysical recognises a divine reality substantial to the world of things and lives and minds; the psychology that finds in the soul something similar to, or even identical with, divine Reality; the ethic that places man's final end in the knowledge of the immanent and transcendent basis of all being - the thing is immemorial and universal. Rudiments of the Perennial may be found among the traditionary lore of primitive peoples in every region of the world, and in its fully developed forms it has a place in every one of the higher religions. A version of this Highest Common Factor in all preceding and subsequent theologies was first committed to writing more than twenty-five centuries ago, and since that time the inexhaustible theme has been treated again and again, from the standpoint of every religious tradition and in all the principal languages of Asia and Europe. In the next paragraph, Huxley summarised the problem more succinctly, saying: "Knowledge is a function of being." In other

words, if you are not suited to knowing something, you do not know it. This makes knowing the Ground of All Being difficult, in Huxley's view. Therefore, he concludes his Introduction with: "If one is not a sage or saint, the best thing one can do, in the field of metaphysics, is to study the works of those who were, and who, because they had modified their merely human mode of being, were capable of a more than merely human kind and amount of knowledge."

4   A pantheon of gods is a common element of polytheistic societies that believe in supernatural gods. The "Greek Pantheon" was a concept developed by the Romans. The ancient Hellenic culture was monistic (monotheistic) accepting the primacy of Mind as its fundamental concept. Monism is the concept that only a single thing exists, Mind, which can only be artificially divided into many things.

5   Parmenides lived in the 6th century, BC, and initiated the study of ontology, the understanding of being.

6   Olympia is located in the Peloponnese region of Greece.

7   Atreus, and his twin brother Thystes were exiled by their father for murdering their half-brother in their desire for the throne of Olympia. They took refuge in Mycenae where they ascended to the throne in the absence of King Eurystheus, who was fighting the Heracleidae. Eurystheus had meant for their stewardship to be temporary, but it became permanent after his death in battle.

8   Thyestes, twin son of Pelops. See, *Atreus*, above.

9   King Eurystheus, a ruler of Argos in the Peleponnese mainland.

10   Artemis, in the classical Hellenic period was often used as a metaphor of femininity. She was associated with childbirth, virginity, protection of young girls and curer of female diseases and fertility.

11   Venus Retrograde, is an apparent reverse motion of the planet in a direction opposite to that of other bodies within the solar system, as observed from a particular vantage point.

12   Pelopia, daughter of Thyestes, by whom, she mothered Agisthos.

13   Agisthos, the incestuous son of Thyestes and Pelopia.

14   The ancient City of Aulis was located on the east coast of Greece, in Boeotia, at the Euripus Strait.

15   Destiny, sometimes referred to as *fate*, is a predetermined course of events. It may be conceived as a predetermined future, whether in general or of an individual.

16   Cassandra was cursed to utter prophecies that were true but no-one believed. A common version of her story relates how, in an effort to seduce her, thought-spirit Apollo gave her the power of prophecy. When she refused him, he spat into her mouth to inflict a curse that nobody would ever believe her prophecies. Another version has her falling asleep in a temple, where snakes licked (or whispered in) her ears so that she could hear the future. Cassandra became a figure of epic tradition and of tragedy. In modern usage her name is used as a rhetorical device to indicate someone whose accurate prophecies are not believed by those around them.

17   Apollo has been variously recognized as a god of music, truth and prophecy, healing, the Sun and light, plague, poetry, and more. However, in the Hellenistic tradition Apollo represented the concept of space; the "separator" of "things" that one

experiences.

18   This story is the major plot line of Aeschylus' trilogy: *The Oresteia.*

19   Menelaos, was a king of Sparta, the husband of Helen of Troy, and the son of Atreus and Aerope. According to Homer, Menelaos was a central figure in the Trojan War, leading the powerful Spartan contingent of the Greek army, under his elder brother Agamemnon, King of Mycenae. Menelaos was a member of the doomed House of Atreus.

20   According to Book II of Homer's *Iliad*, 1,186 ships reached Troy. Helen's was the face that launched a thousand ships.

21   Rhapsodes, in modern usage, refers to an ancient Greek performer of epic poetry and plays. Rhapsodes notably performed the epics of Homer, Iliad and Odyssey, and also the wisdom and poetry of Hesiod and others. Plato's dialogue *Ion*, in which Socrates confronts a famous rhapsode, remains the best source of information on these artists. Often, rhapsodes are depicted in Greek art, wearing their signature cloak and carrying a staff. This equipment is also characteristic of travellers in general, implying that rhapsodes were itinerant performers, moving from town to town. Rhapsodes originated in the Ionian district, which has been regarded as Homer's birthplace, and were also known as Homeridai, disciples of Homer, or "singers of stitched lays". Homer's home is considered to be on Ithaki, near to the remote village of Exoghi, near where the ruins of Homer's School are found.

22   *A New Astronomical Dating of the Trojan War's End* (2013) Papamarinopoulos, S, et al. University of Patras.

23   Ogygio, is today named, Gozo, and is the northern-most of the Maltese Isles. Kalypso's cave overlooks Ramla Bay beach.

24   The Twelve Olympians, in ancient mythology were the thought-spirits - agents of Mind – are now considered to be Zeus, Hera, Poseidon, Demeter, Athena, Apollo, Artemis, Ares, Aphrodite, Hephaestos, Hermes, Hestia or Dionysos. They are called "Olympians" because they were considered to reside on Mount Olympos.

25   Poseidon, was one of the twelve invisible thought-spirits of Mind. As a metaphor, he is god of the Sea and other waters; of land formation and earthquakes; and, of horses. In the Bronze Age, he was venerated at Pilos and Thebes, two ancient capitals, as the metaphor for fear, doubt and terror.

26   Lake Tana, in the Ethiopian Highlands, is the source of the Blue Nile river.

27   Zeus, from the Roman era is the master-father God. However, in the pre-Roman era it was the metaphor for Mind. The name, *Zeus*, translates to: Mind, or, en-lightener by thought; thought giver, the genesis of thought. In ancient Greek culture Zeus' god's were the thoughts that create one's mental activity. One's mental life is directed by the source of thought, the all-seeing, self-pervading Mind.

28   Orestes is the subject of several ancient Greek plays and of various myths connected with his madness and purification through violation of the xenia principle.

29   Agisthos was the son of Thysestes and Thyestes' own daughter Pelopia, an incestuous union motivated by his father's rivalry with the house of Atreus for the throne of Mycenae. Agisthos murdered Atreus in order to restore his father to

power, ruling jointly with him until only to be driven from power by Atreus' son Agamemnon.

30   Agamemnon was the son of King Atreus and Queen Aerope of Mycenae, the brother of Menelaos, the husband of Klytemnestra, and the father of Ipheginia, Electra, Orestes and Chrysothemis. He was King of Mycenae (Argos). When Helen, the wife of Menelaos, eloped with Paris of Troy, Agamemnon commanded the united Hellenic naval forces and invaded Troy, starting the Trojan War.

31   Destiny, sometimes referred to as *fate*, is a predetermined course of events. It may be conceived as a predetermined future, whether in general or of an individual.

32   Atreus, was a king of Mycenae, the son of Pelops and Hippodamia, who fathered Agamemnon and Menelaos.

33   Hermes, from the Roman era, is the god of trade, heraldry, merchants, commerce, roads, sports, travellers, and athletes. In pre-Roman cultures, Hermes was the metaphor for clear-thinking, shame, guilt and conscience.

34   Delphi, is famous as the ancient sanctuary that grew as the seat of Pythia, the oracle who was consulted about important decisions throughout the ancient world. Moreover, the pre-Hellenic people considered Delphi the centre of the world, as represented by the stone monument known as the Omphalos of Delphi. It occupies an impressive site on the south-western slope of Mount Parnassos, overlooking the coastal plain to the south and the valley of Phocis. It is now an extensive archaeological site with a small town by the same name nearby. It is a UNESCO World Heritage Site for its phenomenal influence in the ancient world, as evidenced by the rich monuments built there by most of the important ancient Greek city-states, demonstrating their fundamental cultural heritage and unity.

35   The Oracle of Delphi lists 147 aphorisms for ethical living.

36   Athena, in Greek mythology, was the "metaphor" used for the mental states of *inspiration* and *imagination*. Athena, the name, suggests: *pointed words, rousing, emotive and passionate.* Athena was originally sprung from Zeus' ead; an idea of Mind!

37   Emotion (*synaisthima*) is a *feeling* derived from one's perceived circumstances, mood or relationships with others, which may be instinctive or intuitive as opposed to reasoning or learned knowledge.

38   Kronos is the estranged father of Zeus, was the leader and youngest of the first generation of Titans, the divine descendants of Uranus, the sky, and Gaia, Earth. He overthrew his father and ruled during the mythological Golden Age, until he was overthrown by his son Zeus, and imprisoned in Tartarus. In pre-Hellenic times, the metaphor for Space and Time.

39   The Aegis, in other words, is "reality" being mirrored by our thoughts. A metaphorical shield, a symbol of Mind's work which mirrors an apparently external reality. It is the working out of the plan through one's experience, and it is said to contain the destiny of all. Zeus is the minder of Mind, the "all-seeing, self-pervading one" and uses the dynamic of xenia to control behaviour.

40   Refer to Aeschylus' *Oresteia* for the story of the House of Atreus.

41   Atlas, in antiquity, was the metaphor used for the sensation of gravity.

42   During Odyssey's twenty-year absence, unmarried men start to suspect that Odyssey died in Troy or on the journey home. Under the pretence of courting

Penelope, these unmarried men, called "the 108 suitors", and their entourages, take up residence in Odyssey's palace and vie for her hand in marriage. Rather than simply rejecting the suitors, Penelope devises a plan to delay their courtship. She claims she will choose a husband after she has finished weaving a funeral shroud to present to Odyssey's, Lacerates. For three years, Penelope weaves the shroud during the day and unravels it at night, awaiting her husband's return. The suitors learn of Penelope's delaying tactic when one of her maid-servants, Melantho, reveals it to her lover Eurymachus. Upon finding out, the suitors demand that she choose a husband from among them.

43   Ionian Sea, is an elongated gulf of the Mediterranean Sea, south of the Adriatic Sea. It is bounded by Italy including Calabria, Sicily and the Salento Peninsula to the west, southern Albania to the north, and the west coast of Greece. All major islands in the sea belong to Greece. They are collectively named the Ionian Isles; the main islands being: Corfu, Kefalonia, Anthozoans, Lefkada and Ithaki. The sea is one of the most seismically active areas on Earth.

44   Taphians, mariners, pirates and slave-traders from Taphos, an island off the coast of Arcanania in north-western Greece.

45   Telemakis, in Greek means, literally: away from, or shuns conflict; war-less, peaceful.

46   Phemios, was an Ithakan poet who performed narrative songs in the palace of the absent Odyssey. His audience is made up largely of the suitors (Proci), who attempt to persuade Penelope to marry one of them.

47   Mentes, king of the Taphians.

48   Rithron Cove is probably today's Dexia Cove, close to where Odyssey's palace is believed to have stood. Skartsoubo Island (Sock Island) is just off Dexia Beach, Ithaki, and is said to be the petrified remains of the Phaekian ship and its crew that delivered Odyssey to Ithaki.

49   Temesa, a port in ancient Italy, known today as, Catanzaro, in Calabria.

50   Laertes, was the son of Arcesius and Chalcomedusa. He was the father of Odyssey and Ctimene, by his wife Antikliea, daughter of the trickster and conman, Autolycus. Laertes was an Argonaut. Laertes' title was King of the Kefalonians, an ethnic group who lived both on the Ionian islands and on the mainland, which he presumably inherited from his father and grandfather, Kephalus. His realm included Ithaki and surrounding islands, and perhaps even the neighbouring part of the mainland of other Greek city-states.

51   Penelope, is the wife of Odyssey, who is known for her fidelity to Odyssey while he was absent, despite having many Suitors. Her name is synonymous with marital fidelity. Penelope means: weaver of tears, or pain.

52   Plus, a son of Mermerus and grandson of Jason and Medea, lived at Ephyra between Elis and Olympia. Odyssey requested poison for his arrows, but Ilus declined through fear of divine vengeance.

53   Ephyra was first settled during the Bronze Age and resettled in the 14th century BC by colonists most probably from the coastal western Peloponnese region. The city is about 800 m north of the junction of the Kokytos River and the Acheron River.

54   Nestor, was the wise King of Pilos, who was fond of talking.

55   Penelope's father, Ikarius, was a Spartan king and a champion runner who would not allow anyone to marry his daughter unless he beat him in a race. Odyssey succeeded and married Penelope. After they married, Icarius tried to persuade Odyssey to remain in Sparta. He did leave with Penelope, but Icarius followed them, imploring his daughter to stay. Odyssey told her she must choose whether to be with her father or with her husband. Penelope did not answer, but modestly covered her face with a veil. Icarius correctly understood that this was a sign of her will to leave with Odyssey. He let them go and erected a statue of Aidos (Modesty) on that spot. Icarius was still alive at the time of the events of Homer's *Odyssey*.

56   Polybos, was the father of a suitor, Eurymachus. Polybus himself was one of Penelope's suitors, before she married Odyssey.

57   Taphia or Taphos, is a picturesque island, part of the Lefkada group. The Taphians were pirates and slavers and built a rich kingdom. They were allies of the Ithakans.

58   Eurykleia, also known as Antiphata, is the daughter of Ops and grand-daughter of Peisenor, and the wet-nurse of Odyssey. As a girl she was bought by Laertes, Odyssey' father. He treated her as his wife, but she was never his lover so as not to dishonor his real wife, Antikleia. She later nursed Telemakis, Odyssey's son.

59   Phortune (Phorgyn) Harbour was named in antiquity after Phorgyn, the sea-dwelling merman, its patron god. Now known as Vathy Harbour, Ithaki

60   Mentor, was the son of Alkimus. In his old age Mentor was a friend of Odyssey who placed him and Odyssey's foster-brother Eumaios in charge of his son Telemakis, and his palace, when he left for the Trojan War.

61   Ops, son of Pisonor.

62   Asteris Island is today known as Ligia Island, or Pera Pagadi. Its co-ordinates are: 30° 20' 06 / 20° 44' 58. This tiny island is overlooked by Arethusa's Well and Raven's Rock (Korax) near the ancient site of Eumaios' piggery.

63   Sami is a harbour town on the Ionian island of Kefalonia.

64   Voidokilia Lagoon and beach near Pilos. In the shape of the Greek letter omega (Ω), its sands forms a semicircular strip of dunes that are sheltered from the sea and make an ideal refuge for ships. On the land-facing side of the strip of dunes is Gialova Lagoon, an important bird habitat. The site of Nestor's Palace is on the hill of Epano Englianos, situated close to the road four kilometres south of Chora and 13 kilometres north of the beach with commanding views over Pilos and the Ionian Sea. The "Cyclopean" masonry walls of the sanctuary are of an impressive scale.

65   Patroklos, when the tide of the Trojan War had turned against the Greeks and the Trojans were threatening their ships, convinced Achilles to let him lead the Myrmidons into combat. Achilles consented, giving Patroklos the armour Achilles had received from his father, in order for Patroklos to impersonate Achilles. Patroklos defied Achilles' order and pursued the Trojans back to the gates of Troy. He killed many Trojans including a son of Zeus, Sarpedon. While fighting, Patroklos' wits were removed by Apollo (the metaphor for "separation"), after which Hector then killed Patroklos by stabbing him in the stomach with a spear.

66   Tenedos, now known as Bozcaada, is an island off Turkey, in the northern part of the Aegean Sea.

67   Euboea is an island in the Aegean Sea, east of the Greek mainland.

68   Klytemenstra was the wife of Agamemnon and queen of Mycenae. She was the sister of Helen of Sparta.

69   Souniun is at the southern tip of the Attica peninsula in Greece.

70   Crete is the largest and most populous of the Greek islands.

71   Kydonia, Crete, was an ancient city-state on the north-west coast of the island of Crete. It is at the site of the modern-day Greek city of Chania.

72   Gortyn in Crete, is a municipality and an archaeological site, 45 km from the modern capital Heraklion.

73   Phaestus, an ancient city in south-central Crete, Ancient Phaistos was located about 62 km south of Heraklion, the second largest city of Minoan Crete.

74   The name and location of Therae, has been lost to time. It was probably located in the region to the north of Kalamata.

75   Lacedaemon, or Sparta, was a large city-state in ancient Greece. The location of the palace is not known, however some accept that its ruins are located near the village of Pellana, 27 kilometres north of Sparta.

76   Hermione was the only child of King Menelaos of Sparta and his wife, Helen of Troy.

77   Sinfonia, was a city in ancient Lebanon.

78   Artemis, in the classical Hellenic period was often used as a metaphor of femininity. She was associated with childbirth, virginity, protection of young girls and curer of female diseases and fertility.

79   Peaons were those forced into slavery or organised labour.

80   Phorgyn, is the patron of Ithaki, of whom Phortune Harbour is named.

81   The Nile Delta is the delta in Northern Egypt where the Nile River spreads out and drains into the Mediterranean Sea. It is one of the world's largest river deltas. The Delta begins slightly down-river from Cairo.

82   Shape shifting is the ability of a being or creature to completely transform its physical form or shape. This is usually achieved through an inherent ability of a mythological creature, divine intervention, or the use of magic. Phorgyn was the original.

83   Gyrae Rocks are two hazardous rocks 700 metres east of the of the Promontory of Kafireas on the Island of Euboea, off the east coast of the Greek mainland. The charming church of Saint Gregory overlooks this spectacular landscape. Co-ordinates are: 38°09'32.0" N 24°36'00.9"E.

84   Cape Malea is a peninsula and cape in the south-east of the Peloponnese of Greece. It separates the Lacanian Gulf in the west from the Aegean Sea in the east. It is the second most southerly point of mainland Greece (after Cape Matapan). The seas around the cape are notoriously treacherous and difficult to navigate, featuring variable weather and occasionally very powerful storms.

85   Argos is a city in Argolis, Pelopennese, Greece and is one of the oldest continuously inhabited cities in the world. It is the biggest city in Argolis.

86   Elysian Fields, or Elysium, in Greek metaphorology, is the final resting places of the souls of the heroic and the virtuous. It corresponds to the modern myth of "heaven" as used by organised religions. It's gatekeeper is Hades.

87   Elis is an ancient district in southern Greece on the Pelopennese Peninsula, bounded on the north by Achaea, east by Arcadia, south by Messenia, and west by the Ionian Sea.

88   Ipthime, daughter of Icarius, a sister of Penelope and Perileos, wife of Eumelus from Therae.

89   Skeria is today named, Corfu, and is in the Ionian Sea, some seventy nautical miles north of Phortune Harbour (Vathy), Ithaki.

90   Grace is one of three or more minor goddesses of charm, beauty, nature, human creativity, and fertility, together known as the Charities.

91   Iasion: At the marriage of Cadmus and Harmonia, Iasion was lured by Demeter - Zeus' mistress - away from the other revellers. They had intercourse as Demeter lay on her back in freshly ploughed field. When they rejoined the celebration, Zeus guessed what had happened because of the dirt on De meter's backside, and promptly killed Iasion with a lightning-bolt.

92   The star constellation of The Seven Sisters.

93   The star constellation of The Ploughman. Probably named after Iasion, who is said to have "ploughed" Demeter, the goddess of agriculture, in the, "three furrows" being an allusion to the three sexual cavities of a female.

94   Orion, the Hunter is a prominent star constellation visible throughout the world.

95   Oceanus' star stream: The Milky Way is the galaxy that contains our solar System. The descriptor "milky" is derived from the galaxy's appearance from Earth.

96   Zeus' shield or the Aegis is "reality" being mirrored by our thoughts. A metaphorical shield, a symbol of Mind's work which mirrors an apparently external world. It is the working-out of the plan through one's experience, and it is said to contain the destiny of all. Zeus is the controller of Mind and uses the dynamic of xenia to affect behaviour. The English word: age, is based on the concept of experience through Time.

97   Mountains of Solymi including Mt. Olympos (not to be confused with Mt. Olympos, Greece) are in the Antalya region of Turkey. The site at Yanartas has the Chimaera gas plumes, un-extinguishable flames leaping from the ground which have been burning for thousands of years.

98   Ino, Daughter of Cadmus. In mythology Ino was the mortal queen of Thebes, who after her death and transfiguration was worshipped as a Spirit under her epithet, "white goddess."

99   Albinos, the King of Phaeakia (modern day Corfu in the Ionian Sea) and his court.

100   Aegae or Aigai was an ancient settlement in Achaea located north-west of modern Aigeira, in the north-western area of the Pelopennese Peninsula. It was situated near the river Krathis, between the towns Boura and Aigeira.

101   Probably the Bay of Ermones on the island of Korfu.

102   Nauticca, is the daughter of King Alkinoos and Queen Arete of Phaeakia. Her name means: *wrecker of ships*.

103   The beautiful island of Delos and Apollo's Palm.

104   Marathon is a town in Greece, north of Athens, and the site of the battle of Marathon in 490 BC, in which the heavily out-numbered Athenian army defeated

the Persians. Legend has it that Pheidippides, a Greek messenger at the battle, was sent running from Marathon to Athens to announce the victory, which is how the marathon running race was conceived in modern times.

105   Athenians thought of themselves as *Erechtheidai*, the "sons of Erechtheus."

106   Hephaestos, was the metaphor for emotional and artistic creativity used by the ancients. Later, as a smithing god, Hephaestos made all the weapons for the Invisibles of Olympos. He served as the blacksmith of the gods, and was worshipped in the manufacturing and industrial centres of Greece.

107   Rhadamanthus was a wise king of Crete. In later accounts he is said to be one of the judges of the dead.

108   Demodokos was a poet who often visited the court of Alkinoos, on the island of Skeria. During Odyssey's stay he performs three narrative songs.

109   Was Homer blind? Establishing an accurate date for Homer's life also presents difficulties as no documentary   record is known to have existed. Herodotus and others generally dated him to between 750 and 700 BC. The characterization of Homer as a blind bard by some historians is partly due to translations of the Greek "homêros", meaning "hostage" or "he who is forced (perhaps obsessed) to follow", or, in some dialects, "blind". Some ancient accounts depict Homer as a wandering minstrel, and a common portrayal is of a blind, begging singer who travelled around the harbour towns of Greece and beyond, associating with shoemakers, fishermen, potters, sailors and elderly men gathering anecdotes and stories. A more plausible account suggests he lived on the island of Ithaki, where a school was established in his honour, or the "tradition's" honour.

110   Apollo foretold that Troy would fall to the Hellenes once their mightiest warriors quarrelled. Actually, it was after Agamemnon's feud with Achilles, that Troy was captured.

111   Ares, is the Hellenic god of war and conflict. He is one of the twelve Olympians, and the son of Zeus and Hera. In archaic Greece, he often represents the physical or violent and untamed aspect of war, in contrast to his sister the armoured Athena, whose functions as the Spirit of inspiration and the agent of intelligence and wisdom.

112   Technophiles was a Greek hero, famed as an archer, and a participant in the Trojan War.

113   Herakles was the metaphor for power, strength, will and determination. Later known as Hercules by the Romans.

114   Thrace is a geographical and historical area in south-east Europe. It is now split between Bulgaria, Greece and Turkey. In antiquity, it was referred to as *Europe*, prior to the extension of the term to describe the whole continent.   The name *Thrace* comes from the Thracian, an ancient Indo-European people inhabiting south-eastern Europe.

115   The coastal city of Paphos in Cyprus.

116   The Charities, from youngest to oldest, are Aglaea ("Splendour"), Euphrosyne ("Mirth"), and Thalia ("Good Cheer").

117   Circe is a metaphor of magic, enchantment and intrigue.

118   Epeius, a Greek soldier during the Trojan War had the reputation for being a coward. He built the Trojan Horse, commissioned by Odyssey because Athena

had told him in a dream she would help build it. The horse was hollow and was large enough to hold 30 Greek soldiers equipped with all their armour but Epeius made the Trojan horse so tall that it could not fit through any of the gates of Troy. The trap door of the horse was fastened with a special catch that only Epeius could undo. After constructing the massive horse, he chose the other 29 soldiers that would accompany him inside the horse.

119   Dimorphous was a prince of Troy, and the greatest of Priam's sons after Hector and Paris. Deiphobus killed four men of fame in the Trojan War.

120   The Cicones were a Thracian tribe, whose stronghold in the time of Odyssey (Homer) was the town of Ismara near the foot of Mount Ismara.

121   Kithera is an island lying opposite the south-eastern tip of the Peloponnese peninsula. It was once part of the Ionian Islands' group. It is on this island that Menaloas and Helen had a summer palace. When Paris visited the sanctuary dedicated to Aphrodite, he met Helen. They eloped and sailed to Troy. At the shrine, in the sanctuary, a statue of Aphrodite crumbled into rubble when Helen first entered, so stunning was her beauty.

122   In Greek mythology, the lotus-eaters referred to as the, *Lotophagi*, a race of people living on an island near the coast of North Africa (possibly Djerba) over-run with lotus plants. The lotus fruits and flowers were the primary food of the island and causing the people to live in blissful apathy.

123   Probably Levanzo, a beautiful island located close to Trapani and it is known to be the smallest of islands among the Aegadian group or perhaps Favignana which is situated approximately seven kilometres (four miles) west of the coast of Sicily.

124   The Greek for "no-man" was, "*me tis*". When the two are joined, *me-tis* means: *cunning* or *deceptive.*

125   The plateau topped Mount Eryx sits above the city of Trapani which does seem to be missing its peak.

126   Perhaps the small islet of Formica which sits about 3 kilometres off the coast of Trapani.

127   Perhaps the narrow islet of Maraone which sits adjacent to Formica, as above.

128   The island of Aeolus, is perhaps, modern-day Ustica. In ancient times, the island was populated from about 1,500 BC by Phoenician peoples. The Romans renamed the island *Ustica*, Latin for *burnt*, because of its black rocks. The island is also known locally as the "black pearl".

129   Aeolus was the keeper of the winds and king of the island of Aeolia, one of the rocky Lipara islands close to Sicily.

130   When approached from Goat Island, it appears like a submerged, but floating, upturned hull of a ship.

131   Lamos may be a transcription of the Latin word, *lamina,* meaning: thin layers or sheets of metal, wood, plate or leaf. The English word, *Lames* means layered, defensive armour. The terrain of Bonafacio harbour on the southern coast of Corsica is exposed horizontal layers of rock stratum. E. Bradford gives an account of his efforts to find Lamos in, *Ulysses Found.*

132   Telepylos means: *with wide or high gates, piles or towers.*

133   Artakia Fountain, is a relic of the past and has not been located.

134   Directly east (a "due" course) of the Port of Bonafacio, across the Tyrrhenian Sea, is the cape of Monte Circeo, near the town of San Felice Circeo. In ancient times this headland was separated from the mainland and would have appeared as an island.

135   Perse is an Oceanid, and the wife of the Sun god, Helios.

136   Aeetes was an ancient kingdom located on the Black Sea.

137   Probably the beach below Mount Circeo, at what is today, Torre Poala, under the headland.

138   Eurylochus was Odyssey's brother-in-law and a captain of one of the ships under his command.

139   Ten miles south from the peak of Mount Circeo, at Terracina, was one of the oldest shrines of ancient times; the Temple of Feronia, Spirit of the Wild and of the Forest. Her sanctuary was at the foot of Punta di Leano and its remains are visible today.

140   Polites was a trusted crewman and friend of Odyssey.

141   Pramnian wine is a thick, honey flavoured wine also known as Lesbian wine and has been made around the Mediterranean Sea since the 7th century, BC. The term, "Premium" is derived from this reference.

142   Probably *Datura stramonium.* All parts of *Datura* plants contain dangerous levels of poisons which can induce delirium and be fatal.

143   *Galanthus* or Snowdrop may be the herb "Moly" mentioned as Circe's potion. An active substance in Snowdrop is called galantimine, which could have acted as an antidote to her potions. Medical historians believe that the transformation to pigs was not intended literally, but refers to intoxication and hallucinations.

144   Persephone was the queen of the Underworld. She was married to Hades, the king of the underworld. Similar characters appear in Asian mythologies.

145   Terisias was a blind prophet of Apollo in Thebes, famous for clairvoyance and for being transformed into a woman for seven years. He participated fully in seven generations in Thebes, beginning as advisor to Cadmus, its founder.

146   It was long-believed that the Acheron River was located, as Nicolson relates, that archaeologist Schulten believed that he had found the Homeric hell, ... *West of the straits of Gibraltar, two rivers flow out into the Atlantic at Huelva, Spain; the Rio Tinto and the Odeil* (See page: 128 of *The Mighty Dead, Why Homer Matters* 2014). However, the Acheron is a river located in the Epirus region of north-west Greece. Its source is near the village Zotiko, in the south-western part of the Ioannina regional unit and it flows into the Ionian Sea at Ammoudia, near Messopotamo, Epirus, Greece.

147   The Styx is a river which forms the boundary between Earth and the Underworld, often called Hades, which is also the name of its ruler. According to Herodotus, the river Styx originates near Feneos, a village near Corinth, Greece, however, that is an erroneous translation: it joins the Acheron River at *Fenari* near Messopotamo, Epirus, Greece. The House of Hades (today known as the *Nekromanteion*) is located close to the village and is a stunning historical site, with immense "Cyclopean" masonry walls, dating to the Bronze Age. This complex may be the oldest oracle site in Greece.

148   Erebus was believed to be the original metaphor, representing darkness. Hesiod's *Theogeny* identifies it as one of the first five concepts of existence, born from Chaos.

149   The Cimmerians are believed to have been of either Iranian or Syrian origin and used this region as a trading base with Sicily. It is likely that they established the Nekromanteion complex which can be visited today near Messopotamo, Epirus, Greece.

150   Thrinakia is the modern-day island of Sicily.

151   Not to be confounded with Aeolus, king of the winds.

152   Megara is a historic town and a municipality in West Attica, Greece. It lies in the northern section of the Isthmus of Corinth, opposite the island of Salamis.

153   Kreon is best known as the ruler of Thebes in the legend of Oedipus.

154   Amphitryon was a Theban general, who was originally from Tiryns in the eastern part of the Peloponnese.

155   Jocasta was the daughter of the king of Thebes, Menoeceus, and sister of Kreon. She was the wife of Laius, who was given a prophecy; if he ever had a child, it would kill him and marry his wife. One night, Laius drank too much and had sex with his wife. She bore a son, Oedipus.

156   Oedipus unwittingly fulfilled a prophecy that he would end up killing his father and marrying his mother, thereby bringing disaster to his city and family. The story of Oedipus is the subject of Sophocle's tragedies: *Oedipus Rex*, *Oedipus at Colonus,* and *Antigone*. Oedipus represents two enduring themes of Greek myth and drama: the flawed nature of humanity and an individual's role in the course of destiny in a harsh universe.

157   Chloris was said to have married Neleus and become a queen of Pilos.

158   Orchomenus is the setting for many early Hellenistic myths and metaphors. It is best known as a rich archaeological site in Boeotia which was inhabited from the Neolithic through the Hellenistic eras.

159   Pero was the daughter of Neleus and Chloris, and the wife of her cousin, Bias.

160   Iphikles was the half-maternal twin brother of Herakles, being the son of Alcmene and her human husband Amphitryon. Whereas, Herakles was her son by Zeus.

161   Menelaus was a legendary soothsayer and healer, originally of Pilos, who ruled at Argos. He instigated the worship of Dionysos, according to Herodotus, who asserted that his powers as a seer were derived from the Egyptians and that he could understand the language of animals.

162   Tyndareus was a Spartan ruler.

163   Castor and Pollux were half-twin brothers in known together as the Dioscuri. Their mother was Leda, but they had different fathers; Castor was the mortal son of Tyndareus, a king of Sparta, while Pollux was the divine son of Zeus, who seduced Leda in the guise of a swan.

164   Mount Ossa is a mountain in the Larissa Province of Greece. It is 1,978 metres (6,490 ft) high and is located between Mt. Pelion to the south and Mt. Olympos to the north, and separated from by the Vale of Tempe.

165   Mount Pelion was the homeland of Chiron the Centaur, a tutor of many ancient Greek heroes, such as Jason, Achilles, Theseus and Herakles.

166   Phaedra was the daughter of Minos and Pasiphae. She was also the wife of Theseus, the sister of Ariadne, and the mother of Demophon and Acamas.

167   Procis was the third daughter of Erechteus, king of Athens and his wife, Praxithea.

168   Ariadne is mostly associated with mazes and labyrinths because of her involvement in the myths of the Minotaur and Theseus.

169   Minos was the first King of Crete, son of Zeus and Europa. Every nine years, he made King Aegeus choose seven young boys and seven young girls to be sent to Daedalus' labyrinth, to be eaten by the Minotaur. After his death, Minos became a judge of the dead in the underworld.

170   Theseus was the king and founder-hero of Athens. He battled and overcame foes that were identified with an archaic religious and social order.

171   Ntia Island is an uninhabited island off the northern coast of the island of Crete. The island is approximately seven nautical miles north of Heraklion.

172   Dionysos is the metaphorical representation for enjoyment and self-indulgence. The god of pleasure, ecstasy, revelry, fertility, eccentricity, excitement, male eroticism, male emotion, the grape-harvest, winemaking and wine, of fertility, madness, religious ecstasy and theatre.

173   Maera, daughter of Atlas.

174   Eriphyle in exchange for a necklace given to her by Polynices, persuaded her husband Amphiarius to undertake the raid which precipitated his death by Zeus. She was then slain by her son Alcmaeon.

175   Amphiarius, see above.

176   Achilles' father.

177   Achilles' son.

178   The island of Skyros is an island in the southernmost of the Sporades archipelago in the Aegean Sea.

179   Astyoche was bribed by Priam with a gold vine to persuade Eurypylus to follow his father into the Trojan War, which resulted in Eurypylus being killed in the battle. Along with Aethilla and Medesicaste, she was taken captive after the sack of Troy and set fire to the Greek ships during their stay on the Italian coast.

180   When Neoptolemus arrived at Troy, Odyssey resigned Achilles' armour and gave it to him. This armour Odyssey had received as a prize after the death of Achilles. This is the same armour that caused the death of Ajax; for the latter contended with Odyssey for the honour of owning it, and having lost, he went mad and killed himself.

181   When the Trojans were on the offensive, he was often seen covering the retreat of the Achaeans. Whilst one of the deadliest heroes in the *Iliad*, Ajax has no *aristeia* (excellence) depicting him on the offensive. He was more of a defender than offensive in battle.

182   Tityos was the son of Elara whose father was Zeus who hid Elara from his wife, Hera, by placing her deep beneath the earth. Tityos grew so large that he split his mother's womb, and he was carried to term by Gaia, the Earth. Once grown, Tityos attempted to rape Leto at the request of Hera. He was slain by Leto's protective children the twins, Artemis and Apollo. As punishment, he was stretched out in Tartarus and tortured by two vultures who fed on his liver, which grew back every night. This punishment is comparable to that of the Titan,

Prometheus.

183   Gaia is the metaphor for the ancestral mother of all life on Earth. She is mother nature.

184   Leto is a daughter of the Titans, Coeus and Phoebe. Zeus fathered her twins, Artemis and Apollo, the Letoides.

185   Tantalus was most famous for his eternal punishment in Tartarus, where he was made to stand in a pool of water beneath a fruit tree with low branches, with the fruit ever eluding his grasp, and the water always receding before he could take a drink. He was also called Atys.

186   Sisyphus was the king of Ephyra (now known as Corinth). He was punished for his self-centred ways and deceitfulness by being forced to roll a boulder up a hill only for it to roll down when it neared the top, repeating this action for eternity. Through the *classical* influence on modern culture, tasks that are meaningless and futile are described as Sisyphean.

187   The practice of nekyia is a "rite by which ghosts were called up and questioned about the future, that is, necromancy. A *nekyia* is not necessarily the same thing as a *katabasis*, or trip to the underworld. While they both afford the opportunity to converse with the dead, only a *katabasis* is the actual, physical journey to the underworld.

188   Hebe is the daughter of Zeus and Hera. She was the maid for the Invisibles of Mt. Olympos serving their nectar and ambrosia until she married Herakles.

189   Hera is the metaphor of wives, marriage, family, domestic security and childbirth, and the sister-wife of Zeus. She rules over Mt. Olympos as queen of the gods. A matronly figure, Hera served as both the patroness and protector of married women, presiding over weddings and blessing marital unions. One of Hera's defining characteristics is her jealous and vengeful nature against Zeus' numerous lovers and illegitimate offspring, as well as the mortals who cross her.

190   Cerberus is a many headed dog that guards the gates of the Underworld to prevent the dead from leaving. Cerberus was the offspring of the monsters Echidna and Typhon, and usually is described as having three heads, a serpent for a tail, and snakes protruding from parts of his body. Cerberus is primarily known for his capture by Herakles, one of the Twelve Labours.

191   In the *Centauromachy*, the Lapiths battle with the Centaurs at the wedding feast of Pirithous. The Centaurs had been invited, but, unused to wine, their wild nature came to the fore. When the bride was presented to greet the guests, the centaur Eurytion leapt up and attempted to rape her. All the other centaurs were up in a moment, straddling women and children. In the battle that ensued, Theseus came to the Lapiths' aid. They cut off Eurytion's ears and nose and threw him out. In the battle, the Lapith Caeneus was killed, and the defeated Centaurs were expelled from Thessaly into the north-west.

192   A Gorgon is a mythical creature portrayed in ancient Greek literature. While descriptions of Gorgons vary, the term commonly refers to any of three sisters who had hair made of living, venomous snakes, so horrifying that anyone looking at her would be turned to stone. Traditionally, whilst two of the Gorgons were immortal, Sthenic and Euryale, their sister Medusa was not and she was slain by Perseus.

193   The Galli Islands are an archipelago of small islands off the Amalfi Coast of Italy, between Isle of Capri and Positano. The name, Sirenuse, is a reference to the mythological Sirens, said to have lived there.

194   Poseidon's wife, was a sea goddess, and the queen of the sea.

195   Jason was a mythological hero; the leader of the Argonauts whose quest was to find the Golden Fleece.

196   The Harpies are half-human and half-bird creatures that sound like screeching wind.

197   Phorgyn is the patron of Ithaki, who Phortune Harbour is named after.

198   The Morning Star is the the planet Venus, in its morning appearance.

199   Rithron Cove (Dexia Cove and Dexia Beach) is located just north of the Nymphs Cave (Naiad's) adjacent to Phortune Harbour, or as it is known today, Vathy. It may have been Rithron Cove in ancient times. Skartsoubo (Sock) Island is just off Dexia Beach, Ithaki, and is said to be the petrified remains of the Phaekian ship and its crew that delivered Odyssey to Ithaki. Other theories exist for the location and geography of his landing place, however this location seems the best suggestion as it corresponds with all the references in *Odyssey*.

200   The Naiad Nymphs are a type of female spirit presiding over fountains, wells, lakes, springs, streams, brooks and other bodies of water. They are friends of travellers.

201   Amphora is a type of container of a characteristic shape and size. Standard amphorae were used in vast numbers for the transport and storage of various products, both liquid and dry, but mostly for wine.

202   Idomeneus was a king of Crete and the commander who led a naval force to the Trojan War. He was the grandson of Minos.

203   Perhaps an allusion to the famous battle of 480 BC. Obviously entered into Homer's *Odyssey* later in its evolution.

204   Lazaretto is a picturesque islet in the bay of Vathy (Phorgyn Bay), Ithaki. It has been used over centuries as a quarantine station, prison, leper colony and entertainment centre. A sign reading: "*Strangers are Friends of Ithaki*" was erected on the site to greet visitors arriving by boat, and removed sometime in the 1970's.

205   Eumaios was Odyssey's step-brother, swine-herder and loyal friend. His father, Ktesios son of Ormenos was a king of Syros, located in the Cyklades Islands in the Aegean Sea.

206   Antikleia was the daughter of Autolycos and Amphithea and mother to Odyssey, by her husband, Leartes.

207   Arcesius was Odyssey's grandfather, also a king of Ithaki.

208   Achaens were the inhabitants of the region of Achaea in north-central Peloponnese.

209   Thesprotia or Dodoni, in Epirus, in north-western Greece may be the oldest Hellenic oracle site, possibly dating to the second millennium BC, according to Herodutus. Dodoni was dedicated to Zeus. Situated in a remote sanctuary, it as considered second only to the oracle of Delphi in importance. The "Cyclopean" masonry walls of the sanctuary are of an impressive scale.

210   Kefalonia is the island east of Ithaki.

211   Acastus sailed with Jason and the Argonauts and participated in the hunt for the Calydonian Boar.

212   Aetolia is a mountainous region of Greece on the north coast of the Gulf of Corinth.

213   Maia, the mother of Hermes.

214   Mesaulius is the servant of Eumaios who purchased him during his own master's long absence. He was acquired from the Taphian slave traders. He serves as a waiter during Odyssey's first supper in Eumaeus's hut.

215   Thoas, a hero of the Trojan War.

216   Adraemon, was the husband of Gorge and by her the father of Thoas. He succeeded to his father-in-law Oeneus' power over Aetolia. He and his wife were buried in one tomb in the city of Amphissa.

217   Eurymachos is an Ithakan nobleman and one of the two leading suitors of Penelope.

218   Oxeia Island is located in the Ionian Sea, west of the Gulf of Corinth.

219   Theoklymenos was a seer and could predict the future from astronomical observations. He made several predictions which were proved.

220   Pero's beauty attracted many suitors, but Neleus, her father, refused to give his daughter to any man unless he could raid the cattle of Iphikles of Phylace.

221   Iphikles was the half-maternal brother of Herakles.

222   Phylacus was a town in ancient Thessaly.

223   Erinyes were sometimes referred to as "infernal goddesses" (thoughts). They would haunt any person who swore a false oath.

224   Bias, brother of Melampus.

225   Iphianeira, wife of Melampus.

226   Hyperesia was a town in north-eastern Achea.

227   Ctimine was Odyssey's sister.

228   Syrie, or Siros, is a Greek island in the Cyklades group, in the Aegean Sea.

229   Delos is one of the most important historical and archaeological sites in Greece. The excavations are among the most extensive in the world.

230   Cyklades Islands number about 220 and are located in the central Aegean Sea.

231   Ctesius was Eumaios' father, the king of Syros.

232   A veiled reference to a detected meteor shower on the 28th October, 1207 B.C. visible in Ithaki. Refer to: *The anatomy of a complex astronomical phenomenon described in the Odyssey.* (2013) St. P. Papamarinopoulos, et al. Mediterranean Archaeology and Archaeometry, Vol. 13, No. 2, pp. 69-82.

233   Peiraeus, is a friend and crewman of Telemakis on his journey to Pilos and back.

234   Amphinomos was the son of Nisos, the king of Megara, and a suitor to Penelope.

235   Eupeithes was the father of Antinoos, the leader of the suitors.

236   Aretias is a small island off the coast of Turkey, in the Black Sea.

237   Neritus was a son of Pterelaus of Ithaki, from whom Mount Neriton was named. His sons Ithakus, Neritus, and Polyctor colonised the island of Ithaki (which took the name of one of his sons) and, founded the place names of Ithaki, Neritum and Polyctorium.

238   Polyctor a friend of Odyssey and resident of Ithaki.

239   Melanthios was a goat-herder on Ithaki.

240   Dolios was Penelope's gardener and confidante.

241   Argos was Odyssey's loyal dog, that reached over twenty years of age.

242   Arnaeus, or Irus, was a beggar that ran errands for the suitors in Odyssey's palace.

243   King Echetus was a king of Epirus.

244   Eurydamus was a doomed suitor to Penelope.

245   Melantho is a bad-mouthed, disloyal maid of Penelope, and the sister of Melanthios and daughter of Dolios.

246   Pelasgians were the ancient indigenous inhabitants of the Aegean Sea.

247   Dorians were one of the four main ethnic tribes of the original Hellenistic nation.

248   Knossos is the largest Bronze-age archaeological site on Crete.

249   Deucalion was the son of Prometheus.

250   Aethon was the eagle who tormented Prometheus, and the child of the monsters, Typhon and Echidna.

251   Amnisos was a Bronze Age settlement on the north shore of Crete and was used as a port to the palace city of Knossos.

252   Eileithyia was the metaphor for childbirth and midwifery. Her "birthing" place was Amnisos.

253   Eurybates was a messenger for the Greek armies during the Trojan War. He served as Odyssey's squire. He was described by Odyssey to Penelope as "round-shouldered, dark-skinned, and curly-haired." Odyssey is said to have paid him greater regard than any other of his companions for his honesty and faithfulness.

254   Pheidon was a king of Argos, a city in the Peloponnese in the 7th century, BC.

255   Autolycos was the grandfather of Odyssey, and was responsible for naming him. The name originally meant: trouble, suffering or struggler.

256   Mount Parnassos is a mountain of limestone in central Greece. It towers above Delphi, north of the gulf of Corinth.

257   Amphites was the wife of Autolycos, Odyssey's grandfather.

258   Aedon was envious of Niobe, the wife of her husband's brother, Amphion, who had six sons and six daughters. She planned to kill the eldest of Niobe's sons, but by mistake slew her own son Itylus. Zeus relieved her grief by changing her into a nightingale, whose melancholy tunes are lamentations about her child.

259   The, "*gates of horn and ivory*" are a literary device used to distinguish true dreams (corresponding to factual occurrences) from false. The phrase originated in the Greek language, when the word for "horn" was similar to that for "fulfil" and the word for "ivory" was similar to that for "deceive". On the basis of that play-on-words, true dreams are spoken of as coming through the gates of horn, false dreams come through those of ivory.

260   Hypnos is the metaphor for sleep.

261   Ctesippos was a doomed suitor of Penelope.

262   Oechalia in ancient Thessaly, on the Peneius, between Pelinna and Tricca.

263   Bassae is an archaeological site in Oichalia, in north-eastern Messinia, Greece. In antiquity, it was part of Arcadia. Bassae is located near the remote

village of Skliros. It is famous for the well-preserved mid- to late-5th century BC Temple of Apollo Epicurius (The Helper). Although this temple is geographically remote from major centres of ancient Greece, it is one of the most studied ancient Greek temples because of its many unusual features. Bassae was the first Greek site to be entered on the World Heritage List.

264   Messenia was an ancient district of the south-western Peloponnese corresponding to the modern Messenia region of Greece.

265   Tiryns is a Mycenaean archaeological site in Argolis, near Nafplio, in the Peloponnese, and the location where Herakles performed his 12 labours. The incredible "Cyclopean" walls are a marvel.

266   Leodos, a diviner, was a doomed suitor of Penelope.

267   Eurytion a Centaur attempted to rape the bride of Pirithoos, King of the Lapiths.

268   Dionysos was the metaphor used for enjoyment and self-indulgence. The god of the grape-harvest, winemaking and wine, of fertility, rituals, madness, religious ecstasy and theatre.

269   Nericum, is the island of Lefkada, directly north of Ithaki.

17293843R00249

Printed in Great Britain
by Amazon